ABOUT THE AUTHOR

AND OTHER JENN J. MCLEOD TITLES

Five times published with Simon & Schuster AU & Head of Zeus UK, *House for all Seasons* was **#5 top-selling debut fiction novel**. Simmering Season is the second, with her sixth book, *House of Wishes*, the third and final standalone Calingarry Crossing novel.

As Australia's nomadic novelist, in a purple & white caravan called Myrtle the Turtle, Jenn is ticking things off her bucket list & finding rural landscapes to inspire more friendship & family relationship stories with a backdrop of country life.

(Marie Miller image)

JENN'S OTHER TITLES

House for all Seasons
Simmering Season
Season of Shadow and Light
The Other Side of the Season
A Place to Remember
House of Wishes

www.jennjmcleod.com

Simmering Season

Jenn J. McLeod

wild MYRTLE PRESS

SIMMERING SEASON

First published in Australia in 2014 by Simon & Schuster (Australia) Pty Limited

Second edition published in 2020 by Wild Myrtle Press

National Library of Australia Cataloguing-in-Publication entry

Author: McLeod, Jenn J., author.

Title: Simmering season/Jenn J. McLeod.

ISBN: 978-0-6485708-2-0 (paperback)

978-0-6485708-3-7 (ebook)

Subjects: Class reunions – Fiction.

Dewey Number: A823.4

Cover design: Lana Pecherczyk, Bookcoverology

Wild Myrtle Press does not mass produce books. We print books as required using Ingram Sparks Print On Demand (POD) Publishing because POD books are environmentally responsible, socially beneficial and economically viable management of the world's forests.

Printed and bound in Australia.

To Dad—my moral compass—for letting me travel my own path through life,
for loving me no matter how I strayed, and for letting me make my own choices
even when you didn't understand them.

perfect storm
~ n
Definition

1. a combination of several events which are not individually dangerous until they converge, but occurring together can bring about a devastating outcome.
    2. Maggie Lindeman's summer.

MAGGIE

'I thought the next funeral I'd attend would be mine.'

Maggie responded by dispensing a tissue from her handbag, passing it to the diminutive thirty-eight-year-old with the blonde, pixie-style hairdo. The occasion was hitting Sara harder than Maggie, who'd accompanied her friend to Sydney for the last goodbye. Looking over the fashionable forest of millinery excellence to the front of the church, Maggie wished she'd worn something stylish to cover her very un-coif-fured hairdo, even though she looked ordinary in hats. Some girls who came to the Calingarry Crossing pub wore sweat-lined Akubras like a badge of honour, but Maggie's hair combs, barrettes and crocodile clips, used to keep her hair under control and out of the patrons' beers, didn't sit too well under a hat. To secure her auburn mane into a rough French-twist today, she'd chosen her dragonfly clamp, encrusted with polished turquoise stones; a gift from her husband seventeen years ago on the birth of their son, Noah.

Following the last of four heartfelt eulogies spoken amid sobs and sniffs, mourners filed past the white coffin adorned with frangipani flowers—the biggest floral tribute Maggie had ever seen. Once the daughter of Calingarry Crossing's Presbyterian minister, Maggie was no stranger to funerals, weddings, christenings or communions. Too soon after her mother's death, thirteen-year-old Maggie had inherited the organ-playing duties, learning *Here Comes the Bride*, *The Wedding March*, and numerous pop tunes each couple gushed was 'our song'. The monotonous repertoire of *I Honestly Love You* and *Unchained Melody* had driven Maggie crazy and added to the unbearable task of replacing her mother. When her father had finally agreed to hand the job to one of the congregation, lilac-haired Lorna had stepped up, playing with gusto for years until the organ died.

No crassness accompanied today's service. Amber Bailey-Blair would never have allowed crass at her farewell. Today, mourners left the chapel to the sweet, sombre strains of a string quartet playing *Amazing Grace*.

AFTER THE MAGNIFICENCE OF ST MARK'S CHURCH—A FITTING PLACE TO say goodbye to a much-loved socialite and charity patron—the exclusiveness of the gathering that followed did not surprise Maggie. Sara, on the other hand, fell quiet, like the shy schoolgirl she used to be.

'This sure is nothing like any wake I've ever seen.' Maggie whispered, afraid her voice might echo in the expansive, open-plan penthouse. Even sun-speckled Sydney Harbour seemed dull compared to the sea of bejewelled but suitably subdued mourners now eddying in small groups and muttering platitudes such as 'Lovely service' and 'Terrible shame'.

Though barely noon, champagne flowed, and waiters looking like penguins in their formal black and whites mingled discreetly to create a passing parade of canape trays. Neither Maggie nor Sara refused their offerings, and for the same unspoken reason; their old friend, Amber Bailey, would have insisted.

'Thanks for coming with me, Maggie,' Sara said, her voice small. 'I know you and Amber weren't close at school, but no way could I prise Will from the café and back to Sydney for her funeral.'

Maggie smiled. 'I didn't mind. Driving the open road in that car of yours was a treat after Dad's old clunker. Oh!' Maggie grinned sheepishly at a waiter and snatched up her third smoked salmon blinis. 'One more can't hurt.'

'You really should dump that car, Maggie,' Sara said, inspecting the greenery atop her canape. 'Will swears by the Subaru's safety features.'

Maggie thought the country café owner looked ill at ease in the simple navy dress and strappy sandals that had only ever seen one other occasion —the woman's engagement celebration twelve months earlier. At school, Sara had been an average, quietly spoken student. How the girl had been friends with the outspoken trio of Amber, Poppy and Caitlin, Maggie never understood. It was possible she made them look better. Poppy Hamilton had looked taller and tougher alongside super-petite Sara, and Amber was ten times prettier than them all. Sara did manage to keep up with clever Caitlin Wynter, despite erratic school attendance. No one took much notice of the quiet kid in the corner. Most felt sorry for Sara. Maggie did. There was ample reason.

'I can't blame Will for not coming,' Maggie said. 'I'm impressed he tolerated Amber at all, given the way she and her dad treated him.'

'That was a long time ago,' Sara said. 'Amber changed a lot over the last twelve months. She'd relaxed and seemed happy with so much to do and so much to live for. So sad.' Sara teared up. 'But I'm glad she and Will got to make up. The accident changed his outlook on life. Will reckons the view from a wheelchair puts a fresh perspective on everything.'

'He's a survivor, that hubby of yours,' Maggie said, stealing another yummy bite-sized snack of smoked salmon and roe from the passing tray.

'We're all survivors,' Sara mumbled absentmindedly.

To look at Sara, there was no telling the challenges the woman had endured before she and Will became the picture of domestic bliss. A rogue cell inside Maggie was even a little jealous of how her friend had found her happily ever after with childhood sweetheart and former league star, Will Travelli. Then came the blow of losing Amber.

Sara sniffled into a paper serviette. 'There was so much about Amber —about each other—that we ...'

'Yes, I know, sweetie.'

The truth was, Maggie didn't know much at all. She doubted anyone in Calingarry Crossing would learn the details of what happened at Dandelion House last year when Sara, Amber, Poppy and Caitlin reunited after two decades. Maggie knew what most of the town knew; that the old woman known as Gypsy had bequeathed Dandelion House—a century-old estate on the outskirts of town—to the four women, but only if they each stayed a season in the house.

'Oh, look who's here!' Sara sprung onto her toes, nodding towards the silent flurry as hard-to-miss Poppy Hamilton stepped from the private elevator.

Standing out above the crowd in both height and presence, Poppy— onetime playground prima donna—had butted heads with Amber about being boss of their playground clique. While going home to Calingarry Crossing twenty years later and staying at old Dandelion House had affected all four ex-friends, the experience transformed Poppy Hamilton from hard-hearted reporter to environmental advocate. Immediately following their Dandelion House stay, Poppy wrote an article for the Saddleton Harvest newspaper about the century-old estate changing hands. Rather than satisfying the town's curiosity, however, the piece raised more questions than answers and made clear Dandelion House would keep its secrets.

Maggie never asked Sara about her time at the house. Secrets were just that—secret—and Maggie understood the importance of keeping them. The thin fibro walls of the church residence where she grew up used to muffle, although never completely mute, the voices in the kitchen along the hall from her room. The enclosed veranda—the coolest place to sleep on hot Calingarry summer nights—meant a young Maggie was within earshot of the conversations and confessions of parishioners who dropped in at all hours of the day and night to chat with her father over a cuppa. As ramshackle as the old Manse—their church-provided lodging—had been, Maggie had loved her summer bedroom. When tilted at the right angle, the glass louvres lining all three sides of the wrap-around veranda were like sleeping outdoors, minus the mozzies.

Sadly, around the late seventies when the *Press Buttons* and *Methos*— as her dad had called the Presbyterian and Methodist churches—amalgamated to become the Uniting Church, Maggie's mum died. Soon after, the good Reverend Lindeman gave up looking after the locals' spiritual needs, moved his family from the Manse to the two-storey pub on the corner where, as publican, he'd dispensed a new form of sacred spirits including: Jack Daniels, Jim Beam and Johnny Walker. Affectionately called *The Rev* forever after, locals had continued to seek him out for guidance and forgiveness. During the big drought in the nineties, her father's bar-style ministering had helped countless farmers who were finding life hard. Such tough times had taught Maggie much about the human spirit and, as Calingarry Crossing's publican for the last two years, she understood the importance of keeping those over-the-counter confessions sacrosanct.

'Well, well, well,' shrilled a pretty young woman wearing a flashy black hat with sequined netting suspended above plump, primrose-pink lips. Eyes heavy with mascara scrutinised Maggie from head to toe and back again before the girl took a very unladylike swig of champagne. 'Don't tell me. Another country cousin?' she asked, her tone forced and snobbish. 'I shouldn't be surprised. I've learned my mother's country roots run intriguingly deep.'

'I'm Maggie, an old school friend,' she responded, recognising Amber's daughter the minute she lobbed.

Fiona Bailey-Blair had the same willowy stature and ballsy swagger. Even in a school uniform, Amber had overdressed and oozed priggishness. Fiona's figure-hugging outfit today, including ankle-breaking stilettos, looked more suited to Spring Carnival than her mother's funeral.

'Another friend I didn't know about, eh? Shall I call you Aunty Maggie? I'm getting used to collecting relatives. Although …' Fiona paused, looking Sara up and down, 'I'm still working out what to call you and the others.'

'What do you think your mother would've wanted, Fiona?' Poppy said, having made her way across the room.

'Who really knew what darling Amber wanted?' Fiona gushed. 'She didn't want me. That much I know thanks to you ladies and your Nancy Drew-meets-Hermione Granger adventures at Calingarry Crossing. What a magnificent time you all had together. What a shame once mother finished playing cowgirl and came home she couldn't devote a little more time to me—her daughter. But no. She had to spend the last year of her life engrossed in your stupid Dandelion House project.' Fiona's scoffing cut through the polite whispers. The room stilled. 'What about what she owed me? I'm Little Fiona. Big mistake.'

'Shhh,' said Poppy, attempting to take possession of the glass. Instead, Fiona turned her back, raised the champagne in a mock salute and skolled the contents. Three gulps. Gone.

'Of course,' she continued, waving the empty flute at a passing waiter, 'the only other mystery is who my real father is. So, Nancy Drew …' She glared at Poppy. 'What are the chances of you unravelling that little secret for me?'

'Fiona!' Phillip Blair appeared and snatched his daughter's glass away, dismissing the pimply faced waiter with a disapproving stare. The man had aged since Maggie last saw him with Amber in Calingarry Crossing twelve months ago. 'Enough,' he said, clutching Fiona's elbow. 'This is not the time.'

'Are you quite sure, *Dad*?' Fiona trained her pinched eyes on Phillip. 'I reckon it's the perfect time to discover whose genes are lurking inside me courtesy of a father I didn't know about until last week.' Her words choked on their way out, tears streaming freely down both cheeks. 'Like I give a shit, anyway. Let me go.' She flicked Phillip's hand off, turned, and barged through the sombre gathering like a southerly buster, whipping up a small storm of whispers in her wake.

Maggie rested a gentle hand on Phillip's shoulder. 'Let her leave. She's confused and hurting.'

'She's drunk.' Phillip's shoulders sagged, his voice straining to maintain a cordial tone. 'But generous of you to suggest otherwise, Maggie.'

Maggie's heart broke for him, even though the irony was not lost on her. Phillip's life was the complete opposite to her penny-pinching existence. Renowned plastic surgeon, Phillip Blair, would not need to ignore a strange knocking sound in his car and hope it didn't conk out at the worst time. People like Phillip Blair bought a different car. Fixing a family problem was not so easy. The notion appeased Maggie. Her family was not grappling with a painful secret and about to implode. Maggie's family was far from perfect, but it was intact. Or it would be after this trip; another reason she'd been keen to accompany Sara to Sydney.

'Thank you for coming all this way, ladies,' Phillip said to the trio of old school friends. 'Amber was so …' The perfect smile did not hide his anguish. 'She was excited to be catching up with you in Calingarry Crossing for the big day.'

'The big day?' Poppy looked from Phillip to Maggie. 'I hadn't given the school's centenary celebration another thought. Is it still going ahead, Maggie? Without Amber I didn't think it would. I took an assignment. Can we not postpone?'

Maggie lifted her shoulders. 'The town doesn't have a choice. We're celebrating our centenary, and planning is past the point of no return. Amber had the Saturday reunion sorted.' Heads bobbed in agreement; Amber had arranged everything. 'The only thing left to finalise is the fair day on the Sunday,' Maggie told the group. 'I don't think that will be too hard. The town's put on plenty of those over the years.'

'Sure will miss having Amber organise us all.' Sara said, dabbing her cheeks. 'The reunion was her idea.'

'Yes, it was, and you know our Amber …' A cough did little to disguise Phillip's voice breaking as he spoke her name. 'She wasn't leaving anything to chance, determined the night would go off without a hitch. So, ladies, I guess it's over to you. No pressure, but …' He arched a knowing eyebrow. 'You'd better make sure all goes to plan or else …'

'Okay then.' Sara raised her glass to toast. 'Here's to Amber.'

'And a trouble-free school reunion,' Maggie added. An oxymoron if ever she'd heard one. But Maggie kept that thought to herself.

2

FIONA

Fiona Bailey-Blair shoved the plate of barely eaten Eggs Florentine to the centre of the table. She'd picked out the parsley, poked the sun-dried tomatoes to one side of the over-sized plate and smeared the bright green *salsa verde* across the centre of the ceramic canvas. Downing the last of her skinny soy latte, she let the glass land firmly on the café table before peering over the enormous celebrity-inspired sunglasses at her fiancé and her best friend.

'No!'

'But why not, Fifi?' Luke asked.

'Because I don't want to. Okay?'

'Stop pressuring her, Luke. She's upset.' Fiona's best friend and flat-mate, Molly Myers, had never liked Fiona's boyfriend. 'And in case that thing you call a brain has forgotten already, forty-eight hours ago we were all at her mother's funeral.'

Fiona tuned out to the pair and their bickering. According to Molly, who liked to make inverted commas in the air for emphasis, Luke wasn't 'one of them'. And while her best friend was not the only person to think Luke wasn't good enough, Molly voiced her opinion so often Fiona regretted sharing certain details about her relationship. But wasn't that what those closest to you were for? Didn't siblings forgive your misde-meanours and best friends cheer for you, even when you doubted your-self? Sometimes Fiona wished her brother had lived longer than a day, or that she'd had a sister—younger, of course—even if it had meant sharing her toys. There'd been no shortage every birthday and Christmas. Sharing her mother's affections would not have been a problem either. Fiona couldn't share what she never had.

Sharing her father, though … That might have been different. She loved her father. At least she loved Phillip, until she found out he was a liar.

'Newsflash, *Mol*!' Luke tossed a sugar stick. It landed in Molly's glass, splashing water over her iPhone on the table. 'I know when my fiancée is upset.'

'Geez, you're a jerk, Luke. Grow up.'

'Both of you grow up.' Fiona snatched the container of sweeteners. 'I'm not upset, okay?' If she was—and it wasn't so much upset as angry right now—no way was Fiona falling apart in public. 'I just don't see the point in going to Calingarry Crossing, Luke. What's it supposed to achieve? I'm not my mother. I hardly need to go running off to a hick town to *find* myself or experience some great epiphany. What's important in my life is right here, in Sydney, with you guys.'

Luke clasped Fiona's hand, drawing it to his lips. 'Babe, you must want to know who your real father is.'

She sighed, snatched her hand away and sat back, fully fed up. 'What for, Luke? Is being rejected and lied to by the parents I have not enough?'

For years Fiona had bottled her anger and resentment. Years of pent-up frustration at being shipped off to boarding school and summer camps because she'd had a mother who couldn't deal with her own life, much less her daughter's. Amber Bailey-Blair—as her mother had insisted, as if a hyphenated name elevated a person to some superior status—had been a shit-of-a mother. For that reason, Fiona had moved out of the family's Potts Point apartment and into Molly's Bondi flat the day after her eighteenth birthday. Not long after, and without warning, Amber had walked away from her husband and life of plenty to return to the obscure town of her youth. Fiona had known nothing about her mother's country roots at the time. Amber, it seemed, kept lots of secrets—many even from Phillip, who'd been just as hurt and confused as Fiona when Amber abandoned them both.

Why he'd taken Amber back, Fiona didn't understand and she'd told him as much.

'You're just taking her back, as if she never left?' she'd asked the day Phillip announced her mother was coming home.

'She's been through a lot,' he'd explained. 'She wants to make it up to us, but she needs our help.'

What about what I need? Fiona had wanted to scream. Why was it always all about Amber?

'Promise me you'll try,' Phillip had said.

Fiona did promise at the time. She and her mother had even been making progress until, a few days ago, an aneurism burst inside Amber's brain. Gone. Just like that. Moments before, Amber had been yelling at Fiona's grandfather, Jack. Fiona had stayed hidden in the hallway, listening to father and daughter firing personal pot-shots at each other—Jack with his angry accusations, and a defiant Amber defending her daughter like never before. But the words so painfully carved into Fiona's memory were about Phillip. *We all know the truth, don't we, Amber? Stop pretending Phillip is Fiona's father and tell me about the lucky lad. Who knocked up my daughter? Will Travelli was always my bet.*

The news had shocked and confused Fiona. How could Phillip not be her proper father? The man had cared for her and nurtured her when Amber was too preoccupied. He'd provided for Fiona, spoilt her, called her his little princess and treated her like one—always.

'Hey!' Luke snapped his fingers in her face. 'Fifi, are you listening?'

Fiona swatted his hand. 'As if I have a freaking choice.'

'Well?'

'Well what?' she snapped.

'I asked, what makes you think your real father would reject you? Maybe the bloke doesn't know you exist.'

'Look at me, Luke.' Fiona leaned forward to stare. 'If I can't get a straight answer out of my father—I mean, Phillip—what chance have I got getting answers from complete strangers living in a town I never knew existed? Oh, wait! I have an idea.' She sat rigid. 'Why didn't I think about this before? I'll design a banner and hang it in the main street. Even better, Luke, why don't I set up a Facebook page? I can call it: 'Help Foolish Fiona Find Her Father'. I'll snap a selfie looking all pathetic and plead for likes.'

'So you and Phillip have talked?' Luke asked.

'Barely.' Fiona pictured her normally unflappable father—the same man whose unwavering optimism and smile she'd relied on as a child—sitting in his darkened bedroom, sobbing into cupped hands. Twice in recent days she'd let herself into the apartment to see him. Twice she'd crept out.

'Fi, sweetie,' Molly interrupted. 'If you want an opinion from the person who's known you the longest … You are you and I love you. Just forget it.'

Easy for Molly to say. The Myers' family history was well documented, her lineage an entrée to a world Fiona sometimes struggled to fit into. Now she understood why she struggled, and why even her name—Fiona—seemed out of place among the Savannahs, the Siennas, the Tiffanys and the Taylors. She wasn't Doctor Phillip Blair's daughter. She was the result of a bonk in a bloody hay shed between an unknown cowboy and a drunk Amber—a sad, secret-keeping, prescription-addicted liar.

'This is Fi's decision, Molly,' Luke said.

'Are you for real?' Molly fired back. 'What would she do in a dusty country town? She wouldn't fit in there at all.'

Wouldn't fit in? Fiona twitched at her best friend's words, a bubble of anger floating up and bursting out of her mouth. Where did Fiona fit in?

'Look you two, I can hardly blow into town and announce, "I'm here to find my freaking father". I'm pretty sure that would piss off the locals big time, Luke. Oh, and Molly, maybe I would fit in. Thanks very much for the confidence boost.'

'I'm sorry.' Molly pouted.

'Fifi, calm down and listen. I have a plan,' Luke said. 'Your mother organised that event for her old school, right? And your grandfather got you that marketing job, didn't he?'

Fiona screwed up her face. 'What the hell are you talking about?'

'Doesn't it make sense? You've got skills and experience to contribute and you've just lost your mother. They'll embrace you.'

'I write freaking ad copy and jingles, Luke. Not sure they need either of those for a small-town school reunion.'

'Not the point, babe. You're there offering to help, and they were your mother's friends. They won't turn you away. Who knows what you'll find out.'

'Oh, yes, I made a great impression on those friends at Mum's freaking funeral.'

'Fifi, I wish you wouldn't talk like that.'

'Shut up, Luke,' Molly countered. 'She can talk any freakin' way she wants.'

'Charming, Mol.' Luke turned his back on her. 'Listen, Fifi—'

'She doesn't have to listen to you, *Lukey*. You're not her father.'

'Quit it. Both of you.' Fiona smacked the table, frightening a bark out of the little dog in a handbag under an adjacent chair. 'Luke, I have two fathers. I don't need you telling me what to do.'

'Calm down, Fifi.' Luke kept his voice soft, but there was no disguising the clenched jaw or the way his deliberately slow, controlled breathing expanded his buff chest. Both his hands were on the table, one curled into a fist, the other toying with the chunky gold charm bracelet on Fiona's wrist, a twenty-first-birthday gift from Phillip. 'Let's all calm down, shall we?'

Fiona nodded. The entire café was already whispering about them. She didn't want her relationship woes captured on some loser's mobile phone and uploaded for the world to see.

'You're pure class, Fi,' Luke continued. 'Who's to say your DNA isn't linked to a wealthy property owner out there in Calingarry Crossing?'

'Always comes back to money eh, Lukey?' Molly sprung up so fast her chair fell backwards, smashing onto the footpath. 'You're a sleazebag, you know that?'

'Love you too, Miss Molly.' Luke blew a kiss before leaning down to pick up the chair.

'Molly, wait!' Fiona looped her head through the strap of her macrame beach bag and was about to stand when Luke grabbed her by the wrist.

'Let her go, Fifi. What would little Miss Molly Millionaire understand? The biggest struggle she's had is choosing which shade of bimbo to dye her hair.' He had Fiona pinned to her chair with one hand. The other was tugging at the perfect strawberry-blonde corkscrew curl dangling over one cheek. 'I understand you, babe,' he cooed. 'I'm the only one who truly understands you.' He tucked the wayward strand behind her ear. 'Stick with me, kiddo. Let me look after you.'

3

DAN

Death knocks. No Police College lecture can prepare a copper for that moment: the flash of recognition as the door opens, the worried eyes, the first signs of hope slowly draining from another father's face as he comprehends the well-rehearsed and too often said words, *'I'm sorry to have to inform you that your son—or daughter, or only reason for living—died in a head-on crash this evening'*. And not just died, but died alone, in the dark, on the side of a road, calling your name.

Dan Ireland dropped into the passenger seat and reefed the door of his unmarked police car shut. 'Shit!'

'You can say that again, Sarg. Geez, that sucked. Did you see the birthday cake and the big "Happy Seventeenth" balloons in the living room?'

'Yeah, I saw.'

Dan didn't dare look at his young offsider, staring instead into the lights of an oncoming vehicle and imagining what it must feel like to slam into a half-tonne of speeding metal. Or a wall. Or a tree.

Dan knew how it felt from the other side when first responders moved in to clean up the result of a high-speed crash. Images from tonight's scene played like a horror movie in his head. He'd witnessed the effects too many times before—every bone-breaking, skin-splitting, life-destroying injury. Dan didn't understand why authorities didn't show *that* on the nightly news, plaster *those* pictures on roadside billboards and teach kids about *that* in schools. Would such images slow the idiots down or force different choices? If someone had sat Dan down and shocked him twenty-three years ago, he wouldn't be seeing the scars each time he looked in a mirror—the result of an invincible teenager and a dirt bike tangling with a barbed-wire fence at a hundred kilometres per hour. That day he'd come close to dying. Sometimes he wished he had.

Instead, he was a copper in a car and the bearer of bad news: another death knock, another statistic, another young driver gone. Dan witnessed —often daily—what happened to other kids' faces when they weren't as lucky as he was: noses smashed on steering wheels, teeth rammed through lips like a grotesque stapler. Even when Dan found a picture ID in a wallet, the swelling and discolouration distorting the person's face often wouldn't let their own mother see any resemblance, like a Picasso abstract coming to life before Dan's eyes. Or dying. Only the images didn't die. Like every family, tonight's parents would keep photos of their son on the sideboard, while Dan's images would live on in his head, a cruel kind of mental photo album.

Dan didn't want to think about how many times they'd offered him a transfer out of the crash investigation unit: better rank, better salary, better hours. His wife would've been happy. Lucky for him, Tracy never knew how many times he'd said no to a job that would have meant more time at home being a husband and father. She'd have killed him, and who would blame her? The courts would acquit her of all murder charges. No jury would convict the woman once they heard her side of the story. Justifiable homicide? No question.

'Did you see the mother go white, Sarg?' asked Dan's offsider. 'I was ready for her to pass out. And how about the father?' he added while indicating to merge the car into a queue of peak-hour traffic. 'The man's fist did a good job of that plasterboard wall. Geez, that must hurt. Can't say I've ever had cause to attack a wall though.' As the constable made fists of both hands, the sound of crunching knuckles exacerbated Dan's foul mood.

'Hey, both hands on the wheel, thanks,' he chastised, turning away and catching the faintest reflection of his face in the passenger window.

He pressed his fingers against the old scar on his cheek, rubbing the spot up and down three times before tracing the jagged line from the nick in his earlobe, over his jawline and to the underside of his chin. Yes, he knew pain, both physical and emotional, not that he shared that with his junior colleague.

'Can't think why you wanted to come with me,' the constable said. 'Hey, don't get me wrong. Happy to have you along. It's just most crash guys leave this part of the job to us uniform blokes.'

Dan might have replied, 'I only tag along when they're teenagers', but that would lead to more questions. He instead concentrated on his hand flicking the cover of the leather ID holder with OCD regularity—open and closed, open and closed, open and closed—and reciting the tiny motto on the badge: *Culpam Poena Premit Comes. Punishment Follows Close On Guilt.* The irony was that Dan had been punishing himself for years merely by doing his job. Each time he faced another family to tell them their treasured son or daughter or loved one was gone, he imagined Maggie and her dad twenty-three years ago. This job didn't let the wounds mend, nor erase the memory of his mate's family at the funeral. From as far away as the fig tree that dwarfed the tiny stone church, Dan had witnessed their pain.

Situations like tonight's not only reopened old wounds. They salted them. They had also stopped Dan from going home to Calingarry Crossing. Why he'd told Tracy he'd think about the stupid school reunion he couldn't fathom. Dan Ireland did not believe in going back.

'You're in an eighty zone, Constable. Reckon you can drive any faster?' he quipped. 'Any slower and you'd best put her in reverse.'

'Someone's keen to knock off and start their holidays,' his driver said. 'Geez, can't wait 'til I've clocked up enough years for paid leave. Big plans? Pacific cruise with the missus?'

'Bugger off! I'm not that bloody old.' The spurt of humour was short-lived as the reality hit Dan. He had no idea what he'd do with his leave, except spend time with his kids. They kept him active, and activity kept him from overthinking. 'Just some much-needed time out,' he replied. 'The last few years have been a bastard, and family duty calls.'

'Wives, huh?' the constable quipped. 'Maybe you can hook up the caravan and take a road trip.'

'No caravan, but there's a school reunion in the town where I grew up.'

'Whereabouts?'

'About eight or nine hours drive north-west. You wouldn't know it. Calingarry Crossing.'

'Sounds small.'

'You've got no idea, mate.'

'Not sounding too enthusiastic, boss. What's up?' The constable landed a playful thump on Dan's arm. 'A little Georgie Porgie thing going on back there?'

'What?' Dan was only forty; why did he have so much trouble keeping up with his young colleague?

'You know. A little of that Georgie Porgie puddin' and pie, knocked up a girl then said bye, bye. Am I close? Is that why you're not keen about going back?'

Dan's answer was his all-too-frequent cynical snort. If only it was that simple. He settled into the seat and closed his eyes to yet another bottle-neck of red taillights forming up ahead.

'Come on, have a drink with me,' the constable said. 'We deserve one.'

'Tempting, but no can do. I've got kids expecting me.'

Dan loved his kids. On nights when he couldn't stop thinking about the last crash site he'd attended, or the last parent he'd had to face, Dan's favourite place would be in the kids' room, on the floor between their beds, listening to their breathing while they slept. They were the other reason Dan did what he did—keeping the world safe from bad drivers and bad people. He owed it to Mike and Emily. His kids had saved him four-teen years ago, not that they knew how they'd changed his life. Lucky for Dan, he did.

'G'DAY KIDS.'

'Hey Dad.' The fourteen-year-old twins called back in almost perfect unison from their seated position on the front doorstep.

'Where's your mother?'

'She called a while ago,' his son said. 'The train broke down. She said we don't have to wait.'

'Right, well, best get dinner then.'

'Pizza! Pizza!' Emily pleaded.

'No. Maccas,' Mike said.

'Aww, we had Maccas last time, Dad.'

'Okay, okay, how's this?' Dan rubbed his palms together. 'Put the iPad away and it will be pizza entrée, Maccas mains and a choc-top at the movies for dessert. Howzat?'

'You're the greatest, Dad,' the choir of two sang as they raced each other for the front passenger seat of the car.

'Buckle up.' Dan glanced at his children and tried not to think about the parents tonight with their cold dinner, wilting balloons and unopened birthday presents.

AS DAN DROVE INTO THE PIZZA HUT CAR PARK, THE GOLDEN ARCHES towering over the adjacent McDonalds' restaurant were blinding on his weary eyes.

'Can't we go away with you and Mum?' asked Emily as she unbuckled in the back seat.

'Why would you want to go all the way out to a small country town?' Dan queried. 'A hot, dusty country town at this time of year if I remember rightly.'

'You and Mum grew up there,' Emily said.

'We did, yes, a long time ago. Come on you two.' Dan engaged the Pajero's central locking and herded his pair safely across the busy car park. 'Your mother and I talked. We didn't think you'd be interested bunking down at our old friends' place. They own a farm so you'd be up before the sun. Doubt there'll be any movie channels. Might be mobile phone reception, if you're lucky. But if you want to come ...'

'Crap. Forget that. I'm staying,' Mike said, charging ahead.

'Yeah, Dad, me too. I'd rather stay at Taylor Anderson's place. Her dad's got an X-Box.'

'Is that right?' Dan hugged his daughter to him and felt the day's dirt fall away. 'Okay, pikers. I'm starved.'

4

MAGGIE

Maggie was glad to be heading back to Calingarry Crossing, keen to leave the sadness of Amber's funeral and the craziness of the city behind. She also missed her son. Sometimes it felt like she was still catching up on his childhood. Being the sole breadwinner since Noah was a baby had meant missing out on so much during those early years.

'What a difference a sea breeze makes,' Maggie said, as Sara negotiated the Subaru through the city's shadowy streets, then north across the Harbour Bridge. 'You know the ocean is the only thing I miss about Sydney.'

While twisting her hair into a rough knot, tying it on top of her head with the black elastic—a constant companion on one wrist—Maggie watched a twin-hulled RiverCat on the water below bringing commuters down the Parramatta River from the western suburbs to the city. The fast-moving ferry speared the still blue water before disappearing underneath the bridge, leaving only two lines of white foam in its wake. Out the driver's side, other craft under both motor and sail dotted the postcard-perfect harbour. With a shoulder leaning against the partially open passenger window, Maggie closed her eyes and lifted her nose to a cool breeze tinged with the smell of salt and seaweed. It made her wish she'd spent more time on the water while living here. The occasional weekend Manly Ferry ride hardly counted.

When Maggie opened her eyes again, an enormous red semi-trailer had gobbled up the vista. A tattooed truckie in a sweat-stained blue singlet leered down, a choking cloud of diesel smoke staining the sky above his cabin. Maggie jerked back, raised the window and flicked the air-con vents so they blew directly into her face to make a consistently disobedient strand of hair dance around her eyes.

'You okay there?' Sara asked.

'Do I look stupid?' Maggie blurted, slamming her back into the contoured bucket seat and yanking the stubborn tress behind her ear for a second time. 'Because I am. You know that, don't you?' Even before Maggie had finished saying the words aloud, Sara was laughing and nodding in agreement. 'Dad has a lot to answer for,' she continued. 'Taking people under his wing and guiding them was something he did. I'm not him. What was I thinking when I offered to put her up at the pub?'

'You are like your dad, Maggie—generous and protective, like The Rev. Don't see the offer as helping Fiona. Think of it as doing something for Phillip.'

'Hmm.' Maggie wiggled her butt down into the seat to take advantage of the headrest. 'I suppose when you say it that way. The girl is just spoilt rotten. Reckon I can work that attitude out of her.'

'Work?' Sara whooped. 'Don't go planning any Employee of the Month awards.'

'What's so funny? Is it wrong to expect someone to work for their food and board? We're not all made of money, like the Blairs. Spending time with her grandmother might even help Fiona understand Amber's struggles. The offer wasn't an all-inclusive, first-class getaway. It's an opportunity to experience life in the town where her mother grew up.'

'Not everyone has your work ethic, Maggie.'

Maggie shrugged. 'Oh well, I'd be surprised if Fiona took up the suggestion. It's not as if Phillip can make her come out to Calingarry. The girl is almost twenty-two years old, not that she acts it.'

'You're right, on both counts,' Sara said, as the mobile phone trilled in its cradle. Her smile said it was Will. 'Still, I'd want to get to know my grandmother before it was too late.'

The words 'too late' formed an image in Maggie's head; the frail form of her father the first day she'd called into Saddleton Nursing Home. He'd been sitting in a chair in the common room and wearing the frayed clerical collar nursing staff had said he insisted on every day. In the same room were half a dozen other men and women in varying end-stages of their lives. Having watched from the corridor for a few minutes, blotting her eyes with the sleeve of her shirt, Maggie had managed a brave face and made her way through the semi-circle of recliner and wheelchair-bound residents staring at the old black and white movie playing on a big-screen television.

'Hey there, Dad.' At first, Joe had just stared, like he was looking without really seeing. His eyes, once big and brown and filled with warmth and life, were clouded, and his stare vacant. 'It's me. Maggie.'

Joe beamed. 'My little Magpie?' He reached out his arms and used the word he'd made up when she was a baby. 'Smuddle?'

Afterwards, Maggie had cried for the hour-long trip home to Calingarry Crossing pub. Perhaps that first visit might not have been such a shock for her had she come home for the occasional visit, or if her father or Ethne hadn't kept his declining condition a secret when she'd telephoned. Not that she could have made the trek too often from Sydney. While she thought a lot about her dad, her life was in the city with Brian and their son. Trips back home cost money they didn't have. Now Maggie had no choice, and while trying to make up for lost time with Joe, every week she saw more and more a shadow of a man once wiser than Solomon.

'DID YOU HEAR THAT, MAGGIE?' SARA ASKED AFTER TERMINATING Will's phone call with an audible kiss. 'Will reckons a short stint in the country is what Fiona needs. Look what it did for her mother.'

'He's probably right.' Maggie sighed. 'I wish someone had made me come home earlier.'

'Why didn't you?'

'Sometimes life has other plans.'

She didn't feel the need to go into detail. If anything these days, Maggie avoided specifics. She tried to avoid reminiscing about sliding doors and decisions made and she didn't make a habit of crying in her drink. Maggie Lindeman had never been chatty or demanding and, unlike her husband, she preferred not to be the centre of attention. Maggie's life hadn't turned out particularly exciting, and that was fine, even though as an adolescent she'd dreamed of a fun-filled existence brimming with colour and noise. Real life, as she eventually found out, was never as romantic as the fantasy.

While running her dad's pub meant being more sociable than she'd been in years, Maggie didn't have to make conversation. Most pub patrons preferred talking about themselves, especially after one or two drinks when, for some blokes, bar talk turned into those over-the-counter confessions. Maggie's challenge was skilfully avoiding questions from a curious community about her past, especially her time in Sydney and her noticeably absent husband.

The day eighteen-year-old Maggie had left Calingarry Crossing as Mrs Henkler—The Rev had insisted they marry first—had been so exciting. She'd planned to do it all: marriage, career, motherhood—and in that order. Somewhere in there she'd manage an Arts degree and, after a steady job with a high-profile agency, she'd start her own photography business with world domination in mind. Little Maggie, the minister's daughter, would be the next Anne Geddes. Only she'd revert to the unedited version of her name as her brand. *Magdalene*. Just Magdalene because plain Maggie sounded so … so country.

The reality was far from the dream. Part way through a TAFE course, with a small portfolio of work, Maggie had her own cute-as-a-button baby to photograph; an unplanned pregnancy and way too soon. After losing her traineeship with the portrait studio, she took on the only job she could find. Fairytale Photos operated a small booth outside the Kmart store in Parramatta and the franchise owners had no problem with a pregnant photographer. In fact, they loved the idea, unlike Maggie who found long hours standing played havoc with her legs and back. At least the temporary job had kept money coming in while Brian pursued a never-ending string of what he referred to as 'opportunities within the music industry'. Seven-and-a-half months into her unplanned pregnancy she gave birth to a tiny, fragile baby boy, and a guilt complex that remained just as raw seventeen years later.

Though loving parenthood, a baby had made their already meagre existence harder. For fifteen years they played the same two-steps-forward one-step-back game with their finances. They'd fallen further into debt when, two years ago, The Rev needed fulltime care and could no longer manage the family business in Calingarry Crossing. Maggie had no choice. She gave up work in the city and headed back to her hometown. Selling would help Maggie turn the red into black, but the first lesson as a small business operator was that country pubs don't sell overnight and tyre kickers aren't only in the business of checking out cars. The broker with the slimy smile and sickly sales spiel was yet to produce anything other than sticky-beaks and dreamers.

In the meantime, Maggie was falling in love for the first time in years

—in love with life, her dad's old pub, and a second chance for her family in Calingarry Crossing. If only Brian would make the move permanently. It would be an adventure, like starting over.

'Gosh, that was a big sigh.' Sara laughed. 'Feel better?'

'Did I do that out loud?' Maggie sat up, clearing her throat and fingering the copy of Reality TV News on her lap, her eyes fixed on the magazine's double-page spread featuring *iICON's* top twenty finalists— all so beautiful, all so musically gifted, all so young, and all so not Brian.

'You didn't tell me how lunch went with Brian yesterday. It surprised me to find you tucked up in bed alone when I came back from dinner,' Sara said. 'You know we could've stayed in town longer. I was happy to fill in a day catching up with Poppy. Surely the fancy job your husband's locked into allows overnight conjugal visits.' Sara giggled.

'Fancy job? Oh, ha, ha!' Maggie snapped the magazine closed on her lap. What could she say other than one day of Brian was enough. 'No, Sara, I, didn't stay because I didn't want to be away from Noah any longer than I had to be. Besides, Brian was … He's pretty busy and tired these days.'

'Busy and tired?' Sara shot a brief sideways glance in Maggie's direction. 'Not too busy and tired to make time for his wife, surely? Oh sorry, Maggie, that came out wrong.' After a few seconds of silence Sara asked, 'It is the same job with that music production company? He must be pulling in a special salary, you lucky thing.'

'Ah-huh. Yep.' Maggie turned to look out the side window, not wanting her expression to expose the lie.

Staying in Sydney another day had crossed her mind. There was no need to rush back. Ethne could look after the pub—she'd been running the place for years with Maggie's dad—and an extra day might have helped change Brian's mind. They might've tested the theory that sex really did make the heart grow … *Wait!* Did she say sex? She meant absence. The idea of dinner for two—somewhere cheap and cheerful in the city—then back to their flat had tingled Maggie where there'd been no such tingling for some time. Brian once accused her of losing her passion for sex because they no longer snatched every opportunity to make love. It didn't matter to Brian that Maggie might be sorting laundry or up to her elbows in dishwater when the urge hit him. But she could definitely have shown him some passion last night. Maybe they could have skipped dinner or ordered in and let it grow cold as they had wild sex on the living room floor. Despite not far off the big four-oh, Maggie was still a sensual, vibrant woman. And lonely.

Sadly, there'd been no intimate dinner for two and no fabulous mind-bending sex to tease him away from the city, because Brian had suggested they meet in a crowded Newtown café in broad daylight so he could get to his pub gig around the corner on time.

'Fine, see you there.' She'd pouted and punched the phone to end his call. A quick meeting was probably best. They couldn't argue in public and he couldn't weasel his way back into her good books like he used to with his eager puppy impersonation, which involved whimpering and cavorting around, kissing her feet and licking his way up her legs until she'd giggle and run. He'd chase her to the bedroom, they'd make love, and all would be right again—until the next time they fought over money, or the lack of it. Maggie had learned quickly that parenthood was all about responsibility. Nothing like a long labour and childbirth to squeeze out all remaining immaturity. She'd grown up fast. Brian hadn't. He didn't get it then. He still didn't get it at the café yesterday.

'Sara, do you mind if I close my eyes for a bit?' Maggie pressed a palm against her forehead. 'Shocking headache. We can swap over and I'll drive a bit later, if you like.'

'Sure, Maggie, no problem. I'm kind of enjoying myself being in the driver's seat for a change. Will doesn't passenger so good these days. He likes control. Nap away. I'll wake you if I feel weary.'

Maggie's eyes were already closed and seeing the face of a stranger in the café yesterday. Her husband—Brian.

5

Brian had kissed Maggie hard on the lips where she stood in the middle of the ultra-trendy and very compact café in King Street, Newtown. The kiss felt strange. She didn't know who this man was, even though she'd married him twenty years ago. He sounded like her husband, but that was the only familiar feature of a man whose touch had once flipped her stomach and made her toes tingle.

In the place of a man whose face once held her son's image, was a bad fake tan and an over-bleached smile that made the chipped front tooth—courtesy of a drunken altercation with a club bouncer—more obvious. The sandy-coloured sideburns—edges tinged orange—were new, and the cowboy hat and big buckled belt resting on skinny hips justified the curious stares and the cacophony of *Who is he? Isn't that ...? Wasn't he ...?* Thankfully, Brian's cringe-worthy new look was not as attention-grabbing as the drag queens who sauntered into the café, joining two pink-haired girls sprawled across the corner nook.

As Brian pulled out his wife's chair, Maggie heard a young girl at an adjacent table trying, unsuccessfully, to talk softly on her mobile phone. With one of those voices that didn't know how to whisper, the one-sided conversation wasn't hard to follow.

'He just came in. Not sure. A singer, maybe. Country. Ha! If only he was. Hang on.' The girl quickly looked across at them before returning to the call. 'Pfft! No way. Too old. Besides, she's so *not* Nicole Kidman. He's probably no one. So, what were we saying ...?'

Probably no one. The girl's words acted like two fingers snuffing out a candle. Brian's glow had gone, replaced by the facial twitch, a sniffle and an annoying obsession with his nose and mouth that had developed since Maggie saw him last.

'Maggie, Maggie, Maggie.' Repeating her name three times was a tell-tale sign of the old Brian. Once endearing, it now signalled a familiar lecture. 'You're pulling that face again.'

'What face, Brain? Don't talk to me about faces.' Maggie instantly regretted her words, even though his own expression seemed fixed and unnatural.

'You don't get this business, Maggs. You don't understand.'

'Really?' Those last three words caused the hair on the back of Maggie's neck to prickle, like little Jackpot's fur when old Achilles dared get too close to his dug-up doggy treat.

'Maggs, you know underneath all this I'm the same guy and I still love my family. I've just gotta do this.'

Maggie nodded, her eyes fixed on what looked like a packet of cigarettes rolled up in the sleeve of the black T-shirt stretched tight across a gym-enhanced chest and shoulders.

'When did you start smoking?'

A new tattoo on his upper bicep poked out from underneath the sleeve, the words 'NOWHERE MAN' cleverly etched over the fading letters 'N-O-A-H'. Brian must have seen the early veil of tears in her eyes because he shifted in his seat, successfully turning the arm away from her scrutiny. Not even their son's name had survived this latest makeover.

'Come on, Maggs.' Brian tried a laugh, only it sounded strained and tentative. 'I butted out permanently years ago. You know me better than that. This is to do with the image the *iICON* stylists reckon I need.'

'Image?' She wanted to laugh. 'How does a packet of cigarettes enhance an image these days? The Marlboro Man is no longer considered too smart, you know, and neither is that stylist for suggesting it. The show is paying for all this, right?' A silence hung between them. 'Brian?'

'They said building a brand would help me.'

'Help you what?' Maggie asked, trying to stay in control.

'An artist platform makes me more marketable. I need to stand out from the crowd. Besides, no one wants to know Brian bloody Henkler.'

'Your son does,' she said, evading reference to herself. 'You can come back to Calingarry Crossing and still have your music. We can start over. Without the rental on the flat we might keep the pub.'

'You know not to ask, Maggs. You're the girl who's always saying, "never go back". Why would you want to keep the pub?'

'Something has to go,' she responded. 'The rent on the flat is killing us, and the three of us could live together so cheaply. Plus, you'd be great for business. We don't make enough to afford live entertainment. We have an old Pianola and a poorly stocked jukebox that can't compete with the bands playing at Saddleton Hotel. Bands draw people in. You'd be a celebrity, a country sensation in no time. You already have the hat.'

Brian reeled, his expression—what she could see of it under the shadow of the Akubra brim—unreadable. Not so the restrained roar, like a low growl, that attracted wary glances from diners at adjacent tables. Concerned for her, no doubt, Maggie remained unperturbed. The husband she knew wasn't a violent man. Right now he was hurting and frustrated. She sat back, forced a smile, let café patrons see this wasn't a violent encounter or something to worry about.

Confirming as much, Brian folded his arms and slid his elbows across the table. He peered up from underneath his brim and whispered. 'Maggs, asking me to leave here while there's still a chance is like asking me to walk away from a pokie after feeding the bastard for two hours. You know that feeling, Maggs. Remember the night you walked away and that bimbo walked over, put one coin in and—'

'It's not the same, Brian.'

'Yes. It is,' he said, soberly. 'This gig will do it for me.'

'Brian, you told me the show was over.'

His eyes brightened. 'Next season's series is going into production soon and Reg, one of the producers, is fantastic. He's helping me with some industry contacts. He and I have a bit of a contra deal going. This business has a lot of you-scratch-my-back stuff.'

'Oh?' Maggie was about to ask more about this Reg character when Brian leaned even closer, his voice lowered. 'There's no way I'm giving up and letting some next-season smart-arse move in and take what's mine. This is the break I've been waiting for and it's just a matter of time. I can feel it, Maggs. Besides, I don't fit into small towns anymore. Here I can melt into the crowd.'

Hardly, Maggie thought, trying to ignore the two teenage girls not caring enough to hide their giggles.

'You say the same thing every time I raise the subject, Brian. Noah needs you. He misses his father.'

Brian shook his head and instinctively wrapped a hand over the tattoo that had once been his son's name, rubbing back and forth over the spot. 'I can't. I need to make something of myself and I need my kid to be proud of his old man. What would I tell Noah if I gave up now?'

'Tell him the truth, Brian. Tell him you tried. He'll be happy just having his dad in his life again. Let him have his father back, please.'

Spark fading, Brian mumbled, 'His father doesn't exist anymore. I feel like I need to earn his love all over again.' When Brian was up, he was like a two-year-old on a red cordial diet. After all these years, however, Maggie knew after every up came a down, and the higher the high, the bigger the low; that was when he would suck everyone down with him. 'I've failed him, Maggs. If only I'd—'

'Stop it, Brian.' Maggie was witnessing those first signs of the downward spiral that, if left unchecked, would land her husband in a dark place. Wanting to grab him and shake sense into him, she instead dug deep for the false optimism she knew could stop the decline. 'You didn't fail him,' she said. 'You didn't fail—full stop. You did your best, and you did really well. The show might not want you, but we do.'

'My best wasn't enough,' he droned on. 'It's never enough.'

Why did Brian always make her feel like she had two brooding teenage males to deal with?

'You're enough for Noah,' Maggie said. 'He's growing up, Brian, and you're missing it. I'm missing it because I'm tired all the time. Come home, please. Help me and help Noah. We've raised a smart boy. He'll deal with the truth better than the lies.' Maggie choked a little on the last few words. She needed to remember that herself next time she decided to sugar-coat her answers to Noah's enquiries about his father's so-called 'big-city gig'.

Twitching and sniffing was now part of her husband's anxious leg jig taking place beneath the table. 'I'm enough for you, aren't I, Maggs? You still love me?'

When she saw the cheeky smile, Maggie imagined the sad puppy-dog look in those blue eyes, now shadowed by the hat's broad brim. He might have been rising out of the dark, but not enough that the truth wouldn't plunge him back again.

Maggie's gaze dropped to her lap, her fingers twisting themselves in nervous knots. 'Yes. I love you,' she said.

'Sing it with me.' He urged her to take his hands.

'No, Brian. I'm not singing.'

'Aw, c'mon, Maggs.' The old Brian switch flicked to ON. 'Sing our song with me. C'mon. Ready? Don't tell me you've forgotten the words.'

'I haven't forgotten them, Brian,' she said flatly. 'Just not here.'

He half-lifted himself off the chair to lean closer until their faces were almost touching. '*I love my Magpie, just a little-biddy peck* … C'mon sing with me. *Just a little-biddy peck and a …*'

'*… a love bite on my neck.*' She whispered the final lyrics, determined to not let her husband see the smile trying to burst through. The silly song always made them laugh at the end of a fight.

When they eventually said goodbye outside the café it was as though nothing had changed between them. Brian told her he loved her, and Maggie mumbled the words back. Then he kissed her, hugged her and whispered her name three times. 'Maggie, Maggie, Maggie.'

THE TRAIN TRIP FROM NEWTOWN TO ST JAMES STATION IN THE CITY WAS A crowded one, her carriage painted with graffiti and tainted with a nauseating concoction of suit sweat, sickly scents and sharp aftershave. As the train travelled past several station platforms, the phases of her marriage passed through her mind. They'd been married for more than half her life, but before that, Brian had been there after her brother died. He'd helped her accept Michael's death as an accident when her father had refused. That single, needless tragedy and its aftermath had torn the town in two, and sixteen-year-old Maggie's heart along with it when they blamed one boy for her brother's death. Brian had mended her heart and been there ever since. Often he was too much, too close, too demanding—more a fretful five-year-old than a grown man. Initially drawn by Brian's vulnerability and the music obsession once so endearing, Maggie feared those same weaknesses in the hands of a business that turned people and their passion into a commodity, would be his undoing, especially as she wasn't around to monitor him.

A SHARP SWERVE AND TOOTING OF HORNS JOLTED MAGGIE AWAKE, THE dog-eared gossip magazine sliding from her lap to the Subaru's foot well.

'Moron!' Sara shouted at the overtaking road train. 'Sorry about that.

If only he'd waited a few hundred metres. There's an overtaking lane up ahead.'

'Best you don't argue with those big ones.' Maggie flicked the air vents to interior only to avoid their car filling with road dust. She checked her watch, surprised. 'Good grief, Sara, why didn't you wake me?'

'I told you, I'm enjoying the opportunity to drive. I'm feeling carefree and a little crazy after a weekend away from the café. We're like two girls on a road trip.'

'Maybe not so Thelma and Louise next time you see a road train though, eh?' Maggie laughed and picked up the scrunched magazine from under her feet.

'Okay, some conversation wouldn't hurt now you're awake. Talk to me. What gives?' Sara pointed to the magazine. 'I never took you for a gossip-mag junkie. What on earth made you buy that rubbish?'

'I didn't buy it. I pinched it from the hotel room.'

Sara offered a sideways smile. 'I never took you for a crook, either.'

'There was a pile of them, twelve months or more old. I figured they wouldn't miss one.' Maggie shifted her position to relieve the tension in her back. 'Are you hungry?' she asked, keen to change subjects.

'Starving,' she replied. 'We'll stop for a bite and you can take over the driving.'

Maggie found night driving difficult. Even after leaving the highway with its constant glare of oncoming headlights, looking out for straying wildlife on unlit country roads brought a unique eyestrain. She slowed to pass a stationary four wheel drive, two men in its headlights dragging fresh roadkill to one side.

Her melancholy didn't last too long. The lights dotting the darkness on the outskirts of town were like a jab of energy for Maggie. As she sped up under a corridor of tall eucalypt trees, the glow from an almost full moon flickered like a strobe light. Closer to town, in a corner paddock, she recognised the black mass as a clump of trees where the old mare, past her use by, would be spending the night alone. Had she missed Maggie's morning jog? There would be extra carrots tomorrow morning to make up for the absence.

In the dark, beyond the paddocks, were specks of light. Homesteads filled with the aroma of family dinners and the sounds of contented family chaos. Waiting up the road, beyond two more bends, were the signs of Maggie's life: the illuminated Tooheys New sign, the smell of beer, and the sounds of a social life Maggie watched from a distance most nights. As a publican she lived two lives: the amiable, self-sufficient one in the public bar, and the lonely, after-hours one in the residence at the back of the pub.

As she nosed the car to the kerb outside the hotel, and Sara slipped behind the wheel, Maggie grabbed her overnight bag, wished Sara 'goodnight' and headed towards the pub's veranda. Being home, hearing Jackpot's unfailing excitement made Maggie smile, his yelp causing the predictable chorus of 'Jackpot!' from the main bar as the Jack Russell bounded towards her, tail whipping madly.

'G'day fella,' she said, ruffling the little dog's ears. 'Miss me?'

The attention caused the older dog—a Staffy, still curled up on the beanbag by the pub's main entrance—to lift his head, his tail thump, thump, thumping the doggy bed with lazy reliability.

'Don't bother getting up, Achilles,' Maggie chuckled, delivering a quick pat before heading inside.

From behind the bar, Ethne, the town's long-time barmaid, nodded caringly as Maggie signalled from the side entrance that she was heading out back to the publican's residence. Down the hall from Maggie's room, which by day boasted a splendid view across Rivers-Edge Road to Calingarry Creek, was her son's. With the room suspiciously quiet, Maggie knocked softly three times and called, 'Noah, buddy, are you awake?'

'Sure Mum, I'm studying.'

Studying? Maggie considered the answer carefully. A seventeen-year-old son's room was a scary space for a mother to charge into. Noah's growth spurt this last twelve months had turned his voice deep, his chin spiky and his room into a knock-and-wait-just-in-case kind of place. The cracked ceramic doorknob pressed cold against her fingers and as Maggie peered through the small gap, the fug of adolescent male hit her nostrils.

'Hey, bud.'

'Hi.' Noah's foot kicked his desk to propel the wonky office chair across the wooden floorboards where it snagged on the rug with the frayed edges. 'How was the funeral, Mum?'

Maggie picked up a single sock while scanning the floor for its mate. 'Sad, as expected. Pretty flash. Awkward. Good to be home. What did you get up to?'

Noah shrugged. 'Nothing much. Pretty boring, as usual.'

'Hmm, well, will this make things less boring?' Maggie held out the DVD she'd kept partially concealed. 'I believe you wanted this one.'

The music DVD was of a group Maggie had never heard of before her son's recent fervent interest in them. The band had performed somewhere Maggie had never heard of, supported by an act Maggie had never heard of, but when she'd seen the DVD on a stand outside the little music store in a Newtown laneway, she had to spend the $25.99. Her son's now beaming face made it worth every cent.

'Whoa! Cool! Thanks heaps, Mum.' He was already loading it into his player.

'Had dinner, bud?'

'Yeah, Ethne and I ate early. Saved you some.'

'Thank you, buddy. I think I'll hit the hay.' The urge to kiss her son goodnight came and went. Noah's need for such affection had changed around the same time as his voice.

'Mum?' Noah ventured as Maggie was closing the door behind her. 'Did you see Dad? Is he coming?'

Maggie hoped her face was smiling. 'No, bud, he's not able to yet. He sends his love and ... Of course the DVD is from him.'

Not only was the look on her son's face worth the $25.99, it was now worth the lie.

6

'That her?' Noah asked, scuffing over to Maggie on the pub veranda and swinging an arm over her shoulder with ease. In the last six months her son had shot up to—in the old measure—just on six feet tall, dwarfing Maggie's very average five-foot-eight.

'Sure is her, bud.'

The youthful woman behind the wheel of the canary-yellow convertible parked parallel to the kerb—taking up three nose-to-kerb spaces—seemed much younger without the harsh hairdo, the hat, and the ever-present glass of champagne. After a glance in the rear-view mirror and a quick fluffing of her hair, Fiona slid dark sunglasses onto the top of her head to hold back the fiery mane of curls.

'Here I am,' she called, smiling and waving.

Indeed! But where was the surly, spoilt brat from the funeral? This girl looked all private school, charm and compliance—not counting the parallel park. What had made the difference? Maggie doubted a stern talking to from Phillip would have made any impression on the girl, much less found its way through the veneer of mineral makeup powder and London-look mascara so thick the girl's gluggy lashes were visible from ten paces. With the same natural Nicole Kidman curls Amber had hated, and the next-to-nothing waistline, Fiona Blair looked remarkably like the woman she'd openly criticised for ... *What were the words Fiona had blurted the day of the funeral? Oh, yes—'ruining her life'!*

The girl hardly looked ruined in her flowing sensation of a shirt and with the legs of a praying mantis poured into designer jeans; not that Maggie knew too much about designer anything. She knew enough to know the things she couldn't afford and anything starting with the word designer was right up there on the top of her list. Thankfully, most people around here weren't into designer anything. In contrast to the comfy country curves of most Calingarry Crossing locals—one of whom Maggie now considered herself to be—there was very little of Fiona.

'Nice wheels,' Noah said to Maggie.

'And hardly practical for the country,' she replied aloud, while shaking her head at Fiona's self-righteousness. It was obviously appropriate to despise your dead mother and still take ownership of her car. 'Remember what I said, Noah. She's a city girl and she's just—'

'No wuckin' furries, Mum.' Noah nudged his mother's arm playfully.

Maggie nudged him back with a warning squint. 'Please, Noah, you know I hate those words.' Her arm twitched, itching to smooth the over-gelled hair; the latest addition to her son's gradual transformation from uncool, clean-cut kid, to something from a Twilight movie.

Generation Y. *Why indeed*? Why so much black, and why was it when kids wanted to fit in they did everything they could to make themselves different? How he even tolerated wearing black in these temperatures bemused and bothered Maggie, until she recalled the number of times she'd let vanity keep her warm when she was young and night-clubbing in the middle of a Sydney winter, wearing very little of everything in order to achieve maximum impact.

'What about helping Fiona with her suitcase?'

'Suitcase-*es*,' Noah grumbled. 'How long's she plan to stay?'

'Go. Now,' Maggie growled, distracted by Fiona applying a dab of lip-gloss, and the notion that perhaps all the girl's fat had gone looking for her lips—and found them.

Noah leapt the two steps, hitched the waistline of his jeans up, and swaggered towards the Saab convertible. How long *was* she planning to stay? The invitation, which Maggie had been kicking herself over, was not a two-suitcase arrangement. Calingarry Crossing was sweltering, with higher than average temperatures for this time of year. One bag would have been ample for a short stay: a few light tops, shorts, sandals. Although Maggie had initially offered for Fiona to lodge at the pub, she'd thought the girl might have stayed with her grandmother, rather than a stranger. After all, Fiona was five stars and Maggie's pub might be awarded one, maybe two. Then again, Fiona's grandmother—the one Fiona hadn't known about until recently—was as much a stranger to her as Maggie was.

You've got a big mouth, Maggie!

She groaned at her son's body language: the puffing up of a budding chest and the flick of his head that momentarily shifted the one gelled clump of fringe from his eyes. From memory her son's eyes were a cerulean colour, like his father's, only it felt like she hadn't seen them for so long—his or Brian's.

Ethne came from inside and sidled up to her boss. The brash British barmaid was a pseudo sister, aunty, mother and a friend, with her fleshy, flabby proportions comforting whenever Maggie needed a hug.

'Awright there, love?' she asked Maggie. 'Bit of peacockin' going on, by the looks. Makes you realise how grown up he's gettin'. Not sure which one's puffin' up more, though. Sure is a pretty Miss Priss, and a tempting one.'

'Oh please, do not let my mind go there. Besides, she's too old for Noah.'

'Hmm, yes, older woman and younger man. Never happens.' Ethne nudged Maggie's shoulder.

'He's hardly a man.'

'Look again, love,' the barmaid said, trying to tame the grey fairy-floss hair.

Maggie knew how fast Noah was growing up without looking. The signs were everywhere. 'Don't suppose it's legal to chain your son up to his bed at night, is it?'

Ethne's trill when she laughed always sounded at odds with the woman's very generous proportions. In the purple promotional T-shirt, she was a bulging signboard for bourbon whiskey, while on the bottom she wore a flowing peasant skirt in shades of green.

'It is the first day of October,' she added, looking up at Maggie over her half-glasses.

'What's that got to do with anything?'

'Summer storm season officially starts today,' Ethne announced.

Maggie knew that. Tracking weather patterns was part and parcel of a life in the country where one intense event could mean the difference between bumper crops or no crops at all. They'd had so much rain already this year. One extreme, then the other. Politicians were gleefully announcing, 'No more drought' and 'The drought is over'. The reality was though, now they'd finished lamenting the dry, locals would soon curse a new menace. Too much blasted rain. If the early heat first thing in the morning and increasing grey clouds each afternoon hadn't been enough to let Maggie know storm season was close, the half-dozen men in orange in the beer garden yesterday had reminded her. The week before, there'd been a briefing for the local State Emergency Service volunteers and Ethne had needed time off work to attend. What a remarkable sight. Ethne in the bright orange SES overalls, which she wore with pride and always kept handy so she'd be ready when needed.

'Tell me, Ethne, what's the official start of storm season got to do with anything? Looks like a perfectly beautiful day to me.'

'Some storms are sneaky bastards,' she said. 'The SES suggests people batten down and prepare in advance of an impending catastrophe and, if you ask me, it's looking like we might see our first-ever inland cyclone— called Fiona.'

Maggie chuckled. 'Ha! Ha!'

'Thinkin' I might look up the manual to see what the SES suggests you do with your son when a Category Five storm like that one hits town.'

'Even funnier. Thanks. You're a lot of help, Ethne.'

'I try. Come on, boss. Time to welcome your guest.'

DINNER THAT NIGHT WAS THE QUIETEST ON RECORD: MAGGIE ANGRY AT herself for having created this situation, Fiona apparently angry at the peas for refusing to stay on her fork, and Noah? He seemed less angry at the world and different from the sullen, silent son he'd been morphing into over the last year or so.

'All settled in, Fiona?' Maggie enquired.

'Yes. Thanks.' She added the word as an afterthought, or perhaps because her attention was on something more interesting on her mobile phone.

At the last minute, when showing Fiona to her accommodation earlier, Maggie had changed her mind about the spare room in the residence, instead preparing a single room in the pub. Calingarry Crossing's hotel was much like every other two-storey country pub: a corner position on the main street, decorative balustrades, weathered boards on the outside, high ceilings and fancy cornices inside, and small but comfortable upstairs guest rooms. Recently spring-cleaned, Maggie had added a small vase

with lavender stems she'd picked from the bush growing with little attention at the back of the hotel. As Maggie had left Fiona to settle in, the vase
of lavender was the first thing pushed aside to make way for the Gucci
carryall.

Maggie could only pray that after familiarising herself with the town
in the next day or two, Fiona would feel comfortable enough to move in
with her grandmother. Until then, Maggie would have to be patient.
Tonight's meal was providing practice enough.

'How was school today?' she asked her son, hoping for more than a
one-syllable response.

'Same.'

'Did you remember to feed the dogs tonight?'

'I'll do it after *X Factor*.'

'Dog's first, Noah.' Maggie was learning to dislike reality TV shows,
particularly those that fed false hope to people seeking stardom. What was
it her father always said? 'A person can't be a star. The only stars are
God's creation and they are firmly set in the sky.' In Maggie's experience,
reality never lived up to the dream. At the same time, she didn't want to
quash her son's enthusiasm for his music and while he had talent, she
wanted him to see there was more he could do with that talent than sing on
a stage. 'And homework before *X Factor*, buddy,' she added.

'Geez, Mum, give me a break.' Noah glared, first at Maggie, and then
in Fiona's direction, his cheeks reddening. What had once been an
adorable blush on her baby boy was suddenly an agonising flush of embarrassment.

Maggie took a deep breath. 'I'm sorry, Noah, but you do have homework, don't you?'

'I've done most of it.'

'Well, the rest shouldn't take too long then.'

With a groan, Noah picked up his plate and left Maggie alone with
Fiona, who had one hand still poking peas around the plate with her fork
while the other hand poked her phone. Even from her seat on the opposite
side of the table, Maggie detected the scent of a woman bathed in lotions
and potions meant to allure as much as beautify. She'd noticed the trifecta
of sickly sweet fragrance, hair product and moisturiser waft by as Fiona
swept past her on the way into the hotel earlier. Maggie examined the girl
more closely while she had the chance. Unlike Amber's classic sophistication, Fiona's beauty was in her bohemian look, exaggerated by big gypsy
earrings, eyeliner that turned up at the outer corners of big, blue get-what-

ever-you-want eyes, and a tiny nose stud—diamond, naturally—in the crease of one nostril. Then there was the tattoo of a feather Maggie had spotted on the side of her neck; easy to see tonight with her locks pinned on top of her head with what looked like two small gem-encrusted chopsticks. They probably weren't chopsticks, any more than they were fake gemstones, Maggie surmised. She was, after all, Amber Bailey-Blair's daughter.

'Fiona?' Maggie tried again. 'Did you want to talk about anything?'

'I have a call to make,' she said, pushing the plate with her half-eaten meal into the centre of the table for the invisible servant to carry to the kitchen and wash up. 'I'll be in my room.'

Open-mouthed, Maggie watched the girl leave before letting her own knife and fork drop heavily, the clunk of metal on ceramic covering her huff. *That went well, Maggie!*

'Here ya go, love.'

A glass of red wine came from behind and slid under Maggie's nose. 'Thanks, Ethne, but I shouldn't.'

'Yes, you should. Medicinal,' the woman said. 'Remember, I'm trained in emergency situations and this is an emergency. No different to giving brandy to someone unconscious in the snow.'

Maggie twisted to stare up at the woman. 'Our rural emergency service training teaches you what to do with unconscious people in the snow?'

'Of course not. This one's my personal remedy. Figured you'll be unconscious soon enough if you keep hittin' your head on that brick wall. Wine's less traumatic on the brain.'

'You heard her, huh?'

'Heard what? The sounds of shitty-livered silence?' Ethne waved her cleaning cloth in the air before focusing on a red-wine stain on the adjacent table. 'You know it can take a few days for the new chick to settle in.'

'Hmm, yes, but she's not my chick. Therefore, not my problem.'

'I hope, for your sake, Maggie-girl, she's not going to be a problem.'

THAT NIGHT, THE DINING ROOM SAW ONLY A FEW LOCALS, PLUS AN OLDER couple who were passing through on their way to relatives at a station further west. After warning them about the state of the pot-holed private road and the number of gates they'd have to access to reach the homestead, Maggie offered them a discount on a room if they wanted to wait until morning. They grabbed at the idea and promptly ordered a bottle of sparkling wine. The couple told Maggie they were touring the state. 'Having ourselves an adventure to spend the kids' inheritance,' the man had explained with a chuckle. Then the pair kissed and giggled like newly-weds, while Maggie watched from the bar, envy dragging her down.

'So mother bird,' Ethne said as she sidled up to Maggie. 'You want me to stay on 'til close tonight?'

Maggie signed. 'Would you mind? I'm in no mood to be chatty and no one wants a grumpy barmaid.'

'Best get some sleep then. You've got that brekkie meeting about the centenary fair day tomorrow. More brick walls to hit your head against there too, I reckon.'

'I'd prefer sticking my head in the sand until it's all over. Why, oh why did I volunteer, Ethne?'

'As I recall, you were volunteered, and sticking your head in the sand around these parts will only get it bit by bull ants.'

'Like I said ...' Maggie raised an eyebrow in droll self-mockery. 'Sounds preferable to me.'

Ethne sniggered. 'Awright, you go on, love. Old Barney's holdin' up the bar 'til close. He can make himself useful and help me lock up.'

'Old Barnacle Bill?' Maggie undid her apron and folded it while whispering out of the corner of her mouth. 'He'll help you do more than that if you let him.'

Ethne chirruped. 'Yeah, like that's going to happen at my age.'

Or mine, Maggie mused as she headed off to an empty bed with hopes of something that resembled sleep.

7

S tripped down to her knickers and in front of the open bedroom window, Maggie's body was tantalisingly exposed to the elements, but with the moon hidden behind a thick layer of gathering cloud, only the digital numbers from the clunky clock radio—a sixteenth-birthday present from her brother—illuminated the room. The sash window was propped open with a long chock of wood and a breeze billowed the lace curtaining, teasing her thighs and her breasts. Moving closer, urging the fabric to continue its caress, she imagined a time when Brian's hands had thrilled her.

When she'd met him in the café in Sydney, he might not have looked like the old Brian but when she'd closed her eyes as they'd hugged, there'd been a moment when she remembered a loving man who'd been all spice and sex. Maggie missed sex. Not the orgasm part—she could manage that all by herself—but the intensity and completeness that came from being adored and wanted, as well as that first teasing touch that held the promise of more and warmed everything from her toes to her ears.

'Argh!' Maggie swiped at the curtains, jerked the roller blind halfway down and threw herself on top of cool crisp bed sheets while telling herself this was all stick-insect-skinny Fiona's fault. Fiona not only had Amber's looks, but an inheritance that put a little country pub to shame. Pert, pretty and alluring, the girl was everything else Maggie missed. Even the giggling grey nomads getting cuddly in the bar tonight had stirred Maggie's green-eyed monster.

Maggie's mundane existence and lack of material objects had never worried her as much as they had tonight. She'd always made do, with her mother regularly sorting the family's clothes into boxes and bags. Anything not worn last season went straight to charity. 'Farmers are always needy,' she used to tell her daughter, 'even if they never say it outright.' Such throwaway lines had painted a hopeless picture of farming and convinced a young Maggie that if she was to make something of herself, she'd have to get out of Calingarry Crossing.

She'd grown up hearing about hardship over the dinner table when her parents had talked in a crazy code about which farmer was losing the battle or letting bullying bureaucrats and poor policy decisions push them off the land. Some nights, a sombre Reverend Joe Lindeman would announce another 'accident'. In a small town, death seemed easier to stomach when discussed in vague terms—unless they were talking about Michael. 'Reckless stupidity' was how her heart-broken father had referred to the act that killed her brother. Although he'd stopped saying it aloud a long time ago, her father thought about it still. At least he had up until the moment he could no longer remember the tragedy in much detail at all.

Maggie fell back against her pillow, wishing she could shut out the memory from her sixteenth birthday. They didn't let her see him. They didn't let her say sorry: sorry for being a brat; sorry for the time she'd faked bruises on her arm with purple eye shadow, telling everyone he'd given her a horsey bite; and sorry for writing *I hate you* in indelible ink on the wall above his bed one day. Even though Michael's death would change her life forever, they never let Maggie say goodbye.

Her sixteenth had started out predictably enough—predictable for Maggie who, for the last three years, had looked after a house, a father and a brother. Homework was always the priority after each school day, followed by the chooks, the dogs, the laundry and other household chores. How three people could dirty so many clothes was beyond her understanding. Each evening she cooked, usually for two—her and her dad—as Michael was ... Well, he was a restless teenage boy and who could control them? Her father couldn't; everyone's favourite ex-minister was always preoccupied fitting his life around the needs of his congregation, and later his customers. There was nothing left for family.

If only he'd been there the day that big brown snake had sought respite from the burning summer heat by coiling up under the laundry copper on the back veranda of the Manse. It took a sleepy snake to strike down the otherwise indomitable Mary Lindeman—keystone of the Lindeman family—two weeks before Maggie's thirteenth. Maggie was desperately sad, her father sadder, while Michael—two years older—coped by taking a bull-by-the-horns approach to life. If her father noticed, he did nothing to curtail his son's unruliness. Their mother had been the only one who could control Michael and she was gone.

Maggie missed everything about her mother, including her kisses. Mary Lindeman was the kisser in the family: good morning, goodnight, hello, goodbye. In town, she adopted the European double-cheek air kiss thing because she'd dreamed of one day going to Italy and to the opera. Mary loved to sing, and her soprano voice and strange medley of church hymns, Italian opera and Broadway musicals used to be audible several houses down. When she died, Maggie's father struggled to meet the most basic of his clergyman's duties, let alone domestic chores. That's when nurturing and housekeeping responsibilities fell to his daughter. After a quiet dinner each night, The Rev wordlessly but methodically wiped as Maggie washed and stacked the dish rack. Often Maggie tried to hold off serving dinner in the hope her brother would lob with his hungry hangers-on, even though stalling usually meant singed or soggy food. Her father didn't seem to care, and Maggie didn't. She craved noise and the chaotic clamour that Michael and his mates brought into the house and her humdrum world. They came mostly on a Sunday when The Reverend, occupied with his religious duties in the adjacent church, didn't have time to worry, or the inclination to care about the mischief his son might be up to in the Manse.

Maggie's sixteenth birthday happened to fall on a Sunday, with the all-male invasion taking over every chair in the living room where they watched 'Wide World of Sports', swigged on cans of beer and Pepsi, and ate Cheezels straight from the box. Pesky younger sisters—birthday girl or not—were definitely barred. Not that Maggie was interested in her poser brother's chorus of swearing and farting while carrying on like a dork in front of his mates. Michael was not the reason she wanted to hang around.

If Maggie could have wished for anything that birthday, it was that sixteen was old enough to drink beer, make noise and get up to no good with the boy she liked. That brooding mate of Michael's—the one her father would later label reckless—who always acknowledged Maggie with a smile and silent *G'day* when his mates weren't looking. As mates, the boys were cool and loud and blokey, constantly making mischief around the town, staying up late, playing drinking games by the river and taking girls to Cedar Cutters Gorge. Yes, even *he* apparently did that, although Maggie chose not to believe everything she heard. Maggie didn't want to be cool as much as she did loud. Wasn't life meant to be big and colourful and exciting? Not in Calingarry Crossing, it seemed, especially at night when country-town silence did the opposite of soothe.

✿

MAGGIE'S SIXTEENTH HAD BEEN NO DIFFERENT TO ANY OTHER SUNDAY. After scoffing down dinner, the boys left the house, ejected by The Rev whose tolerance for tomfoolery—any kind of fun—had died along with Mary. From behind her louvred bedroom windows in the Manse, Maggie watched her brother and his friends go, their drunken attempts to hush each other only making more noise. As usual, she stifled her giggle behind a hand to remain undetected. But tonight—maybe because it was special —*he* turned around and looked towards her window. Then, walking back-wards, he doffed his hat and promptly tripped, falling flat on his bottom.

Maggie fell on her bed, burying her laughter in the pillow and when she lifted her head to the louvres again, the boys were gone, the night was silent, and she was alone. She lay on her bed in the dark for a long time, staring at the bright red numbers of the new digital clock radio she'd unwrapped over breakfast. She must have fallen asleep because when she looked again the little LED numbers read 11.30 pm. They kept turning over, until at 2 am all the familiar night noises changed, and a curious, curved beam of light travelled over the foot of her bed. The white glow illuminated the bedside table, passed over the walls and striped the ceiling until the room was black once more, the night noises normal.

Then a car door banged, and the front gate clanged back against the old milk can mailbox. Feet shuffled over the gravel path, and a fist pounded on the front door. The crickets that chirped unfailingly each night quit, as if they wanted Maggie to hear the voices. The only night noise that continued was the muted and ominous oom-oom, oom-oom sound of the tawny frogmouth with its bird's-eye view of the porch from its perch in the gnarly tree out front. Sneaking a peak through a gap in the louvres, and under a full moon, the police car was easy to make out in the street, the sight of it speckling Maggie's neck and arms with goose bumps despite the warm September night air. The bare bulb on the porch flickered before spotlighting the uniformed figure at the front door. As daughter of the local minister, she'd woken plenty of times to a late-night visitor, or to the shrill of the telephone. Maggie didn't need to hear the policeman's words tonight to know a visit at such an hour generally meant bad news. Someone, somewhere in town, or on a property, needed consoling or counselling. Any minute her father would invite the policeman in while he quickly changed out of his pyjamas and into the clothes he customarily laid out, kind of like a fireman's outfit, ready to slip into when time was of the essence.

Tonight, her father didn't swing into action. Rather, he sank back into the darkness of the doorway and she heard a sound she had never heard before.

'Not my boy!' came the inconsolable roar. 'Not my Michael!' The cry rose from the shadows, ripping through the early morning calm and sending a flurry of squawking birds from their perches.

MAGGIE HAD SOBBED SILENT TEARS THAT NIGHT AND EVERY NIGHT FOR months, scared that her life would never again be loud. To this day, when she closes her eyes, Maggie can picture the policeman walking away from the little church residence. He'd stopped to stare at the glass louvres as if sensing her there, and Maggie saw his face. It was one of those sad, tired faces. Tired of being the bearer of bad news. But things were to get worse. The aftermath of Michael's funeral tore the town, and Maggie, in two. The incident left half the folk shaking their heads in disbelief, while the other half condemned one young man.

That memory from long ago wouldn't allow Maggie to close her eyes tonight. The little pub bedroom was no longer dark, the combination of moon shadow and pressed tin on the ceiling creating strange shapes and playing with her mind. Maggie's life had changed forever on that sixteenth birthday. The only thing to help her cope then, and now, was to tell herself Michael was with Mum.

God had had them both for so long, but what did Maggie have? An absent, fame-obsessed musician husband, a stagnant marriage, an ailing father, a dwindling bank account, and now an all too alluring twenty-two-year-old female occupying a room not far away from an increasingly restless seventeen-year-old son.

8

'Uh-oh!' A grinning Will Travelli poked his head around the side of Big Bertha. The shiny red coffee machine had been the love of his life—until the day Sara Fraser came home to the country. 'Now, that's a give-me-the-strongest-coffee look if ever I saw one, Maggie.'

Ordinarily, she loved Will's coffee. 'Caffeine may exacerbate my foul mood, Will,' she said. 'I hardly slept last night.'

'New guest giving you grief already?'

'Ha! Have you *seen* my new guest? She's her mother all over again.'

Will laughed along. 'You mean trouble?'

'I mean too damn gorgeous. When I wasn't having nightmares about female praying mantises eating their unsuspecting mate after sex, I was awake and ready to pounce the moment I heard Noah sneaking down the hallway. It's not funny, Will.'

'Hi Maggie! What's not funny?' Sara stopped in the kitchen doorway, a plate of muffins in her hand.

'You know you married a joker?'

'Um, yes.' She laughed. 'Sit down. Jennifer will be here soon. She's found another marching band. You know the first band bailed? They figured we'd cancelled the event when Amber didn't return their messages.'

Maggie slid along the bench seat that ran the length of the café, admiring as always the difference Will's makeover had made to Nick the

43

Greek's old takeaway from their youth. No more speckled laminate tables trimmed with chrome; no more vinyl-covered booths that stuck to your legs so badly in summer that you had to slowly peel your flesh away or else treat it like a Band-Aid and suffer the sting. The café's exterior was like most other shopfronts in the street: scarred facades, some thick with multiple layers of old paint, and all with the same drab corrugated tin awnings. Inside was a different story: fancy spotlighting, all-stainless-steel countertops, and a long, fabric-covered bench seat with a dozen or more multi-coloured cushions as ad hoc backrests. Maggie shoved a blue oblong pillow in the small of her back.

'Did Jennifer explain to the band people that the event organiser passed away?'

Sara shrugged. 'They said they were sorry but they'd already booked another gig.'

'Are you talking about that lousy band?' Jennifer huffed and let her notebook drop heavily onto the table. She slipped into one of the wood and chrome chairs across from Maggie and hooked the heel of one foot on the edge of her seat, hugging a knee to her chest. Jennifer always sat that way. The woman was the same age as Maggie, but like a string of spaghetti—and about as supple. 'Can we have the meeting after work next time? I don't do mornings.'

'Nine o'clock is hardly early morning, Jen,' Will chimed. 'Most of the locals have done half a day's work by now. Sara's baked muffins.' He said the words with such pride, anyone would have thought his wife had single-handedly grown, harvested and stone-ground the wheat. Knowing health-obsessed Sara, she probably had.

'Okay, everyone, let's get on with it.' Sara took charge. 'Jennifer, you're taking notes this morning I assume?'

Sara was different to the girl constantly ribbed at school for having an annoying don't-make-me-cry whine in her voice. But if anyone was allowed to moan, she was, and if anyone deserved a happily ever after story, Sara and Will did.

'We have a week, folks,' Jennifer said, referring to handwritten notes in front of her. 'And I can confirm the following regarding the fair day. We've received another float entry for the street parade and I'm waiting to hear from interested Saddleton businesses. I've had confirmation from the school that every class, except Year 12, will enter a float, or they'll march. Some senior boys have put together a band and both Saddleton and

Rainbow Ridge schools are sending kids to join in. Oh, and Glen Innes is sending a marching band as well.'

'Really? Glen Innes? Wow. That's a trek for them. What sort of band?' Will asked.

Jennifer snorted. 'Bagpipes! What else would come from the Celtic capital of New South Wales? We were lucky to get them, too. Turns out they're on their way home from an event on the Saturday. Twenty men in kilts might not be all bad, although it could be more excitement than the CWA ladies can handle if it's a windy day.'

'Minds out of the gutter please,' Sara said, keen to curb the smutty turn in conversation due to the arrival of said Country Women's Association ladies—two of them, at least.

'Hi Val, hi Lorna.' Jennifer waved at two empty seats. 'Thanks for coming so early.'

The two women looked at each other as if to say what Will already had: Nine o'clock is hardly early.

'Good morning, lovely ladies,' Will said, wheeling across the cafe to slip a coffee in front of his wife. 'Your presence is a delightful addition to what is already a bevy of beauties.'

Sara shoved Will's wheelchair so it rolled away, her stern look lasting all of two seconds until he winked.

'Ignore my husband,' Sara said. 'We were just about to discuss the family fun events scheduled for the sports ground. The Lions Club is running Cow-Pat Bingo throughout the day. The school hall is accommodating artworks and we have several pieces already stored behind the stage in the assembly hall. The afternoon outdoor events will be a tractor pull and hay bale hurdles.'

'Shouldn't we have the tractor pull in the morning before it gets hot?' Maggie suggested, wishing she'd thought to suggest they schedule the fair day for the Saturday, not Sunday, which was after the reunion night. 'It doesn't matter so much about the kids' stuff in the afternoon. They'll all hit the swimming hole afterwards.'

'Excellent point,' Sara agreed. 'And the tractor pull boofheads won't be so full of brew before the event that way.'

'You wanna bet?' Will contributed from the back of the café.

'Fine.' Jennifer sighed and scratched several lines through her care-fully typed event schedule. Then, in case no one noticed the sigh and the frantic scribbling, she huffed long and loud. 'I'll take it from here, thanks Sara,' Jen said, brandishing her pen and a rainbow of highlighters. 'The street will be closed from seven in the morning so the stallholders can set up. We've got four tables allocated for the jams and baking entries. The CWA ladies will judge them; Cheryl Bailey is happy to arrange that part. If it's raining, they'll shift into the school hall. There are two tables for the Lions Club sausage sizzle. That leaves one, two, three ... about four spare.' Jennifer's finger ran over the paper in a double check. 'Yep, four. The bottom end of the street is where we'll set up the farmers' market.'

'Having the farmers setting up fruit and veggie displays on the back of tray-top trucks is a great idea, but shouldn't we keep them under the trees? Unless we want roasted pumpkin,' Maggie quipped.

'What about the pigs?' Will added. 'You can't race pigs in the heat.'

'What are you on about?' snapped Jennifer. 'What pig race?'

'The one Charlie and Cricket were talking about at the pub. The Pork Crackling Cup and the Ham and Bacon Stakes.'

'Ignore him,' Sara said, trying to bring Jennifer back from boiling mad to her usual simmer. 'Will is joking and he'll stop now, or else. Won't you, Will?'

'Sorry, yeah, pulling your leg, Jen, but you'll be pleased to know I have arranged the bucking bull ride,' Will added as if he'd somehow single-handedly scored a one-on-one interview with America's talk show queen. 'Three players from my old footy team are keen to come out and do a teaching clinic on the day. Brashnee, Fitzi and Gilbertson.'

Jennifer stopped scribbling and stared across at Will. 'Paul Brashnee? Here? In the flesh?'

'Yep! Here we go, lovely ladies. Two Earl Greys.' Will squeezed his chair in between Lorna and his wife. 'And I do know Brash will be particularly keen to try out a bucking bull or two while he's in town, Jen, so ... Ouch!' The crack of Sara's hand against Will's shoulder made Maggie smile.

'Can we get back to business?' she asked, checking her watch.

'Good morning! Noah said I'd find you all here.' A fresh-faced Fiona stood in the doorway. Obviously she'd experienced no problem sleeping last night, unlike Maggie.

'Ah, good morning, Fiona. The café's not actually open yet. Is there something wrong?' A problem at the pub was always Maggie's first thought these days.

The girl replied with a shrug. 'I don't know. Is there? I'm here for the meeting.'

Her matter-of-fact tone silenced everyone except Jennifer, who suddenly resembled a meerkat on high alert. 'Meeting? What do you mean by meeting?'

Fiona's gaze took in each committee member. 'This *is* the planning meeting for the centenary, isn't it? Naturally, I'll be taking my mother's place and managing the reunion event.'

Arming herself with highlighters and quickly staking her claim as Chief Organiser of Everything Jennifer said, 'We have that event under control. Your mum and I started on those details a while ago and we've—'

'Yes, Mother always knew how to throw a magnificent party, and as I'm her daughter—as far as I know,' Fiona added for effect, 'I'm sure I can add value. Maggie said you needed help. Let's start with you telling me which portfolio you're each in charge of. Maggie? You start.'

'Portfolio?' Maggie sat straight-backed as if the class teacher had called on her for the homework she'd left on the dining room table. Last night, within Fiona's earshot, Maggie *had* asked Ethne to cover a couple of her shifts as the committee needed as much help as possible with the final planning.

'The reunion is organised,' Jennifer repeated, her tone as firm as the pen tip now gouging lines through the notes on her sad, scribbled-over page. 'Everything is absolutely under control. Ticket sales are covering catering costs; there'll be drinks and canapes on arrival; after which, all other grog will be from the bar, manned by SES blokes who've got their responsible service of alcohol certificate. We have a DJ, who comes with a sound system, and I negotiated disco lights and a mirror ball—no charge.'

'Well,' said Fiona, seemingly unperturbed. 'My father … I mean Phillip—of course we all know by now he's not my real father—told me I had to make myself useful. So here I am.'

'I believe he meant at the pub for experience or helping your grand-mother,' Maggie said as plainly as possible. They already had weekend casuals, while Monday to Friday, Ethne both cooked and delivered meals, with Maggie dividing her time between the bar and the kitchen. Maggie was happy to have help and company during the week. Fiona might be inexperienced at waiting tables, and she'd never been forced into menial tasks to further her education, but to know how to carry multiple plates, especially laden with Ethne's generous servings, was a skill worth learning —in Maggie's opinion.

'I am extremely qualified, Maggie. I can call you Maggie, can't I?' Fiona didn't wait for an answer and Maggie had a feeling that happened a lot. 'I work in marketing and I'm very experienced with product launches and the media. I'm sure you'll know some of my work.' The girl hardly paused for breath. Ethne was right. Fiona was like a windstorm, sweeping through the town, taking everyone by surprise and spinning them around until they no longer knew which way was up. 'You know the television commercial with the cat and the talking goldfish …?' Fiona continued.

Will chuckled. 'Not the one with that little ditty about the—'

'It's not a *ditty*,' Fiona barked. 'I write advertising jingles and design slogans. I've done a million launches, making me better equipped for event management than table waiting.'

'All very impressive, Fiona.' Jennifer steamed. 'But with my vast food and beverage experience, the event management side of things is in hand.' Jennifer didn't mention her 'extensive experience' was courtesy of *Will's Wheely Great Café*. 'Perhaps, Fiona, you'll *manage* the coat-check table?'

Maggie and Sara rolled their eyes at each other, while Will snorted. 'Get real, Jennifer. Have you checked the temperature of late? Who's going to be wearing a coat? Not me, that's for sure.'

'I did a long-range weather check. They're predicting rain,' she said.

'So what? They've been predicting rain in these parts since Noah was a boy.' Will nudged his wife and laughed. 'Get it? Since Noah was a boy?'

'The idea has merit,' Sara said, rubbing her arm. 'The school does have a cloakroom, and *some* men,' she added, her eyes on Will, 'and I'm referring to the sophisticated ones interested in making a good impression, might wear jackets and take them off once they're inside.'

'You mean those metro males coming from the city?' Will scoffed. 'The ones who think the rest of us are lesser human beings because country sweat makes us smell like real men?'

Sara's ski-lift nose twitched and scrunched. 'Is that what I can smell, Will?'

'A man in a jacket cuts a dashing picture,' Lorna offered, cheered on by Val's nodding head. 'I think somewhere they can put hats, or even the lady's handbag, is a splendid idea, Jennifer. Just splendid. Don't you agree, Val?'

'Yes,' Val agreed. 'And if it rains they might check muddy gumboots.'

'I'm sure you can add value to our planning, Fiona,' Maggie said, keen to finish the meeting.

'I agree,' Sara said. 'Grab a chair and join us, Fiona. Will can make you a coffee, unless you prefer tea?'

Fiona sat and picked up a spare water glass from the centre of the table. She held the glass up to the light, no doubt looking for traces of garish lipstick that would clash with the garish red lip print Fiona was about to stamp on the rim. 'I only ever drink skinny soy milk. GMF.'

'Well, you've come to the right place,' Will called back as he wheeled over to Big Bertha. 'Just yesterday we got ourselves a skinny, genetically modified-free cow for the backyard. You guys carry on. I'll be back once I've worked out how to milk a soy cow.'

෧

ETHNE WAS WAITING ON THE PUB VERANDA WHEN MAGGIE AND FIONA walked separately across from the café. When Fiona disappeared up the internal stairs to the guest rooms, Ethne asked, 'Is that a blunt stick poking out of your eye, love?'

Maggie rolled her eyes and grunted. 'I'd prefer poking my eye with a blunt stick than sitting through another meeting like that. I was tempted to grab one of those chopstick things sticking out of Fiona's hair. As if Jennifer's not difficult enough so early in the morning. Did you know Fiona is too qualified to wait tables?'

Maggie looked down at Ethne sitting on the old church pew, one of eight running the length of the pub's veranda, each varnished cedar seat bearing three decades of scratched-in graffiti. Once taking pride of place in the town's Methodist church, the Reverend Lindeman had called the pews 'souvenirs', acquiring them after both town churches amalgamated into a single entity.

'Am I the only one silly enough to think she would pull her weight, Ethne?' Maggie asked. 'Everyone works here, and we'll have a full house for a few days.'

'A full house. Woo hoo!'

'I'm not cheering yet,' Maggie said. 'I have a terrible feeling.'

'About what exactly?'

'The reunion, the fair day, the—'

'The fair Fiona?' Ethne chuckled.

'Argh! Don't joke. How could I be so—?'

'So caring?' Ethne stood and wrapped one arm around Maggie's waist, squeezing tight. 'You're just like your dad, girl, always seeing the good in people, always willing to give strays a second chance.'

'I'd hardly call Amber Bailey-Blair's daughter a stray. She's the most overindulged, spoilt brat.'

'Doesn't mean she's not a little lost,' Ethne said. 'Being abandoned isn't just physical. Kids all too easily get overlooked and forgotten.'

Wives too, Maggie wanted to say.

'And remember this.' Ethne waved her index finger at Maggie before turning it into the centre of her own chest. 'Your dad took this old stray dog in how many years ago? About the same age as the fair Fiona, I was, and not exactly the model of diplomacy—or anything else back then.'

Maggie did remember the feral-looking British backpacker with the weird accent who—much to her father's ire—had told a teenage Maggie it was possible to calculate her cycle to avoid getting pregnant. *For all the good that lesson did!* The Rev had paid Ethne cash-in-hand, with food and lodgings on top. He'd told Maggie she was a hard worker and keen to learn, so she waited on tables, assisted in the kitchen, and serviced the guest rooms, while Joe Lindeman manned the bar with its cast of characters. Maggie wasn't sure when Ethne had started running the place solo; she was just so very glad the woman had been there for her dad. Keen to maintain the status quo when Maggie took over the pub, she'd suggested putting Ethne on the books officially. The woman had declined, respectfully, and for a time Maggie worried about the legalities, but she never broached the subject again.

Always let sleeping dogs lie, Maggie told herself, looking at old Achilles splayed out on the cool veranda boards: mouth open and panting, a dangling pink tongue dancing up and down. The old mutt was never too far away from Ethne these days; probably because she smuggled treats from the kitchen in her pockets.

'I do remember you back then,' Maggie said.

'Then you'll know the most capricious will eventually calm and settle into country life.' Ethne hand-batted a bug from her face. 'Fiona's young, given too much too soon. Let her see how the other half lives. It'll work out.'

Maggie smiled. 'I hope you're right, my friend.'

'I am, love. What could possibly go wrong?'

9

E thne's arms and lily-white wing flaps were in full swing as she helped Maggie re-stock the cans in the main bar.

'How was this morning's torture, err, I mean meeting?' asked Ethne. 'Day two of Fiona-phobia any better or did Jen put her in her place?'

'That smile of yours may wane when I tell you Miss I'm-qualified-to-manage-a-function suggested we add a 'Centenary Cocktails' event on the Friday night. A kind of welcome to Calingarry Crossing for those arriving in town early. She suggested we have it at the pub.'

'Did she?' Ethne's wing flaps wobbled to a stop. 'You said no, I assume?'

'The thing is ...' Maggie passed two VB stubbies to Ethne. 'The pub could do with the income. There could a few people in town on the Friday night and if *we* don't offer them something to do, Saddleton will. Fiona suggested going through the RSVP list and emailing those with tickets, in case they want to come a day earlier. Not such a silly idea. We'd provide finger food and they'll buy their own drinks.'

Maggie had volunteered to help with the RVSP list, hoping to glimpse one name in particular. The list, however, remained Jennifer's well-guarded secret to add "a sense of mystery and surprise" on the night. Maggie did not agree, and she didn't need more mystery and surprise in her life. With a little lobbying, and with Sara and Will onside, Maggie had achieved a small victory before the meeting closed. She'd managed to secure a majority vote that name tags be issued so reunion attendees might avoid embarrassing *Do you remember me?* moments.

While she would have little trouble identifying most of the students from her era, as the event was turning into more than a simple class reunion, any student or teacher, past or present—or even people with merely a fond memory of the old school—were welcome. Name tags, therefore, were a must in Maggie's opinion. She felt queasy enough just thinking about the potential perfunctory platitudes she'd have to endure, like, 'You haven't changed a bit, Maggie'.

What if she had and people didn't recognise her? She was no Jennifer Jones. Put that string of spaghetti in a school uniform today and she'd hardly look out of place in the school assembly. If only Maggie could magically airbrush her worry lines and the shadows from under her eyes in time for the reunion. The years had been kinder to her body because she'd maintained a reasonable level of physical fitness. Spending most mornings running up and down the stairs to the accommodation level and rolling kegs between the cellar and the car park helped.

'And so did carting cartons of beer,' Maggie mumbled while lugging a crate into the main bar.

What was making her think about her looks so much? Was it the presence of a pert and pretty Fiona, or the fear of ending up with Ethne's bingo arms?

'Awright, come on,' Ethne persisted. 'Yes or no to this silly cocktail shindig?'

'Let me put it this way ...' Maggie ripped the flap from the carton to avoid Ethne's glare. 'I said yes, but don't worry,' she added. 'Noah and I will help in the kitchen. We'll buy in a load of those frozen catering packs from the wholesalers: crumbed prawn cocktails, dim sims, meatballs, that kind of thing. We could whip up a few dipping sauces, a cheese platter and—'

'And you think whipping up wholesale party pieces will satisfy Miss Fancy-pants' idea of cocktail snacks?'

Maggie stopped stacking to look at Ethne. 'It will have to. The idea might be hers, but the pub is mine. If I want tacky snacks, we'll have tacky snacks.'

'Ah, now you're talkin' my language,' Ethne chirped. 'Come on, boss, I've got tacky product catalogues buried in the kitchen somewhere.'

10

FIONA

'F'iona followed the sound of a guitar and found Noah sitting on an old church pew, one leg bent and resting on top of his other knee, his head lowered, focused on placing his fingers on guitar frets and strings.

'Nice sound, cowboy!'

He looked up from under a black felt cowboy hat. 'Sorry. I forgot we had a guest. I'm killing time until Mum's ready. We're going to Saddleton.'

'You weren't loud and you don't have to stop.' Fiona finished a text message to Molly and slid the phone deep into the front pocket of her shorts, forcing the pocket's white lining to stick out below the frayed denim cut-offs. 'I was sitting in my room texting Molly and wondering what the hell I'm doing all the way out here.'

The heat, combined with a sticky night in a stifling room smaller than her closet at home, had Fiona regretting her decision to stay at Maggie's pub, even though it was better to have her own space in the hotel than to share a house with a dead grandmother. Not that her grandmother was actually dead; just another of her mother's lies that had surfaced when she returned home after her stint at Dandelion House.

'I don't recognise the tune,' Fiona said. 'What is it?'

'Something I put together.' Noah tilted an ear towards his strumming fingers and closed his eyes. 'Needs work.'

As he plucked at strings, Fiona swatted bugs, wiped sweat from her top lip and brow, and wondered how every freaking fly was managing to find her face. What wouldn't she give for an air-conditioned shopping mall or the cooling breezes off Sydney Harbour that sometimes called for a sweater in the middle of summer. Even her moisturiser had turned to liquid this morning—in the jar and now on her face.

There's nothing keeping you in this dump, she told herself. She could get back into her air-conditioned car and return to Sydney, to her her life and friends and a father who loved her.

Father? Ha! Phillip was partly why she'd come. Fiona had never even heard of Calingarry Crossing until autumn two years ago when Amber had walked away from her city life and from her family. At the time, her mother's leaving had barely registered a blip on Fiona's emotional radar. Once Amber came home, everything was different. She was different; a woman on some bizarre mission, desperate to make up for lost time and be a better person, a better wife, a better mother.

All of a sudden Fiona rated in Amber's life and the various shrines scattered throughout the house for fifteen years—should any of them dare forget baby Christopher—disappeared one by one. Fiona and her mother started to reconnect, mending their ragged relationship a single stitch at a time—Fiona cautiously. She'd been a witness to her mother's rollercoaster life and her battle to stay beautiful for too long. Despite Phillip's efforts, Calingarry Crossing was the only thing to bring Amber out of her spiralling lifestyle of pills and booze, and to leave behind the reluctant socialite, the artificial wife, the crap mother. Now, crap or not, her mother was gone.

Noah had stopped playing and laid his guitar down flat. 'Was there something you wanted, Fiona?'

'This place you're headed to soon—Saddleton. What is it exactly?' she asked. 'Sounds like something you get from riding a horse for too long.'

Noah squinted up at her from under his cowboy hat, his mouth a crooked smile. 'Saddleton is a place. The biggest town around. You drove right by the turnoff, about fifty clicks that way.' He thumbed. 'The hospital is there. My Pop is in hospital, kind of.'

'You two close?'

Noah shrugged. 'He's my grandfather, but he doesn't really know me. You close to your granddad?'

'With mine you don't get a choice,' she said. 'Thinks he's the centre of the freakin' universe.' Fiona wasn't about to admit that the man who'd been more important than her mother while growing up was turning out to be a major control freak and really pissing her off. 'God! How do you people live out here with these temperatures?' She pinched the front of her shirt between a thumb and index finger, fluffing it about, letting air circulate over sweaty skin. 'It's not even summer.'

'You get used to it.' Noah shrugged and positioned his guitar again, as if the instrument was some kind of security blanket. 'No good complaining about something you can't do anything about.'

While his fixation on the instrument annoyed Fiona, the guy was weirdly cute. 'So, what do you country kids do all day, besides sit around strumming your *ghee-tars*?'

Noah plucked out a comical country riff. He ended with an exaggerated 'Yee ha!', a stomp of his feet, and a smart alec smile. 'By the way, Fiona, I'm not a country kid.'

'Is that so?' She'd wondered about the confusing concoction of baggy black shorts, a New Moon: *Team Edward Sucks* T-shirt and a felt cowboy hat.

'Grew up in Sydney,' Noah said. 'Came back to sell the pub after Pop got sick, but it's taking forever to sell.'

'I'd completely die if someone forced me to live out here. Don't you just miss everything?'

Noah shrugged. 'Like?'

'Shops, restaurants, nightclubs, the theatre. The beach! Need I go on?'

'Not really into that stuff. Besides, we've got our very own restaurant in the pub and Ethne cooks as good as any place. There's a pool and a cinema in Saddleton. Did you want to see a movie?'

'Not quite what I meant.' Fiona smiled. 'I hear your mum's planned a dinner with my grandmother one night. A good ol' sit down around a giant table of cook's re-fried pub-style food so we can all pretend to be old friends. I assume you'll be there. I could do with a friend at the table.'

Noah strummed a chord and sang a line from the song: 'You've Got a Friend'.

Fiona grimaced. 'I'm not short of friends usually, but I don't want to be alone at a table of country hicks.'

'You know something, Fiona—?' Noah started, then stopped.

'What? Did I say something wrong?'

Noah shook his head. 'Doesn't matter. Forget it.'

'Call me Fi, if you like.'

'Nah, don't reckon I will,' Noah said. 'Reminds me too much of a girl at school back in Sydney. She had a fancy French poodle called Fifi.'

'Oh yeah?' Fiona retorted. 'Well, does having a biblical name like Noah make you a good boy?'

'For a start, I'm not a boy. Soon I'll be eighteen.'

'Kinda cute for *seventeen*,' Fi said. 'Got a girlfriend?'

'Nope.'

'Boyfriend?' Noah looked at her as if she had two heads. 'Just checking.'

'You got a boyfriend?' he asked.

'Fiancé.' She thrust her left hand out to show off the diamond solitaire ring.

'Aren't you young to be marrying?'

'I'm almost twenty-two.'

He grinned. 'Still twenty-one then.'

'What would you know anyway?' she snapped.

'No way I'm hooking up with anyone until I've done everything there is to do.'

'Really? Well, Luke and I plan to do everything together. He's very ambitious. My grandfather introduced us. Granddad says 'he's going places'.' She picked at the fire-engine-red polish on one thumbnail with the other thumbnail. 'So, about dinner then.'

'What about it?' he asked.

'Well, since you're Noah and Noah saved all creatures great and small … He did, didn't he?'

'You wanna get to the point, Fiona?'

She straightened and tugged on the legs of her shorts. 'You, Noah, will soon have the pleasure of saving your favourite French poodle from a flood of bland food and boring dinner conversation. If you do that, tomorrow I'll let you help me out with something I'm planning for the reunion. Deal?' She turned on her heels without waiting for a response. She didn't have to wait. No one said no to Fiona. 'I'm off,' she called, heading back to the stairs. 'Gotta get polishing my best boot-scooting boots in case we all go line dancing afterwards. *Toodles!*'

Back in her room, Fiona scrolled the contacts list on her iPhone, punching out a text message to Luke: *Being here sux. Do I have to go through with this?*

MAGGIE

'Is he having a good one, Roslyn?' Maggie asked the sister-in-charge at Saddleton Nursing Home.

The nurse squeezed out a cautious smile. 'Not too bad today but give us a minute. He's all fed and Linda is getting him squeaky clean.'

'He likes Linda,' Maggie commented. After eighteen months of visiting her father, Maggie knew all the nurses' names. 'It was nice to see her and the family at the pub for her birthday last weekend.'

Roslyn nodded. 'I'm looking forward to getting out that way again myself. Let me know next time Ethne has that yummy risotto on the specials board.'

'I'll do one better and put in a request for the weekend.'

'Deal. Ooh, that buzzer is for me. See you on Sunday.'

As the nurse waved a hand and strode down the corridor, Maggie helped herself to a pen and Post-it sticky on the desk to write a reminder. She was having to remind herself of lots of things lately. *Roslyn. Sunday. Risotto.* While the hotel's dining room menu featured the usual pre-prepared food items: frozen fish pieces, salt and pepper calamari, mince patties and crumbed schnitzels, Ethne enjoyed creating weekly specials. A self-taught cook, she told Maggie she'd picked up most of what she knew from the procession of self-proclaimed chefs that had passed through the pub's kitchen over the years. One of them, Luigi, was a stocky Italian whose favourite saying at the end of food service when he walked out, leaving a sink full of dirty dishes behind, was 'Finito mosquito!' The tricks Ethne had learned from Luigi were why her weekend pastas and risottos now brought diners from a hundred clicks or more away.

After the food, the next best thing was the location. Positioned across from the river, the water view from the beer garden and dining room had always been a draw card. Now the town was part of an official tourist drive, thanks to a push by locals, and the hotel was busier than it had been in years. Why someone didn't snap the business up for a bargain price baffled Maggie. The broker had suggested a small renovation to 'bring the place into the twenty-first century' might attract more interest and ultimately a higher offer from buyers, but the list of reno options was extensive. Some tasks, such as rust-proofing and repainting the lace ironwork on the top veranda, sanding and re-varnishing the floors and wood bar tops, and landscaping the beer garden were not too difficult for a handy woman, but even if she had money for the materials, Maggie lacked time and opportunity. As it was, there was hardly enough hours in the day for front-of-house duties, kitchen and admin tasks and visiting her dad. Even if Maggie found money, time, and the required enthusiasm, given there'd been no offers and no genuine interest since listing the business with the broker, renovations seemed a waste.

Had her father's decline not been so swift, Maggie might have approached the sale of the hotel with a little less knee-jerk and a lot more planning, although no amount of research would have told her how long things would take; nor would any crystal ball have foretold how, with each passing month, Maggie would settle into the familiar comfort of country life. That was until she saw two things: the bills mounting up on the dresser in her room, and Noah's face every time he asked when they were going back to Brian and Sydney—or when Brian was coming out to Calingarry Crossing. Her dad would love to see him.

The aged-care home, a privately leased annexe of Saddleton Hospital, was a little sad and worn out, much like its occupants. The rooms weren't big, but each one had a glass sliding door leading to an enclosed porch where residents could get fresh air without wandering too far. Some people kept outdoor pot plants. One had a guide dog, and another kept a cat which apparently made for interesting times. Her father had kept his one home comfort, and it sat on the small slab of stained concrete. The wooden rocker had been Mary's favourite. Often when Maggie visited, her father would be asleep in the rocker, and sometimes she would sit outside, mostly to escape the potent scent of antiseptic that barely masked the smell of musty carpet. As she rocked back and forth, Maggie would pretend she was still at home in the tiny fibro house adjacent her dad's church—the Manse—waiting for the Reverend Lindeman to wake up from his afternoon nap so her mother could start singing.

This tiny room was home now, and not even the sprinkling of picture frames and family memories could disguise the very basic, easy-clean cocoon where people like her father spent their final season waiting for wings so they could fly away, finally freed from the pain and uncertainty. Her father's room—number twelve—was at the end of the long corridor. The door was open, and Linda was mopping water on the en suite floor. According to Roslyn's latest official report, The Rev was becoming less enamoured with shower time. Maggie smiled apologetically as the young nurse in the disposable plastic pinny held open the door while juggling a mop and bucket.

'Come on in. Squeaky clean, we are,' Linda shouted, as though Joe were hard of hearing, which he wasn't—until it suited him.

'How you doing, Dad?' Maggie walked over to the bed, leaned down and pressed her lips to her father's forehead. 'I brought more PJs,' she announced with verve, as though doing her father's laundry was the highlight of Maggie's day. It was more rewarding than office work, which only identified the dwindling funds in her bank account.

She shook the plastic shopping bag and freshly laundered clothes fell onto her father's bed. After refolding the pile of lemon-scented pyjamas, she gathered up the dirty ones from the bottom drawer of his bedside table. Yes, the in-house linen service could take care of such things, but it was an added weekly expense Maggie could avoid. Besides, it wasn't an extra chore. She'd done the family laundry since she could reach the dials on the old machine. Without warning, her father's hand strangled her wrist so tight Maggie flinched.

'Get away from that,' he growled, making a sudden grab for the shopping bag. 'Mine! Mine!'

'It's okay, Dad.' Maggie startled. 'I'm taking your dirties. The clean ones are right here. In the bottom drawer. See?' Hoping to calm him, she dangled the once-folded pants in the air.

Her father blinked and screwed up his face. 'Mary?'

'No, it's me, Dad. Maggie,' she said, propping a pillow behind his back.

'Oh, my little Magpie. How wonderful. You just missed your mother.'

'Did I, Dad?' By about twenty-seven years, she might've added.

According to her father these days, Mary Lindeman was visiting at least once a week. When Maggie had mentioned his hallucinations to nursing staff, they'd nodded and flashed hurried, empathetic expressions to remind Maggie that even the experts didn't understand the cruelty of dementia on a sufferer's mind. At first she would try explaining to Joe that Mary was dead—that she'd died a long time ago—but to have her father relive the same anguish repeatedly broke both their hearts. Maggie now let herself believe her mother really was visiting Joe, rocking in her chair, singing to him and urging him to join her, and Michael.

'I have your lottery scratchy game, Dad.' Maggie plucked the two-dollar scratch 'n' win tickets from her pants pocket and waved them as if she'd already won. The strategy had proven to be the perfect distraction in the past when she didn't know how else to deal with his irrational outbursts. It worked today. 'So, Dad, do you remember Amber Bailey?' Maggie chatted as she pressed her father's thumb and index finger around a ten-cent piece.

'Trouble,' he muttered as his brain struggled to coordinate his grip on both the small cardboard square and on the coin.

'Yes, well, you'd probably say the same about her daughter, Fiona. She's staying at the pub with me.'

'Amber?'

'No, not Amber, Dad. Amber's daughter. Fiona's taken on her mother's centenary committee role. Do you want to sit outside for a bit, Dad?'

Joe was having one of his close-to-coherent moments and Maggie wanted to make the most of it by getting him out of bed and outside where, for a short time, he would look like the old Joe, the happy Joe, the healthy Joe. Something about the stark whiteness of bed linen made his skin look grey, except for his nose—a bulbous reddish-purple beacon of broken capillaries—and the nicotine-stained teeth. A quick stop in the garden would put some colour back into the rest of him.

After helping Joe into his wheelchair, they passed through the common area with the hypnotic TV screen. The adjoining dining room had only two occupants: a man sat alone at a table, his head hanging limp, drool escaping his mouth to form a dark spot on the pale blue seersucker cloth, while the withered body of a frail, grey-haired lady—one who Maggie determined would have been a real beauty—sat hunched and sobbing wretchedly. It took all her strength to not go to her, wrap an arm around her and tell her it's all okay. It wasn't. *Getting old sucks.*

Maggie quickened her pace. Why was life so cruel? Why make people wait so long to die all alone, while others—like Amber—got snatched away too soon? Joe didn't want to be in this place. None of these people wanted to be here. No wonder her visits three or four times a week, and the monotony of repeated conversations, were exhausting Maggie, both physically and emotionally. Trying to remain upbeat and pretending everything was fine when it sometimes felt like life could not get any *suckier*— as Noah would say—was draining. Then there was the confounding combination of both sadness and amusement Maggie felt at her father's increasingly bizarre behaviour.

A blast of the predicted thirty-four-degree heat was a shock against the cool, temperature-controlled atmosphere left behind in the hospital corridor. But once settled in the shade of the leafy camphor laurel tree— Maggie on a white plastic chair and Joe in the wheelchair—the heat was less intense, the fragrance heady.

'I've invited Cheryl Bailey for dinner. Figure it will help break the ice with her granddaughter.'

'Terrible shame. Terrible.' Joe's head wobbled a little more than the usual dementia tick. He was letting Maggie know he remembered what Cheryl had silently endured for years before her husband ran off, taking their daughter, Amber—pregnant and sixteen at the time—away to Sydney.

'Did I tell you Noah's playing in a band at the fair on Sunday? And of course, Saturday is the big party to celebrate the school's one hundred years. I found out today that someone called Charlotte Gilbertson is coming. No relation to the footy player, I'm told, but at ninety-two she's possibly the oldest living ex-student. Can you believe it?'

Joe harrumphed. 'That boy'll be there.'

Maggie sighed. How was it that Joe sometimes failed to recognise his own grandson, while never failing to remember Dan Ireland who'd worn the town bad boy label unfairly? 'I don't know if he'll be there, Dad. I doubt it.'

To Maggie's knowledge, Dan had never come back home. He had no reason to. The only thing he'd left in Calingarry Crossing was a father who'd abandoned him in the worst way a father could. He'd sided with the town that ostracised his son. Accident or not, some seemed to believe the blame had to be levelled at the living, not the dead—even though in Maggie's heart she knew better.

'My boy!' Pain tempered her father's words, the weight of remorse making him shrink into himself as he relived the night that policeman had knocked.

'Please, Daddy,' Maggie cajoled, reaching for his hand while the other stroked his arm. 'Please try not to go there. Michael's safe with Mum and it was so long ago.'

Joe snatched his hand away. 'That boy killed him. His own father thought so, didn't he?'

To his eternal detriment, Maggie wanted to say.

She saw Dan's dad in town from time to time. For all his 'she'll-be-right-mate' sanguineness, when Maggie looked closely, it was the old man who looked forsaken nowadays. She even felt sorry for Charlie Ireland.

'Okay, Dad, let's get you back inside.' Either her father's continued agitation or the heat had turned Joe's face as red as his nose. 'Noah should be here any minute,' she told him. 'He had a twenty-dollar voucher to spend from Bingo last month. I left him at Hartford's Co-Op. He should've found something to spend it on by now.'

As predicted, Noah was a messy lump leaning slovenly against the wall outside his grandfather's room. Maggie lifted one hand to wave, while pushing the wheelchair along the corridor. Applying the foot brake once in his room, Maggie tapped Joe's hands where they rested on the small pot of his belly, exaggerating the rise and fall of each sleepy breath.

'Wakey, wakey, Dad. Look who's here.' Maggie's stare and eyebrow arch were enough of a nudge to scoot her son off another wall and to his grandfather's side. As always, it broke her heart to think Noah hadn't known the strong, funny and wise man. 'Say hello,' she instructed Noah, hoping Joe would remain alert enough to enjoy the rare visit.

'Hi, Pops.'

Joe Lindeman's head bobbed up, and he peered through the all-too-familiar squint of confusion. 'Is that our boy?'

'He's growing up, isn't he?' Maggie stopped fussing with the bed sheets to fluff up with pride. Despite everything, she and Brian had done a good job. She nudged Noah again, this time with her elbow, muttering, 'Hug. Now.'

'That's my boy. My Michael.' Joe's hug was firm from the look of Noah's squirming. 'Look at you and your mother.' Joe held Noah at arms' length. 'Where's my other little angel today? Where's my Magdalene?'

Noah pulled away and looked to Maggie, uncertainty clouding his eyes, while in her father's face she saw confusion shift to frustration, then anger. She needed another distraction.

'Okay, so how was lunch today, Dad?' She waved away one persistent fly that must have hitched a ride in on one of their backs. It settled on the half-eaten meal still on the tray-table.

'Damn chicken,' he snarled. 'Always chicken. Chicken, chicken, chicken. Any more chicken and I'll damn-well be layin' eggs. *Bwark. Bwark. Bwark.*' Her father flapped his arms like a crazed bird while Maggie eyed the leftover fish and rice on the plate and tried to ignore Noah's indiscriminate flicking through TV channels with the remote.

Someone save me!

❧

'THAT WAS WEIRD,' NOAH SAID ON THE DRIVE HOME. 'HE THOUGHT I WAS Uncle Mike.'

'Pop gets mixed up some days. You don't visit enough, Noah. We'll go again next week—without the twenty-dollar shopping spree, I'm afraid, buddy.'

'Do you still think about Uncle Mike, too?'

'All the time.' Maggie wondered how much to say. Sometimes Noah seemed so grown up that the idea of burdening him with her concerns and sad memories was acceptable. Other times he was her baby boy; the one she wanted to protect from everything hard, or sad, or painful. 'It's difficult to not miss someone like Michael,' she said. 'The bigger the personality, the bigger the hole they leave behind ... in here.' Maggie flattened a palm over her heart. 'The night your uncle died left such a gaping hole. But then—'

'Dad came along, like a knight in shining armour, and filled the hole, right?'

Suddenly he was that eager boy who needed her protection more than he needed the truth. 'Yes, buddy, Dad was there for me, but better still, you came along and took my whole heart.'

'You miss Dad all the time, too, though, don't you, Mum? I do.'

'I know,' she blurted, grateful he hadn't waited for her response to his question. 'He misses you, too.'

'So, why don't we talk about him more?' Noah asked. 'You hardly said anything about seeing him in Sydney. You don't even tell me when he calls. I hear you on the phone sometimes late at night; I know it's Dad.'

'Do you?' Maggie's hands tightened around the steering wheel. What did he hear? Yelling? His mother's exasperation? The slamming down of the phone on the dresser?

'You tell me I have to spend more time with Pops, but what about Dad? When's he coming? Each time I ring, he says the same. "Not long now".'

'Your Dad's busy,' Maggie said, staring at the road ahead, trying to sound convincing, and craving those years where the answer to every 'But why?' could be, 'Because I said so'.

'Are you and Dad breaking up?'

Maggie stared dead ahead, unsure how to answer and asking instead, 'What would make you say that?'

'Just checking,' Noah said.

She might've seized the opportunity to prepare her son, or was Maggie struggling to accept the truth herself; that the family unit she'd worked so hard to build was coming apart, stitch by sad stitch.

'Well, I'll tell you what. I'll make of point of pinning Dad down to a date next time he calls. Okay?'

IN THE SANCTUARY OF HER BEDROOM, MAGGIE PROSTRATED HERSELF ON the bed, her mind reeling from Noah's perceptiveness about Brian. Were they breaking up? How would Maggie know? She'd never broken up before. She knew how it felt to fall in love—all those nerve-tingling, body-shuddering, scream-it-from-the-rooftop moments—but why was it she hadn't noticed falling out of love with Brian? Was it because falling out of love had been so excruciatingly slow? Or was it because she didn't feel much of anything any more? Maggie merely existed, numb from years of disappointment. To *fall* out of love sounded insufferable—a gradual, awkward and agonising end—which meant the only way to avoid the fall was, perhaps, to brave up and jump.

'I wonder where Fiona is,' Maggie said as she sat opposite Noah at the permanently reserved staff table in the corner of the dining room.

Noah's head stayed bent over the giant bowl of pasta, his fork twirling long strands of Ethne's spaghetti carbonara. He twirled, stopped, stood the fork upright, then let it fall to the rim of the bowl with a clunk—repeating the manoeuvre twice. By the second clunk Maggie sensed trouble.

'You normally love Ethne's pasta. Not hungry tonight?'

His reply was a lazy lift and drop of his shoulders—the internationally recognisable symbol of adolescence. Was it Maggie's imagination or were her son's shrugs becoming more frequent since their visitor's arrival? Two years ago, when Noah had been going through a tough time at school, shrugs had been the answer to every question. Back then, Maggie had too easily dismissed her son's moods as nothing more than a boy pushing through puberty. The truth was, she later discovered, a school bully was doing the pushing, leaving her once-outgoing son withdrawn and moody.

It saddened rather than surprised Maggie that teenage dynamics nowa-days meant high school could be a challenge for the studious, the shy and the not-overly sporty. Students like Noah who opted for more creative courses, such as art and music, became prime targets for bullies. When her son had come home with a torn shirt and grazed knee, he'd shrugged the incident off and insisted it was nothing he couldn't handle himself. With Brian badgering Maggie over the phone to let him work things out, she'd reluctantly agreed. This fresh batch of petulance she'd been witnessing of late had Maggie's mind kicking into overdrive as it sorted through the million other possible teenage son problems, hoping none of them had anything to do with Fiona.

Only two years ago, a clumsy and slightly gawky fifteen-year-old Noah had needed a nudge to make new friends in town. He not only seemed to have hit it off straight away with Fiona, Maggie believed he was spending way too much time in her company. The last person Maggie wanted her son hitting it off with was a spoilt city girl who spent her days sitting around—usually in the beer garden—playing with her fancy phone and driving around the town in her fancy car. Seventeen-year-old boys, even good ones like Noah, were too easily impressed and generally by all the wrong things.

Unable to tolerate the clunk of the fork for the third—but who was counting—time, Maggie intercepted the utensil. 'Please Noah, quit with the fork thing. What's worrying you? Talk to me. Tell me what's up, buddy.'

There followed a few seconds of silence with her son staring down at his untouched dinner long enough for a disconcerting lump to form in Maggie's throat.

'Did you and Dad want me?' Noah asked the bowl. 'I mean, like, was I planned?'

'Were you …?' Maggie gulped, almost gagging on the mouthful of half-chewed pasta. 'Of course,' she quickly added, followed by a strategic sip of lemon squash. Two more sips and she could blame the sparkling, ice-cold liquid for her hand grabbing at her palpitating chest. 'Bubbles,' she spluttered, trying to stall, to think, to focus.

In the protracted silence, she coached herself in the controlled breathing the midwife had encouraged her to use throughout labour—*In through the nose, two, three. Out through the mouth, two, three.* She tried again—*In through the nose, two, three. Out through the mouth, two, three* —but the only thing Maggie was giving birth to tonight was a nine-pound lie.

'Of course you were planned, Noah.' Maggie tried to laugh; it came out as a croak. 'Why would you ask such a thing?' Another shrug and Maggie braced for the clunk of a falling fork for the fourth time. She wanted to scream or run far, far away, but there was more to endure first— more shrugs, more moody silence, more clunking forks. Maggie had the sudden urge to drive the prongs of that bloody fork into the back of her own hand. The pain had to be preferable to this conversation. 'For good-ness' sake, Noah. Put the cutlery down and talk to me. Tell me what this is about?'

Clunk. Huff. Slump. So like his father. An exaggerated huff and puff regularly conveyed Brian's exasperation.

The man had begun calling twice a day to talk—make that argue—with Maggie. The second call usually contained an apology, with words over the phone a sorry substitute for the puppy play and lovemaking that once used to quell Maggie's anger and frustration at something her husband had said or done. This afternoon's call had ended with another tantrum—Brian's. He was turning more demanding than a five-year-old, when what Maggie needed was a partner to share the load, to share the financial and emotional burden, and to be here, in Calingarry Crossing, to deal with their son's questions.

'Noah? I asked you why you think you weren't planned?'

'Because, Mum.' He raised his face to hers. 'I know that kind of stuff happened in your day.'

'My *day*?'

'Yeah, you know, condoms and stuff weren't around back then so girls got themselves pregnant all the time.'

'Girls got *themselves* pregnant?' Maggie was glad she'd pushed her plate aside because her throat was about to seize up, along with her mouth and her brain. Where was her son going with all this and did she want to know?

'Fi and me were talking this afternoon,' he said. 'She reckons she was a mistake and basically unwanted. That's why her mum sent her away to school and they didn't talk for a long time. Then her mother walked out.'

'I'm not following you,' Maggie said. 'Amber and Fiona are nothing like us.'

'But we moved out here, right? And I hardly talk to Dad.' Moistening eyes and the visible sweat breaking out and mingling with the downy fuzz on her son's top lip seemed so incongruous; the clash of a man in the making, yet still a child in need of his mother's reassurance. If this phase of her own life wasn't so bloody problematic, Maggie might find joy in witnessing her son's manly metamorphosis.

'Will a *smuddle* help, buddy?' she asked. But it seemed, for the first time in sixteen years, the Lindeman version of a cuddle had failed her. Noah remained silent, his gaze back on his over-poked pasta. 'Listen to me.' She reached across to prise the fork out of his fingers. After she placed it on the plate—without the clunk—Maggie rested her hand on his. Left to stare at the zigzagged parting on the top of his head, she tried to explain. 'No one has sent anyone away and no one's walking out. You and I are here for Pops and to sell the pub.'

'But he doesn't know us and the pub's not selling.' Eye contact restored, she saw tears glistening. 'So Fi and I were talking today—'

'*Fi-ee-eee* ...?' Maggie dragged the name out, her vocal chords taking the little moniker on a quick rollercoaster ride to add more resentment than she'd planned. 'That girl doesn't know anything about us or our family, Noah, and I don't want you—'

'Chill, Mum, geez! I was talking to *her*. She listens. She hasn't said anything.' He balanced the chair on two back legs and looked at Maggie. 'Actually, that's not true. She never shuts up.' He grinned and Maggie felt some relief. 'Most of the afternoon she talked about herself and *her* problems. Some problems! I wouldn't mind a few of them.'

'Like?' Maggie enquired, glad to leave the seriousness of their discussion behind, for the time being at least.

'A car like hers would be a pretty cool problem,' Noah huffed. 'A flat with a view of Bondi Beach would be a major problem, too. The only thing we share is our dads aren't part of our lives.'

Maggie faltered. 'You have a father who loves you, Noah. Dad's just not here at the moment, and I'm hoping, by Fiona getting to know her grandmother, she'll see Phillip is a good and caring man.'

Noah let the chair drop back onto all four legs. 'Fi went to see Mrs Bailey today.'

'I'm glad,' Maggie said. 'That's what her visit here is about. Finish your meal, Noah.'

'You reckon that's really why she's here?'

While Noah slurped pasta into his mouth, Maggie's glass hovered at her lips. 'What do you mean?'

'She keeps going on about finding her real father. Do you know if he lives here?'

'I can't tell you anything about him.'

That wasn't exactly true. Thanks to the rumour mill, Maggie almost knew too much about the night Amber had fallen pregnant. The tricky bit was knowing which version was true. Jack Bailey's account had been the loudest—and the most unlikely. No local male under forty had been safe from suspicion, making Amber's so-called rape claims a major scandal. Poor Will and his family had suffered the most. Not even when Jack whisked his daughter away to marry her off did the town's tongues stop wagging. Maggie wondered if Phillip knew Fiona was poking around in search of her father. Should she tell him? *No!* She closed her mind to the idea. Maggie's simmering pot of problems was already full to the brim. Any more and it was bound to boil over.

'Let's not make Fiona's trouble our trouble, Noah. Who her real father is has nothing to do with us. Okay?

'So, about Dad ...' Noah ventured.

'Hmm? What about him?'

'If Dad's so busy and always working, how come we don't have more money to buy cool stuff?'

'It's a contract job, Noah.' Maggie couldn't believe how quickly and how easily her lies formed. 'Contract jobs can mean no payment until the work is completed. We have to make do.'

'Or we might get a buyer,' Noah corrected.

'Yes. We can only hope.'

She could see her son considering her explanation. How she wished she'd never abided by that ridiculous *iICON* confidentiality clause, as if they couldn't trust their son to keep a secret. Explaining to Noah that the contract Brian had signed did not allow her to tell him would only suggest she hadn't considered him grown-up enough. Telling him the truth now would expose her lies, and Maggie had to wonder. Was he smart enough and mature enough to understand that sometimes a lie is the right thing? What was she talking about? A lie is never acceptable, although Maggie readily accepted her husband's countless explanations to her enquiries, happy to bury her head in the sand to avoid confrontation. Or was she simply trying to glue the cracks in her relationship?

'Are you going to eat more of that, or are you planning to probe the pasta to death?' There was something going on inside her son's head and Maggie was desperate to join the dots.

'I'm done.' Noah rubbed a hand on his stomach as if to satisfy his mother that he'd eaten his fill, even though he'd eaten very little.

'Are we good, buddy?' Maggie's finger dared reach out and touch the dangling fringe. 'Love me?'

'*Muuum!*' He jerked his head away.

Maggie sat back and smiled. 'Okay. Last one out of the dining room is on dishwashing duties.' The strategy worked every time. Situation defused. But for how long?

In a couple of hours, Maggie would go through her nightly routine of locking up and turning off lights. First she'd phone through any food and beverage orders. Most suppliers had tried to convert Maggie to online processes. She preferred leaving her order on answering machines because some parts of the business she wanted to keep the way Joe had done them. Finally, she would walk by Noah's room to say goodnight, albeit under protest.

'Get a grip, Mum,' he'd say as she attempted to kiss him goodnight.

Maggie would laugh, pinch his ear and say, 'Am I *ear-i-tating* you?'

Noah would attempt to grab his mother's nose and say, 'You *nose* you are.' But Maggie would be too fast, jumping out of the way and leaving the room laughing, her heart full.

On those nights she needed no other toddy to make her sleep. The elixir of her son's love was enough.

13

DAN

Dan scanned the small round dining table covered with beige manila folders. He'd spent the week tidying up loose ends for the job that had become his life, noting every adjourned court case had been rescheduled for hearing the week before his leave was due to start. With several other ongoing investigations to hand over to his colleagues, Dan had to make sense of the scribbled notes and make file notations. He also had to clear the family paraphernalia from his desk: the kids' photos, *I Love Dad* coffee cup-cum-pen holders from several Christmases in a row, and school projects, like the ceramic hippopotamus paperweight that looked like no hippopotamus Dan had ever seen.

Preparing for leave was not only turning out to be more work than staying around and doing the job, truth be told, Dan Ireland would do a better job of all these cases, even though he'd recently started questioning his capabilities and his commitment. Impatient, quick-tempered and intolerant of fools who didn't care enough about themselves to not break the law—often breaking themselves in the process—were not the qualities required of a crash investigator; hence the need for an unprecedented amount of time off to clear his head.

If anyone had tried telling a loutish young Dan he'd hold a job long enough to qualify for long service leave, he would have laughed in their face. Actually, he would have mumbled some profanity and made a crude gesture before downing another beer. That's how Dan was, and mostly what he did before wising up and joining the police service; that and terrorise his hometown with his mates in the early hours of the morning because there hadn't been much else to do in Calingarry Crossing. That's what had made Dan Ireland such a good cop. His childhood had made him an expert at getting himself into trouble, and out of it again. Every choice had made his father angry, including almost garroting himself when he ran his dirt bike at full throttle into a barbed-wire fence. No sympathy there. A swift smack across the skull had been as close to a fatherly hug as Dan got as a kid. The one time his mother, armed with a rolling pin, had tried to intervene and protect her youngest, she'd copped a black eye for her trouble.

Two days later his mother had sat both sons down on the floor in her bedroom. Dan remembered dodging flying coat hangers as she ripped clothes from the wardrobe, crushing them into a suitcase. She was crying and shouting words Dan's older brother, Mark, would get a clip over the ear for using.

'I'm not living in this shit of a town one more day,' she'd spat. 'Some things are worth loving. Some things aren't. I'm sorry, boys.'

Mark had run from the room and Dan didn't know why until his brother returned with his own clothes spilling out the top of an old duffel bag he dragged behind. By then, however, the family station wagon was already on its way down the drive, their mother at the wheel. Mark had run so hard to catch up, falling over twice and calling out, 'Mummy! Mummy! Come back, Mummy!'. Dan had stood on the little front porch looking over the piggery, and squinted through the billowing dust cloud—waiting.

No brake lights. Not a flicker. She didn't slow down. Not for a second. Their mother never did come back, so Dan never did work out which things were worth loving and which things weren't. News of her death a few years later filtered through to the Ireland family farm on the outskirts of town. 'Hit by a Melbourne tram in the early hours of the morning,' they were told. Dan had been young at the time and remembered not understanding what a Melbourne tram was. His older brother taunted him with stories of monster machines in Melbourne that gobbled up mothers and left fathers crotchety old men.

When Mark was old enough, he ran off with a shearing team that was passing through town one year, leaving Dan alone to endure his father's anger. From that point onwards, for every clip over the ear Dan received at home, some kid at school would cop the same. And so began an innocent boy's progression to bully, troublemaker and eventually—to use his father's favourite term—no-hoper. Blame had come too easily to Charles Ireland, who only ever saw his son as trouble. Years later, Dan realised what made Detective Dan Ireland such a dedicated cop was his need to provide true justice for others.

With a sudden urge to hug his children, he left the dining table under its blanket of beige folders and walked over to where the twins sat side by side on the sofa, immersed in the new Nintendo game.

'*Daaad!*' Emily squirmed as her father's arms wrapped around her from behind. 'I can't play with you doing that.'

'Oh, that's too bad. How about if I do this?' Dan tugged gently on her ponytail so her head bobbed back and he laughed as she tried to slap his hand away. 'Or how about like this?' With a poke to her ribs, Emily squealed and dropped the game controller into her lap.

'*Yesss!*' Mike hissed. 'I win.'

'Okay, well, the winner gets to choose dinner,' Dan announced. 'Fish and chips or Chinese takeaway?'

'That's not fair.' Emily huffed and slammed back into the chair. 'I'm telling Mum. Being a girl around here sucks.'

'Ah, but the loser,' Dan added, grabbing the notepad from the side table, on which he'd started writing his list of things he'd need to do before leaving for the weekend. 'The loser gets to pick the DVD.'

Emily's life suddenly didn't seem so sucky. 'Mamma Mia! Mamma Mia!' she chanted.

'Oh, no, kill me now.' Mike thrust a make-believe knife in his chest and feigned an agonising death on the living room floor.

Even Dan wanted to groan over a cheesy musical about a girl finding her actual father. *Load of rubbish!* Speaking of garbage ... Dan returned the notepad to the very busy dining table and added to his pre-trip to-do list: *Put rubbish bins out.*

'Okay, you lot, get a move on before I change my mind and we have eggs and ABC News.'

Dan felt blessed to have Emily and Mike. They were great kids who had missed out on the reckless and rebellious genes that attracted trouble. Dan had once been a beacon for the blasted stuff, even though he'd mostly kept to himself. Later in life, he'd turned into a lighthouse—perched on a wind-swept rock, watching for danger, and keeping everything and everyone at a safe distance. As hard as he tried, it was inevitable someone, or something, would crash against him—like Michael Lindeman. Calingarry Crossing's local minister's son would dare everyone and try everything. Another mate was Nate Parker, grandson of a Saddleton police sergeant, but he hadn't been much better. And people had labelled Dan as trouble! 'A product of his environment and a bloody troublemaker,' they'd spouted.

Dan scribbled another reminder on his to-do list—*bolt window locks*—while recalling his mates and their harmless antics. Bored kids, they were, ignorant of the consequences until the night of Michael's accident. How many times since had Dan cursed his stupidity? If he'd downed one less stubby, taken one less turn around the paddock, called it quits one hour earlier, everyone's life, including Dan's, would have turned out differently. Forced into a corner, and with the town blaming him for Michael's death, Dan's final act of defiance had been leaving—if you can call sneaking away in the dark of night without a word an act of defiance. He added to the list: *Let neighbours know you're going away.*

Marrying had quelled any leftover defiance, which was how come Dan was going back to that same town to celebrate one-hundred years. Tracy was so desperate to visit and show off to her old school friends and, Tracy being Tracy, she couldn't go to a reunion alone in case she looked unloved; not that anyone who went to school with Tracy Rose would think she was anything but adored.

Dan remembered his wife as the girl everyone wanted to be around. Why someone hadn't snapped her up between school and when Dan had bumped into her years later in Sydney, he never understood. He told himself their meeting had been fate. She was what he'd needed at the time: the life of the party, a lover of life, always optimistic. Tracy took an empty shell of a man and filled him until, for the first time since his mother left, Dan was one of those people worth loving. Trace had brought out his best and been good for him ever since, even when Dan wasn't good to himself. After twenty years married—while he, it had to be said, was married to his job—Tracy deserved his support when she asked for it. He could hardly refuse her this one small request. He'd go to the reunion. He'd do it for Tracy and try damn hard to not dwell on any thing or any person from the past.

Dan's pen hovered over the latest, unconscious addition to his to-do list and saw he'd doodled the words: *Maggie Lindeman.*

MAGGIE

As Maggie intercepted Noah and Fiona at the bottom of the stairs, the thought of chaining her son in his room again crossed her mind. 'Where have you two been?'

'Just cruisin', Mum,' Noah said.

She'd started worrying after returning from Saddleton to discover Noah and Fiona had gone out driving. The pair was spending far too much time together, and the growing friendship and age difference was concerning Maggie. She'd seen Fiona's alcohol intake during the awkward and uneventful dinner with Cheryl Bailey, then later in the beer garden. The sight had taken Maggie back to those occasions she'd sneaked an under-age Amber Bailey into the pub. There'd been no shortage of farmhands willing to buy Calingarry Crossing's most popular girl a drink. Fiona had seemed just as popular in the beer garden.

'Cruising where, Noah?' Maggie asked.

'Saddleton. Got my first tat. Whadaya think?' Noah gripped his bicep and slid the T-shirt sleeve high to expose the black skull and crossbones. 'Like it?' Her son laughed. 'Chill, Mum. We ran into Jennifer. She'd just picked up the face painting stuff and Fi suggested we test the temporary tattoos to make sure they worked. They look legit, eh?'

'Your expression just now, Maggie, was priceless,' Fiona contributed before leaving mother and son at the foot of the stairs. 'I'll be in my room, texting.'

'Quit with the weird face, Mum,' Noah chided in a whisper. 'I'd never get a tattoo for real.'

Was that supposed to make Maggie feel better? She wondered. 'What else did you do today, bud?'

'Like I said, we cruised for a bit and I showed Fi the swimming hole and Cedar Cutters Gorge. Later, we went to her grandmother's. Mrs Bailey makes the best scones and jam.'

Maggie's mind couldn't get beyond Cedar Cutters—Calingarry's answer to Lovers' Lane.

'Mum?' Noah was standing on the bottom step, staring, while Maggie reminded herself she could and should trust her son. He wasn't silly. 'Mum, your face is all weird again.'

'Today's heat has knocked me around,' she said. 'Would you mind popping into the bar and asking Ethne for a lemon squash?' Maggie needed a minute alone.

Sitting at the corner table, she chastised herself for overreacting. Fiona was female, yes, but she had nothing in common with Noah, unlike her son's other female friends and they didn't sent Maggie into a meltdown. The giggling pair Noah hung out with after school were from respectable families. She knew because both had stuck their heads in the main bar one morning to let Noah know they were waiting; Ethne had recognised both girls. They lived on adjacent properties about ten kilometres out of town. 'Gigglers' is how Ethne had described the pair, assuring Maggie that their interactions seemed platonic. Recently, both girls had made friendship bands. Plaited from leather strips, they'd knotted one each around Noah's left wrist. Noah didn't have one girl vying for his affections, he had two, so Maggie could stop worrying about Fiona.

In addition, Maggie and Brian had raised Noah well, although not as a family should—together. When Brian had been a stay-at-home dad during his I-can-make-money-writing-songs phase, he and Noah had spent every day together, while for Maggie, parenting became a tag-team event. Depending on the day of the week, and if the timing worked in her favour, she might get to catch-up with her husband and share a quick bite together before he left for a pub gig. The rest of her night was spent preparing food for the next day and attacking the laundry and housework. When Brian came home in the early hours of the morning, eager for sex and smelling of smoke and alcohol—despite his ardent denial that neither had touched his lips—Maggie feigned sleep.

In the early days of their marriage, she accompanied Brian to gigs.

Most places allowed for partners, although usually at tables located at the back of the room, or even in the kitchen when the arrangement included a meal. Sometimes, other entertainers' wives or girlfriends provided conversation, while bouncers on their break entertained with their repertoire of funny drunk stories. A bar tab was usually part of the backstage provisions and no one back then thought much about drinking and driving. Consequence was not a word that ran off their tongues when it came to drink, drugs, or even unprotected sex. Such dangers had not existed to the invincible and unthinking. Yes, even a young Maggie.

'Here you go, Mum.' Noah presented the frosted glass. 'Can I go now?'

Maggie took a quick sip of lemon squash. 'Actually, Noah buddy, we need to talk.'

'Yeah, I see you've got your serious face on. Is this about Dad?' Noah asked. 'Is there something wrong?'

Maggie fingered the two vertical frown lines above her nose. Were they responsible for creating the so-called serious face? 'No, everything's fine, bud.'

A smile lit her son's face. 'So, he's coming here?'

'Ah, well, it's not about your dad, and no, he's not coming to Calingarry Crossing—not yet,' she added, seeing the flash of disappointment, before her son's youthful optimism kicked in again.

'So we're going back to Sydney? When?'

'Slow down, Noah.' Maggie pictured those frown lines deepening. She positioned a second dining chair opposite her and slapped a palm on the seat, waiting until Noah plonked himself down. 'You know our leaving here can't happen any time soon. We have no other choice with Granddad like he is, and with the pub not selling I thought you understood living here is practical. You were okay with the idea before ...' Maggie stopped herself. Criticising Fiona would not help her cause. 'The other night, buddy, you were talking about your father and, well, you worried me. I know you miss him.'

'I miss Sydney,' Noah stated firmly.

'Since when?'

Accompanying her son's predictable shrug and confirming her fears was his furtive glance up the stairs towards the accommodation level. The city that Maggie had been happy to take her son away from had arrived in town and found *him*. Intentional or not, Fiona Bailey-Blair and her highfalutin attitude was having an impact. Worse still Maggie felt powerless to do anything except kick herself for inviting the girl.

'Noah, you wanted to get away from your old school.' Maggie recalled the conversation. The changing of schools had clinched the deal, she thought. 'Do you no longer like it out here, bud?'

'No. Can I go? Upstairs,' he clarified. Maggie's face must have been doing that thing. 'I have homework and Fiona's helping me.'

'With what exactly?' Maggie chastised herself for stereotyping, but she couldn't help it. Fiona was Amber Bailey's daughter and the only thing Amber had been good at was ... Maggie groaned inwardly. 'Noah, look at me.' She leaned across, rested a hand on her son's knee and adopted her in control mothering tone. 'Fiona is visiting, Noah. She'll go soon. I know you're friends and she's attractive—'

'Get a grip, Mum.' Noah's face flashed red, mirroring his father's the day Maggie had asked Brian to pick up a box of tampons. 'You're not about to give me a sex talk, are you?'

'I, ahh ...' Maggie struggled with the simple trifecta of breathing, swallowing and speaking all at once. 'Do we need that talk, bud?'

'No way! Geez, Mum. Besides, Dad kinda took care of that already.'

'Your father did? When?'

'Yeah,' her son replied. 'Like a decade ago.'

A decade ago? Brian gave a seven-year-old a sex talk? Maggie feigned a cheery face for her son's benefit. 'Okay, well, if there's ever anything—'

'*Muuuum*, quit with that stuff and chill?'

'I'll *chill*, Noah, when I know you're okay about being in Calingarry Crossing.'

'You mean only until someone buys the place, right?'

Tell him, Maggie, the voice in her head nagged. Tell him you want to stay. But as she went to speak, her boy's expression stopped her. Not until Noah, had Maggie understood how capable a child was of breaking a mother's heart. Each year, realising her son needed her less, another piece chipped away. One day Noah would fly the nest and Maggie's heart would crumble into a million impossible pieces. He'd marry and become a father with his own family. He'd have left Maggie behind to witness his own children's lives and Maggie would be alone. Seeing Brian during her recent Sydney trip had confirmed as much. Later in life, if she was to be alone, she selfishly preferred to be in Calingarry Crossing. *Tell him. Noah will understand. He'll be fine.*

'You said "until someone buys", Mum,' Noah persisted.

'Yes, that was the plan. The thing is, bud, maybe we need to take the pub off the market for a while. It's not smart to keep advertising a place that's not selling.'

'You mean we're stuck here?' Noah kicked at the air, his foot nudging a nearby chair. 'No way! We live in Sydney, with Dad. You can't make me stay.'

'Please, Noah, I don't have a choice.'

'I do. I can live with Dad. I'll get a lift back when Fi goes home.'

Chink went one tiny piece of her heart. The look on her son's face, the thought of losing him to Sydney and to his father, could have changed her mind, made her reduce the pub's asking price to secure a quick sale, and let them both get the hell out of town.

'Noah, I'm sorry.'

'I have a life too, you know, Mum. What about what I want? What about our deal?'

'Well, sometimes life comes up with a different idea.' Maggie tried to take her son's hand, but he folded belligerent arms tight across his front. 'I'm not understanding this at all, Noah. You've got girlfriends here, and what about Cory and the other boys you play music with?'

'They're all right. They don't want to play my music though, especially since that dickhead Dave joined the band. Thinks he knows everything. I told them if they toned down the heavy metal sound we might get a gig in the pub.'

Maggie let that go without comment. 'But you're all sorted for the fair day, right? The band is playing?'

Noah nodded. 'Yeah, we're powering our gear from Will's café and using the back of Gus Markum's semi. He'll park it that morning and roll the vinyl cargo cover up on one side to give us a covered stage.'

'Smart thinking,' Maggie said, seeing her son's frustration lessening. Just like his father, music was the ultimate distraction. 'Was that Will's idea?'

'Nah, mine. The boys are worried about the rain wetting their gear.'

'You're my clever boy.' Maggie stood and successfully tugged Noah into a bear hug.

'Quit it will you, Mum.' He squirmed. 'I'm not a kid.'

'Oh, I know. I see that every day.' Maggie reluctantly let go. 'I'm sorry, buddy. I've got a lot on my plate at the moment with the pub, the sale, the centenary planning, your granddad ...' *Your father and Fiona,* she silently added. 'Let's get through next week and then talk again. You head off—and leave those clothes you're wearing on the floor,' she called out. 'I'm doing a load of ...' She was talking to herself.

With one more situation defused, for the moment anyway, Maggie sighed away the unexpected urge to cry.

When had her son stopped needing her hugs?

When had her husband stop needing her by his side?

When had she stopped needing her husband?

15

With less than a week to go, the committee met at the drop of a hat —Jennifer's hat—with Maggie and everyone else bending to Jennifer's frantic demands. Ethne covered the pub's opening and closing times as they were set in stone. The framed tapestry stuck to the wall behind the bar reinforced them: *The Eleventh Commandment*, it read. *Thou shalt open the bar on time.* God help her should Maggie open late, close early, or not open at all.

This morning's early meeting was being held at the pub, even though Lorna and Val looked uncomfortable about the insalubrious surroundings of a public bar. Like bookends on either side of Maggie, they sat like nervous church mice. It's just a pub, lightning won't strike, Maggie was tempted to say, but with talk of an electrical storm building to the east, she decided not to tempt fate. Maggie was a big enough lightning rod for worry.

Meeting adjourned, and more things ticked off the list this time than added to the list, Maggie scooted Will and Sara away so she could help Ethne.

'You head off, Will.' Sara kissed her husband goodbye as if the guy was leaving for Antarctica rather than across the road to the café. 'I need a chat with Maggie.'

'Talking about me?' Will grinned.

Sara waved him away with a smile. 'We've got better things to talk about.'

Maggie had a million things to do and no time to talk at all, but to-do lists and timetables did not feature prominently in the café owners' lives; something else about the couple that occasionally awakened Maggie's little green monster. Hunky hubby, Will, especially didn't take anything too seriously and with Sara in remission, both embraced life, love and their second chance at happiness. The pair carved nothing in stone, including the hours the café kept. The business hours sign on the door was a reminder to all:

Open most days around 8 or 9, but sometimes as late as 10 or 11.
We close about 4 (maybe 5) but occasionally at 3.
Some days or afternoons we aren't here at all, especially when the fish are bitin'
or the mercury reaches 40. But at all times we appreciate your company.

Maggie watched Sara's gaze follow Will as he crossed the street. 'You pair still act like a couple of love-struck kids.'

Sara sniggered. 'But when we *were* kids, I was tongue-tied dork and Will was Mr Popular. We were never going to get together back then. What about you, Maggie?' asked Sara.

'What about me?'

'I don't recall your school crush,' she clarified. 'Who was he?'

Mr Unpopular, Maggie mused while collecting used water glasses.

Sara's voice dropped to a whisper. 'Do you know, for years I used to imagine it was Will and not my ex when we … You know?'

Maggie nodded, but didn't confess to doing the same. On those nights of perfunctory sex with Brian, she'd spiced up the experience with thoughts of the boy who'd both captured then broken her young heart. A few years after Dan had left town, an invitation arrived by mail. Tracy Rose, a good friend from school, was marrying Maggie's school crush.

'Some couples are meant to be, Sara. You found each other in the end.' Maggie tied her black apron, crossing the ties at the small of her back before bringing them around her middle

'I wonder what would've happened if I'd been braver and we'd got together twenty years ago …' The thought made the petite blonde smile as she rinsed cups, yelling over the running water. 'I thank Gypsy every day for the Dandelion House inheritance: for the truth, for the family she gave me, and for bringing me back to Calingarry Crossing.'

Sara had coped amazingly well, Maggie thought. She had an instant family, a small business, the ever-present threat of breast cancer, a paraplegic husband, *and* his overprotective, pain in the butt mother—all of which made Maggie's pot of problems small by comparison. Maggie had one thing Sara didn't. From the minute the midwife had put Noah in her arms, the enormous responsibility of caring for another human had hit her with staggering force.

Both she and Brian were totally and instantly besotted, with Noah quickly becoming the reason for everything: to stay home, to go out, to save, to spend, to get up, to sleep in—all three of them in the double bed. Morning sex became a thing of the past, eventually petering out almost completely. Strangely, it didn't bother Maggie. By then, even if Brian had been capable when he'd slipped between the sheets in the early hours of Saturday and Sunday mornings after his gigs, the lingering stench of smoke and booze had been an instant turn-off. Besides that, making love was the last thing Maggie wanted after working full days Monday to Saturday, especially knowing she had to get up early for a job she hated, while her husband and baby stayed cuddled up in bed. Planned or spontaneous, she missed sex. She missed both the tender touches and hurried and hushed humping while her son did homework in his room. Maggie needed to feel beautiful and sexy and adored, especially given the milestone birthday creeping closer.

'Better go,' Sara was saying. 'Monster-in-law's tonight. After that I might take Will home and—'

'Okay, okay!' Maggie flapped both hands. 'I get the picture. Now scoot. I have a pub to open.'

AFTER A CHECK OF THE BEER TAPS, MAGGIE DID A TEST POUR AND WAS loading the glass-washer when she caught sight of her reflection in the pitted old Perkins Stout mirror hanging behind the bar. Touching a hand to one cheek, then the other, she considered paying more attention to her skin, but with no one to impress except a bar full of blokes, and given she *was* married—information Ethne had quickly disseminated to anyone with amorous notions about the new "not-bad-looking" female publican—Maggie saw little benefit in wasting time and money on lotions, potions and perfumes designed to keep a woman youthful and radiant.

'No product on the planet had such power,' she mumbled. All any of them did was allow the glow of a woman in love to shine on the outside. With Maggie basically celibate these days and left to her own … ahem … devices—supported by a rather limited imagination given she'd only ever been with Brian—there wasn't too much glowing of late.

While her beauty regime may have taken a back seat over the past couple of years, she had made an effort to keep her body and mind active. If she'd needed any reminding about the importance of physical and emotional fitness, the nursing home hallways echoing the creaks and regrets of worn bones and jaded minds did the job. This morning's centenary committee meeting, unfortunately, had meant missing her morning run, which also meant no scraps for the old mare that had seemed particularly frisky yesterday.

'The bloody horse has probably seen more action in her lifetime,' Maggie grumbled as she marched the tray of washed glasses from the main bar to the dining room.

'Did you say something, Maggie?' An overly cheery Fiona called across from a table covered with paper. 'Sorry I missed the meeting. I needed to get a start on this project.'

Maggie's interest piqued. Had Fiona brought work to do during her stay? Was there a mature, conscientious side to the girl with the mobile phone fetish?

'Looks intense,' Maggie called from the kitchen, adding hot water to eke out the last of the filter coffee before leaving the kitchen again.

'Noah and I are working on something for the reunion,' Fiona announced.

Maggie not only faltered part way across the dining room, she managed to fit a mountain of concern into a single syllable. 'Oh?'

'It's a memory wall,' Fiona said. 'A photographic retrospective.'

'A retro—?'

'A retrospective,' she repeated. There was definitely an unusual level of enthusiasm in the girl's attitude, as if someone had told her Myer was setting up shop in the town's main street tomorrow. 'I'm very good at visual displays.'

I'll add that to the list, Maggie mused, burying her grin in her coffee cup while examining the myriad photographs on the table. She recognised the old class pictures; the kind in which tall students like Maggie, Poppy and Tracy found themselves standing in the middle at the back—a position that only served to accentuate their towering statures, thereby confirming for the entire school that they truly were freaks of nature. The petite, pretty ones like Amber and Sara got to sit front and centre: straight-backed with hands on knees and butter-wouldn't-melt smiles.

'Where did you get all these?'

'Cheryl gave them to me,' Fiona replied. 'We've had a good couple of days talking about Mum and stuff.'

'Cheryl,' Maggie echoed. 'As in your grandmother?' It had taken Maggie twelve months to start calling Mrs Bailey by her first name, and only after the woman had insisted.

'Yep! These are all of Amber when she lived here.' Fiona poked the pictures around on the table, a trace of sentiment in her voice cutting through the usual forced sophistication. 'Naturally, I didn't know the pictures existed, on account of I didn't know this town existed. Or, for that matter, that I had a grandmother.'

'A lovely grandmother,' Maggie added. 'I'm glad you're getting to know each other. It's been hard on her ...' She let the sentence trail off. Sharing Cheryl Bailey's hardships was not appropriate. 'Remember, Fiona, she didn't know much about you until recently.'

'Whatever.' The girl flapped a dismissive hand, sentiment squashed, stomped on and ground to nothingness like a spent cigarette. 'I figured if the school is a hundred years old there must be heaps of stuff hanging around. Not sure why no one else thought to arrange a display.'

The girl's arrogance might be vexing, but she had a point. Why hadn't anyone thought about a pictorial account of the school's history? Why hadn't Maggie? She could tell *Miss I'm qualified* that she, Maggie Lindeman, was a skilled photographer. A single TAFE term 20,000 moons ago counted, didn't it?

'I might have photos to contribute.' Maggie didn't elaborate. She certainly didn't tell Fiona her box of photo albums was always the first thing she'd packed each time the family had moved.

Even now, her box of precious memories remained tucked away in a cupboard under the stairs, always close to the door in case Maggie should need to risk life and limb rushing back into a burning building to rescue them. The catalogue of albums scrolled through her mind: one brag book for every year of Noah's life, one wedding album, and one box of miscellaneous pictures from her youth when the family finally bought a camera on Maggie's twelfth birthday. Until then, friends had captured special family moments. These days, Maggie's album box was everything: her memory, her companion, her sanity on those long nights alone lamenting her choices—choices that had always considered someone other than herself. Every now and then she would pick a random album, take it to the hospital with her and find a picture to reignite the spark in her father's face. Memory was a gift, unappreciated until it was gone.

'Fiona, be sure to run the idea of a display by Jennifer.' Maggie could picture the mad scribbling and tsk-ing that would take place. 'Jen might even help you collect more contents. Coffee?' Maggie called on her way back to the kitchen, her own cup calling out for a refill.

'No, thank you, but …' Fiona said, 'I was kind of hoping you and I could go through Mum's pictures. You can tell me who some of the people are.'

'I could try.' As Maggie returned with a cup half-filled with desperate dregs, she peered down at the array of photographs. 'Not sure how good I'll be at remembering names. While it was a small school in our day …' *God, how ancient does that make her sound?* 'There were still cliques and I definitely wasn't in the same circle as your mum.'

'You mean not as …' Fiona fashioned quotation marks with her fingers, "popular with the boys".'

Maggie didn't respond or tell Fiona a door in the girls' toilets had chronicled Amber's popularity. Silly scribbles like: *Amber Bailey thinks safe sex means doing it where she won't get sprung.* Had there been any truth to some school scuttlebutt, even Maggie's brother had taken Amber to Cedar Cutters Gorge.

'What I mean, Fiona, is that your mother and I weren't close friends.'

While the annoying girl with her fresh face and obsessive hair flicking was trying not to care, the fingering of old photographs suggested otherwise. Maggie was about to apologise for not being helpful when guilt tugged at her conscience. She could try.

'I'll take a look after dinner,' she told Fiona. 'With Ethne off I'll be working the bar. Mid-week we're generally quiet. We'll see how we go'

What harm could come from looking at old photos?

16

Maggie had been spot-on with her prediction of a quiet evening at the bar, making Fiona and her project a welcome distraction. With few patrons and no meals to serve, staying awake was difficult. Two regulars propped up one end of the bar and a couple of long-haul truckers passed time with a game of pool at the table in the adjacent lounge. Maggie delivered their beers and on her way back stopped to fix the black velveteen curtain that concealed the tiny corner podium. The dust-covered Pianola next to the stage provided the occasional drunk with an opportunity to accompany him or herself singing—usually too loudly and almost always out of tune.

At the bar, Fiona sorted photographs into two piles: clear and not so clear. Some were old instant Polaroid photos, faded from age, their ghostly subjects unrecognisable. Maggie had always wanted one of those fancy cameras that whirred and clunked and poked out a glossy tongue of black film. The magic of self-developing pictures had made her first fall in love with photography.

'Good grief.' She picked up a photo from the school dance with girls dwarfed by shocking shoulder pads and a sea of chiffon.

'Whatchya got there, girlie?' Barney asked from a few bar stools away. 'Looks like thirsty work.' He leaned across and up-ended his empty glass onto the tray of dirties—his standard ready-for-a-refill ritual.

'School photos of Amber Bailey,' Maggie replied. 'Have you met,

Fiona?' She cocked the handle on Barney's brew of choice, half filling the fresh schooner glass before banging it twice on the bar towel to settle the frothy head. 'She's Ambers daughter.'

'Heard a young thing had blown into town,' Barney said. 'You got your mother's looks.'

Fiona swivelled on her bar stool. 'Do you really think I look like my mother?'

'Bloody oath! Need more meat on them bones is all.'

'And do I look like anyone else you might know from around town?' Fiona asked. 'My father maybe?'

Caution crumpled Barney's brow, telling anyone who bothered to see beyond his town-soak act, as Maggie did, that he was wiser than he let on. 'Can't say I know too much about that, missy.'

'Funny that!' Fiona sneered, turning back to the photo spread. 'Me either.'

Sensing danger, Maggie formed her next words to Fiona carefully. 'I gather this interest in old photos isn't about a display for the reunion. Have you come to Calingarry Crossing thinking your father will be here?'

'Would that be so wrong?' the girl asked without looking up.

Maggie eyed the room for any impending orders before lifting the servery and stepping through to the public side of the bar. A stool scraped like chalk on a board as she positioned herself next to Fiona. Hooking a heel of her work boot on the foot rail, Maggie perched one butt-cheek on the edge of the seat and leaned close.

'The answer, Fiona, depends on why you're looking. It was a long time ago.'

'I think I know how long ago it was, Maggie.'

'Are you sure you want to go down that path so soon after your mum's passing? You might find more disappointment. A wise person focuses on your future.'

More silence. More sulking—at least that's what Maggie thought was happening as she stared at the stripe of strawberry blonde regrowth in Fiona's hair. The colour was hardly a shade different from the fashionable foils that no doubt cost a fortune. The girl was her mother. *Au naturel* was never good enough for Amber either, no matter how well she wore it.

'Have you thought about Phillip?' Maggie ventured. 'How difficult this search might be for him? Your mother's barely—'

'Why?' she blurted. 'They both lied to me my whole life.' As Fiona slowly lifted her face, her eyes, cheeks and nose—tinged red—showed the first signs of a sob held in for too long. 'Do you know how I found out Phillip wasn't my real father? There was an argument. Mum, Phillip and Granddad. They didn't know I was there. Nothing new about that!' She huffed, sniffed back the sob, straightened her back. 'But I was there, in the hallway; I heard every word. When Mum saw me, she said my name and …' Fiona clicked her fingers before her hand fell back onto her bare legs with a smack. 'She died.'

Fiona was trying so hard not to care, but Maggie knew better. 'I understand you're upset about your mum dying.'

The girl shrugged, although no amount of bravado could stop the tears that finally tipped over and rolled down her cheeks, washing a faint trail through the mineral makeup powder that did an amazing job of masking her freckles. 'It's not as if she was around much when I was growing up. Even when she was there, she wasn't. You know what I mean?'

'She wanted to make amends, Fiona. She tried.'

'Well, I wish she hadn't.' The girl's chin puckered, her voice cracking under the pressure of another sob. 'I wish she'd never come here and had whatever freaking epiphany it was to make her change. Hating her was easy. Hating her wouldn't hurt so much now.'

Maggie rested a hand on Fiona's shoulder, her heart aching for the girl. Whose wouldn't? Fiona might be a snotty-nosed brat, but maybe that was because she'd been spoilt with everything but the truth.

'Have you talked to your father about how you feel? He understands loss and heartache, too.'

'He's *not* my father. Phillip lied to me. I knew my mother didn't give a shit when I was growing up, but I thought he loved me. I mean really loved me, like a real father loves a real daughter.' Despair overrode the rage in her words. 'I don't know anything. I don't know my mother or him. How could they keep such a secret? When I confronted Phillip, he told me he didn't know my actual father. Was he lying then, too?' When Fiona's hands covered her eyes, Maggie moved in for a hug because hugging was what she did best, even though Noah was fast growing out of them.

Fiona stiffened, pulled away from the embrace within seconds and dragged the disintegrating napkin across her nose. 'I hate them both.'

'Maybe it was his love for you that stopped him from telling,' Maggie said. 'Parents protect their children for as long as they can, any way they can.'

'And that makes lying acceptable?'

Yes, Maggie silently confessed. Aloud she said, 'Some things are best left in the past.'

'Luke said I needed to come out here and find the truth for myself.'

'And Luke is …?' Maggie asked.

'My fiancé.'

How had Maggie not noticed the serious bit of bling before? 'You're engaged?'

Fiona reclaimed her hand. 'That's what they were arguing about with Granddad. Mum and Dad—I mean *Phillip*—never liked Luke.'

'They must have had their reasons, Fiona. You are still young.'

'Whatever!' As sorrowful as she'd been only seconds before, the tears dried, the spine stiffened—the brat was back. 'At least Granddad's on my side. He's so cool.'

Cool is one word, Maggie thought. Hopefully, while Fiona gets to know her grandmother, she'll learn how un-cool Jack Bailey used to be— and probably still is.

'So, what's Luke like?' Maggie was curious and keen to get their conversation away from Amber and Phillip.

'Granddad calls him his protégé.'

'Does he?' Maggie stifled a smirk. 'And where is Luke?'

'I told him I wanted to come on my own.'

So, she had the gumption to stand up to this Luke. Maggie still smelled a rat. 'It was your idea, Fiona?'

'Of course! Where were we?' A final sniff and a hair flick closed the discussion down. 'Are these photos all we have? What about the albums still in your box?' Fiona pointed to the carton Maggie had deliberately kept to one side.

'Those aren't from school,' she explained.

'And that?' Fiona cocked her head at the protruding A3 folder with the top portion of black vinyl showing a yellowing business label with curling corners.

'My old portfolio,' Maggie said. 'I studied photography a long time ago.'

Fiona wiggled *gimme-gimme* fingers. 'Show me.'

After a moment's hesitation, Maggie lowered the black folder directly into Fiona's upturned palms as if it was an ancient artefact, not old photos from a still-life collection she'd done in a different lifetime. Expecting nothing more than a cursory glance before the girl lost interest, as Fiona turned each tissue-separated page with near reverence, a muddle of satisfaction and self-doubt permeated Maggie's every pore. No one had shown such intense interest in her photography. Not when she was kick-starting her career and not now her gallery remained packed—along with her dreams—in the banana box she'd picked up from the greengrocer's store when she and Brian had lived briefly in Sydney's inner west.

'Wow, Maggie, you were good when you were young.'

Were young? Assuming the slight was unintentional, Maggie focused on the 'wow' part, pride puffing her up a little. 'I took pictures of anything that got in the way of my lens. My dream was to be the next Anne Geddes.'

Fiona grimaced. 'Who?'

'Another beer, thanks,' came Barney's voice from the end of the bar. 'And one for my mate.'

'Oh, hello there! It's been a while,' Maggie said to Charlie Ireland—the father of another teenage dream that never eventuated.

Ordinarily, she might stop for a chat but conversations with Charlie were never easy, or as uplifting as Fiona's praise just now. Through their mutual love of photography, Maggie and frosty Fiona had found a connection. The girl might appear cold, but maybe, if Maggie kept chip, chip, chipping away, the ice might crack—if Calingarry's heat didn't melt it away first.

THE EVENING HAD BEEN UNSEASONABLY HOT, WITH LITTLE RELIEF STILL BY ten-thirty as she closed up for the night. In her bedroom, in the cottage behind the pub, the breeze barely ruffled the lacy curtains where Maggie sat, cool drink in hand. The television remained muted—for light only—with the late-night, sleepy country town noises music enough: the chorus of cicadas, the frog refrain drifting across from the river, and the effervescence bubbling in Maggie's glass. Chiming in occasionally was a hooting owl, mewling cattle, and the thud, thud, thud of old Achilles attempting to scratch his ear, but with his arthritic leg falling short of its target and dropping heavily on the veranda boards.

In a few weeks—maybe days—the rumble of thunder would add to the cacophony. The accompanying showers would initially do little more than add moisture to the air and to a thirsty ground baked dry during the day, but a humid heat was a change from a dry one. As always, the hope was enough rain would fall to make gauges overflow overnight. On the TV screen, the late-night news had switched to the cute weatherman pointing to his synoptic chart showing a cold front blowing in from the south. Behind the front was another high-pressure system expected to move towards Saddleton, with a ridge extending further towards the north-east. The icons suggested scattered showers and isolated thunderstorms for the next few days.

This morning, when checking the weather station Joe had installed after a horrendous season, the gauges had showed twenty-nine degrees Celsius—barometer rising. Maggie couldn't recall if the same scatty weather patterns had existed when she'd lived in Calingarry Crossing as a girl. Then again, the last thing a teenager thought about was weather patterns. There seemed to be no pattern at all these days, with the erratic and all too often extreme conditions affecting both crops and cattle. Fruit trees were no longer fruiting when they should and Cricket was in the bar earlier tonight complaining that even his best cluckers—the chooks he claimed 'yous can set ya watch by'—had stopped laying each morning.

'Predictable as flies on a Christmas dinner, them common brown hens,' Cricket had announced. 'Bleedin' global warming muckin' 'em up for sure. And that's not the worst of it. There's a perfect storm headin' our way, Maggie.'

'What are you on about?' another old-timer grumbled.

Cricket sighed. 'I'm talking about when a whole load of events converge at once. On their lonesome, they're not a worry, but bring 'em all together …' The rumble of laughter in the bar got Cricket worked up. 'You blokes laugh all you want.' He grabbed his hat from a stool. 'You can also mark my bleedin' words. There's a storm brewing; big enough to blow the lid of God-knows what.'

Much joshing followed, along with comments like, 'Old Barnacle Bill's boat might come in bloody handy,' followed by 'If the old bastard ever gets it finished.'

In her room, while draining the last cool dregs of her drink, Maggie smiled at the image of Old Barnacle's parting finger gesture and prepared for bed. No doubt she was in for another restless night filled with thoughts about a life that never varied, weather patterns that never stayed the same, and storm season building up just in time for next weekend's reunion. Any out-of-towners who'd forgotten how sticky the place could be were in for a not-so-subtle reminder. Ideal conditions for beer sales, she thought.

'Not so good for hair.' Maggie inspected herself in the dresser mirror and released her mane from its elastic band.

A storm was definitely brewing somewhere. The air was thick with static, her hair crackling and sticking out at odd angles as if someone controlled each strand with invisible strings. After stripping down to her knickers, she turned the ceiling fan up high, flopped on top of the sheets, and sprayed water from a trigger bottle to glaze her skin with a fine mist. Sleep tonight would be more challenging after an evening with Fiona, and with her photographs turning Maggie's mind into a slide show of her younger years. In a matter of days, Maggie's youth would catch up with her, the past and present converging with the unpredictable. Would celebrating Calingarry Crossing's centenary be Maggie's perfect storm?

School reunions made Maggie think about a swollen river about to burst its banks. Both terrifying and fascinating, the simple act of venturing too close for a look could be disastrous, but it was also impossible to stay away. The true danger of reunions, however, was making Maggie question her worth and her achievements. She might not have a lot to show, other than Noah, but at least her life was real and honest. She was who she was: no living beyond her means, nothing fancy to show off, and nothing to prove. Amber, on the other hand, had come from very ordinary beginnings and changed everything about herself to measure up to a society that judges a person on their appearance. Like Brian, Maggie supposed.

Now Amber's daughter was the uncomfortable and unsettled one, as though who she was and what she was no longer fitted in her world. For that reason, Maggie would cut the girl some slack—starting tomorrow. The connection the pair experienced tonight had been mutual, she was certain of it, and the two of them were not so dissimilar. They'd both faced rejection, but in different ways. The people meant to love Fiona had sent her to boarding school and holiday camps, whereas Brian hadn't rejected or abandoned Maggie as much as he'd forgotten her.

17

The tune *Old McDonald Had A Farm* blared from the portable handset by her bed. Maggie snatched up the receiver before the *ee-eye-ee-eye-o*.

'Hello?'

'Maggs?' Brian sounded tired and nasally, the 'M' of Maggs muffled.

Of course it's me, she wanted to say, stifling a groan. Who else would it be at …? She eyed the clock ticking over to midnight and groaned aloud. At least she'd learned to ignore the gut-wrenching pull of dread that had once accompanied late-night wake-up calls and door knocks.

'What is it, Brian?' She kicked the tangle of sheets from around her ankles, a sure sign of restless sleep.

'Aw, Maggs.' He sniffed. 'Do you know how much I love it when you call me Brian?'

It's your name, she might have responded, but laughing at his comment was counterproductive. Brian was busy having his very own pity party. She knew by the namby-pamby pitch in his voice—the one that had all the bounce of a solitary helium balloon the morning after the party. She also understood the nuance in his comment. Her husband, Brian Henkler, no longer existed. He was Reece Naylor, wannabe country rock performer and failed *iICON* contestant desperately clinging to the dream. She'd seen his desperation at the Sydney café: the hair, the outfit, the attitude. Now she heard it in his voice.

Crazy, funny, clever and, like Maggie, a romantic, Brian had once held the promise of a big, colourful, exciting life for a country girl. She'd been missing the noise her brother brought into her world, and with her crush on Dan Ireland quashed by grief and an unforgiving father who'd forbidden Maggie from seeing him, it was Brian who'd swept into Calingarry Crossing, swept her up, then swept her away.

'Do you know the time, Brian?' Maggie cringed at her tone. If the call was to say he was coming to Calingarry Crossing because he could no longer live without her, then she had probably just blown it.

'Give me a break. Can't a guy call his wife?' The nasally quality in his voice was not about being tired. He was drunk, or stoned, or something in between. Maggie never knew which, and Brian constantly denied using. Whatever the habit, it was yet another reason to keep Noah in the country. 'I miss ya, Maggsy.'

'Well, Brian, there's one way to get over missing me.' She didn't bother to hide the sarcasm. 'Calingarry Crossing is not the end of the earth and it wouldn't be the end of the world to be a country singer in a country pub. You want people to appreciate your music, don't you?'

'You don't understand, Maggs.'

Maggie bristled. 'You know I despise those words, Brian.'

'But it's true.' His whine made him sound like a foot-stomping four-year-old rather than forty. 'Global is the only way to go. This country doesn't appreciate what I have to offer. They don't get my music—or me. But people in America would get Reece Naylor. I'm doing everything the producers are telling me to do. The timing has to be right, is all. They say, "opportunity plus preparedness equals success". This business requires patience. I need to wait my turn.'

Maggie bit down so hard on her bottom lip that she flinched. She wanted to scream. *There's nothing to wait for. There are no more auditions. The show went on without you. They weren't interested, Brian. You weren't good enough, Brian. You need to work for actual money, Brian.*

Instead, she breathed deeply, hoping to sound genuine. 'You've tried so hard, Brian. You were amazing to get as far as you did. How many hopefuls were at that original open audition and yet you made it through.'

'The auditions were in Sydney, Maggs. I never even made it out of the fucking country.'

'But you made it into the top one-hundred potential Australian contestants. You were better than so many, and you did everything they asked. But Brian, the show's over. It's time for family.'

'Well, good to know how little faith you have in your husband.' Brian was doing his usual three-sixty and turning the argument into Maggie's fault. 'The show might be over for you, my disbelieving wife, but I'm no quitter. You can't ask me to give up my dreams.'

'*Your* dreams,' she hissed. 'Where do you think we'd be if I hadn't given up my dreams when Noah came along? One of us had to keep food in the refrigerator. If I'd left it to you, Noah would have been burped on beer. Do not lecture me about dreams. I gave up *everything* to have Noah.'

Maggie slammed her fist into the mattress, desperate to hold back the sob brought about by her husband's derision. He'd pushed and pushed, ripping the roof off that place inside her—that place that had hidden the teensy-weensiest sliver of resentment all these years. *Damn you, Brian*. He'd forced her to add her son's name to a list of dream-wreckers, and hearing herself say the words aloud broke her heart. At that moment, she'd never felt so precarious, so unprotected, so over-whelmed by her son's moodiness, her unexpected houseguest, her father's continued decline, and this stupid school reunion. Now her husband.

'I can't do this alone, Brian.'

'You forget I have a contract, Maggie.'

'Break it,' she yelled, tempted to add, *break it like you've broken every promise you ever made your family.*

'You know me better than that, Maggie.'

No, she was tempted to tell him. Her husband was a stranger. She'd barely recognised the man who had greeted her at the café.

'Brian, I need sleep. I have a pub to open tomorrow. It's late and—'

Click! The line went dead, but her husband's words stayed. *You forget I have a contract.*

Yes, the contract! She fell back against the pillow, recalling how she'd questioned the agreement that had arrived via courier to their Sydney flat. Even to her uneducated eye, the terms had seemed too open-ended, too ridiculous, too risky. The more she'd questioned, however, the more adamant and defensive Brian had become.

'Where's your sense of adventure?' he'd demanded.

At first Maggie laughed. 'You don't call diving into two weeks' worth of yours and Noah's dirty laundry adventurous?' She closed the bi-fold doors on the hide-away laundry that took up half the kitchen.

'You don't get it, Maggs. You're always thinking small-town. This is the ultimate adventure.'

Brian guzzled his third VB, courtesy of the latest pub gig that had paid in kind rather than in cash.

'Maybe I am small town,' she said.

'Well, Maggs,' he burped the words, crushing the empty can in a powerful fist. 'Time to think big. This could be the break I've been working towards.'

'The break *you've* been working towards?' Maggie imagined her expression: stunned and confused, like she'd whacked her head on an invisible pane of glass. Since when was playing guitar for two hours then drinking for two hours working towards anything but a hangover the next morning? She was the one putting actual money in the bank, only to watch the cost of living and a growing boy siphon it back out.

'What are you implying?' Brain pouted.

'Never mind.' She was wasting her breath.

Brian's gigs around town were as haphazard as the method of payment, which Brian never questioned, accepting whatever the pub owners dished out and telling Maggie, 'What's the diff? If we got cash, we'd still have to buy beer.' Maggie wanted to suggest they might buy fresh vegetables, or even eat out as a family occasionally. She always refrained. Brian acted like an eager puppy most times and such statements were like a smack on the snout for peeing on the carpet. He never understood what he'd done wrong. Those same big, Weimaraner-blue eyes had beseeched her the day the *iICON* contract arrived.

'AND YOU WON'T GET THIS CONTRACT LOOKED AT BY A SOLICITOR?' THEY were the first words to come out of Maggie's mouth after seeing the costs the production company seemed prepared to cover: aeroplane fares, personal stylists, PR advisors, new wardrobes, new hair, new everything. The *iICON* people claimed to be the first-ever no boundaries global talent show: their goal to discover an international music sensation. From the look of it, the production budget was just as boundless and smacked of 'too good to be true'.

'What the hell do we want a solicitor for?' Brian said. 'Why spend hundreds of dollars we don't have so some pompous, overpaid prick can tell us what we already know? This is a once in a lifetime opportunity. You need to relax, Maggs. I know how this biz works,' he said, going for another beer in the refrigerator. 'Production costs don't come out of anyone's pocket. It's all advertising dollars. Companies buy exposure, and this show is global. Forget Tamworth, Maggs, we're talking Nashville.'

'Shhh,' Maggie said, but it was like asking an excitable dog to bark quietly. Instead, she moved to shut the door to the hallway so Noah wouldn't hear them.

'Come 'ere, you.' Brian grabbed a hand as she passed, tugging her onto the sofa beside him. 'Imagine what this could mean for us—for Noah. Our dreams don't have to stay dreams. Don't you see, Maggs?' He shifted to kneel on the floor in front of her. Forcing her knees apart with his body, he nudged her skirt higher and peered up into her eyes. 'Ordinary people like us finally have a chance. That's the great thing about reality television. Someone has to win. Why can't it be me? Look at that Susan Boyle chick. Look how it catapulted her to fame and fortune.'

And look how people treated her. How wrong it could have gone for the woman, Maggie wanted to add. She smoothed the hair falling around her husband's ears, loving the power of his body pushing between her thighs and the gentleness of his teasing fingers tantalisingly close to their mark. At the same time, she wanted to hate it and push him off her, but Brian's wild side had captured an innocent country girl with a big heart and bigger dreams. He'd been young, impetuous, exciting, and exactly the sort of distraction Maggie had needed following her brother's accident and Dan Ireland disappearing.

'Susan Boyle was a nobody, Maggs. Until suddenly she was the biggest star in the world. I could be next.'

There was an element of truth to Brian's words. Reality TV pulled nobodies from obscurity and let them shine. Ordinary people with a passion for cooking, renovating—even game show participants—could achieve their fifteen minutes of fame. That's all Brian wanted; to have his moment in the spotlight. Imagine if he realised his dream and won prize money. What might that mean for them as a family?

'We're so close, Maggs.' He pushed against her legs, his breath laced with beer, although it wasn't his breath that had Maggie's attention. It was the hand working its magic higher and higher between her thighs. 'Feel it, Maggs. Feel the fame.'

'Brian,' she breathed. 'Brian, stop, we can't. Not out here.'

'We can do anything, Maggs. I'm so close I can touch it. Let me taste fame, Maggs. Let me taste you.' She gasped as his finger found its mark inside her knickers, the seriousness of the conversation quickly losing importance. 'Shhh,' he said, his breath warm on her wetness, his hand moving to his trousers.

No! Maggie dragged her skirt back down. He was doing it again, being Brian, being the naughty puppy, and she was rewarding the behaviour. 'Stop!' She tried shoving his shoulders. 'Noah is in his room and we're trying to talk.'

Brian barely faltered, stopping long enough to lift his face to hers, to smile, then tug her skirt back up her thighs. 'You talk. I can do this and listen at the same time. I'm talented that way.'

'Brian, please.' Maggie tried to untangle herself, but he had her pinned against the sofa. She groaned and squirmed, the words 'stop' and 'don't stop' fighting for top honours. 'The contract says you agree to your communications being monitored. Why would they want to do that?'

Brian sat back and huffed. 'In case you didn't notice, I'm trying to make love to you and all these questions are kind of killing the moment. What's got into you?'

'I'm tired, Brian, and I'm worried about Dad. Ethne was on the phone the other day. I need to get out there. A pub doesn't run itself.'

'Yeah, well, Ethne looks after the place. About time the lazy old bag earned her keep. My career is more important.'

Maggie drew a knee to her chest, planted the arch of her foot on Brian's left shoulder and shoved. 'Ethne is an employee, and in case you didn't notice, Brian, I'm trying to have a conversation about our family's future.' She adjusted her shirt and skirt, sat straight-backed and stared her husband down. 'So, tell me why the show would want to monitor our telephone conversations?'

'The surprise element is everything in these situations,' he said. 'That's why they keep everyone together for the duration, and why there's a family confidentiality agreement to sign. We can't tell Noah because he's under eighteen.'

'And what do I say to our son about your absence? What if I slip? Lying doesn't sit well with me.'

'Everyone knows how to lie, Maggs—even you. You're keeping a secret. Secrets can be fun.'

'Until someone slips up,' Maggie muttered.

Brian was still sitting obediently on the floor and looking up with those Weimaraner-blue eyes. 'You won't slip up if we create a story that's easy to stick to.'

'Like?' Maggie asked, trying not to dwell on his 'even you' addition.

'You'll figure out something, Maggs. Better to be in your words. Makes a lie easier to remember.'

'Whatchya doing in here with the door closed?' said their fifteen-year-old with one eye, half a nose and thick fringe of mousey brown hair poking through the gap in the lounge room door.

Maggie leapt off the sofa, while Brian chuckled and winked. 'We weren't doing nothing at all, mate. Mum and me were talking.'

'About what?' Noah nudged the door open.

'You should be asleep,' Maggie said, fussing with her skirt, her shirt, her hair. 'Back to bed.'

'Hang on, matey.' Brian waved his son over, pointing to the op-shop armchair with the tapestry fabric. 'Your dad might go away for a bit.'

'What?' Both fear and confusion melded into one heartbreaking expression on her son's face.

Maggie didn't want to lie, but she wouldn't cement his fear by arguing or nit-picking. She feigned a smile. 'Everything's fine. Your dad is—'

'I might have to go OS for work, mate.'

'You mean like another country?' Noah asked with the same puppy-like eagerness. 'Me too?'

'No, mate,' Brian said, standing. 'I might be incommunicado though.'

'Huh?' Noah's excitement fizzled out, replaced with questioning glances between his father and Maggie.

'Means it could just be you and Mum for a while.' Brian roughed up his son's hair. 'You can take my place as head of the family. What do you say, big boy?'

'No wuckin' furries,' Noah replied, meeting his father's high-five.

Brian always thought the phrase hilarious. Maggie remained unimpressed. 'I really wish you wouldn't let him think that phrase is funny.'

'Isn't it?' Brian laughed, watching Noah walk over and bury his head in the fridge.

When Noah emerged with a crunchy green Granny Smith apple in his other hand, rather than a fizzy drink, Maggie found a reason to smile. At least Noah wasn't all his father.

'It wouldn't hurt you to follow your son's example, Brian.'

'No way, Maggs, you gotta be wary of them apples. You know what happened in the Garden of Eden.'

'Brian!' Maggie shushed.

'Aw, come 'ere, wife. You worry too much.' He pulled her close and kissed her the way he always did—a finger pressed to her lips, a tap on her nose, and their song in his best Count Dracula voice, '*I lurve my Magpie, just a little-biddy peck and with a love bite on her neck. Bwah ha ha.*' The ritual always ended with him sucking her neck and Maggie pushing him away and laughing. 'That's my Maggs. I love it when you laugh. Everything will be great. You'll see. Have I ever let you down?'

⁊

ALONE IN THE PITCH-BLACK BEDROOM WITH ITS BARELY THERE BREEZE, Maggie found she was mentally listing the many failed moneymaking schemes, but with Brian's pre-schooler attention span, each one was discarded quickly in favour of something more exciting. When Noah came along, things in the Henkler household changed. Nothing delivered a reality check like a baby and a zero bank balance. When Noah started coming home from high school scuffed up and bruised, adamant Maggie didn't need to intervene and insisting—to his father's amusement—the other kid always came off worse, she'd been contemplating what to do when news came of Joe's decline. Guilt over having delayed numerous trips to Calingarry Crossing caused more arguments with Brian. How had she not recognised each time she'd telephoned that The Rev's vagueness was something more sinister? With no choice, she left Sydney with Noah, bundling a few weeks-worth of gear for her them both in bags and leaving her husband behind to follow as soon as practical.

Where has the time gone?

Maggie tossed and turned for a while, feeling the smallness of the stuffy little room she now called home. As she was turning her head off to Brian, the *Old McDonald Had A Farm* ringtone sounded, and in her haste to silence the noise she smashed the receiver into her jaw and cursed.

'Hello to you, too,' Brian responded. 'I rang to talk to Noah.'

'Oh, for goodness' sake!' Maggie rubbed the spot, imagining the bruise she'd have by morning. 'Why this late, Brian, and why when you won't even remember what he—?'

Click! 'Goodbye to you, too, Brian.'

At least his phoning late allowed Maggie to answer, and not her son. To her, Noah was still that little boy who idolised his dad and wanted to grow up to be just like him. Maggie shuddered. Whether intentionally or unintentionally, Brian would never hurt their son. Protecting Noah came first, protecting Brian came second. But as Maggie closed her eyes to wait for sleep, she wondered, *Who's protecting me?*

18

Despite Brian's last call causing sleeplessness three nights in a row, Maggie woke on the day of the cocktail party oddly optimistic, rested and keen to attack her to-do list. With no more praying mantis nightmares, Maggie convinced herself Noah's puffing up around Fiona was nothing to worry about. Her son was not into pretentious princesses, thank goodness. With better things awaiting smart, funny, affable boys like Noah, Maggie wanted—no, she needed—her son to have the big, exciting life with colour and noise, and the freedom to make his own choices in his own time. Noah could marry at thirty and it would still be too soon for Maggie to let him go, even though a grandchild would be nice.

First things first!

To think Amber had been Noah's age when she'd fallen pregnant with Fiona; the boy responsible, probably not much older. *Who was he?* No one ever figured it out. The actual father might not have known because Jack Bailey had whisked Amber out of town. Maggie shuddered at Noah getting a girl pregnant before marriage, but knowing her son, he would be many years, several girlfriends and a million adventures away from the responsibilities of fatherhood.

Denying such thoughts entry to her mind already full to overflowing, Maggie attacked the laundry basket—similarly overflowing—plucking a top from the bottom of the pile and giving the indestructible chemise a shake. The flimsy, no-iron cheesecloth fabric had been *the* best op-shop find. Teaming the burnt-orange-coloured top with a pair of cut-off jeans that sat at her knees—as opposed to Fiona's that barely covered her backside—Maggie twisted her hair, securing the lot with the gift one of her regulars had handed her. Known by locals as Uncle Neville, he'd handpainted the palm-sized flap of bark with white, yellow and ochre dots to surround the central image of a black and white magpie. Securing the bark piece around her ponytail by threading a sanded twig through opposing holes, she paused to look out the window and to wonder about the weather.

For five days, climate change had remained the talk of the bar, prompting louder than normal conversations over whether it was La Niña, El Niño, climate change, or the 'same-old, same-old'. Maggie found the passionate debate amusing and a refreshing change from talk of sheep dip and stock prices. As she crossed the small courtyard separating the residence from the hotel, billowing storm clouds were teasing the town with a promise of reasonable rainfall. The same cloudiness built each afternoon, but the only thing to fall were a few extra swear words off the tongue of drought-weary locals.

This morning, Fiona and Noah were hard at work decorating the beer garden for tonight. Although a more accurate description might be Noah and his mate, Cory, were hard at work, while Fiona demonstrated her ability to issue orders. She'd done much the same during every committee meeting, much to Jennifer's chagrin. But, to the girl's credit, she'd kicked Noah into action. Maggie still struggled to get him to feed the dogs each night.

The outdoor beer garden venue was Plan A for the cocktail party. Should the heavens open, however, Plan B was the dining room, once Fiona's centenary retrospective was fully relocated to the school hall. News of the display's progress had circulated around town, calling the curious into the pub for a sneaky squiz at the collected paraphernalia. A few old-timers also dropped off memorabilia, including the old school bell —the heavy brass type with a wooden handle that only the prefects got to ring—as well as trophies and sports day pennants. Someone dropped off a set of the colourful, although faded, wooden Cuisenaire rods from maths class, while Frank Ryan contributed a milk crate crammed with old chalkboard dusters and a story about keeping every one the teachers threw at him for mucking up in class.

Around lunchtime, having eradicated at least ten Daddy Long-leg spiders from the cornices of every airing guest room, wiped a tonne of dust from each ceiling fan, and sprayed each window with spray-on silicone, Maggie took a break, hoping for a breeze on the veranda. She knew telling Ethne about her looming headache would result in an aromatic brew when only one cure existed; getting tonight's little shindig over and done and letting her anticipation over Saturday's reunion subside.

Perched on one of the old pews outside the main door to the bar, were a couple of regulars.

'G'day Uncle Nev! Barney!' Maggie said. 'The temp's not much better out here.' She plucked at the drawstring around the low-slung neckline of her cheesecloth top and blew a long stream of air down her cleavage.

Uncle Nev doffed his hat, while Barney nodded and said, 'Old Nev and me are chattin' about that display young Noah and his friend have started at the school. They're hittin' it off, too.' He winked.

'Terrific display, isn't it?' Maggie said, ignoring the gossip about her son.

Dropping by the school assembly hall yesterday for a look, a mix of pride and surprise had warmed her heart as she'd watched Fiona and Noah putting together the exhibit. When she'd sneaked in the side door, Noah had been adding computer-generated thought bubbles and embellishments to the display boards, to make a collection of old photos resemble a giant scrapbook.

❦

MAGGIE'S IMMEDIATE THOUGHT WAS HOW CLEVER NOAH WAS WITH HIS hands. She wanted to think he'd inherited her passion for visual arts, but music was his obsession and that came from Brian.

'Nice work, guys. What a great selection of—' Maggie almost gasped aloud as her eyes locked onto one photo, his image unmistakable. But how would Dan Ireland look today?

Would his scar be as obvious? Maybe facial hair covered the jagged line—a beard as brown and as unruly as his hair. The quiver in her sigh worried Maggie. If looking at a picture made her edgy, what sort of mess would she be if Dan showed up in person? *Damn Jennifer for not sharing the RSVP list.* Maggie's gaze moved to another photograph. Small and crinkled across the centre, one subject was definitely Dan. Behind the old school maintenance shed, sitting back to back like bookends on the grass, he and Amber posed for the camera, their bodies mirroring each other: legs bent at the knee, chins tilted skyward—crowns touching—and two perfect smoke-rings hovering in the air above their faces.

'Looks cosy!' Fiona said as she sidled up to Maggie. 'Found that picture in Cheryl's collection. Who's the hunk and what would the ladies at Mum's day spa say?'

Maggie refrained from telling the girl how Amber Bailey had taught the entire class to blow the perfect smoke ring. She was too concerned about the display and the number of photos featuring Amber with a different boy. More photos sat at the far end of the worktable and as Maggie perused the pile she noticed yellow Post-it Notes stuck to the back of each image, with names scribbled in pencil. Fiona's intentions were becoming clear. No one else had thought about a photo display because no one had an agenda like Fiona. What better way to dig around and identify your mother's many beaus—and possible birth fathers?

'Fiona, about these—'

'Spares,' she blurted, scooping the pictures into a yellow envelope.

Maggie had been about to probe a little deeper when the mobile phone in her pocket buzzed against her left buttock. She answered. Ethne was having a catering crisis trying to fit the delivery of frozen finger food into the one small box freezer. Fiona would have to wait.

❧

'YOU LOOK A MILLION MILES AWAY STANDING THERE, MAGGIE-GIRL,' Uncle Nev was saying.

'Hmm? Oh, yes, my break is over. Tonight's cocktail party won't run itself. See you fellas later.'

Maggie left the pair on the veranda to find Fiona in the beer garden where she was instructing Cory on how to blow up a balloon. Not far away, Noah was filling glass jars with layers of different-coloured sand and singing along to a song coming out of Fiona's fancy phone.

'Check out the candlestick holders, Mum.' Noah held aloft a single, white tapered candle before plunging the base into the jar. 'Fi calls it "The Sands of Time".'

'Does she?' Maggie raised an eyebrow at the three buckets on the floor. One held the deep orange-red sand found around Cedar Cutters Gorge. Another was a creamy yellow, probably from the sandy beach down by the swimming hole. While the third lot of sand, which Maggie thought looked like garden soil, was probably from nowhere terribly exotic at all. But candles, Maggie learned from Fiona, were crucial to any evening event, 'adding much-needed ambience to an ordinary beer garden'. What the event manager extraordinaire hadn't considered was the effect of hot daytime temperatures on long, tapered candles. If this heat got any worse, limp candles could be quite the conversation starter.

'Not so much air, Cory,' Fiona gushed, followed by a dramatic Scarlett O'Hara swipe of her sweaty brow. 'These conditions are impossible to work in. Please, can't we do something about the temperature?'

'No worries, Fi.' Noah fashioned a pretend telephone with his fingers and pressed it against his cheek. 'I'll call God and get the temp turned down 'cause our Fifi's feeling the heat.'

As Fiona poked out her tongue, and another balloon popped, she yelped and thumped Cory's arm, shouting, 'It's not rocket science, moron! Don't blow so hard.'

'Don't blow so hard,' the boys mimicked, both faces flushing red.

'Hey Cory, mate,' Noah called, 'leave the balloons and come help me with the amplifier sound check.'

Fiona had suggested Noah play guitar at tonight's function and Maggie was looking forward to showing off her talented son and greatest achievement.

'Forget it, cowboy,' Fiona said. 'Cory has the balloons to finish and I'm in charge.'

'Ah yes, but I have the power.' Noah twirled an electrical extension lead over his head, pretending to lasso Cory.

'And I'll be pulling your plug if you don't stop mucking around Noah —both of you. The clock is ticking.'

Maggie laughed inside. Despite a long list of negatives, Fiona was turning into a positive influence. Seeing Noah goof around, smiling rather than moping—maybe even showing off a little in front of a mate—left Maggie hopeful her son would forget about Sydney, at least until the end of school.

'I'll leave you to finish,' she told the trio. 'If you need me, I'll be in the kitchen giving Ethne vodka shots.'

The mobile phone Maggie had left on the main bar was ringing as she headed towards the kitchen. 'Hello? Maggie speaking.' The super-calm voice on the other end of the line flipped her stomach. 'I understand. Tell him I'll be there soon,' she said, almost running through the dining room, passed the kitchen where Ethne hummed, and towards the laundry outhouse. While petty matters set her father off, restoring order to his world was not difficult. On this occasion, a blue bathrobe—freshly washed and returned to its rightful place on the hook in his room—would do the trick. Unfortunately, the task would mean an unscheduled, ill-timed, two-and-a-bit-hour round trip by car for Maggie.

19

FIONA

'Just what I need,' Fiona said, accepting a tall lemonade and ice. 'I'm parched.'

'Parched?' Noah snorted. 'Geez, you can put it on, Miss Fancy Pants! Then again, I guess parched is more ladylike than freakin' thirsty.'

'Are you always so annoying?' she retorted. 'And thanks for reminding me—again—why I enjoy being an only child.'

'You do? Seriously?' Noah asked. 'I think it sucks. Having a sister— nah, make that a brother—would be cool.'

'I had brother,' Fiona muttered. 'Christopher. He didn't live a day. Afterwards, Mum lost the plot. She blamed herself. He was Phillip's, so that made him more special. Anyway ...' Fiona fixed the last knot in the last blue balloon and batted it into Noah's head. 'Your mum was okay about you playing tonight? I got the impression she wasn't keen at the start.'

'Nah, she likes it when I play,' Noah said. 'But she worries about music interfering with my schoolwork. Playing reminds her of Dad. When he wasn't much older than I am now he played at this very pub and wrote her love songs. Dad and I are alike.'

'Oh yeah? You can write me a love song?' Fiona asked.

'As if I'd want to!'

'Whatever!' she said, looking around the once tired-looking beer garden. 'It must be nice knowing you're like someone. I look like my

mother, but never saw Phillip's traits in me. Now I know why. Anyway...'
She brushed her hands together. 'We've got this place looking good, no
thanks to your mate.' She'd sent Corey packing earlier, unable to tolerate
any more exploding balloons. 'Speaking of looking good, Noah, is your
dad as cute as you?'

'Nick off!' Noah smacked Fiona's hand where it ruffled his hair. 'He's
all right, I guess. Haven't seen him in a while.' Noah shrugged. 'Mum
reckons I have the best bits of them both.'

'Lucky you!' Fiona said, twirling a loose ribbon of paper streamer that
hung over one shoulder where she sat. 'I don't know any bits about my
father: what he looks like, what he does, what he loves. I'm not sure he
even knows about me.' Fiona coughed to disguise the sob and blamed the
first thing that came to mind. 'Can it be any dustier or hotter out here?'
She gathered her hair, twisting and knotting it tight like she had the
balloons and felt instant relief as the air cooled the sweat on the back of
her neck. 'Tell me,' she said, slumping back against the chair, 'what *are*
the best bits of Noah? Tell me everything. Where's Noah from? What's he
doing? Where's he going?'

Noah stood, turned his chair, straddled it. He rested one arm on the
back and glugged the remaining lemonade, staring at Fiona from over the
rim. '*He* comes from about as far away as you can get from Potts Point—
not geographically, just every other way.'

'Potts Point is a long way from perfect,' Fiona said. 'Some of us just
know how to nip and tuck our ugly bits to hide our imperfections from the
neighbours. At least that's what I've discovered; a perk from having a
plastic surgeon in the family. Besides, my growing up wasn't as great as
you might think, Noah. Like I said, they sent me away to school. A kid at
home messed with Mum's social engagements.'

'Boarding school?' Noah queried.

'A *laaaaaadies*' college,' she said, striking a pose and poking out her
tongue.

Noah laughed. 'They teach you those classy acts at your fancy
school?'

'You'd be surprised what I learned at an all-girls school.' She winked.
'But that is all strictly on a need-to-know basis. The place wasn't all bad,
though. Better than being at home, not that I told Mum. Far more lucrative
to milk my misery act so's every time I did go home for the holidays they
showered me with apologies.'

'What do you mean by 'apologies'?'

'Presents 'n' stuff.' She thrust the gold locket under Noah's nose. 'I deserved this one, and more, for putting up with my parents' crap in my final year.'

'Oh yeah, sounds like a crap home life all right.'

She sighed. 'You have no idea, Noah.'

Their banter turned into a game. What was the most embarrassing thing your parents made you do? What was the worst bit of advice, the weirdest present? Fiona knew she'd win.

'As a kid they made me perform for their friends, like the lost freakin' Von Trapp kid.'

'My dad and I used to sing together,' Noah said, 'until people in the other flats complained, except the two guys downstairs. They were cool. On the weekends Dad and me would play somewhere like Centennial Park or the Domain, and Mum would pack sandwiches and bring them down. Dad liked it when people stopped to listen. Some threw coins on the blanket and my Mum …' Noah laughed, stood up and walked over to where his guitar rested against the small amplifier. 'Poor Mum would try handing the money back.'

'So, your parents met here, then moved to Sydney?'

'Dad was born in Wagga Wagga, but he and his dad toured country towns. They came here and played at this pub. One year he proposed to Mum, they married and moved to the city to crack the music business.'

'And did he? What's his name?'

'Brian Henkler,' Noah told her, 'but you won't know him. He's working behind the scenes on a big project.'

'Oh, yeah? What kind?'

'Sorry, Fi, the details are on a need-to-know basis.'

Noah's lips slipped into a supercilious smirk and Fiona barked a laugh so genuine she hardly recognised the sound. 'Do you like it here?'

'I wish I was back in Sydney,' he said, 'but Mum says no way while Pop is sick and until the pub's sold. Not seeing Dad sucks big time.'

'You at least have a father,' Fiona said, watching Noah adjust the tuners at the head of an instrument that had seen better days.

'It really sucks,' Noah said, 'them not telling you about Phillip. I'd be furious.'

'Yeah, well, come on. We still have to finish the photo display. So here's your hat, cowboy, let's hurry.'

Noah caught the hat she frisbee'd. 'You still planning on doing that thing?'

Fiona paused. 'What thing?'

'I heard you on the phone to your boyfriend. Something to do with the photo display. I don't want to be done for being an accomplice, or anything. I have to live in this place.'

'Well, I don't give a shit what anyone thinks of me, cowboy.'

'I think you do care.' Noah strummed a few chords. 'Your problem is you act tough when you're not.'

Fiona was not about to admit he was right. Yes, she cared. She cared that the man she'd loved and looked up to all her life was not her real father. She cared that her mother had lied about a grandmother—still kicking and living in a dusty country town. The best thing would have been never overhearing the argument between her mother and grandfather that day. Phillip would still be Fiona's father and she wouldn't have to torture herself about what was real, or trying to fit in when she couldn't possibly any more. That awful day had had one clear and comforting outcome. Amber had defended her daughter, which was not something Fiona remembered witnessing before. They were never that kind of mother and daughter.

The day her mother had walked out and returned to Calingarry Crossing, hadn't drawn a single tear from Fiona's eyes—not one anybody saw. Fiona had been crying all her life in such a way that nobody noticed the tears. A few months later, however, when Phillip brought Amber home, her mother was a changed person. She even tried being a better parent and Fiona's memory of Amber standing up for her during the argument would haunt her forever.

※

FIONA HAD LET HERSELF INTO HER PARENTS' APARTMENT AFTER A DAY shopping with Molly at Bondi. She was about to dump her bag and drop her keys in the Murano glass bowl on the entry table when she heard her mother's voice.

'No, you listen to me, Dad,' her mother was saying, 'Phillip and I have discussed Luke and we don't want you encouraging this relationship. He's not right for her.'

'Don't you think Fiona is old enough to make her own choices?' Jack said. 'He'll be good for her. I've been right before.'

'She's too young to be engaged, Dad, and Luke is too old and too ... Oh, I don't know. Pushy?'

The door was ajar enough for Fiona to catch glimpses of her grandfather prowling around the study with its wall of books, enormous L-shaped desk of smoked glass and chrome and with reading chairs that looked like red spaceships. The same predatory stare she'd seen him use on his staff was fixed on her mother, who stood with one hand on the edge of the desk. Fiona couldn't see Phillip.

'Pushy is not bad,' her grandfather said. 'The lad knows what he wants, and he's smart enough to know in which order: engagement, marriage, babies. Luke will settle my granddaughter. He's not spoilt. None of this growing up and getting everything. Like me, the lad's had to work hard. He has ambitions. I'm mentoring him myself.'

'And that's supposed to make us feel better?' her mother mumbled into the water glass.

'I'll pretend I didn't hear that, daughter dear. You weren't so against my guiding you in a certain direction once. Young Luke will keep Fiona in line, which she'll need, assuming she's her mother's daughter.'

'He's not *young* Luke. He's thirty, Dad. Don't you have a problem pushing your granddaughter onto someone almost ten years older?' Amber's expression and slight pause suggested she'd heard the irony in the question. There was twenty years between her and Phillip. 'And before you shoot me down, Dad, it's not only his age. Luke is very … intense.'

'You mean determined. Yes, you can bet he is. I even see a little of me in him.'

Phillip Blair moved into Fiona's frame and with a nod from his wife— almost an approval to speak—he wrapped an arm around Amber's shoulders in an obvious show of strength in unity.

'I'm agreeing with Amber, Jack,' Phillip announced. 'Fiona is—'

'—not your concern, Phillip. This matter is between me and my daughter. You don't get a say.'

'Dad, please.' Amber seemed to stiffen until Phillip's arm moved to her waist as if pinning his wife against him. 'Don't treat Phillip like he doesn't have a say. We both want Fiona to make her own choices, but she needs time to know herself first. I won't have you manipulate her life like you did mine. I am her mother and Phillip *is* her father.'

'Bullshit!' Jack spat.

The burst of profanity forced Fiona to draw breath and clasp a hand to her mouth, while Phillip calmly disarmed his wife of the water glass.

'Butt out, Dad,' Amber said. 'Fiona is *my* daughter, therefore *my* responsibility.'

Fiona frowned, confused. What was going on? The old Amber would never have stuck up for her. In the past, she would have caved, retreated to her room to pop a pill—or a cork—and wiped herself out. The new Amber, the one who'd had some great epiphany in Calingarry Crossing, was not taking any crap, despite an indomitable Jack Bailey rearing up like a snake about to strike.

'You expect me to butt out?' Jack hissed into his daughter's face. 'And just where do you think my butting out would've left you all those years ago? I'd hate to think.'

The room pulsed with angry, heaving breaths and unsaid words until Amber spoke. 'You love Fiona,' she told Jack, her voice soft, her words measured. 'We all do and we want what's best. Please, can we not dredge up the past, Dad? We're talking about Fiona's life—her future.'

'Yes,' he returned. 'Fiona's future is important. It's why I've invested so much—'

'Invested?' Phillip interjected. 'I've seen the way you play the market, Jack. One sign of things not going your way and you drop disappointing investments without regard. My daughter is not a commodity.'

Jack Bailey smashed a fist on the desk so hard the decorative vase wobbled and a pen spilled from its holder. 'Stop with the bullshit, Phillip. And Amber, don't you dare tell me what's important and what's not. You think you'd be better off today if I hadn't taken control, taken a risk, and made the hard decisions? What would life be like in Calingarry Crossing with you shacked up with whichever deadbeat fathered the kid?'

'Don't,' Amber growled. 'Phillip *is* Fiona's father.'

'We all know that's not the truth and why on earth you haven't told the girl by now—'

'When and what I tell my daughter is my business, Dad.'

'Now you're being ridiculous, Amber. You've no more been a decent mother to the girl than he's been her real father.'

With a hand still firmly covering her mouth, Fiona half-expected Phillip to punch her grandfather but, despite a body swollen with anger, the generous, gentle man Fiona had known all her life backed away.

Then, in a conciliatory voice Phillip said, 'Everyone take a deep breath and remember we're talking about what's best for Fiona. Amber and I are expressing our concerns, Jack. Luke seems to be moving quickly and we want her to make her own choices. You've made a career out of convincing others, but it's better to steer Fiona to set her own course.'

Her grandfather had numerous gestures and Fiona had learned them all over the years by observing him in action. This one—hand raised, palms thrust forwards, usually accompanied by a slight shrug—said, I don't agree, but I'll give in for now. Phillip Blair, perennial peacemaker, had successfully played up to his father-in-law's arrogance.

'I wonder, Phillip,' Jack said, 'if I might have a quick word with my daughter.'

Fearing she'd be caught snooping, Fiona was about to turn and run when Phillip exited the study via the deck, closing the glass sliders on the chilly south-easterly blowing in off Sydney Harbour.

'You have to agree, Amber,' Jack said, 'I knew what was best for you back then. I have a track record so I know what's best for Fiona, too. The girl's spoilt rotten but strong-willed. She'll need someone to support her financially and keep her in check. Someone she can support in return. That's what dutiful wives do.'

Amber groaned as if she'd heard the same lecture too many times. 'Seriously, Dad? What's that supposed to mean?'

'I mean dutiful wives do not run off after twenty years of marriage without explanation and leave their high-profile husband to lose face. I'm surprised Phillip stuck by you. The man has no balls, if you ask me.'

'Do not talk about Phillip that way,' she snapped. 'By all means criticise me. What's new? But Phillip has done nothing wrong.'

'Amber, my dear, what in God's name was so important that you had to go back to Calingarry Crossing? Was it a sudden attack of conscience? Did you go back and see *him*? Who was it anyway? Which lucky lad got to knock up my daughter? Will Travelli was always my bet.'

'Stop, Dad, I'll not let you do this.' Amber was doing her best to stay calm, yet looking strangely fragile, brittle almost, like kindling taunted by Jack Bailey's struck match.

'At least agree your father knew what you needed, Amber, and it was not some small-town boy in a dead-end corner of the country so you could turn into a pathetic drunk like your mother. I knew what you wanted from life and not even Will Travelli was good enough back then. You had to have it all and I don't recall any complaints when we came to Sydney and I got you this grand life.' Jack waved his hands around the room. 'You were as keen as I was to say goodbye to that town and everybody in it.'

'You've got a hide talking about running away and leaving people, Dad,' Amber retorted. 'What you did to Mum, all those things you said to make me think she didn't care and didn't want me was cruel. Then you stirred up the town about Will. It was wrong and unforgivable, Dad. I'm glad I got to go back and make things right with Will and Mum. My daughter need not live with regret like me. I'll protect her if it's the last thing I do.'

Fiona's grandfather laughed, but in a strange, nervy way, as if he was doubting himself. 'Come on, Amber, what are you dragging up all that business for? Your mother was never sober enough to know you were even there. You remember how she was.'

'And who bought the booze, Dad? Even when she told you "no more", you bought it and you put it where she'd be tempted. She was sad and lonely and bullied into being what you expected, and when she didn't meet your standards, you made her feel inferior and useless.'

Jack guffawed and spit sprayed out of his mouth. 'Is that what she told you? For God sake, Amber, your mother was irresponsible and careless and you'd be exactly the same if I hadn't married you off. Like mother, like bloody daughter, I say. Except history will not be repeating itself with *my* granddaughter. I will win, Amber. I always win.'

'Get out!' Her mother swung around to point at the hallway door. 'I don't want you anywhere near me or—' Amber's eyes widened. 'Fiona?' A lifeless, grey mask fell over Amber's face. 'Oh my God! Darling, I'm sorry, I ...'

They were her mother's last words before she clasped her head with both hands and folded to the floor.

෪

'YOU OKAY, FI?' NOAH WAS STARING, HIS FINGERS FROZEN ON THE GUITAR frets.

'Hmm? What? Oh, yeah, sure. Except this freakin' heat wave is making my eyes perspire.' With the heels of both hands, she blotted her cheeks before engaging fake Fiona again. She might not be Phillip's daughter, but she was as good at hiding her emotions as Phillip was at hiding his patients' flaws and scars. A nip here, a tuck there, and *voilà*! All the unpleasant stuff gone—from the surface, anyway. 'Let's tidy up, cowboy. I need a shower to wash off this dust.' She began collecting empty cellophane wrapping and snatching bits of broken balloon and streamers, cursing Cory in the process.

'Fi?' Noah said, unmoving. 'You said something before about not giving a shit.'

'Your point?' she asked, both hands planted impatiently on her hips.

115

'Well …' Noah strummed a chord. 'Like …' *Strum* '… I think …' *Strum* '… you're hoping the reunion will find your father.' *Strum, strum, strum.*

'Wanna know what I reckon, Noah?' She scrunched the garbage bag into a ball and launched it at his head. 'You should stop thinking and quit with the guitar and guesswork.'

'But I'm thinking it's pretty good guesswork,' Noah dared.

Fiona pondered the chips in her toenail polish while thinking about what to say. Finally, she looked up, her eyes narrowed. 'So, cowboy, tell me you wouldn't be just as curious to know who your actual father was if not the person you've known all your life.'

Noah shrugged. 'There's no way. We look too alike and Mum reckons I sound like him when I sing. But Fi, back to the reunion. Will you let me in on your plan? I gather you've got one. Or are you going to stalk every bloke ever pictured with your mother? Maybe you think some dude will arrive with a nametag that reads: "Fi's father".'

'Or maybe, smart-arse, I'll know straight away because we'll look alike.'

'I thought you said you look like your mother. You can't look like both of 'em.'

'I do look like Amber, except I have blue eyes. Mum's eyes weren't blue, which means his must be.'

'Gee, that should narrow down your search,' Noah quipped. 'Did you think to ask your gran when you were talking?'

Fiona shook her head. 'I tried. She gave me some photos, but from what my grandfather used to say, Cheryl had a fairly foggy view of the world back then. And by foggy I mean she was off her face heaps.'

If the old lady did know, she never told Fiona, redirecting her back to Phillip. But he didn't know Fiona was here looking for her biological father and she wouldn't want to hurt him. She loved Phillip. He'd been the one stable person in her life.

'You know the worst thing about all this, cowboy?' Fiona asked. 'I finally understand why I've struggled to fit in with Molly's crowd, and I told her. I had to tell Moll. Her and Luke are the only true things in my life. Molly's been my best friend since pre-school, and Luke looks out for me. He knows me better than I know myself. It was his idea to find my father.'

'So, you're doing this find-my-father thing for him or for you, Fi?'

Fiona contemplated the question, plonking back down in the chair.

What was she doing hanging around with Noah and letting the kid interrogate her motives and make her second-guess her choices? Then again, he was right about the reunion. What made Fiona think she could rock up to a stranger—a face from a photograph—and ask if he'd screwed around with her mother twenty-two years ago? Did she honestly want to know? And what would she do if she found the guy? Hug him? Probably not. Fiona Bailey-Blair didn't know how? Knowing what to say was equally challenging. Fiona was an expert at talking about herself, not so at ease with deep and meaningful conversations, although Noah seemed to be an exception. He listened and told her what he thought straight out. None of her Sydney friends would dare be so blunt, unless they wanted the cold shoulder. Kid cowboy had a maturity Fiona didn't see in the skateboarding, beach-loving seventeen-year-olds back in Bondi, and he was growing on her.

She leaned in and gave him a solid nudge with her shoulder. 'You're so pushy, Noah. Anyone told you that?'

'Are you going to answer my question or change the subject?' he countered. 'I recognise avoidance tactics, Fi. Mum's a good subject changer whenever I ask about Dad. So, which one is it?' He persisted. 'You doing this find-my-father thing for you or for this Luke guy?'

'I'm doing it because I want to know and because I'm angry about the lies. Satisfied?'

'Angry enough to want to hurt people who love you and maybe ruin the party your mum planned?'

'For a kid, you're pretty smart, Noah—and cute,' she added. 'How come some girl hasn't got her hooks into you?'

'My turn to change subjects and make you a deal,' Noah said with a grin. 'I'll help finish the photo display this afternoon if you forget about crashing the reunion. Mum's already about to blow a fuse.'

Fiona shrugged. 'Not sure I want to bother now.'

'T'riffic! We can do something together tomorrow night instead. We'll have the pub to ourselves and there's a jukebox with some real classics.'

'No karaoke machine?' Fiona asked. 'Molly bought one for a party and it was totally *brill*. Not so the singing. Poor Molly has everything *except* a voice.'

'And you?' Noah asked.

'Oh, I can sing. I love it.'

'Yeah, but do you mean like oops-I-can't-hold-a-note singing, or can you really sing? I've been working on a song.' He plucked at the guitar's strings. 'No lyrics yet, but ...'

'I'm great with lyrics,' Fiona announced.

'Then we'll collaborate—music and lyrics. Gotta be more fun than a room full of old farts. Whatdaya say?'

Again, Fiona hardly recognised her own laughter. 'I say, Hugh Grant and Drew Barrymore, eat your hearts out.'

20

MAGGIE

'My, my, aren't we in a mood,' Ethne said, finding Maggie on all fours and cursing over the contents of the commercial cutlery tray strewn across the kitchen floor.

'I'll have to put these through the damn dishwasher again.'

'Leave 'em to me.' Ethne righted the toppled cutlery basket.

'I could but you've got enough to worry about today, thanks to my inability to say "no, Fiona".'

'You mean tonight's little shindig?' Ethne trilled.

'I'm angry I let that girl and her snooty remarks get to me. "I totes understand if you don't think the pub's sophisticated enough, Maggie ..." *Argh!*' Maggie growled. 'You should've seen me puff up in that meeting. Anyone would think I single-handedly had to defend small pubs from snotty-nosed assumptions that country people aren't classy enough to do cocktail snacks. I'll give her bloody sophisticated,' Maggie grumbled as a handful of forks clanged onto the metal bench above her. 'I'll stick sophisticated right up her—'

'Awright, love, relax.' Ethne said, filling a teapot from the hot water urn. A calming brew was in the making.

'Best make mine a double.' In a little over six hours, Maggie's not-so-classy little pub would be on display to what felt like half the world. 'Dear God!' A violent churning in her stomach was making her want to vomit.

'It's only forty-four people for cocktails, love. Not worth getting your Cottontails in a tangle.'

'Four or forty-four is hardly the point, Ethne. Why did I agree to cocktails of all things? As if I don't have my hands full enough sprucing up eight claustrophobic little guestrooms. I've never had sixteen people staying.' She was back on all fours, her arm and fingers stretched to the max under the stove to retrieve a lone fork, only to find another chore: cleaning under kitchen appliances. Maggie crouched and stared at the floor drain, hoping it would suck her down along with the mismatched cutlery so she could disappear for the duration.

Dragging herself up, her body aching from doing four loads of linen and cleaning four rooms—four more to go—she looked at Ethne. 'We're a bloody country pub with dusty floors, wobbly bar stools and warped tables. Look at this.' Maggie plucked two random forks from the basket Ethne had loaded. She waved them about like a crazy person. 'We don't even have matching cutlery!'

'Steady on, love.' Ethne rescued the forks from Maggie's throttlehold. 'For a start, we won't be needing cutlery.' The woman spoke in the same soothing voice she used each time Maggie returned from seeing her dad in the home. 'It's finger food and serviettes, and we have plenty of both. The place never looked better. You've worked like a Trojan to keep the pub looking good.'

'I suppose,' Maggie grumbled.

The place scrubbed up okay, except for the previously unnoticed cracks and peeling paint that typically, like an infestation of pimples, had waited until the night of the party to make themselves obvious. Except under the stove, the hotel was the tidiest and the cleanest it had been in a long time. Maggie told herself as long as the forecasted storm held off, the night and the weekend would be a success. The beer garden looked festive draped in bunting and balloons, and Ethne was a dab hand at catering. She'd also rostered Noah to help in the kitchen between song sets, with any argument about a musician's hands needing protection from dishwater falling on Ethne's selectively deaf ears. As self-appointed maître d' for the evening, Fiona would be responsible for … Well, not much in Maggie's estimation: welcoming people as they arrived, checking them off the guest list, and pointing them towards the beer garden. Cory had offered to help as drinks waiter while Maggie worked the bar and filled orders for him to collect on trays. With an aversion to small talk with strangers, she was more than happy to have a legitimate excuse to avoid the social scene completely.

'Thanks for the brew, Ethne,' Maggie said.

'Not sure I've seen you so worked up, Maggie-girl. It's not the first time we've had a mob to feed. Unless ...' Ethne's eyes narrowed. 'Unless it's not about the forty-four people, but one person in particular.'

As Maggie sipped more tea, the rising steam from the mug heated her cheeks. 'I don't know what you're raving on about,' she said, her voice hitting an unusually high note at the end. 'Pass the cutlery basket.'

Ethne chuckled. 'That's what's making you all twitchy, eh?'

'I'm not twitchy.'

'Oh yes you are! What about? Better still, which one? Unrequited love? Dumped you for the cheerleader, did he? Hmm?'

'You have a vivid imagination, Ethne. I'm not at all worried about bumping into anyone tonight.'

Tomorrow night's school reunion was a different matter, Maggie reminded herself. Unlike Jennifer's school reunion RSVP list, which she treated like a yet-to-be-published Harry Potter Reunion novel, Maggie had studied tonight's guest list.

'Ethne, if I appear twitchy it's because I'm keen to impress and I feel awkward selling tickets, like asking people to pay for a party I'm holding.'

'No different to the dining room, and no one's twisting arms, love. A ten-buck ticket for food is neither here nor there to most folk. Think of the drinks they'll buy. Tonight's little shindig will be good for business.'

'We could do with that.' Maggie hid how tight finances were at the end of each month, but Ethne would know. Management of the pub had fallen on her for years.

'We've had check-ins already,' Ethne announced.

Maggie gulped the remaining hot toddy. Time to panic—again. 'But I have more rooms to prepare.'

'Two couples came up from Sydney and stayed in Saddleton last night. Drove in early this morning. You didn't see the cars out back? Not even a layer of Calingarry dust can make those babies look bad. Makes The Rev's old HQ stand out like a horny horse though. You got those brakes looked at like Barney said to do?'

'Not yet.' Maggie lowered her voice, hoping Ethne would follow suit. 'That's my point, though. These people aren't locals. They'll have expectations.'

'Love, if they're here from the city for the Centenary they must have a

connection and fond memories. Who's to say they won't look at you with
envy, wishing they ran a quaint pub in a country town.'

'Quaint?' Maggie's gaze swept the room, convinced the peeling paintwork and cracked cornices were getting worse by the minute. 'Then
maybe I'll hang a few For Sale signs. We might get lucky.'

'Awright, love. Whatever you want.' Ethne turned to the sink and
rinsed plates from breakfast, no evidence of her having shared Maggie's
amusement.

'Hey, I *was* joking.' All the times Maggie had moaned about the
useless broker, she'd never considered Ethne's feelings or her situation.
Twenty-odd years was a long time in any job, especially as she'd given
more to the place than an ordinary employee. Ethne had never complained
about the extra load as Joe deteriorated. She was family, even though
Maggie had left town before getting to know much about the wild-looking
backpacker who had kept to herself. But the pub was more than a job to
Ethne. This was home. She wouldn't want it sold. Brian did. Noah did.
And Maggie …? Well, that was a question for another time. First, she
needed to reassure Ethne. 'The sign idea is a *sign* I'm brain impaired at the
moment,' Maggie said. 'A potential buyer need only see the haggard-
looking publican and that'll be that. The grass always looks greener on the
other side of the fence.'

'Out here it usually is.' Ethne's tone remained as flat as her expression.
Even her painted on eyebrows had flat-lined. 'I know you've had it hard,
love: packing up your life, uprooting your son, taking on this pub… You
should feel proud of what you've accomplished, and be proud of your boy,
as well.'

'Thanks, I am proud, on both counts.' I'm also close to broke, Maggie
might've added.

Every week that passed, every month that her penny-pinching kept the
creditors at bay, made Maggie more determined to hang on, more determined to stay, and more torn when Noah begged to see his dad. So, if
Maggie was twitchy, as Ethne claimed, it was only that she had a full
house for the weekend, a cocktail party tonight, and it was likely, in the
middle of the mayhem, her father's blue bathrobe was bound to disappear
at the most inconvenient time.

❦

AS THE FIRST GUESTS TRICKLED INTO THE BEER GARDEN, NOTICEABLY impressed with the effort Noah and Fiona had put into decorating, Maggie let herself breathe. Sharing a good-luck glass of white wine with Ethne in the kitchen relaxed her a little more, but soon enough she'd be too busy behind the bar to worry.

People met, mingled and munched on Ethne's scrummy assortment of finger food, which amply satisfied the unexpected extras. Appearing unfazed, maître d' Fiona handled each additional guest with grace and humour while from behind the bar Maggie could only glimpse the revelry, the hugs, and the handshakes. She filled champagne glass after champagne glass with bubbly while feeling none of the effervescence herself. Instead, she wished Brian had acted on her invitation to come for the weekend. Maggie was recalling the conversation in which she'd suggested he and Noah could perform together when a sound carried in from the beer garden. Brian's very distinctive voice—an echo of John Williamson—was singing Maggie's favourite song.

'Brian?' Despite being mid way through pouring a beer, she darted out from behind the bar while stripping the elastic band from her hair and shaking it loose. At the door to the beer garden she stood on tiptoes to look over the crowd and there he was—Noah—propped on a bar stool and singing his father's number.

'Oh!' she whimpered as her heels crashed back to earth and disappointment turned bittersweet, her tears at odds with bursts of laughter and pride.

'Found you,' Ethne said, wrapping a comforting arm around Maggie's waist. 'You okay? Want Cory to cover the bar for a bit?'

'Thanks, but I'll be fine. I'm just so damn proud.' After a final sweep of the crowded beer garden, Maggie returned to the bar.

There would be no Brian tonight or, as she'd suspected, no Dan Ireland. Calingarry Crossing was the last place either of them wanted to revisit.

❦

MAGGIE RAISED THE COFFEE MUG IN A MOCK TOAST TO HERSELF AND muttered in the now darkened and deserted beer garden. 'One event down. One to go.'

Apart from her dash to the hospital earlier, all had gone to plan. Even Noah's 'Sands of Time' candles had stood the test of time, with many still burning, their light casting strange shadows along the tired weatherboard wall of the hotel. Cory, Ethne, Noah and Fiona were long gone, leaving Maggie alone to come down from the buzz of a successful event and enjoy some quiet time. Tomorrow would be hotel business as usual until, at 5 pm on the dot, she would lock the doors early for probably the first Saturday-night early close in the pub's history. From Sunday, however, Maggie's seven-day-a-week business would resume, which meant seeing little of the daytime fair and living vicariously off the people dropping in for a cold beer and to escape the heat. At least she hoped the day would bring heat rather than rain.

Missing the festivities didn't faze Maggie. The fair day was simply a giant church fete with craft stalls and games. Non-locals would no doubt enjoy the hay bale sculpting and tractor pull. Maggie was less sure about watching cows crap on numbered squares in Cow Pat Bingo. For locals, fetes days were about loading their utes with coolers chock-a-block with beverages and catching up for a chinwag with families from neighbouring stations. Most local businesses were closed on Sundays, but some had hired a stall—like Saddleton's Greener Pastures Realty who considered an influx of out-of-towners an ideal marketing opportunity. Again, the strate-gically placed For Sale poster idea niggled Maggie. Would it be so wrong? Selling meant money in the bank, and posters might generate enquiries. At this stage, even a tyre-kicker was better than no interest at all.

If only securing the pub's sale held a sense of relief for Maggie. It didn't. Her connection to the country had grown stronger than ever. She and Noah were a part of something special. They were a part of this town's past and its present. Why not the future? She told herself Noah needed to experience both country and city life so he'd be able to choose the life right for him. At the same time, she envied her son. He would have those choices ahead of him, whereas circumstances had dictated much of Maggie's decision-making over the years. While the downside to living in a small town was the curiosity factor and gossip mongering, the upside was some news items, including reality TV exposés, were of little interest —unless the show was *Farmer Wants a Wife*. Maggie hoped her husband's involvement in *iICON* stayed under the radar, but she couldn't think about Brian right now. Tomorrow—reunion day—would be an early start with a full house for breakfast. Weather permitting, they'd again set up in the beer garden, with the trestles only needing a wipe down in the morning and fresh paper tablecloth. After breakfast, Maggie would deliver the promised platters and back-up glassware to the school and do whatever else she could to make the reunion as successful as tonight.

Sipping her lukewarm coffee and feeling a smug satisfaction, Maggie recalled Ethne's face when Fiona had taken over dishwashing duties so Noah could return to the stage. Fiona's freckle-covered arms drowning in sudsy dishwater was the feel-good image Maggie would hang on to if she ever needed a laugh. Maybe it was the country air, but Calingarry Crossing, it seemed, was having a similar effect on Fiona as it had on Amber. The girl was more relaxed, more natural, softer and prettier—if that was possible.

Daunted by the prospect of people remembering a pretty young Maggie at tomorrow's reunion but seeing a tired local publican in her place, Maggie would make an effort with her outfit and her hair and hope her mascara hasn't dried up.

'Like the rest of you,' she muttered, flinging the coffee dregs into a nearby pot plant.

'Talking to yourself?' said a gentle female voice.

Startled straight, Maggie spun around and squinted into the darkness. 'Sara?'

'Sorry, I thought I could sneak into the beer garden and sneak out again. I didn't mean to scare you.'

'What are you doing back?' An hour ago, Maggie had watched her friend leading Will and two of the promised NRL stars from the pub. Brashnee and Gilbertson had arrived in town from Sydney and the drinking had begun early.

'Escaping, for one.' Sara groaned and flapped a hand. 'Will has been promising the boys an introduction to "Big Bertha" all night. He's now teaching them the finer art of espresso, although I'm fairly sure the boys weren't expecting Big Bertha to be a coffee machine.' The pair shared a giggle. 'Also,' Sara added, poking around several pot plants, 'somewhere in one of these pots is my husband's mobile phone. Ahh! Got it!' She wiped the device with the tail of her T-shirt. 'I swear, if it was possible to lose a wheelchair, he would. He's drunk enough.' Sara plonked on a chair. 'You happy talking to yourself, or do you want company for a bit?'

'Company would be good,' Maggie said. 'I'm too awake for bed, even though it will be a big couple of days.'

'Tell me about it.' Even in the dimness of candlelight, Maggie could see Sara's eye roll. 'Thank goodness the monster-in-law has the kids. My hands are full enough with Will planning on staying drunk all weekend.'

'You are the most understanding, patient and capable woman I know, Sara.'

'Huh, tell that to Will's mother. The woman questions every decision and has an opinion about everything, even the darn dress I'm wearing tomorrow night. But …' Sara's gaze dropped to her lap.

'But what?' Maggie asked, tentatively.

'I guess a grandmother questions a lot when there's a new bub on the way.'

Maggie jerked straight. 'You're pregnant?'

Sara nodded. 'Found out when I came back from Sydney.'

'Oh, Sara.' As the pair leaned into each other and hugged, Maggie felt happy tears welling. 'I'm thrilled for you both, really. How wonderful. I gather the doctor has assured you everything is good?'

'I'm fine,' she reassured. 'Will is fine—more than fine, obviously. Talk about against all odds.'

'Love prevails, eh?' Maggie offered, fishing out a tissue from her trouser pocket to wipe her nose and pat her cheeks.

'We're not telling anyone else yet, in case, but I know you can keep a secret, Maggie. Even in this town. Speaking of … Is your outfit for tomorrow night a secret?'

'Not at all,' Maggie said with a laugh.

'Oh,' Sara added. 'Let's not forget to get a planning committee photo of us in our finery. I changed my mind three times already. You?' Sara asked.

'Oh, an unexceptional wardrobe made the decision easy.' Maggie joked, but she looked forward to feeling feminine, appreciated, admired, and a part of something—none of which she'd felt in a long time. 'Getting out of the same old work gear will have a sense of Cinderella dressing for the ball, don't you think?' she asked.

'I've got the wicked mother-in-law.' Sara winked.

'Oh, well, in that case, should you come across a fairy godmother to turn a pumpkin into a carriage and a rat into a footman, send her my way. And I wouldn't say no to a prince sweeping me off my glass slippers.' Maggie instantly regretted the throwaway line.

From the day she'd arrived in Calingarry Crossing with Noah, Maggie had hidden behind a careful smile; one she could confidently and comfortably maintain for the brief time needed to settle her dad into the home and sell the pub. She would be gone before anyone in town got to know about her or her small, uneventful city life. As time went on, friendships formed and that careful smile hid more and more lies. To protect them and create a picture of happy domesticity, Maggie had built a pretend bubble around her and Noah. The trouble with a snow globe existence, however, was the tiniest shake could whip up a storm, and with Maggie's storm not looking like settling anytime soon, the lies couldn't stop—not even for Sara.

'Maggie?' Sara reached out a comforting hand. 'If you want or need an ear at any stage ...'

Maggie's return smile was restrained, while on the inside she longed to off-load on someone as understanding as Sara. The woman wasn't a gossip and she could put a positive spin on the worst news. She'd done so all her life, even giving breast cancer the credit for helping reunite her and Will. Maggie could tell Sara about her stagnant marriage, her guilt as she watched The Rev's deterioration, her lack of honesty with Noah about his father, and not wanting to sell the pub. But simply talking to a person about the weight of responsibility Maggie felt these days, even if that person was Sara, was not the same as having a partner to share the burden. Maggie missed that most of all. But these problems were hers to deal with, and she would—eventually. In the interim, she'd try some of Sara's positive thinking.

'I'm fine, Sara. You're probably best to check on those blokes and get a good night's sleep. You're carrying precious cargo.'

'True, but remember, the offer is always there.' She bent down and kissed Maggie on the cheek. 'Good job tonight. See you tomorrow, Cinderella.'

2 1

W ith no glass slippers magically materialising the next morning, Maggie shoved her not-so-delicate size nine feet into pink scuffs, threw on jeans and a shirt, and glanced out the window at the rolling grey storm clouds. She needed to deliver the glassware and catering equipment to the hall before the rain.

OUTSIDE THE SCHOOL BUILDINGS, PATHS WERE BEING SWEPT AND STUDENTS carried stacked chairs inside the assembly hall, lining the perimeter in a way that reminded Maggie of school dances and wallflowers. Teachers helped primary students adorn walls with a collage project depicting Centenary celebrations and what the occasion means to them. There will be proud parents here tonight, Maggie mused. Amber could be proud, too. Fiona's contribution had gone beyond the photo display. Her media release about the oldest ex-student, Charlotte Gilbertson, attending had resulted in last-minute enquiries and boosted the town's profile considerably. Other feedback, including promises to visit and support their old hometown later in the year, came via the Calingarry Crossing Facebook page she'd set up. While the additional numbers had sent those overseeing the catering into a flap about the lack of bowls, Maggie's offer to provide commercial-sized platters had gone some way to helping reduce the panic and palpitations.

'G'day, girlie,' Barnacle Bill called as Maggie slammed the portable cool room door closed. 'You got a cold one in there for three hard-workin' men?'

Maggie laughed, feeling sorry for Barney and his mates stooped over red-hot coals and lamb carcasses in this heat.

'I'll see what I can do later,' she yelled, taking in the brand-spanking-new awning over the quadrangle. Combined with a marquee, there was ample space and protection for the 200 ticketed attendees. Better than cramming everyone into the musty school hall—the home of uninspiring assemblies and cacophonous renditions of 'Advance Australia Fair' for twelve years of Maggie's life. 'Smelling good, fellas.'

Three whole lambs cooking on homemade drum spits took Maggie back to her mother's festive lunches. Christmas had been a busy time for the Lindeman family and the day usually a stinking hot one, but Mary would insist they all find time to sit and eat as a family, at least once. While The Rev carved the meat, and Mary metered out the vegies, Maggie would whip the pan juices into a thick, fatty gravy. First, a sprinkle of flour and hot water turned the meat dripping into an insipid goop, followed by a good serving of Vegemite to adjust both the colour and the taste. As wonderful as the meal had tasted with lashings of gravy, the memory was making Maggie queasy.

'Oi! Maggie!' Barney called as she started towards her car. 'While you're checking on those coldies, you might check your young visitor.'

Maggie winced. *What's Fiona done?*

'The girl was lookin' green around the gills when she bumped into the lamb carcasses coming off the trailer,' Barney added. 'Not a fan of meat, maybe?' All three men roared as Barney re-enacted Fiona's vegetarian frenzy.

Maggie bit back to urge to laugh. 'Very funny, boys. Now, how about one of you jokers give me a hand unloading the car and I'll see about rustling up those beers. Then I'm off to make myself look eighteen again. That could take a while.'

'Nah, you'll knock 'em dead just the way you are.'

'Ha!' Maggie hooted. 'You must be desperate for those beers, Barney.'

'WELL?' MAGGIE TWIRLED FOR HER AUDIENCE OF TWO. 'HOW DO I look?'

Noah had lifted his head from his guitar to watch. 'Like you're gunna chuck your guts up.'

'Really?' Maggie abandoned the sophisticated pose and slumped against the wall, both arms cradling her sucked-in stomach to quell the bilious sensation in her tummy. 'Maybe I am.'

'What have you got to feel sick about, love?' Ethne asked. 'Belle of the ball. Very classy.'

'I may have to stand all night,' she said while smoothing the little black dress that hadn't been off the hanger for a while. Five years was Maggie's best guess. 'Not too tight, bud?' she asked, turning again.

'Uh-oh!' Ethne said, arms flailing in a crazed robotic dance. 'Warning Will Robinson. Your mum's about to ask that question, and if you haven't learned already, Noah Henkler, there's no right answer when a woman asks, "Does my bum look big in this?"'

'Oh, ha-ha!' Maggie adjusted the shoestring straps for the umpteenth time and fiddled with the string of pearls sitting snug enough to accentuate every nervous gulp. 'What about the pearls? Too much?'

'Fine on someone your age,' Fiona said, joining Noah at the table and helping herself to the last piece of toast from his plate.

'Hey, get your own,' Noah grumbled, trying to snatch the triangle back, but the girl moved away too quickly and was now circling Maggie as she munched.

'Don't you want to wear makeup?' Fiona asked.

'I am,' Maggie replied without thinking.

'Err, no, Maggie, I don't think so.'

TEN MINUTES LATER, MAX FACTOR'S MAXIMISING SOMETHING-OR-OTHER had revitalised Maggie's caked-on mascara; fresh kohl eyeliner—drawn on and smudged off—defined her eyes; mineral powder—dusted on and brushed off—concealed her complexion flaws; and lip liner created a border for the glossy Siena Sunset.

'Ta-dum!' Fiona announced, stepping back to admire her work. 'Now you're ready. Perfect!'

Strangely, the girl's final tick of approval eased Maggie's anxiousness. Her tension further abated when Fiona announced she would not attend the reunion on behalf of Amber after all.

'I've got better things to do,' she said when Ethne asked her why not.

Maggie had wanted to ask what better things. She didn't. Fiona had either heeded the advice about not making a scene and upsetting Phillip, or the announcement was a ploy to put Maggie off the scent. Maggie opted to think positive thoughts about what was, ostensibly, positive news for the evening.

'Noah and I will be working together on a song,' Fiona said. 'I'm good with lyrics.'

Ethne muttered a blasphemous alternative to praising the Lord, smiled and announced she would be leaving for her own big night soon—her first Saturday night off in years. She offered to deliver Maggie to the school on her way, saving her a walk in the impressive but impractical high heels Fiona had insisted she wear, but Maggie declined, telling her, 'I need the practice.'

While the strappy shoes were not glass slippers, her feet felt special, her ankles slim. That had to be worth some foot pain. It was only one night—and an early one. Maggie would make an appearance, make sure everything was going to plan, and make an exit. First, she had to make her entrance.

§&

HAVING DECLINED ETHNE'S OFFER, MAGGIE WALKED THE SAME PATH SHE'D taken as a schoolgirl, pausing several times to adjust the sandal's straps and look beyond the pitched marquee roof at the blackening western sky bleeding layers of orange and crimson. To the left, columns of sunlight ascended fan-like from a gap in the clouds, while to the right of the school grounds, one giant and ominous cloud hovered overhead. The walk home later could be a wet one. Maybe she should've driven herself. The dirt paddock next to the school amply accommodated the overflow from an already packed bitumen area out front.

A steady but straggling line of partygoers tiptoed across the dirt like an unwavering line of ants keen to find shelter from an impending storm. Most were couples, chatting and laughing, with only the odd single person. Maggie fidgeted in the dress that was tightening by the second and imagined the string of pearls around her neck rising and falling with each anxious swallow. The single strand, with matching Mikimoto pendant earrings her mother had worn on her wedding day, added a touch of sophistication to the dress with its simple sweetheart neckline. Fiona the Fashionista had confirmed as much as she'd swept Maggie's hair into a proper French twist and secured it in place with her favourite turquoise clip, plus a million bobby pins that would take four hours to find. But that was a problem for later.

'First things first, Maggie,' she muttered.

The old school looked fabulously festive, and the cooler, overcast conditions perfect for showing off the flickering fairy lights festooning veranda railings. Coloured strands of bunting, that tomorrow would line the street parade, laced the pathway to the assembly hall where handsome couples were herded in front of a banner displaying the school emblem and the words '100 Years'. Why hadn't Maggie thought to volunteer for the photography job? Hiding behind a camera lens would've been the ideal school reunion survival tactic. Rather than taking photos, however, Maggie was taking a deep breath, sucking in her stomach and striding towards the entrance—all smiles.

'My, my, if it isn't the publican's daughter,' a voice shrieked. 'Maggie Lindeman. *Fab-u-lous*, darling. How are you?'

Maggie flashed her best Colgate grin, stopping long enough to offer her cheek for the first inescapable air kiss of the evening. 'Genevieve Genford? You don't look any different.'

She took in the familiar jet-black hair, pasty complexion and predictably plain long-sleeved black jumper. While these days Gothic was considered fashion, at school the girl's unexplained predilection for long sleeves had resulted in the nickname: Genevieve Jumper. Maybe, after a few wines, Maggie could cleverly work the jumper into a conversation. What good were reunions if they didn't satisfy all those childhood curiosities?

'Are you here alone, Maggie?' Genevieve was asking.

'Ah, yes, I am—*tonight*,' she said, hoping to sound like travelling solo was a once-off. 'Hard enough getting myself organised,' she quipped, deciding indifference and humour were her best defence for the more awkward questions. 'By the way, Gen, it's no longer the publican's *daughter*. Just publican. I've been running the place since Dad moved into the home in Saddleton.'

'I heard,' a voice behind cut in. 'Imagine you running the pub, Maggie, darling.' Kimberly Freehill's effusive hug was such there was almost a popping sound when Maggie pulled out of the embrace. 'I'm afraid the pub will always be The Rev's to me,' said Kimberly. 'Say hello from me when you see him next.'

'Will do,' Maggie said, genuinely pleased with the comment. 'We'll chat later, Kimberley.'

After passing her just-in-case brolly to the spotty-faced boy Jennifer had roped in to man the makeshift cloakroom, Maggie slipped in behind two couples to follow them through the assembly hall, past the bejewelled DJ happily partying all by himself, and into the food marquee. A table of welcome drinks sat inside the tent and, with Houdini-like stealth, Maggie snaffled a glass of champagne before joining other guests sniggering at Fiona's Memory Wall. Even Maggie smiled at her old class photograph. Bumbling boys with big ears and graceless girls with centre parts and pigtails smiled back. How innocent and unaware they were.

But catching Maggie's eye was a much smaller collection of pictures and memorabilia beside the main display. *So, this was what had occupied Noah and Fiona today!* The bleak high school obituary, a tribute to those with lives cut short, seemed an incongruous addition to a night of celebration. Framed photos, yellowing newspaper clippings, emails and handwritten notes from relatives also adorned part of the display. Below them was a printed sign: *We Miss Them*. While respectfully done, the morbidness was shocking, especially the photo of a stunning sixteen-year-old Amber Bailey at the centre. Perhaps Maggie had read Fiona wrong, and the girl deserved more credit and less flack. She was clearly hurting more than she let on. But Fiona was her mother's daughter; Amber had also hidden so much sadness.

Among the array of photos, Maggie spotted another student from her year, remembering the short boy with a pudgy face, dimples in both cheeks, and his hair shaved with military precision to avoid lice. Stephen Lowry had been funny and smart—much smarter than the kids who'd teased him over the plastic aeroplane he'd kept in his school bag. On tonight's display, pinned next to the picture of a proud man in uniform—and with dimples, the same crew cut, and wings on his breast pocket—was a fresh-faced young Stephen Lowry. The handwritten card from his mother squeezed tears into Maggie's eyes. No explanation for how he'd died, just 'suddenly'. Someone else snatched away too soon.

While the display's concept was commendable, and the finished product impressive, Maggie needed to walk away, get another drink, and start having fun. But she didn't do any of those things. She couldn't. Her feet were heavy, her heart too as she breathed her brother's name. 'Michael.'

Maggie's next breath in was a sob and, despite her efforts to hold it inside, she couldn't. So she exhaled and plucked a tissue from down her cleavage. Just as she was wondering what Max Factor's Maximising something-or-other would do with an onset of tears, two hands wrapped around her eyes from behind and the urge to cry was siphoned away.

'Guess who?'

Too easy, Maggie thought, hearing the very distinctive laugh that followed. 'Elizabeth Taylor, if you don't let me go I'll be forced to tell that big secret about you and Derek Hurley.'

'You remember *that*?' When the woman giggled and snatched her hands away, Maggie breathed deep, forced a smile and turned to see Elizabeth and …

'Derek? Wow! What a … surprise.' Had her tears spilled over moments ago, the heat now prickling her cheeks would surely have dried them.

'Nice to see you again, too, Maggie. You're looking good. A little surprised right now, but good.' Derek's laugh was almost as memorable as Lizzie's—Woody Woodpecker meets Porky Pig. 'I'll leave you and my lovely wife to catch up while I suss out the bar.' He winked, then kissed Lizzie and disappeared.

'Grab me one, too, hon, and I'll find you.'

'You married Derek?' Maggie asked. 'Weren't you going to run away to Hollywood and be a movie star?'

'Hey, I went from little Liz Taylor to Elizabeth Hurley—and got a gorgeous and faithful husband in the process. Speaking of gorgeous, I wonder if Tracy'll be here?'

Maggie's stomach hitched at the thought. 'When did you arrive, Lizzie?'

'This morning,' she replied. 'Tried for a room at the pub.'

Maggie grimaced. 'Sorry, we booked out quickly.'

'We?' Lizzie's eyes bugged. 'You're back living here?'

'Yes, Dad went into care a couple of years ago. The place has been on the market ever since. People want the dream, but all the regulations make a pub hard work.' Maggie stopped short of admitting aloud how much she loved it.

'Someone will fall in love with the old place and take it off your hands,' Lizzie said, her eyes busy scanning the room for familiar faces. 'Derek and I ended up in *Bris-vegas*. We have a business. We design portable homes. We love it and we can run everything from home, which means lots of time with the kids. We have four.'

Maggie tuned out momentarily, trying to recall when she'd used the word 'we' so many times while describing her life.

'Since the January floods, Derek's been flat out,' Lizzie continued until a commotion on the other side of the hall drew her attention. 'Oh! My! God!' She yelped. 'Anne Wallace and … Good heavens, is that …? Oh-Em-Gee, it's Will Travelli. Bloody hell, would you look at the guy! But who's he with? That's not …? It is!' Lizzie stood on her toes, craning her neck, desperate to confirm the sighting. 'Guess I'll know where to find my husband all night.' She chuckled. 'Ask Derek who his football god is and he'll tell you Paul Brashnee. I'd better get over there before he makes a scene. Plus, I need a drink. Catch you later, Maggie. Derek! Honey! Hold on.'

At school they'd called her Dizzy Lizzie; Maggie remembered why as she watched her cross the empty dancefloor. On the far side of the hall, standing back from the scrum, Sara was waving at Maggie—make that beaming. A proud, adoring wife basking in the glow of her husband: sporting legend and all-round good guy of football. Their story was all heartache and hope. People loved those stories.

Every attendee tonight would have his or her story to tell, with many summing up their achievements in a synopsis and spruiking it like Lizzie had. Although curious about the lives of those same bumbling, beaming children from the early school photographs, Maggie had no desire to compete. Having made an appearance, and with little to shout about, she began planning her exit.

2 2

FIONA

'This is absolute magic!' Fiona sung out as she pumped the Pianola's pedals, which turned the paper music roll and drove the keyboard to play its own tune. 'Look, no hands!' She laughed. 'I can play music *and* do a thigh workout all in one.'

Grabbing both knees, she urged her aching thighs to peddle faster until Noah slipped alongside her on the piano seat and she slowed.

'Cool, eh?' Noah said as the melody slowly died.

'Not as cool as you and me making sweet music together.' She flicked a forefinger at the lump of gelled fringe hanging over his eyes. She was excited to have a pub all to themselves. Why didn't Luke do fun, romantic stuff, like when Patrick Dempsey takes Reese Witherspoon to a closed Tiffany's store in *Sweet Home Alabama*? Fiona loved that movie.

Feeling weirdly content about dropping the search for her father, she gave Noah a shoulder nudge and said, 'You wanna know something?' Then she stood, walked behind him and tickled the back of his neck. 'I'd go for you—if you weren't gay.' She waited for a reaction, but when Noah kept fingering the strings she knew. 'I'm guessing no one knows?'

Plonking herself next to him again, facing away from the piano, she leaned back to rest her elbows on the keyboard, crossed her legs and let one foot kick the air. 'Hey, cowboy, if you don't want people asking then ditch the T-shirt. Team Edward? Really? I would have picked you for a Jacob guy.' Fiona drove her fist into his shoulder, but he brushed her hand away. 'Come on, cowboy. Talk to me. I understand. I have lots of gay friends.'

Noah turned sideways to straddle the piano stool, putting his back to her. 'Don't call me cowboy.'

A few more awkward moments ticked by before Fiona nudged him. 'What's it like? Being gay, I mean.'

Noah swung back around to face her, a smile creeping into his expression. 'Quit the dumb-arse questions, Fi. How would you feel if I asked you "what's it like being blonde"? Oh wait,' Noah grinned. 'You probably fake that.'

'Yeah, like you pretend to be funny.' She smacked his hand from the guitar's strings, clasping his wrist. She liked a person's full attention when she talked. 'Does anyone know?'

'What do you reckon?' With his hand trapped, Noah fidgeted, his legs doing a nervous jig.

'And you're not faking it?'

Noah reefed his hand from hers, drew back and pulled a face like she was crazy. 'Why the hell would I?'

'Hey, don't go all weird on me, Noah. I know people who swing both ways because they can. They're not gay—not all the time. They're having fun, experimenting, considering their options. Lots of people do it, or they think about trying it. Not me, though. What?' she asked, bemused by Noah's expression.

'Discovering you're gay isn't all fun and games, Fiona. Being out in a small town is—'

'Wait! You mean, you're not out? Not even to your mum? That's a hell of a thing to keep to yourself,' Fiona said. 'How have you managed?'

'Ah, it's called keeping a secret,' Noah replied. 'Besides, lies are easier than the truth.'

Fiona wanted to disagree. Thanks to everyone around her sharing that opinion, her life is turning out to be one huge lie.

'You got a boyfriend?' she pushed. 'Cory, maybe? He's cute enough, in a pain-in-the-arse kind of way.' The tinge of red creeping up Noah's throat suggested she wasn't far off the mark. 'Please tell me he knows at least.'

'Quit it,' Noah snapped. 'He's not, so just shut up, okay?'

'Relax, cowboy, I'll keep your secret,' she cooed, letting Noah begin his strumming again. 'Did you have a boyfriend in Sydney?' she ventured.

'Not really.'

'Not really as in never?' Fiona queried. Noah didn't respond. 'What makes you think you're gay then?'

The redness in Noah's throat spread until both cheeks were beacons. 'Are you always such a nosey pain in the arse, Fiona?'

'No need to be rude. If you'd rather not talk about it …' She shrugged. 'You look like you could do with a drink.'

'I'll get us a Coke.' Noah said on his way to the fridge behind the bar.

'If that's as good as it gets.' Fiona closed the Pianola lid and walked to the bar, eyeing the Vodka Cruisers from where she perched her butt on a stool.

'Don't even think about it,' Noah said, handing her the can of soft drink. 'Mum would kill me.'

'Maybe she'd never notice, like she hasn't noticed her son's gay.' She guzzled the fizzy liquid and imagined the taste of Bundy. 'When did *you* know you were gay?'

Noah set the servery counter in place, took up his guitar, and sat on a stool adjacent Fiona. Resting the cutaway section of the instrument on his thigh, he strummed a few chords. 'The kids at school in Sydney knew before I did,' he said. 'One guy let me know by beating the crap out of me.'

'Why?' Fiona asked.

'I guess because he could and because that's what some kids do.'

'What did you tell Maggie?'

'Scrum collapse. I thought coming here, to a new school, might be different.'

'Is it?'

Noah sighed. 'Not as intense and people seem friendlier, especially the older kids. Owning a pub makes me popular with them. But I miss my dad and his cool muso friends. And I miss the two gay guys in the downstairs apartment. I sorta talked to them once.'

'Why not come back to Sydney for a few days to see your dad? I'll take you clubbing, introduce you around. And don't worry about my friends not liking you. In my circle, gay is the new gorgeous.' Noah did a thing with his eyes while looking at Fiona over the rim of the Coke can. 'There's a great wine bar in Cremorne with an amazing piano player and an open mic night. We can perform our song. We'll be fabulous together.'

'Who's being fabulous with my girl?'

Both Fiona and Noah jumped at the voice coming through a partially open window.

'Luke!' Fiona recognised the nose and lips pressed comically against the pane of glass.

'You want to open a door and let me in?' he asked, rapping his knuckles in a playful rat-a-tat-tat. 'Or do I climb in here?'

'Go 'round to the beer garden.' Fiona waved him in the right direction and ran over to unlock the screen door, launching herself at him so hard she almost knocked him off his feet. 'What are you doing here?' she squealed as Luke's hands cupped her buttocks and he spun her around.

'Can't a guy miss his girl?' he asked, staring across the room at Noah while Fiona's feet found the floor again. 'I didn't think I'd have to travel to the middle of nowhere to find her, and I didn't think she'd be getting all cosy with some bloke. You going to introduce us, Fifi?' He made his way across the empty lounge area towards the bar.

'This is just Noah. His mum owns the pub. Noah, this is Luke.'

'Her fiancé,' Luke added smugly, overzealous handshake in progress. 'What's going on, Fifi? The place is deserted.'

'Everyone's at the reunion.'

'Oh yeah?' Luke stalked the bar area like a lion at feeding time. Then, as he stopped to eye Noah from head to toe, Fiona covered her smirk with her fingers on her free hand. The other hand Luke held tight. With her fiancé acting like a wary dog, she half expected him to lift a leg and mark his territory.

Dragging a chair out from a table, she patted the seat and said smugly, 'Come, Luke. Sit! Perfect timing.'

'For what, my little Fifi?'

Ordinarily Fiona liked the way Luke pinched her chin and called her Fifi, but his voice held a strange sarcasm.

'We're writing a song together. Want to hear it?'

Noah shot her a panicked look and shook his head. 'We're not ready for an audience.'

'Sure you are,' Luke said. 'I'd love to hear your little ditty. But, um, one question, babe. Shouldn't you be at the reunion with everyone else, like we talked about? All your text messages had me thinking you needed my support. So here I am—and here you are in an empty pub. The reunion you've been banging on about is tonight, right? There's not another reunion, is there?'

'You're the one who's been banging on ad nauseum, Luke. Of course there's only one reunion. That's why the pub's closed. Everyone is there.'

Fiona glared, expecting him to recognise her growing irritation. Rather than back off, he seemed intent on being a jerk.

Luke draped a possessive arm over Fiona's shoulder and plucked the elastic strap on her tank top so it pinged back. 'Let me get this straight.' He played with the strap again, letting it slide down her arm before repositioning it on her shoulder. He repeated the ping several times. Then he tugged her body a little too roughly, his fingers digging into her waist. 'Everyone is there except you two. *Every*-one ...' he stressed in a hushed voice, '... maybe even the father you've travelled several hundred kilometres to find.'

Fiona squirmed out of his grip, needing to distance herself before explaining. 'About that find-my-father thing, Luke.' Swiping the back of a hand across her mouth and transferring the beads of perspiration and face powder to the back of her shorts, Fiona was suddenly conscious of her state of dress. Had she known Luke was coming she would have showered and slipped into something more than shorts and a singlet. She would have done her hair and smell of Dior right now, not dust. She glanced towards Noah to see his head lowered, his eyes focused on the strings of his guitar. 'Luke, I've been talking to Noah, and we agreed the reunion wasn't the best approach.'

'I see,' he replied. 'So while I've been dodging your grandfather's inquisition, you've been playing music with Noah? Cute!' He was circling the room again, reminding Fiona of her grandfather's overbearing behaviour in the study on the day her mother had died. 'And you decided on a little pub party for two. Guess that makes me the gate crasher. Stupid Luke! The third bloody wheel. How about that?'

Anger drove the temperature in Fiona's cheeks up again. The evening was no longer fun, and she was wishing Luke had never arrived. 'What the hell's wrong with you?' she demanded. 'Why are you acting all weird?'

'Am I, Fifi? Must be I'm tired after driving all day so I could support my fiancée at this very emotional and traumatic time, only to discover I'm redundant.'

'Listen, mate, you've got it wrong,' Noah piped up. 'Fi and I are hanging out while the oldies are at the reunion.'

'He's right.' Fiona squared her body to Luke's and slapped defiant arms across her chest. 'Quit being a jerk.'

'You're right,' Luke said, his easy submission throwing Fiona. 'And I'll apologise. Sorry, mate,' he added. 'Now Fifi, can we speak in private?'

She matched his stride, stopping at the pool table in the adjacent room where he grabbed her waist, lifting her onto the wooden surround.

'What's got into you, Luke?' she said with her punch to his shoulder barely registering.

'Hey, stop with the cross act, Fifi.'

'I'm not acting, Luke, I'm seriously angry.'

Luke said nothing, tangling his fingers deep into the mass of curls before gripping the back of her neck with force. The hold didn't frighten her. Luke was playing, wanting her to give in and make up but, as always, she resisted the pressure to kiss him. Luke's behaviour had displeased her, and she'd let him know just before his lips met hers.

Jerking her face to one side, she whispered her warning in his ear as he nuzzled her neck. 'Don't push me, Luke, or else.'

He pulled back. 'You can't blame me for being disappointed. I thought finding your father was important.'

'It is and I've asked around a bit, but the town will clam up if I gate crash the reunion. It's how they are out here. Besides, there's no urgency, and it is my decision.' With both hands flat on his chest, Fiona deflected another kiss and shoved him off her. 'Now stop treating me like a naughty little girl.'

'But you are. It's what I love about you, Fifi.' He tried to move in, to kiss her again, but Fiona slipped under his arm and off the pool table.

'Well, I don't appreciate you barging in here and speaking to me like that in front of my friend. And don't call me Fifi,' she added haughtily. 'I sound like a poodle.'

'I thought you wanted people to call you Fifi.'

'Stop telling me what I want. Quit it, Luke! I've had enough of guys telling me what to think and do.' The resentment Fiona didn't realise had been simmering inside her boiled over. 'Granddad might think I need someone to keep me in line, but I assure you I do not.'

'Hey, babe, shhh!' Luke dragged her into his body, his hug pinning her, his lips pressing against her ear. 'I've embarrassed you and hurt your friend's feelings,' he whispered. 'I'm an insensitive jerk. But I've missed you.' He kissed his way to her mouth and Fiona felt herself giving in to him until she glanced over Luke's shoulder and saw Noah in the main bar lost in his music.

'Let me go, Luke.'

'After I remind myself what I've been missing.' He purred the words into her neck. 'I'm so in love with you, Fi. What's a guy to do when he walks in and sees his girl with another guy?'

Fiona wiggled out of his grasp and straightened her top. 'You can't be jealous of Noah.'

'Why not?'

Through a hush finger at her lips she whispered, 'Because he's gay, silly. But don't tell him I said so. It's a secret.'

Luke did a thing with his face; the same curious squint and knitted eyebrows she'd seen in her grandfather.

'Seal my lips with a kiss,' he said, 'and we'll get the party started. Your friend is over there on his own. Come on.' Luke led her back to Noah in the main bar. 'Sorry to be rude, mate, put it here.' The pair shook hands again, and Luke slapped Noah on the back. 'You understand that Fifi—I mean Fiona—is my special girl, right? But to show there are no hard feelings, it's my shout. I need to loosen me up after that drive. Then I'll hear this song of yours.' Luke flashed the contents of the leather billfold Fiona had given him last Christmas and walked over to the bar. 'Line 'em up,' he ordered, whacking a fifty on the counter.

'Sorry, Luke,' Noah said. 'The pub's closed and I'm not eighteen 'til—'

'Don't sweat it. I'm legal. I'm also experienced on both sides of a bar. What'll it be?' He leapt over the counter and landed on the other side like an action figure coming to the rescue. 'Shall I whip up a Screaming Orgasm for you, babe, or save that treat for later?'

Fiona giggled and frisbee'd a drink coaster at Luke from where she stood with a nervous Noah. She would have hit the target too had he not ducked his head below the bar.

'Don't be a wus. One drink won't hurt, Noah,' she said. 'You can bet the entire town is part way to pissed already. Please, please,' she cooed as Noah continually shook his head. 'One Vodka Cruiser. Just one.'

'Too easy.' Luke moved to the fridge, opened the door and handed Fiona a bottle. Then he grabbed two cans. 'I can be a can man.' He snapped the ring-pulls on two Bundy and Cokes, releasing a fine spray of fizz as he walked towards Noah. 'Get this into you, mate. To new friends!'

Fiona first clinked drinks with Noah, then tugged on his shirt to make him sit. In contrast to Noah's sullenness, a hyped-up Luke paced to room, pausing to examine the black and white retrospective of Calingarry Crossing set in picture frames and hanging on one wall. Fiona recalled looking at a photo from 1959 and thinking not much had changed.

'Relax, it's called having fun, cowboy,' she whispered through a giggle. 'Or has living out here made you forget what fun is?'

'Wouldn't mind some food,' Luke said, having already finished his Bundy and Coke. 'Long time since breakfast. Can we order in pizza?'

Fiona choked on her drink, and Noah snorted Coke from his nose.

'We can try ordering in from Saddleton,' Noah said, wiping his shirt-sleeve across his face, 'if you don't mind cold pizza.'

'You're kidding me!' Luke fell onto a chair and kicked another closer to elevate his feet. 'So that *was* the black stump I saw on the way here.'

Fiona moved to Luke's lap, sitting sideways and draping one arm around his neck. 'There's a vending machine. I could get us some chips.'

'Sure, why not? Best not to drink on an empty stomach. I'll shout us another one,' Luke said, attempting to tip Fiona from his lap. 'Then I want to hear your song.'

'We can't,' Noah said soberly. 'Mum will know they're missing.'

'Don't worry about upsetting *Mummy*, mate. Old Lukey, here, knows how to shuffle a self. She'll never notice, but one more might put hair on that chest of yours.'

'Quit it, Luke.' Fiona's warning was double-edged. 'No means no, which is exactly what I'll be saying to you tonight if you make me mad. Let's go for a drive instead.'

'In bloody big bird?' Luke scoffed. He joked often about her yellow Saab. 'I bet she flies along these country roads. You had a drive of the her yet, mate?'

Noah shook his head. 'No licence.'

'Bad luck about that, but she's still worth a gander under the bonnet. It's always good to know what makes 'em purr. But only if you're into that kind of thing,' Luke added, slyly. 'Personally, I prefer the roar of a hot and throbbing Harley between my legs as I lean back and enjoy the smooth ride.' Several thrusts of his hips sent Fiona flying off his lap and feigning disgust.

'You're filthy, Luke.' She said, putting extra sway in her hips as she walked away. 'I'm off to the loo while you, mister, quit with the smutty talk.'

'Take your time, gorgeous. Me and Noah have a little bonding to do,' Luke called out. 'And I've got just the thing, mate.'

23

MAGGIE

One hour into the reunion and Maggie had one regret. She wished she'd pushed Jennifer harder for the RSVP list. To know for certain Dan Ireland was not coming was better than wondering if he was here somewhere, or if he'd planned to come but changed his mind. He could simply be running late, held up in highway traffic and about to walk through the door.

Argh! She swallowed another mouthful of champagne and frustration. Had Maggie thought to scan the table of nametags as she'd collected her own, she might have already processed her disappointment and made an excuse to leave early, like an urgent call from Saddleton Nursing Home; another missing-clothes catastrophe. She would say her goodbyes and leave the function, but having learned several things: her sixth-grade teacher was now shorter than she was and nowhere near as frightening; the boy with the glasses and big ears they'd nicknamed Wingnut had made a fortune in real estate and, in the looks department, would give Hugh Jackman a run for his money; and Mitch Matheson, whose mother had described her twelve-year-old son as having 'a good face for radio', was in fact the high-rating Mitch Matheson from 2SC drive-time radio.

Sara sidled up to Maggie. 'What's your excuse for not drinking?' she asked, nodding at the empty champagne glass. 'I've never been so annoyed that I can't have a drink. Then again, never so happy.'

'I'd say Will's drinking your share tonight,' Maggie said.

'Not sharing our news is taking all his strength, but I've warned him. I'll pull Big Bertha's plug if he breaks the news to anyone.'

Maggie loved how the pair made her laugh. 'If running a pub has taught me anything, Sara, it is how alcohol loosens lips, and loose lips—'

'Sink ships. I know. I know.' Sara smiled. 'But I want him to relax and enjoy the night. You should too, Maggie. I saw you checking your watch. Are you worrying about Noah?'

'He's hassling me about going back to Sydney.'

'Oh, don't tell me,' Sara said. 'Cyclone Fiona influencing him?'

'I wish I could blame her. But he's been moody for a while—one of the fifty phases a teenager goes through. You'll understand one day.'

Sara beamed, about to rub her tummy when she stopped and scanned the room. 'Will's hoping for a boy, but all I know is he or she will be a brilliant swimmer after all the water I'm drinking. And on that note, I need to pee again.'

Sara darted off as a rowdy rendition of ABBA's 'Ring Ring' prompted someone to grab the old school bell from Fiona's memorabilia display.

'And I need to drink again,' Maggie mumbled en route to the service bar in the marquee where a young barman busily dispensed liquid confidence into tall flutes.

'This makes a change. Me serving the publican,' he said. Maggie recognised the face, but he wore no nametag. 'What'll it be?'

'Champagne, thanks. I'm celebrating.'

'What are you celebrating?' he asked, handing her a glass.

'Me.' She raised the flute. 'To making it here tonight.' The cynical toast was lost on the young barman, adding to Maggie's unease. All she needed was Tracy super-spunk Rose to turn up for all those gawky, high school, late bloomer reminiscences to resurface.

'I knew I'd find you here,' a voice said from behind, right on cue.

'You mean at the bar?' Maggie joked. It was all she could do as she turned ever-so slowly to find a rose resplendent in red, her face radiant, eyes sparkly and with a grin wide enough to lift those perfect cheekbones into place. Tracey Rose was glowing.

'Not at the bar, you dag, at the reunion. Give us a hug.'

Bittersweet nostalgia cut through Maggie's opening sarcasm as the pair embraced, reminding her they'd been good friends.

Maggie pulled away first. 'Wild horses had to drag me here, you know?'

'Well, speaking of wild horses ...' Tracey said, taking Maggie's hand. 'Come over here and see who *I* dragged along.'

Maggie's first thought was to pull out of the tight hand grip and dig her heels in, but the combination of champagne and stilettos kept her teetering unsteadily forwards to the memorabilia display. The crowd had thickened, all giggling, all pointing, all intent on the photographic array.

Tracy stopped behind a tall man with a white shirt sitting snug across broad shoulders. 'Honey, look who I found.' When the man turned around, Tracy tugged him closer, like the interfering mother foisting a fella on a wallflower at the school dance. 'You remember Dan, Maggie.'

Having tottered into position, Maggie's mouth twitched into what she hoped was more smile than grimace. 'Sure, I remember Dan,' she said with exaggerated gusto. 'You promised me a corsage, but you gave me broken toe.' Maggie's and Dan's laugh melded beautifully into one as they locked eyes. 'Good to see you.'

'And you,' he responded predictably. 'It's been a long time.'

'Great night so far,' Maggie added quickly, not giving him an opportunity to say something as perfunctory as 'You haven't changed a bit.' That would be insincere, and she needed the spark of recognition and surprise in his face to be genuine.

'I totally forgot about you two going to the dance,' Tracy said. 'Fancy being back in the same hall altogether. I was sad to hear about Amber, but so glad she got the ball rolling on this reunion. About time, I say.' Tracy's eyes were suddenly everywhere else, like she couldn't wait to get amongst it all. 'Dan, honey, I can see Anne and ... Oh, there's Lizzie.' Tracy's face lit up. 'I can finally return this.' She pulled a bulky package from the small handbag. 'It's only taken me twenty-odd years. I'll be back soon, okay?'

'Go, go!' Dan's chuckle and the roll of his eyes suggested he knew better.

It had only taken twenty-odd years for Maggie to be alone with Dan Ireland, but here they were as alone as they could be, notwithstanding the couple of hundred guests and the DJ cranking up the volume in the auditorium where a hired mirror ball was hypnotising eager couples into thinking they could dance. Maggie craved a drink—something to do with her hands, something to look at other than Dan. Gone was the teenager with the unkempt hair that hung over his eyes in greasy strands, and who loitered in the living room with her brother—two troublemakers who farted and burped and constantly drove Maggie crazy. They'd been about

146

Noah's age now, and Dan had the same beautiful bluebottle blue eyes as her son.

'Earth to Maggie?' Dan raised his voice against the doof-doof sound of speakers. 'I said, you probably need reminding about my dancing prowess.' He reached out a hand and took hold of Maggie's, squeezing tight. 'Are you game?'

She returned the squeeze, her hand feeling safe in his. Her toes, not so safe perhaps. 'Should I have steel-cap boots?'

Laughing, he led her into the centre of the crowd and began gyrating and miming the song; *You Make Me Feel Like Dancing*. The years hadn't altered his dance technique. The man's moves were still like a Leo Sayer puppet on speed. There was the occasional hug from a stranger, the familiar face that smiled, and the predicted 'You haven't changed a bit' remarks while they danced.

After a little 'Jive Talkin', 'Boogie Fever', and some essential ABBA, Maggie clutched her parched throat to signal time out, hoping she didn't look as hot and as sweaty as she felt under the clingy black dress.

'I'll get us a drink,' Dan yelled in her ear, the buzz of warm breath causing a rush of goose bumps to speckle Maggie's neck. 'I'll come find you.' He pointed to the open fire exit by the assembly stage that led to the playground area and much-needed fresh air.

Her first breath of warm night air rising from baked asphalt did little to revive her; nor did the thick scent of fatty lamb and burning tin foil. To her right, illuminated by a stand of SES spotlights, was the smell's source— the three homemade spit roasts, surrounded by a pack of beer and testosterone fuelled blokes taking turns to test their manhood by prodding the fire. At the edge of the darkness lay a dozen hopeful dogs with orange eyes glowing eerily. Achilles and Jackpot would likely be among the mob, snouts lowered and positioned between paws, eyes watching, pleading, ready.

With most of the outdoor tables and chairs occupied by bodies, jackets or handbags, she ventured beyond the monkey-bars and fell against the balance beam she'd once dreaded—anything to take the pressure of the balls of her feet. Maggie had never enjoyed sports period at school, nor understood how learning to balance on a lump of wood might prepare her for anything as an adult. It sure hadn't helped her balance a career with marriage and motherhood.

She waited, watching out for Dan to make sure he found her, glad to be away from the crowd with their constant hellos and shrieks of

'Remember me?', only to follow up with, 'Geez, haven't we been lucky with the weather?' *The weather!* Topic of last resort. Maggie disliked small-talk or forced conversations, and yet here she was setting herself up for an intimate tête-à-tête with the man making his way across the playground—two glasses and a bottle hanging from one hand, a paper bowl of something balanced on the other. Suddenly nervous and questioning her intelligence, Maggie adjusted her bum on the balance beam, tugged at the hemline creeping up her legs and tried to come across cool as her still gorgeous, still married schoolgirl crush stopped in front of her, close enough to feel cruel. Maggie was a child again, being handed a bag of lollies and told, 'Don't touch. They're not yours to eat.'

'Thanks, Dan.' She took both empty glasses and waited for him to balance the bowl of Cheezels on the beam beside her.

After filling both their glasses and balancing the bottle next to the bowl, he loaded four fingers with Cheezels, held his hand towards her and said, 'Hey, remember we used to do this?'

'I do,' she replied, waving his offer of Cheezel away. Maggie remembered every mad and bad thing Dan had got up to. When not mucking around in the loungeroom with her brother, the pair had turned the town upside down with their shenanigans, not that anyone proved who was behind the regular late-night drag races, the firecrackers or the exploding mailboxes.

Dan reloaded his fingers with four more Cheezels. 'Mmm, I forgot how good these little buggers are. Sure I can't tempt you?'

Maggie shook her head. 'Once I start I won't be able to stop.'

'Well then, while I'm stuffing down Cheezels, give me the Maggie Lindeman story in five-year increments.'

Maggie Henkler, she should have corrected. She didn't. 'How about I give you my life story in three words so we can move onto more interesting topics: TOO. BLOODY. BORING. Besides,' she added, 'we're here to reminisce about the good ol' days, like this playground. She lifted her chin and sniffed the air. 'Remember the smell of rain hitting the hot tarmac? Thank goodness the weather's held tonight.'

Was it her imagination or did Dan's expression have that Oh-God-not-the-weather look as he brushed Cheezel dust from both hands? Then he moved the bowl and the bottle further along the beam to settle beside Maggie.

'I heard about Amber,' he said.

Maggie hung her head in a kind of reverence. 'It was so sudden.

Totally devastated her husband. The funeral was moving and befitting Amber, but Phillip looked shattered. The daughter didn't help matters. I met her at the wake. She goes by Fiona Bailey-Blair.'

Dan eyed Maggie. 'Fiona is the baby that caused the kerfuffle?'

'Yep, and she's all grown up and staying in my best room at the pub. So like her mother—or I should say, like her mother used to be. Amber changed after she and some friends from school came back home briefly. Old Gypsy passed away recently and left Dandelion House to her and the others.'

'I heard,' Dan said. 'Is Fiona's here tonight?'

'No—thank goodness.' The surprise in Dan's eyes demanded Maggie explain. 'For a while Fiona looked like causing a bit of trouble.'

He smiled. 'Like mother like daughter.'

'Maybe, but with Amber gone, Fiona is intent on finding her biological father. She's assuming he's in Calingarry Crossing and the reunion is a likely place to look. Tonight's photo display is—was—part of her plan. She's very good at visual displays, you know?' Maggie chuckled. Dan did not.

'You really think that's what she's doing here?' he asked.

'Who knows? She's a twenty-two-year-old version of Amber. No one ever knew what was going on behind the pretence and pretty face?'

Tomfoolery at the barbecue spit took Dan's attention, and he laughed at two hairy mutts running in crazy circles for no reason. Maggie might've found the antics humorous, too, had the small spark in Dan's face at the mention of Fiona not unsettled her. On the list of potential catch-up topics with this man, Fiona had not featured. Then again, any topic, including the weather, meant avoiding the subject of her marriage. For one night, Maggie preferred to forget her husband in the same way Brian was forgetting her.

When Dan resumed their chat, he wanted to know about Noah. Maggie bragged shamelessly. And when she told him about her praying mantis dream, Dan laughed so hard he almost choked on his champagne.

'Are you serious? Praying mantis? That's hilarious, Maggie.'

'Not from my perspective, Dan.'

When the conversation changed to his children, the man turned to mush, with the first mention of his twins stripping all the stiffness from his body until he was leaning into Maggie, shoulders and arms brushing against hers. The balance beam never felt so good.

'My two keep me grounded,' he told her. 'They keep me doing what I do to make the world a little safer.' There was such joy in Dan's face as he recounted the moment he and Tracy had discovered they were having twins—one of each. 'Emily and Michael teach me something every day.'

Michael! Maggie closed her eyes.

'You okay?' Dan was leaning forward, craning his neck to look at her. 'I was saying how the kids keep me active but wear me out emotionally.'

'Well, be thankful you're not Phillip Blair,' Maggie said. 'Twenty years older than us and dealing with Fiona. He was the reason I invited her to stay. I figured he needed time to grieve in his own way while Fiona … Had you seen her at the funeral you'd swear she was experiencing all seven stages of grief at once. Turns out she's not so bad. Don't tell her she's actually growing on me.' Maggie responded to Dan's raised and ready-to-pour bottle by holding out the glass growing warm in her hand. 'And don't ask her to admit this, as I'm certain she never will but, like Amber, Fiona is glad she came to Calingarry Crossing.'

'As am I right now.' Dan smiled that smile etched in Maggie's memory; the one that was so much more than a simple curve of the mouth and two tiny twitches at the corners of his lips. Dan Ireland had had a George Clooney grin before Maggie knew there *was* a George Clooney grin, and it was still impossible not to be drawn in and smile with him. Dan and George had one more thing in common. Neither man would never be anything more than Maggie's fairy tale. Soon the clock would strike and Maggie's Cinderella moment would end, sending her scurrying back to her lonely broom closet at the rear of the pub.

'You have that look on your face again,' Dan said.

'I don't have a look,' she re-joined. 'I have a numb bum from sitting on this bloody balance beam.' She wiggled her frame straight, repositioning the shoulders she'd unconsciously let slump a little too close to Dan's. She might be near forty and married to a man choosing fame over family, but she was allowed this one fairy tale. Wasn't she?

Dan stood and held out a hand as if asking her to dance. 'I have the perfect way to get that numb bum moving again. My legs could do with a stretch, too?'

'No,' Maggie said a little more vehemently than she'd planned, her fingers clawing the edge of the hard wooden beam. 'I mean, I'm fine for now.'

More partygoers spilled out of the hall, probably needing fresh air and a break from the DJ's song selection. One group disappeared into the dark, the glow of cigarettes and the distinctive smell of pot pinpointing their location.

Maggie flicked her head in the same direction. 'Shouldn't you be doing something about that, Detective?'

'Oh, sure, the word hypocrite comes to mind. I might be a police officer, but I'm no poster boy for good in this town.' He tried, but the smile didn't quite curl Dan's lips. 'I also think the teachers busted me smoking in that very spot,' he went on. 'Wasn't there a maintenance shed?'

Dan's question torched her cheeks. There was danger in sharing such memories with him, she decided. He was too close, too wonderful, too married.

'You know there was, Dan.' And what kids got up to behind it, she added under her breath. 'What do you suppose Tracy is up to inside?' Maggie deliberately spoke her friend's—his wife's—name.

'Oh, you know Trace.' He sounded almost dismissive. 'She'll be monopolising the conversation, playing her part in a game of pass-the-picture, gushing over photos and showing off the kids. Isn't that what reunions are for?'

Maggie nodded, not that such rituals interested her. She'd long ago lost the need to monopolise a conversation—especially one about her life and marriage—or gush over other people's baby photos. Her son remained the one thing in Maggie's life worth showing off. That was, she thought, until a grandchild happened along. How Maggie longed for the day her son and his wife would present her with a beautiful grandbaby to spoil and gush over. Finally, Maggie will have understood all she'd had to do and endure in order to reach that ultimate milestone in her life. Thinking of Noah at home, she drew a deep breath and let it rush out in a continuous sigh with her confession.

'Dan, I have no idea what I'm doing at this reunion.'

'You're keeping me company,' he said. 'And while I'm grateful, I am monopolising you. You should be inside showing off like Tracy. Weren't you "Girl most likely to succeed"?'

'That was Tracy's title,' Maggie grimaced before gulping the last of her champagne. 'I wasn't much of a standout at school.'

'You're sure making up for it now.'

His forensic fascination with her little black dress flipped Maggie's stomach. 'I think the years are testing your memory, Dan.' Was the man flirting, or was it the alcohol stirring her imagination?

'Weren't you going to be a photographer?'

'You remember that? What else?' she asked, playfully.

'Truth is, Maggie, I remember too much about living here. The good and the bad.'

She didn't want to tell him 'me too'. She didn't want to go back to morbid topics.

'How about after Calingarry?' she asked. 'What's the Dan Ireland story in five-year increments? What did you do, besides marry my friend?'

'Ah, yes, well, like you, Maggie, I've also got three words for my life story—my professional one, at least,' he clarified. 'NOT. BORING. ENOUGH. There isn't a minute I'm not wishing for a day without a single crime and no one to save.' Dan reached to the back of his head, his hands working down to his neck. 'On a personal note, if I'm honest,' he added. 'Trace saved me.'

Maggie followed his gaze into the crowded marquee. If they looked hard enough, they might glimpse the all-rescuing Tracy Rose resplendent in red. 'Did you need saving, Dan?' she asked.

'I'll put it this way. I was halfway to hell when I bumped into her at a university party. And before I give you the wrong impression, Maggie, I wasn't smart enough to be there as a student, which makes me wonder what she saw in me. The uniform probably.'

'Uniform?' Maggie queried.

'Part-time campus security. Call sign Tango-Foxtrot-Twelve. Bad boy Dan Ireland had a two-way, a baton and a licence to take out his frustrations on any moron who messed up. Highly qualified in detecting trouble-makers, though,' he added.

'Not everyone in Calingarry Crossing thought you were trouble, Dan.'

A clump of dandelion weed poking out of the ground bore the full force of Dan's frustration, the toe of his brown leather boot grinding the green leaves to mush. Maggie's eyes traced the line of blue denim all the way from his boots to the snug fit over his hips and wondered how the rebellious Dan had got away with jeans and a chambray shirt given the sophistication of Tracy's stylish red number.

'If I was going to marry Trace,' he began, 'I needed to straighten myself out. Her mum accepted me, but lowly security guard would not cut it with her father. Next thing I know, strings were being pulled and I was headed to Goulburn Police Academy.'

'Dan Ireland a policeman!' Maggie hoped the incredulousness in her voice hadn't offended him.

His laugh said no. 'Best thing I could've done. Like I said, she rescued me—and I made good after my misspent youth.'

Maggie shook her head. 'You were no different to half the town, Dan, and that includes my brother.'

'I know you stuck up for me with The Rev. Do you still think the town was wrong for kicking me out?'

The words 'I do' sat just behind her lips—two words that brought back images of schoolbooks and a pencil case emblazoned with: Mrs Lindeman-Ireland. 'Accidents happen, Dan,' she said.

Yes, Michael's death had devastated her. Was she surprised? Not really. She'd witnessed her brother and his friends do dumb things over the years. Any grief she'd experienced over Michael's loss had been confused and diluted by her anguish over the town's determination to have someone pay the price.

'I used to call them accidents before I joined the force,' Dan said. 'General Duties officers attended so-called accidents all the time. I branched out a few years later, studied and got a job with the Crash Investigation Unit. First thing I learned is there's no such thing as an accident.' Dan's smile flickered, faded, never happened. 'Even today, whenever I have to confront a family with the news I ...'

'You think about Michael?' Oh, Dan, Maggie cried inside. Every protective and nurturing instincts kicked into overdrive, her arms aching to reach out and tell him it was all right.

A comfortable silence fell around them, except for the unrelenting doof-doof and occasional spray of drunken laughter escaping from the high-set windows in the old school hall. Jennifer had done a superb job; tonight's DJ was playing all the popular numbers. Tina Turner's *Nutbush City Limits* was the current guaranteed crowd-pleaser, with everybody rushing the dance floor for a spot in the line. Not Maggie. Not with these shoes.

'I think about you and your Dad,' Dan said.

'How do you mean?'

He pushed a hand into his hair, exhaling loudly. 'Ever since learning how it works: the dreaded late-night knock and the words that sound so cold ... I see your dad. I see his pain—and yours, Maggie—and I hate myself.' Dan's boot sent a stone skipping across the quadrangle, followed by another. 'Geez, I'm one hell of a fun date, aren't I? Laugh-a-minute Ireland, that's me.' He jammed his hands in the pockets of his jeans, pouted a little, and too quickly was out of Maggie's reach; the hand she'd wanted to hold finger-combed his hair. 'Tell me to shut up, will you? Coming back here was bad idea. I came to make Tracy's night and I'm spoiling yours.'

'No, you're not. You've made my night, if you really want to know. So sit.' Maggie patted the balance beam while she worked the heel straps on her shoes down with her toes. 'And you don't have to shut up.'

Dan eased back into the space beside her, his hand resting on the beam next to Maggie's. So close. One tiny movement and their little fingers would touch, and like live wires they would flash equal to the lightning she could see in the sky. How beautiful, but how dangerous a spark could be near a tinder box like Maggie. Despite the temperature, a shudder rippled through her body.

'You're cold?' Dan asked with a curious lilt and an expression to match. But when his arm made a move to wrap around her shoulder, Maggie launched herself off their makeshift seat.

'I, ah, may be coming down with something,' she said. 'I should keep my distance. It certainly has been nice catching up, Dan. Will you be stopping long in town?'

'Back home tomorrow,' he said. 'Kids rule my life these days. I've taken long service leave to spend time with them. I want to make up for working when they were little.'

'What about you and your dad?' Maggie enquired. 'Did you have time to see him today?'

Dan's childish shrug said enough. Charlie and his boys had been like oil and water.

'The old bastard's still around; I'm getting regular bills for the mobile phone I sent him a few years back. I stopped by the property on our way into town. The place looks like crap. Left a note with my mobile number. Told him I wanted to come out again in the morning. Tracy will make sure I don't leave without trying again. She's like that.'

'I hope he calls,' Maggie said. 'You both need to get re-acquainted. You should. I know what it's like to lose that connection with a father.'

'Oh, sorry, Maggie, I didn't know. I should've asked. When did he die?'

'No, it's dementia, but he's not doing well,' she told him. 'I came back to Calingarry all a bit too late. Even though we talked over the phone often, he never let on, never complained, and I never realised. Ethne called me when it happened—a sort of mini stroke. He recovered, but it fast-tracked his decline. By the time Noah and I got ourselves organised and out here ...' By the time I'd done trying to reason with a selfish husband, she might've added. '... Dad was no longer the same person. You wouldn't recognise him.'

'That doesn't compute, Maggie. Your dad was as tough as they come.'

'That's what he let people see. He wasn't though, and especially after ...' Maggie stopped herself. She didn't want to go there. She didn't want to remember what she knew she could never forget; how a stupid stunt had ripped Michael from their lives and changed their paths and her world. She steered her thoughts back to her dad. 'Strange how he could counsel and comfort others, but not his own daughter. When I needed him the most, his grief kept him distant. I remember being so angry and confused when they blamed you, Dan. Then you all but disappeared. I never saw you.' Maggie stopped short of mentioning how she'd found the solace she'd craved in the young musician called Brian who'd played at the pub with his dad on several occasions.

'I didn't get much say in the matter,' Dan said. 'Figured it was better to disappear—for you and your dad.' He swept his fringe to one side in the same way as Noah. 'Sorry, Maggie, I didn't want to go there tonight.'

'Then let's not,' she said as an alarm-like laugh pealed over the early strains of yet another disco favourite. Inside the hall doors was Tracy with a group of woman half dancing, half talking.

'Tracy's looking as gorgeous as ever,' Maggie said, heeding the high-pitched warning. Might as well face it, she told herself. The man was married.

'Maggie, about Tracy and me ... I'm under strict instructions tonight. I did promise her—'

'Yes, oh, yes, Dan, I understand. You'd best hop to it.' Maggie smiled. What else could she do? 'Promises are important. Why else have I never forgotten your promised corsage?' She laughed, but it sounded as awkward as the moment felt. 'It's been great seeing you again, Dan. Really great. I'm so glad you came.'

'Sounds like you're saying goodbye.'

'I am. I need to go.' Maggie lifted her feet one at a time, brushing her soles to wipe away small bits of bitumen and sand.

'Don't. Stay with me, please.' His voice dulled. 'Let me check with Tracy and I'll be right back.'

Check what? she mused. For her permission to be a needy woman's fairy tale for the rest of the evening?

'It's getting late,' she said. 'I've already been here two hours longer than I planned.'

Dan looked perplexed. 'It's hardly late. The event only got started two hours ago and there are speeches and—'

'Exactly! I hate a fuss and I've never been good with crowds.' And she did not feel like being part of one anymore tonight. 'I think I *am* getting a cold, Dan.' She had to make a move before she changed her mind or made a move she'd regret. 'Besides, I have the breakfast shift at the hotel. I'll slip away. No one likes a party pooper!'

'You know what happens to a crowd when one person leaves?' he said.

'This crowd?' She scoffed. Visible through the open doors was the strobe lighting that exaggerated the jerky dance movements of mid-life bones that hadn't boogied for years. Maggie might've laughed at the sight, but there wasn't a laugh left inside her. 'If you think my going will have any effect, Dan, you're mistaken.' Struggling to slip swollen feet back into the strappy sandals without losing her dignity, she added, 'No one will even notice I'm gone.'

'I'll notice.' His words floated out on a whisper.

'But, Dan …' Maggie stumbled, despite her grip on the balance beam, then she stammered, even though she was rarely lost for words. Her English skills were as good as her maths skills and this was simple maths. Four drinks, multiplied by one old flame, divided by twenty-five years and a marriage equalled Danger with a capital D. 'I'm going, Dan. It's been great.' She kissed his cheek like a finger tests a hot iron. 'Good night.'

Good decision. Right decision. Only decision.

24

Maggie had almost reached the school gate when the first drops of rain prompted her to collect her umbrella. Had the soles of her feet not hurt, she would've made a run for the hotel and left the brolly behind until morning. No person would steal a lime green promotional umbrella with 'Midori' printed on every panel.

With no sign of the spotty-faced attendant in the cloakroom that, remarkably, still smelled of stale sandwiches and bad banana, Maggie immersed herself in the collection of coats and bags. How the humble country cloakroom had changed over the decades. Gone were the gumboots, Globite cases and plastic raincoats. In their place tonight were Sass and Bide, Collette Dinnigan and Hugo Boss. When Maggie emerged, the garish umbrella hooked over one wrist, there was Dan.

'What are you doing?' she asked.

'Looking for an umbrella,' he replied, straight-faced. 'My party trick is Charlie Chaplin impersonations.'

'Dan!' If he'd noticed the censure in her voice or her expression, it didn't show in his smile.

'I checked in, Maggie, and Tracy will be happily holding court until lights-out. Had trouble getting a word in, actually. Given I lost my dance partner, I decided on a walk along the river. Join me?' The way he asked made a simple stroll sound harmless. 'What do you say? Not a big decision, Maggie. It's the Calingarry riverbank, not the Kokoda Trail.'

'It's raining, Dan.'

He glanced outside. 'Haven't you heard the saying? Rain always looks wetter through a window. Come for a walk with me. We'll share your brolly.'

'No,' she said.

Dan cocked his head. 'No—you haven't heard the saying, no to sharing your brolly, or no to the walk?'

'No, Dan. I mean yes. I mean … my shoes. They're hard enough to walk in on a hard surface.'

'You'll manage,' he grinned. 'You're a problem solver from way back, Maggie Linderman.'

Maggie *was* a smart girl, a straight-A student. Rarely had there been a question in class she didn't know the answer to. But if she was so clever, where did her reply come from?

'Okay. A short one.'

Light rain fell as they set out, crossing Rivers-Edge Road and the open green space with a playground and picnic tables. By the time they made the track, worn by years of foot, horse and bicycle traffic, the cloud cover had thinned, taking away the rain and revealing an almost full moon. By not straying from the path, the stroll was relatively easy, even in high heels, but Maggie would have to stay on her toes—in more ways than one —because this was crazy. Maggie should be back at the pub, checking up on her son who, as trustworthy as he might be, was at that unpredictable and impressionable age; no longer a boy but only partway to being a man. At least he'd kept Fiona occupied and away from the event. All night, Maggie had been expecting trouble. Getting back to the pub would ease her mind once and for all and yet here she was moonlight strolling in fantasyland with Dan Ireland.

'A penny …' he said.

'I was thinking about Fiona's need to find her father,' Maggie replied. 'I wish I could help her. She asked me the other day, but Amber and I weren't that close—in or out of school. Except for nights she wanted to sneak into the pub. Then we were best friends. If Amber knew who the father was, she never told me. You?'

'Not likely,' Dan replied. 'I recall most of us blokes were drunk or stoned on the night she claimed it happened.'

Maggie baulked. 'Us? You were there?'

Dan huffed a laugh. 'In body, not in brain. Me, Nate and …'

'What?' Maggie said, stopping in her tracks. 'It's okay. Tell me. Were you going to say Michael? Was he there with you and Amber? The three of you?'

'Sorry, yeah,' Dan said, sheepishly. 'Amber was off her face when she and two blokes busted the three of us over there ...' He nodded to a point further along the river and the pair continued their moseying. 'Through those trees is the place we smoked joints.'

'You, Nate and Michael smoked joints?' Maggie sounded prudish. 'I never knew that.'

'Because you were a good girl.'

She pouted. 'I didn't want to be good.'

'And I didn't want to be the one corrupting The Rev's daughter by introducing her to marijuana. Amber Bailey, on the other hand ... Her not-so-good reputation was no secret.'

'Do you think it was rape like her father said?' Maggie asked.

'Hmm, Jack Bailey's allegations were all about stitching up Will Travelli. Out of all of us, he was the one with potential. But nobody could force Amber to do anything she didn't want to. From what I heard, she offered it up freely most weekends. Some would say she was all tease with little follow-through. Others bragged about home runs, but I doubt many got past first base.'

'Do you know which blokes *were* with her that night?' Maggie was curious about how close Dan might be to having known the truth. 'Can you name them now?'

'You probably don't want to know, Maggie, and I truly don't remember the details. I smoked a joint, finished it and ...'

'And what?' Her stopping was as sharp as her words sounded. 'What did you do, Dan?'

'I don't recall, Your Honour,' he replied, then chuckled. 'Are we done with the cross-examination, Madam Prosecutor?'

'Sorry,' she said. 'I'm shocked and wondering what else I don't know about you, *and* about my brother.'

'Let's keep walking, shall we?' Dan said.

Strolling so close to Dan, and so far down memory lane, had Maggie on edge and with a heightened sense of awareness. Every noise, every smell, every feeling was sharper, spicier, stronger. The nutty, fresh scent of spring rain on dry earth still lingered in the air, and the gum trees and eucalypts seemed more potent, as if washing away the layer of dust let them breathe. Maggie was also so busy trying to breathe, to slow the evening down, that she'd failed to realise her fingers had woven themselves between his. She dared a sideways glance to search out the details of Dan's face in the moonlight. What was going on in that beautiful head, behind that perfectly sculpted face, masked by the fine, late evening stubble?

'Dan!' She halted, shifting in front of him.

She wasn't going any further down this path—the literal or the figurative. But before she could tell him so, Dan drew her into his arms, the urgency of their kiss reminiscent of impetuous youth. They were teenagers again, heading home from her Year 10 school dance, walking a slow zigzag; stalling, stumbling, happy and unprepared for midnight to strike and turn her back into plain Maggie.

'Stop!' She pushed back. 'I can't. I'm married, Dan.'

'Sorry, Maggie, I-I wasn't thinking.' Dan raked a hand through the mop of hair and cursed at the ground. Then his head snapped back up, and he fixed his stare. 'Actually, that's not true. You're all I've thought about.' He squinted in the moonlight at her nametag, confusion crumpling his brow. 'I didn't notice until just now and you didn't correct me when I called you Maggie Lindeman. I assumed it was just you and Noah. Doh!' He smacked a hand to his forehead. 'How stupid am I? Of course you're still married. Who in their right mind would not want to be with you forever? So it's Brian?'

'Of course,' she snapped, angered at Dan insinuating she'd not corrected him on purpose.

'It's just, when you weren't wearing a ring, I ...'

'Oh, that,' she mumbled. The single gold band encrusted with diamond chips that she'd picked and paid for herself served as both engagement and wedding ring. Due to constant hand-washing and dirty dishwater, Maggie kept the ring in a drawer. When she'd slipped it on tonight, it was too loose. She'd dropped almost two dress sizes since taking on the pub.

'I am married.' She spoke with pride, but it sounded like an apology.

'Sorry,' Dan said for the umpteenth time, the words annoying Maggie. What was he sorry about? Kissing her? Sorry she was married, maybe? Sorry it wasn't to him? He hung his head, stubbed the toe of his shoe into the ground and shoved both hands into his pockets. 'I've totally messed up, Maggie. I should've asked. I didn't.'

Poor Dan. She could fix the situation, tell him the matter required no apology and confess to enjoying every sexy second of his mouth on hers. Instead, she arched an enquiring eyebrow. 'Asked me what exactly, Dan? If I was married? Or if you could kiss me?'

He breathed a sigh—relief most likely that she'd smiled. 'Maybe both. All night I've been like a silly, love-struck teenager.' He grinned. 'And I purposely didn't ask about Brian because if I you told me he was still on the scene I'd have to behave myself. Seriously, Maggie, had you mentioned his name I would never—'

She silenced Dan with the tips of her fingers pressed to his lips. 'You're not silly, or a teenager, but you are married.'

He took her hand in his. 'I am tonight,' he said distractedly. 'It's just, well, things with Trace are not quite that simple.' He moved to hold her, but Maggie held both hands out in front, her force field firmly in place. 'I promised Trace that for tonight we'd be the happy married couple we were for sixteen years.'

'What do you mean?'

'Trace and I have an arrangement—and if you tell her I told you …'

'Go on,' Maggie urged.

'Trace has this image she wanted to project. She wanted us to be married tonight. We still are, sort of. We're keeping together to avoid the big divorce thing for Em and Mike. Starting high school has been a big enough adjustment. We want to stay together for them. It isn't hard,' he added. 'We'll always love and care for each other.'

'Okay, so you and Tracy are *whatever*,' Maggie said, sounding like her son. 'But, Dan, I am married to Brian. It's not perfect, but I'm hopeful …'

'Hopeful?' Dan looked expectant; like Achilles when Ethne opened the treat jar. It didn't matter that the treat was a tiny sliver of dried liver. A smart dog knew, with the right moves, there was always more. 'Hopeful of what?' Dan asked her.

Maggie stepped away and turned both palms skyward. 'Feel that? It's starting to rain again. We should go back. You promised to be the doting husband.'

The skin on her shoulders burned under his hands. 'Maggie, please—'

'Shhh!' Maggie's four fingertips again pressed his mouth as frustration opened the floodgates and twenty-five-year-old tears fell. 'Keep your promises, Dan. I've enjoyed seeing you.' More than you know, she told herself. 'But this stops here—now.'

He suddenly looked and sounded beaten. 'This is crazy, Maggie—'

'Shhh!' This time her head motioned towards the school. 'What's that?'

'What are you hearing?' Dan asked.

'Nothing,' Maggie replied. 'Not even music.'

'I think someone's calling you,' he said.

'Maggie? Maggie, can you hear me?' Sara's sing-song voice carried easily through the stillness of night.

'Wait here, Dan.' Maggie thrust a stop hand at him, panic taking precedence. 'I'll go first.'

'You're kidding me!' He sounded angry, or it was frustration. Maggie understood both. 'We are *not* school kids sneaking out one at a time from behind the maintenance shed.'

'You're right, Dan. We're grownups who should know better.' As she turned, her stupid stilettos snagged in the grass, and she stumbled. Dan lunged, prepared to steady her, but she fended him off with a shove of hand. 'We're also married, only not to each other.'

'Because we allowed people to keep us apart,' Dan countered. 'Did you ever wonder what might've been if they'd let us choose?'

He said 'us', but Maggie knew he meant *her*. The Rev had not let his daughter have anything to do with Dan after Michael's accident and Maggie would never hurt or disrespect her father. The man had lost so much. No wonder he'd latched onto the young musician. Brian could be a kind of surrogate son.

Maggie shook her head. 'We can't do this now, Dan. We can't do this ever. Calingarry's a small town; one I have to live in when you've gone back to your life in the city.'

'That's the thing,' Dan said. 'I—'

'Maggie?' Sara's voice was clear now and panicked. 'Are you out here?'

'I have to go, Dan. Goodnight and goodbye.'

Both cursing and thanking Sara in one breath, Maggie hurried along the path, her mind sifting through all the possible reasons someone would call for her. Did they need help tapping a new keg? At least she'd hoped it was about beer and not about Fiona.

25

No music. No party sounds. Nothing.

'Someone pull the party plug, Sara?' Maggie opted for humour. She needed a smile to reassure her things weren't as serious as Sara's face was suggesting. There'd been enough seriousness for one night.

'Quick.' Tugging Maggie down the path to the school gate with its twinkling fairy lights, they hurried along the main street.

'Sara, slow down.' Maggie worried: for her stupid stilettos, for her friend, and for the tiny life inside Sara that would complete the woman's fairy tale.

'Gangway!' Sara shouted.

Beyond the sea of onlookers was Fiona's Saab parked at an odd angle near one of the massive fig trees. At first, Maggie groaned. Did the girl not understand the basic nose-to-kerb parking rule? Then she noticed two deployed airbags and the Saab's passenger door wide open.

'What's happened? Where's Fiona? Tell me she's all right.'

'Fiona's fine. She's over there.' Sara pointed.

Huddled under a blanket on the far side of the canary-coloured convertible, her face covered in a white powder, was a sobbing Fiona in the comforting embrace of a well-dressed partygoer. Standing over them was a man Maggie didn't recognise. In shorts and a T-shirt, he was hardly attending the school reunion.

Who was he? What had happened? Where was—?

'Noah!' Maggie didn't recognise her own shrill voice. She shook Sara's arm away and rushed to her lifeless son, dropping to her knees. Oblivious to stones gouging flesh, she fingered that damn fringe to one side of his bleeding forehead and saw Noah's blue eyes wide and staring. 'Oh my God!'

'Are you his mother?' a voice asked.

Maggie nodded, bracing for grave news as she looked across the body of her son and into a stranger's face. 'What's happened?'

'You probably don't remember me. I'm Rosie McDonald,' a woman said. 'Mum is a doctor and I'm a paramedic. We'll get Noah to Saddleton Base Hospital faster than an ambulance.'

'Lucky?' Maggie said, feeling both irritation and terror bubbling inside her.

'Breathe, Maggie. We've got this. It's important to keep him still. The backboard will fit fine in a station wagon.'

Major incidents out this way usually brought the Air Ambulance, Maggie thought. No one was talking about summoning them for Noah. That had to be good. Didn't it?

'I have a station wagon,' Maggie said. 'This is my son.'

Car headlights shone into the crowd, casting light on the grazes colouring her son's legs and arms a dirty brown. One side of his face already showed signs of swelling and bruising.

'Maggie.' Sara leaned down with a soothing hand on one shoulder. 'Think about it. You've said the brakes aren't good in the wet and you're in no state to drive. Accept the help being offered, Maggie. It's best for everyone this way. Best for Noah.'

'Noah? Noah, buddy, it's Mum.' No response, his eyes fixed and staring, but not at her. *Why?* Maggie tried again, hearing the confusion in her voice. 'Noah?' She looked across her son's body into the sympathetic face of the doctor. 'What's wrong?' Someone had to tell her what the hell had happened so she could stop feeling as empty and as useless as those bloody airbags flapping inside the Saab. 'Was he run over?'

Rosie McDonald shook her head. 'Seems he fell out of the car.'

Only slightly relieved, but still confused, Maggie sat back on her haunches and rubbed both dented knees. 'Fell?'

'His physical injuries from the fall are superficial,' the doctor added. 'His condition isn't the result of a fall, so the backboard is merely a precaution. The hospital will be able to identify the cause.'

'Cause?' Maggie blinked, squinting into harsh headlights. 'Of what?'

'He'll be fine,' the doctor said, standing. 'But very sore and very sorry once he comes down from his high.'

Maggie rose to eyeball the medic. 'What?'

'I can't be sure what it is he's taken,' the doctor said, not under-standing Maggie's question. 'Without knowing which drugs, he—'

'Drugs?' Maggie barked. 'Oh no! He-he doesn't … He wouldn't. He …'

Maggie looked over the doctor's shoulder, zeroing in on the fair Fiona still cowering under a blanket and sobbing. Her next breath rattled with rage. Her next thought was to race across and rip into the girl before drag-ging her back to the pub and calling her father, Phillip. But how small-town did that make Maggie? What if Noah had taken something? Only tonight she'd criticised locals for condemning Dan when, truth be told, Michael had made a mistake and taken a risk. Did Noah have a drug prob-lem? Was that why he'd been so moody and distracted this past year? Had she been naïve to think Noah would never do drugs? Michael had smoked pot and Maggie never knew. As for Brian …

Hands clasped her shoulders from behind. Sarah was whispering, telling Maggie to relax and attempting to massage the knot of tension from her neck. Maggie was too intent on the local police officer to relax. Callum had moved the unknown male away from the crowd and was standing over him, notebook in hand. Maggie could see the stranger's bloodstained mouth moving, and while she couldn't make out any words, smugness smeared his face like a dirty stain.

Dan moved into the frame, producing a small wallet from his trouser pocket to present to Callum. The police badge glistened under Callum's torch light before both policemen shook hands. When Dan looked over his shoulder and across at Maggie with a smile that said 'It's okay, I'm here' she let herself imagine, ever so briefly, that for once someone was helping her carry the parenting responsibility and protecting her, rather than her protecting everyone else.

A sprinkling of rain cleared the crowd, while a blur of bodies moved around her son with the backboard from the SES storage sheds behind Mick's garage. The three women—mother and daughters, they'd said—and three men first rolled and then, in one seamless movement, slid the suddenly small and fragile frame of her son onto the device.

'Just a precaution,' someone again reassured Maggie her as all six transported Noah to the flashy Volvo station wagon that would take her son to hospital.

Her son. Her everything. 'Noah!' she gasped behind a cupped hand. For the first time in years, Maggie's trusty coping mechanisms were close to failing. She raced across to Dan, dragging him by the arm and finding it impossible to whisper when all she wanted to do was scream.

'They're telling me Noah's taken drugs, Dan. Who is that man? What's Fiona said? Have you spoken with her?'

'Calm down, Maggie.'

'Do *not* tell me what to do. Do not!' Twenty minutes ago, Maggie had been enjoying Dan's attention and warm touch. Now she couldn't stand it. 'They've run over my son.'

'He wasn't run over,' Dan said. 'He fell out of a moving vehicle when the tyres hit the median a bit hard.'

'A bit hard?' The noise to erupt from her mouth was a crazy woman's cackle. 'That's ridiculous, Dan. How does a person fall out of a car?' She looked at the Saab. 'It was enough to deploy those fancy airbags. Don't fancy convertibles have fancy seatbelts, too?'

'Yes, Maggie, but for them to be effective you have to be sitting *in* the car, not perched on the back of the seat.' Dan gripped her arm softly, protectively. Meant to sooth, she shook him away.

'And which one of them was driving while my son was … Oh, I don't know …' Maggie's voice hardened, and like a Magpie sharpens its beak on the top of the fence, she honed her words for maximum hurt. 'What do you call reckless behaviour these days, Dan? Is it Saab surfing? The good ol' ute surfing with a belly full of beer and pot not stylish enough for city idiots? You must know.'

The words were a stinging slap to Dan's face, his hurt as plain to see as the sheet lightning turning the sky from night to day. Big, plopping drops of rain fell, hitting them and speckling the surrounding ground. Maggie couldn't care less about getting wet; it was only water and she'd been drowning under the weight of responsibility for months. So, like any sinking person fearing for their life, she lashed out, grabbed the nearest person, and took them down with her. Dan Ireland was closest.

'Isn't that's right?' she insisted. 'Michael was stoned. Were you, Dan? Is that why you clowned around in a ute and why Michael died?' Silence hung between them as she waited, wanting to grab Dan and shake him and demand he admit—

Admit to what? Dan wasn't to blame, Maggie. Her anger recoiled, snaking away to that dark corner of her heart where it would again hibernate. Was she really comparing this incident to Dan's role in Michael's accident, after defending him in her head for years? Unless, deep down, she had always blamed Dan, and that's why she'd been so easily swept her away by another man. Maybe, just maybe, Maggie could blame her brother's death for everything—for the whole bloody screw-up that was her life. If Dan and Michael hadn't been hooning around, if Michael hadn't died, if her father hadn't banned her from seeing Dan, if Dan hadn't given up and left town on the back of blame. *If, if, if!*

'I know you didn't mean that, Maggie,' Dan was saying. 'You're upset.'

Maggie huffed loud and purposeful before shoving him in the chest and adding a look that clearly hurt more than any words. But she couldn't deal with Dan's pain. She had Noah to think about. Her precious son. The one person she could rely on to never abandon her, hurt her, or lie to her. The son who would not exist had life been different.

As thunder rolled overhead, a lifetime of self-doubt, disappointment, and failure converged. This was Maggie's perfect storm. She needed someone to blame, someone to hang on to, someone to rescue her. What a shame it can never be Dan Ireland. Maggie had known that much even before seeing his wife sidle up and slip a possessive hand into the crook of her husband's arm. As Tracy cast a concerned smile in Maggie's direction, she was on the verge of screaming; *I don't want your sympathy, Tracy. I want your husband.*

'Time to go, Maggie, honey.' Sara hugged her from behind. Beautiful Sara. She and Will were Maggie's reality check; a daily reminder of the difficult challenges life could have thrown at her but hadn't. Not yet, at least. 'There's room in the back, right beside Noah.' Sara directed Maggie into the split-fold seat where she'd be able to sit and stroke her son's forehead all the way to Saddleton, an impossible hour away. 'I'll follow in our car and bring you back. The benefit of all that water I drink is I'm sober.' Sara tried a smile.

Maggie reached out and took her friend's hand. 'No, I don't want you doing that. Not in your condition.'

'Stop protecting everyone else, Maggie. Think about what *you* need.'

'I am, Sara, and I don't need the responsibility of you driving at night. Besides, I won't be coming home until Noah's all right, and I'll worry about how I do that later.'

26

Rain had bucketed down all night and throughout Maggie's return drive from Saddleton in the early hours of the morning. With little sleep, other than a few naps at Noah's bedside, she'd sat on the edge of her bed and tried rubbing the heaviness from her eyes with the heels of her hands. All the action did, however, was make her eyeballs burn. They probably resembled the handset's red light that blinked each time Maggie replayed Dan's voicemail recording. How many more times would she press play before erasing the message? Before erasing last night from her own memory bank.

A loud 'Yoo-hoo' startled Maggie, catapulting her across the room without stopping to think who it might be at this hour. 'Maggie? Hello? Oh, there you are,' Tracy said, doubling back towards the now open door. 'I heard you'd made it home, finally, and Noah is okay. I'm relieved. And I realise I'm probably the last person you expected to come knocking this morning,' Tracy added. 'But here I am, Maggie, and, well, here you are. We should talk. Don't you think?'

'Talk?' Maggie blinked away the Dan Ireland Flicker-Fest that had been playing on a loop in her head all night. 'Umm...'

Where did she start? An apology for drooling over the woman's husband was probably appropriate. It just seemed utterly inadequate— laughable even. Maggie *had* flirted unashamedly. Goodness knows how far she might have let things go had it not been for Sara's calling out.

Making matters worse, Maggie had made a spectacle of herself while blaming Dan for her troubles. Tracy must have wondered what the hell was going on. If a sleep-deprived Maggie was capable of coming up with a reasonable explanation, she would use it and add a simple 'sorry' at the end—a blanket apology for both declining the invitation to talk this morning and for not declining the invitation to disappear into the darkness with the woman's husband last night.

Instead, stupidly, bewilderingly, she said, 'Sure, yes, we can talk, Tracy.' As desperate as she was to get back to Noah at the hospital, Maggie had to allow the woman an opportunity to speak her mind.

'I won't keep you long,' Tracy added as Maggie instinctively checked her wristwatch. 'You're keen to get back to your son. It's just ...'

Maggie held her breath.

'We were mates once.' Tracy smiled. 'And this was a school reunion. I meant to catch up last night, but you know me—chat, chat, chat. Plus, I need to apologise.'

'Apologise? To me? For what?'

'For not rescuing you from Dan right at the start, or at least warning you he's never been Mr Sociable. As such, I'm afraid he grabs hold of the first person who'll give him an ear. I tried finding you, but each time another person snapped me up and I lost track of time—and Dan. Forgive me?' She stopped talking long enough to laugh. 'That's why I had to catch up with you before leaving town. Flying visit. Kids, you know?'

Maggie was watching Tracy's lips move, hoping a visual would aid her comprehension, but the words barely registered. 'Kids. Yes.'

'So, here we are finally catching up—the two of us.'

'You just want to catch up?' Maggie queried.

'And to see how you are after last night's, ah, events.' She sounded almost apologetic. 'I'm relieved Noah's okay.'

'Yes, they've kept him for observation, but he refuses to wear a hospital gown so I'm picking up his sweat shorts and a T-shirt.'

'Teenage boys, eh?'

Maggie nodded. 'Callum, our local policeman, gave me a lift back a few hours ago. With a full house, I could hardly leave Ethne on her own for breakfast.'

'The dining room was empty when I came through,' Tracy said. 'The entire town must already be at the fair day. How about it?'

'How about what?' Staying awake and keeping up with Tracy's constant chatter was testing Maggie.

'A quick bite and a coffee,' the woman said. 'I can't dilly dally either.'

At any other time Maggie would have happily reminisced with an old friend, but not this friend, not now, and definitely not after last night.

'Oh, um, I planned on grabbing leftovers from the kitchen before setting off again. Maybe—'

'I used to love your leftovers,' Tracy interjected. 'I'm starved and knowing Dan once he hits the road …'

'You're leaving today?'

'That's why I hoped you'd be back from Saddleton before we headed off.' Tracy took Maggie's arm and giggled. 'Hey, remember when we used to swap lunches? Yours was heaps tastier …'

FOR FIFTEEN MINUTES TRACY HAD PRATTLED, SWITCHING THE conversation from Tracy and Maggie, to Tracy and Tracy's children, while shovelling food from her plate like a Tonka truck in a sandpit.

'Oh dear.' The woman slumped back in her seat, groaned, rubbed her stomach and belched loudly and almost proudly. 'Whoops!'

Maggie pinched back an unexpected grin. 'Too much food, maybe?'

'More like too much baby.' Tracy smoothed the fabric of her shirt to show off a barely there baby bump. 'Completely different, this one. Some mornings are worse than others. I'm just grateful my dress fitted okay last night. I was determined it would, otherwise I wasn't going to come. Poor Dan bore the brunt of my panic. I swear the man is a saint,' she added, talking while nibbling a corner of her toast. 'I shouldn't have forced him to come with me either, not that I had to force him. Dan had seemed keen, which was, well, weird, but I had been on at him for ages about his father.'

'You're pregnant?' Maggie had heard nothing else.

'Crazy, I know. And at our age. I mean, Emily and Mikey are almost fourteen,' Tracy giggled. 'Not planned, of course, and we're not telling anybody yet. Are we, sweetie?' She dropped her gaze to her belly and coochee-cooed while rubbing her palm in tiny circles. 'I'm glad I could peel Dan away from the kids to break the news gently. You know Dan.' Maggie must have been pulling a nonplussed face because Tracy went on to explain. 'What I mean is, you and he were talking a lot last night so you'd know what a fuddy-duddy he's turned into. I call him "Do the Right Thing Dan",' she chortled. 'He's a long way from that bad boy we all swooned over. He turned into a bloke who does what's expected before he does what he wants. I figured if I told him about the baby while

170

we were here and away from the kids we could nut out what happens next.'

What does happen next? Maggie wanted to ask.

'But,' Tracy continued, 'with morning sickness hard to hide, what better time to come clean than while Dan's holding my hair back as I chuck up in the toilet bowl. Come to think of it,' Tracy said with a slight tilt of her head. 'Dan looked about as shocked as you when I told him the news.'

Maggie had opened her mouth to speak but closed it again when no words came out.

'It's the age thing, no doubt. People worry,' Tracy continued. 'And men like Dan worry more than they like to let on. Best I get used to being mollycoddled again.' She giggled, child-like. 'You now, I once heard a pregnant woman describe herself as a hormone with a hairdo. Too true, if you asked me!' She slapped a hand on the table and whooped. 'If anyone had said anything about me looking fat last night, I would have exploded and blurted out why on the spot.'

Maggie didn't know how the woman was managing to breathe, eat and talk, while she struggled to watch in silence from the opposite side of the dining room table. What she did know was spending time with Tracy this morning had been a huge mistake. Spending time with Dan last night had been a bigger one.

'Maggie? Can we talk?' The voice over Maggie's left shoulder sounded familiar, only smaller, less assured.

She exhaled. *What now?* And twisted in her seat. The last face she wanted to see stared back forlornly, the usual peaches and cream complexion now a puffy, red, tear-streaked mess.

'Not a good time, Fiona. Really not good.' Maggie turned back, hoping the girl would go. She couldn't look at her. She couldn't even look at Tracy. Right now, Maggie had trouble looking at herself. 'Let me out of here!' She pushed back from the table so abruptly the chair fell over, smashing onto the floor. 'I don't want to deal with any of this. My son is my priority and he needs clean pyjamas. Tracy?' The woman's mouth hung open, the last of her toast visible. 'I am truly, truly sorry,' Maggie cried. 'About everything.'

❧

MAGGIE SLAMMED THE CAR DOOR, LOWERED HER FACE TO HER WHITE-knuckled hands clenching the steering wheel and counted to ten. She couldn't drive with tears stinging her eyes. The blistering wind and dust that would soon fill her father's old Holden would make concentrating on the road hard enough. A knock on the driver's window made her jump. It was Ethne. Maggie cranked the old window winder and blotted her cheeks with the back of her wrist.

'You okay, love?' the barmaid asked.

'You heard?' she asked.

'Love, they would've heard you in Timbuktu.'

'I'll be fine once I get back to Noah.'

'Well, I've got a Dan chappy on the phone insisting I find you.'

Maggie hesitated, considering her options. While this was the perfect time to take the call, congratulate Dan on the baby and end the nonsense, she couldn't be sure she'd make it through the first sentence without slipping back into last night's love-struck teenager. And she was far from being one of those. Maggie was a mother, and Noah was her first and only priority.

'Ethne, do me a favour and deliver a message to Dan ...' Maggie paused to reflect on her conversation with Tracy; the way she'd glowed with news of a new baby. 'Tell him family and children come first. All of them, always. I'm giving my child all my love and attention. He should do the same with his own. And tell him not to ring me again.' Maggie turned the key in the ignition. The engine rumbled and died. 'And no,' Maggie responded to her friend's curious expression. 'You can't ask, Ethne. I'm fine, but I'll be better when I'm back with Noah.'

'Awright, love,' Ethne spoke over the complaining engine Maggie forced into life. 'But try to be home before this afternoon's storm. And you'd be wise to avoid the shortcut through Cedar Cutters Gorge with those brakes of yours.'

'I'll be careful,' Maggie said. 'I want us both home safe.'

27

FIONA

Tracy took several napkins from the metal dispenser on the table and handed them to Fiona in one thick wad. 'Blow your nose, wipe your eyes, and I'll sit with you for a bit.'

'I only wanted to apologise,' Fiona spluttered.

'Maggie's upset,' the woman said. 'Understand what it's like for a mother. Children come first.'

'Not always,' Fiona mumbled. 'Mine never knew or cared if I scraped a knee.'

'I'm Tracy, and you're Amber Bailey's daughter, aren't you?'

Fiona nodded. 'How did you know?'

The woman's smile said what Fiona already knew. 'It's not hard to tell. We all went to a small school, which meant we were all friends at one point. Some better than others. Let me grab us some water.'

Tracy was back in a flash with two glasses full to the brim.

'Small-town schooling meant we were so into each other's business. Who liked who? Who didn't like who? Who liked you only because their parents, with property values in their eyes, had thrust them on you? Know what I mean?'

'I guess. Thanks for the water,' Fiona took two long gulps. 'The way my grandfather tells it, everyone liked my mother, especially the boys; only sometimes they liked her a little too much. Do you know what *I* mean?'

Tracy's eyes widened. 'Your grandfather said a thing like that about your mother?'

'Then he'd remind me I was all the best things she wasn't. "A genuine Bailey girl",' she snorted cynically. 'Nothing genuine about me at all, though.'

'But I bet you have young men fighting for your attention, just like her,' Tracy said. 'Maybe to your grandfather it looked like she dated a lot. Or he listened too hard to the school rumour mill. There were rumours, and even more bragging going on in that place. Every boy wanted to date Amber. Come to think of it,' Tracy laughed, 'even my adorable husband, Dan, went out with your mother at one stage. We were all around the same age, give or take. Dan was a little older and quite the spunk.' The chatty woman sighed, or she was stopping for air. Fiona didn't know which one. 'And I'll let you in on a little secret, too,' Tracy went on. 'While our present-day Detective Dan is both loyal husband and devoted father, he spent his youth being Calingarry Crossing's bad boy. He and his mates got into all kinds of trouble, but had he not been such a lout, Maggie and Dan might have ended up together. She had a huge crush, only her father wouldn't have a bar of him—even before the unfortunate thing with Maggie's brother. Not long after, Dan left town, went to Sydney, and a few years later we ran into each other on campus. I've always been a sucker for a man in a uniform. I see you're engaged.'

Fiona extended her hand to let motor-mouth *ooh* and *ahh* over the engagement ring.

'How lovely,' Tracy said. 'I wish you well and hope you, too, experience the euphoria of being adored. I so remember the first time Dan asked me on a coffee date. I didn't think to mind when he asked in the middle of our chat if I knew how Maggie and her dad were doing. Only later did I realise he was still punishing himself for what happened to Maggie's brother. Still holding a candle for Maggie, too, I reckoned.'

'But *you* married him,' Fiona said.

'Hell, yes!' Tracy whooped. 'I told you. Dan was—is—a spunk. But,' she said, her tone suddenly serious, 'people's lives go in different directions for different reasons and opportunities open up. Dan and I have had a fabulous life. We're both still happy and we love our kids, but I have a new guy.'

Fiona was intrigued and desperate to keep Tracy talking. This was more information about Amber's past than she'd unearthed since arriving in this tight-lipped little town. 'You and your husband are not together?'

Tracy shook her head and gulped the last of her water. 'Heavens! I do go on. Best erase half of everything I told you. Time I left.'

Tracy slid the napkin holder closer to Fiona before standing, but there were no more tears to wipe. The possibilities swirling inside her head had siphoned them away. 'Are you sure you have to go?' she asked.

'Yes, Fiona dear, I shouldn't be talking out of school—pardon the pun —but I hope my rabbiting on has helped and made you feel better.'

'Oh, it has. Thanks.'

Tracy stood and paused, both the perpetual smile and earlier unbridled banter reined in. 'If I can say one more thing before I leave you, Fiona. In my experience, the past is best left in the past. Make your own memories. And most of all, make wise choices. Dan and I loved each other but love is not a feeling as much as it is a decision. I chose to make us happen. If I'd let Dan's past with Maggie—or the fact he'd dated your mother—get in the way, I would not have enjoyed so many wonderful years with him. And I wouldn't have two gorgeous kids waiting at home to see their parents. Oh, and one more thing, Fiona. If I were you, I'd act scarce after Maggie brings Noah home. You know her nickname at school was Magpie. She's fiercely protective as a friend. I suspect even more so as a mother. You know how mothers are? I'd best get home to my own fledglings. All the best. Lovely to meet you.'

Fiona slumped back against the chair to mull over everything motor mouth had told her about Dan Ireland. The man with the police badge and the blue eyes who'd comforted Maggie last night once had a thing for her. He'd also dated Amber at school. Crossing Fiona's mind was the notion she'd been looking in the wrong place all this time. She'd let what her grandfather had said about the boy from the school footy team sway her. And while Luke had desperately wanted ex-football hero Will Travelli to be the one, the more Fiona saw Will and Sara, the more she discarded the possibility. Will was short and stocky, blond, and with nondescript greenish-brown eyes.

Luke had been the one to talk Fiona into visiting this fly-filled freaking town to look for her father, but there was nothing to say the man— whoever he was—had stayed in Calingarry Crossing after school. It was entirely possible Dan Ireland's name needed adding to the list of potential fathers, and he lived in Sydney.

'Hello Fifi.' Luke's appearance started Fiona. 'How very accommodating of the local constabulary to give me board and lodgings, only to kick me out before the sun was up. Had to sleep in my bloody car as I had no idea which room my princess was sleeping in and her phone was off.' He nodded at the leftover food on the table. 'I can see you've been worried sick.'

'They should have locked you up and thrown away the key,' Fiona said. 'What sort of moron are you, Luke? Why would you do such a thing to Noah?'

Luke smirked and straddled the seat backwards, resting his chin on his hands and feigning innocence. 'I did nothing to your boy, Fifi.'

'You gave him something. What was it?'

'He needed loosening up. I never forced the pill down his throat. I suggested he'd feel like the king of the *worrrrrrld!*' Luke threw his arms wide and laughed through a lousy impersonation of Leonardo de Caprio on the bow of the Titanic. 'Or should that be *queen* of the world?'

'Shut up!' Fiona barked. 'I told you that was a secret.'

'I was joking, Fifi. You need to loosen up, too. Luckily I had this stash hidden in my car.'

'Put those away,' she chided, taking a swipe at his hand holding the little pink pills. 'You're lucky the copper didn't find them. Time to get out of town, Luke.'

'I agree, Sherriff,' he joked. 'As did Officer Officious when I came in under the limit. Dumb-arse copper. Come on, get your gear. I've checked the Saab's good to go, but I'll drive her. Here, you take mine.' He dangled a key-ring in her face.

'You're going, Luke. Not me.' She snatched at the key-ring and sauntered away from the table, leaving him to trail behind. She exited the dining room via the beer garden and stopped in the dirt parking area out the back.

'What the fuck's going on with you, Fi?'

'I wish you wouldn't talk like that—*Lukey!*' Fiona mimicked, ending with her best smart alec smirk.

'Don't you go pissing me off.' There was nothing playful in his tug on her arm. 'Get your gear and let's get out of this dump.'

'No,' she said defiantly. 'Get your hands off me and understand no means no. Or has my grandfather programmed the word from your vocabulary? Mum told me he never liked her saying "no" to him, only at the time I didn't believe her. I believed Jack.' Fiona felt herself choking up. Who was telling the truth? Who did she trust? Who loved her consistently and unconditionally? She had thought Luke was that person.

'Fi, are you hearing me?' Luke was saying. 'If you're sticking around waiting for some epiphany to change your life like your mum did, you need not change one bit. And you sure as hell don't owe these people any explanation. You're too good for them, Fi.'

Did she tell Luke her metamorphosis was already happening? She was different and the anger and hurt she'd dumped on her mother and on Phillip was shifting—first to Jack Bailey and now to Luke.

'I'm staying in Calingarry Crossing until I know Noah's okay,' she announced. 'I owe him.'

With the hotel no longer an option, she'd stay at her grandmother's. Cheryl was nice. A little distant and, Fiona had gathered from their chats, abused by Jack and hurt by her daughter. Being hurt by Amber gave the pair something in common. Cheryl would make her granddaughter welcome. Certainly more welcome than Maggie would when she returned from the hospital with Noah.

Fiona snatched the Saab keys out of Luke's hands and jammed them into her jeans pocket. Then she walked across the car park and threw his keys on his driver's seat. 'Just go.'

'And tell your grandfather *what*? You don't want to piss him off and you know he won't be happy.'

'Tell your boss whatever you like and tell yourself and him this.' Fiona wrangled the diamond ring off her finger and forced it into Luke's palm. 'We're over.'

28

DAN

D an again swore under his breath, but the Ethne woman had already hung up, telling him—quote: 'Family and children come first. Don't ring again.' End of quote.

He wanted to believe Maggie's diktat was not in response to last night, but that of a worried mother who'd needed to be with her son. People had nicknamed her Magpie for a reason. She'd slipped into the nurturing role young, pushed too early into caring for her father and brother after Mary died. Dan understood. He knew first-hand how dysfunctional a household became without that maternal glue. No wonder the magpie had flown the second that wandering minstrel had offered her a way out. But she was back in Calingarry Crossing and what Dan had seen at the school reunion, was a Maggie not too different from the girl he remembered—tougher than she looked and fiercely protective.

Sheltering under the same porch that, as a boy, he'd sat with his father, Dan checked the time and imagined Charlie Ireland not too far away, hidden in one of the numerous sheds that dotted the old pig farm and waiting for the visitor to leave. Dan would stay fifteen minutes and not a second more. Looking from his watch to the maze of old fencing, the still and stench-free surrounds jarringly unfamiliar, Dan recalled the hard-working farmer who'd come home one day to find his wife gone. A no-nonsense third-generation man of the land, loneliness had eaten away at Charles, with hurt further shaping him into an angry, unforgiving father.

Each afternoon, when his dad stank from sweat and dust after a day in the sow shed or wrestling weaner pigs into pens, Dan would sit beside him swigging a cordial, while his father downed a bottle of home-brew. With no hugs, little conversation and less eye contact, Dan remained unnoticed; a little boy made invisible by sorrow and bitterness.

Dan had been in high school when word got out about the king brown snake that had killed the local minister's wife while she did the laundry. Dan had known little about the Lindeman family; church had never been high on Charlie Ireland's list of things to do each week. 'Don't need no one interfering with how I live,' he'd tell his sons. Only because Dan needed to connect with someone—like Maggie Lindeman who knew what life was like without a mum—did he sneak out on Sunday mornings. He'd make his way to town on the discarded dragster he'd found, resurrecting the bike by stealing parts off other kids' bikes—the kids he didn't like. If a bike was his only way of getting to church, Dan figured God would understand. He'd stop by the sprawling fig tree that dwarfed the stone church and drop his bike behind one of the alien-like buttress roots—the creepy, crawling protrusions that snaked out along the ground. Then he'd climb onto a low-slung limb and wait with his bird's-eye view as the congregation trickled out to the sounds of an organ. Only once everything went quiet did Dan know to watch the side door for the pretty organ player—the girl people called Magpie.

He snorted and shook his head, smiling at the memory of that first laughable attempt to get her attention by laying red fig tree berries in a line from the church's side door to the nearby tree. When Maggie had paused where the curious line ended, intent on finding the bird responsible, Dan had launched his round of berries.

'Quit that!' she'd yelled, clutching her head.

'I KNOW YOU'RE NOT A BIRD, SO COME OUT WHEREVER YOU ARE.'

'I didn't do it to hurt you,' Dan said from his perch, legs dangling and kicking the air.

'In that case,' Maggie rammed both hands on her hips. 'I'd suggest you shouldn't be throwing things at people.'

As he jumped from the branch, Dan slipped and landed on his backside, the jarring stop enough to rattle his brain and send his teeth deep into his bottom lip. His pride, and everything else, hurt like blazes and he felt his tears welling. He braced himself for her taunts; like his father didn't suffer sooks, neither did the kids at school.

'So, why did you?' Her arms were crossed now, her eyes—the colour of Dan's favourite Chocolate Buddies—staring at him from under the heavy fringe.

'Why did I what?'

'Throw berries at me.'

'Dunno. Coz.' Dan kicked a small stone at his feet harder than he'd intended, forgetting he only wore thongs. His boots had worn out a long time ago and he was yet to score himself a replacement pair—by hook *or* by crook. As his kick followed through, connecting with a buttress root, more searing pain and a broken thong added to his acute embarrassment.

'That'll teach you, Dan Ireland,' the girl giggled.

Dan wondered how his name flowed so readily off her lips. Was it his reputation or his father's drinking? Or perhaps his brother's running away, or his mother walking out? The Ireland family had provided plenty of fodder for the town gossips.

THE FOLLOWING SUNDAY, DAN WAS BACK IN THE FIG TREE, AND EVERY church day thereafter. Each week, after the congregation dispersed, Maggie would emerge from the church and stop on her way to the Manse. They'd talk, have berry tossing contests, ride his bike or, when it was hot, sneak down to the river. When every Sunday was no longer enough, he started hanging around Michael Lindeman. He needed more of what Maggie provided Dan. She understood losing a mother and he could be himself around her while, to the rest of the town, Dan was 'the adolescent Ireland boy'. For lots of reasons, even when puberty pushed and goaded him into making a move and asking her to the movies, Maggie and Dan never got closer than mates. He was young and insecure, she was younger still, and to townsfolk Dan would always be trouble. Besides that, her brother, Michael, became Dan's best friend and that, in best-mate-land, made little sisters off limits.

⁊

JUST AS DAN TOLD HIMSELF COMING BACK TO THE FARM HAD BEEN A monumental waste of time, a movement by the sow shed tightened the tangle of anticipation and anxiety in his stomach. Realising it was a dozen

180

wallabies standing erect and wary, he studied the the mob until they resumed their grazing. All but one.

'Look at you!' Dan spoke to the glaring buck with his muscly bulk making the animal double the size of any other. 'You're a lucky bastard to have such a brood and a good dad for protecting them.'

About ten years ago, after some gentle persuasion from his benevolent wife, Dan had re-established contact with his father—a word he'd used reluctantly in the past. He now sent occasional letters, with Emma and Mike providing ample material: birthdays, sporting achievements, class photos. One year—the kids were around four or five—the Ireland family sent a photograph taken on Santa's knee. That same year, the twins received their first-ever Christmas card reply from Grandpa Charles. Communication from both camps increased to include a call on the day, but Dan had warned Tracy not to get her hopes up for more contact than that. He'd been right.

Dan was studying his mobile phone, wanting to press the call button each time he scrolled over the Calingarry Crossing pub listing, when he checked the time.

'You win, Dad,' he called, as if Charles was avoiding him, rather than simply being old and forgetful.

Should Dan forget catching up or suggest he and Tracy stay in town and try visiting again? But with his wife always the first to flutter home once the party lights switched off, she'd be keen to go and Dan would not let the mother of his children leave alone. Of all the things this town might have labelled Dan Ireland, insensitive, untrustworthy and disloyal were not among them. He was none of those things. Not now and not when he'd taken hold of his best mate's hand, taken him to hospital, then taken the blame.

While waiting on the front porch of his childhood home, because physically setting foot inside would whip awake the demons that Dan's wife and children had kept dormant all these years, Dan contemplated moving from their friend's farm into the pub accommodation for a night. Dan might bump into his dad, or into Maggie. He'd known she was living back in Calingarry Crossing. He'd made enquiries about her through his detective network. He'd done so because Dan didn't like surprises. Facts were an investigator's best friend. If his conscience had let him, he would have delved deeper. Instead, he convinced himself hearing Maggie's story from her own lips held a lot more appeal for a man in need of a distraction. And distraction he'd achieved, even though kissing Maggie had not factored in any plan. Then again neither had Tracy's baby news, which Dan was still coming to terms with. Was he surprised? *You bet.* Happy? *Of course.* Frustrated? Confused? Concerned? *Yes. Yes. Yes.*

At least the woman on the phone earlier had been gracious enough to let Dan know Maggie's son was doing okay after his clash of pills, booze and joy riding. Last night's contributing factors hadn't been hard to spot for a seasoned investigator. If only there was a way to put old heads on young necks Dan would happily not have his job. He'd start a new career; one that didn't involve scraping kids off the road and telling their parents the sad news.

For most cops, the death knock was a task that happened too frequently, even in the country where young driver casualties and deaths out-numbered the city stats, but after twenty-odd years of trying to effect change, nothing was different. More young drivers died from crashes than any other driver group, and those figures didn't include the close shave or near miss that went unreported—or was just not remembered in the morning. The difference between kids and older drivers? Experience. The difference between one kid dying and the next? Luck. Even the brightest, most-loved and best-raised kids, like Noah, became idiots once alcohol and pills entered the mix. One drink will make a kid feel invincible and any sense of right and wrong, good and bad, smart and stupid will be dangerously compromised. They just didn't get the fragility of life because being reckless was part of growing up. Extreme sports and extreme risks meant extreme consequences. Noah knew all about those; now so does his poor mum whose anguish last night haunted Dan still. He'd wanted to comfort her, but she'd shaken his attempts away, wanting no part of him then, or in the harsh light of day, according to Ethne's message.

'And she has a blasted husband. Who's the idiot now, Ireland?' Dan slammed the door on the borrowed ute, buckled up, turned the ignition, and put his foot down. 'Take that, you old bastard,' he shouted as spinning wheels sent a cloud of dust billowing over the roof of his father's old house.

Driving away like a petulant youth, Dan had to acknowledge everyone took risks. The risks were just different when you were older: right and wrong, good and bad, smart and stupid. Dan knew all about those now, too. But Maggie *had* kissed him back. The thought calmed Dan, his foot easing off the accelerator. She had … Hadn't she?

29

MAGGIE

'Do you want some lunch, Noah?'

Her bruised and battered son didn't speak or attempt to move his head on the pillow. He didn't even open his eyes to see Maggie dab away her anger, her disappointment, and the urge to interrogate her son. There was, thankfully, no rush. They had time to address all those issues once Noah was well.

Slowly and quietly she slid his bedroom window closed before switching the rarely used air conditioner up a notch. The hospital discharge notes mentioned bed rest, but with the menacing sky that had followed Maggie from Saddleton growing more ominous, her son's west-facing room would end up a sweatbox.

'Mum?' Noah was groggy still. 'I'm sorry.'

'Hey, you have nothing to be sorry for, Noah. You need to rest. We'll talk later,' she said while fussing with the sheet speckled brown with Beta-dine ointment. 'I love you, no matter what.'

Leaning over to kiss his forehead, Maggie liked that he didn't pull away, screw up his face or complain. Then, with a sneaky glance, she drew the door closed behind her and let out a shaky breath, relieved the weekend was almost over. More than anything, Maggie Lindeman wanted her quiet country life back.

☙

NORMALITY RETURNED SLOWLY—MAGGIE'S VERSION OF NORMAL, THAT IS. Ethne had returned from her Saturday night off all sprightly and smiling and happily covering for Maggie while she fitted her nursing home trips around Noah's needs; Will and Sarah stayed low, unsurprisingly, given Will's big weekend, which left Jennifer to bask in the glory of a successful event to the point of implying she'd somehow, miraculously, kept the rain at bay for the fair day. While work had meant Maggie missed the entire Sunday event, the reports filtering into the pub over the days that followed were all good.

Dan was long gone but remained a constant thought in Maggie's mind, and in the text messages on her phone. His latest asked her to call him. She didn't. Another request to call arrived via the hotel email address. Again, Maggie didn't respond, pressing delete before Ethne or Noah saw the contents. Her son, still contrite and physically hurting from the massive bruising down one side of his ribs and thigh, was moving about more freely but not venturing far from his room. Grazes on both legs, superficial and drying nicely, had needed regular saline baths, but he'd refused his mother's help, suddenly sensitive about his privacy and his mother's inability to 'chill'. When Maggie raised her concerns with Ethne over Noah's unusually coy behaviour, the wise old barmaid had suggested it was likely an acute case of embarrassment.

❧

'I'M BACK, ETHNE!' MAGGIE CALLED THROUGH THE KITCHEN SERVERY. She'd woken early to visit her confidante—the old mare down the road— before a flying visit into Saddleton to sort her dad's dirty clothes from clean ones and play tug-o-war with the putrid blue bath rob. As a result, it was past the lunch rush by the time she'd parked the old Holden behind the residence, stopping at the laundry on the way in. 'Sorry I'm so late.'

'All okay here, love' the woman replied. 'Our boy is doing fine.'

Our boy! What a lovely thing to hear. Someone else caring, someone else being there for Maggie gave her a lightness of step as she slipped behind the bar and noticed Ethne's hands were crimson from peeling beetroot.

'He's learned a hard lesson,' Maggie replied.

'Still sore and sorry,' Ethne added.

'Hmm, not so sore he can't sit up and Facebook, or whatever it is he does on that old laptop.' As Maggie shoved a rack of glasses into the washer and pressed the green button, the soft whir of motor helped mute the meagre mid-week mob in the main bar.

Straightening, a hand pressed to the small of her back, Maggie scanned the reassuringly familiar faces sitting—some standing—in their usual spots in the bar and lounge area. The only anomaly was Fiona: primped and painted and loitering in the doorway to the beer garden. Against a backdrop of dusty work shirts and dungarees, she looked like a mournful swan in a pond full of quacking ducks.

As if waiting for permission, and with Maggie too shaken to deny her, the girl made her way towards the bar, her once conceited chin not so proud. 'Can I see Noah, please?'

Maggie's first instinct was to strike out a warning paw, like a lioness protecting her cub. 'No, Fiona.'

'I can't blame you for being mad, and I *am* so sorry, Maggie.' The girl took two tentative steps closer, but Maggie didn't lift her gaze from the tray of steaming glassware. 'I didn't know what Luke had done, or that he had pills. Honestly. Besides, they weren't dangerous.'

Maggie slammed the glass-washer rack on the bar with such force the room fell silent, albeit briefly. 'Not dangerous, Fiona?'

'No! They were only supposed to—'

'Only what?' Maggie growled. 'There is no *only* with drugs, Fiona. What is it kids don't get?'

'Noah was anxious about something and Luke thought—'

'Wrong, Fiona. Luke didn't think, and neither did you. That's the real problem. And if Noah was anxious, I'd know.' Maggie picked up glasses one at a time from the rack, strangling each one with a tea towel. 'My son is my life. I've protected him since he was a baby and I will do anything to protect him until my final breath. That's what mothers do, Fiona. It's also what friends do for friends.' She flicked the tea towel onto her left shoulder and stared down the pathetic-looking princess. 'Genuine friendship comes with trust and for some reason Noah's taken a liking to you. Then you let this happen. Mates care about each other. At least, we do out here in the country.'

Fiona's face turned the colour of Ethne's beetroot fingers, her eyes bulging and her lips so thin her Siena Sunset looked well and truly set.

'Oh, yeah, sure, everyone's holier than thou out here,' she hissed the words. 'Must be something in the freaking water that makes all mothers freaking saints.'

'Fiona—' Maggie wanted to warn, but the girl cut her off.

'Mothers like to think they know everything about their children, Maggie. Even bad mothers like mine.'

'Amber wasn't bad, Fiona, your mother just—'

'My mother didn't see me.' Fiona was shouting. 'The most important thing in Amber's life was Amber. I was invisible to her, until twelve months ago when suddenly it was acceptable to interfere with my life and tell me what I can and can't do, like marry Luke.'

'I'm sure it wasn't about interfering. Amber was trying to connect with you, Fiona.'

'Why?' The girl stiffened. 'I've managed perfectly fine without a mother. I didn't need one. I didn't need *her*.'

Max Factor's Maximising something-or-other was evidently *not* tear proof as the combination of anger, perspiration and tears played havoc with the girl's perfect paintwork. The mother in Maggie wanted to walk over to the miserable melting mess and give her the kick in the pants she needed, while the magpie's instinct was to gather Fiona up in her protective wings and shield her from predators like Luke. Instead, fearful the anger simmering away inside would boil over, and intent on saving her compassion for her son, Maggie didn't do either. 'Where is this Luke person now?' she asked.

'He's gone back to Sydney.'

'Good. I suspect you'll be following him soon, Fiona. That would be best.'

'Not until I've seen Noah,' Fiona said.

Maggie bristled. 'Obviously I can't force you to leave town, but I can tell you to stay away from my pub and my son.'

'Mum, please!' Noah's voice startled her.

He stood in the doorway between the kitchen and the bar, still wearing his track-pant pyjamas, his hair jutting out at strange angles, and shadows under his eyes darkened further from the bruising. He'd heard her tirade. Old hard-of-hearing Joe probably heard it in Saddleton.

'To bed, Noah.'

'But Mum—' He pleaded all the way back to his room with Maggie on his heels like a working dog mustering a wayward lamb. 'I have a killer headache.'

'Is it any wonder?' she snapped. 'The doctors said rest, and that doesn't mean staring at a computer. Get into bed and I'll get tablets for the pain.' Maggie closed down the lid on the laptop while her son huffed, fell back on the unmade bed and crossed muscled arms across a broadening chest sprouting downy hair.

'You don't have to treat me like a kid. I'm not.'

'Oh, so you grew up overnight?' Exasperated, Maggie began collecting clothes from the far reaches of the floor and from door handles and hooks. 'Do alcohol, drugs and betraying your mother's trust make you an adult?' She grunted the last few words as the defiant top drawer of his tallboy—jammed with a black T-shirt—finally gave in to Maggie's unrelenting tug. Not bothering to remove the offending garment and refold it, she punched the bulge and slammed the drawer shut again. 'I don't think so, Noah Henkler.'

'But, Mum, it wasn't Fi's fault. Luke is a dickhead.'

'You got that right,' she quipped. 'I trusted you, Noah, and I thought I could trust Fiona.'

'I was wrong to let them have the drinks, but that's all I did,' Noah said. 'Fi didn't know about the pills. You can't blame her. It was my fault. Blame me.'

Maggie staggered to a stop and stared at her son, not knowing whether to be angry or proud. He was everything his father wasn't: loyal, honest, accepting, trustworthy, caring. 'Why are you protecting her, Noah? I know you told me you're just friends, but ...' She eased herself onto the mattress as if the bed might bite. 'Oh Noah, you're not ... You and Fiona aren't ... You're not ...?'

'Geez, Mum. No way!' Noah's face looked like it was about to explode and Maggie was sorry she'd asked, although kind of relieved. 'I like her, but not that way. She's more the sister I've always wanted. You know, someone to give a hard time.' Noah shrugged, smiling sheepishly. 'We get on like mates.'

'Good.' Maggie scanned the room, looking for more things to straighten, to pick up, to fuss over. At least having asked the question, her praying mantis dreams might stop. 'Mind you, Noah, mates don't let mates nearly kill themselves doing a Leonardo di Caprio off the back of a car.' She smiled while smoothing his fringe off his face to look into the blue eyes she loved so much. 'I gather you don't recall what happened; maybe that's just as well.' Maggie wanted to forget it herself, while Noah had learned a hard lesson. In a way not too different from when the Rev had made her smoke an entire packet of cigarettes after catching her puffing away in the toilet out the back. She'd been sick as a dog for days. 'You could have really hurt yourself badly, bud. You might've …' She avoided comparing the incident to Michael's accident aloud. That had been about mates having fun, too. Yes, there'd been alcohol, and whatever else.

'But I'm okay, Mum, and even though it wasn't her fault, Fi said she wants to make it up to you.'

'To me? You saw Fiona? Before today?' Maggie tensed. 'When?'

'She messaged me on Facebook to say I could go back to Sydney and stay with her sometime.'

Panic catapulted Maggie off the bed. 'Not in my lifetime, Noah, and if she makes more ridiculous offers there'll be no more Facebook for you. Understood?'

Noah huffed, slammed his arms tighter against his chest and sank back onto his pillows. 'But I could stay with Dad.'

'No,' she answered, even though it wasn't a question. 'Your father's in no fit state. He can hardly look after himself, let alone …' The words had slipped out before Maggie could stop them and she found herself staring at her son's luxuriously long lashes blinking in bewilderment.

'What's "no fit state" mean?' he asked.

'Nothing. That's not what I meant. I'm tired and annoyed and not thinking.'

Maggie slumped back down onto the bed, prepared to give anything for one *smuddle* with her son. The adorable fusion of a smell and a cuddle was her favourite thing, born from those early days when, as a freshly bathed baby, all warm and sweet-smelling, she and Noah would cuddle until he fell asleep. How Maggie longed for those days again. Puberty had meant settling for a hand on her son's arm—an arm with wounds that would likely leave visible scars. More grazes littered Noah's chin, making her think about Dan Ireland's jaw. Hardly a badge of honour. He'd ridden his dirt bike into a boundary fence, the barbs tearing the flesh off his cheek. Doctor Wynter had said, if the wire had pierced his skin any lower, Dan could have died. And because it happened not long after Michael's accident—which everyone blamed on Dan, as the driver of the ute—some locals seemed convinced Dan had ridden his bike into that fence on purpose.

Only after seeing him at the reunion had Maggie recalled the bike incident, the berry throwing, and the almost-broken toe, but that's what reunions did. They brought home memories, and not all memories were pleasant ones.

'Mum? Mum, are you listening?'

'Hmm?' Maggie's attention switched back to her son. 'Sorry. What?'

'Dad … Is he all right?'

'Your father's fine, Noah. He's working and under a lot of stress.' The lies were back and flowing.

'Well, if he's stressed and in no fit state, what are we doing out here?'

Tempted to reply *making a living and keeping this family afloat*, Maggie clamped down on the sarcasm, offering instead, 'Your father can look after himself.'

'But, Mum, how do we know if we're living in this crummy town?'

In a burst of impatience Maggie said, 'All of a sudden it's a crummy town, Noah?'

'There's nothing to do here. I got my Ls first go, but I can't get my licence because you say you can't give me enough driving practice on all road types, and you don't trust anyone else. If I was in Sydney, Dad could teach me to drive in the traffic.'

'Noah, I've told you before, it's the car. Until I can afford to get the engine and brakes checked, I don't want you driving it.'

'Just 'cause Uncle Mike died in a car accident doesn't mean I will. I'm eighteen soon; you can't stop me doing what I want.'

Maggie dragged in a sharp breath along with the sob hidden in it. 'Then act your age, Noah, and don't test me today. I'll bring your dinner up,' she said, walking away so her son wouldn't see the tears in her eyes.

❧

ETHNE POKED HER NOSE AROUND THE CORNER OF THE KITCHEN WHERE Maggie stood, staring at the plate of soft cheese and crackers. 'Is it safe in here yet?' she asked, smiling.

'I'm not sure what will be my undoing. Noah or living off cocktail party leftovers. How long does cheese last?'

'Not as long as wine keeps, so eat more and go easy on the vino, eh?' Ethne suggested. 'I've finished closing up. Can I do anything else for you? Make a proper meal?'

'Tell me you think I'm a good person, Ethne.'

'Awright, love, easy enough. You're a good person. What this about?'

'Noah said something earlier today about me not being there for his father.'

'Listen, love, you know me,' the barmaid said. 'Kids, real ones—not those overgrown louts at the bar every night—aren't my area of expertise but I doubt your son means anything by it. He loves you and his dad. Maybe he's worried. Kids pick up signals.'

Maggie nudged a cracker around the plate with the tip of her finger. 'Noah's always been so easy-going. When he got to seventeen without drug and alcohol problems I thought I was one of the lucky ones. I know he loves us both, but that's all I seem to know about him lately. He promised me that night was his first experience with party drugs, but something's changed in him and I'd hate to think it was me dragging him out here.'

Ethne walked over and wrapped Maggie in an effusive embrace. 'Every kid pushes the boundaries when they're growing up,' she said. 'Even the good ones.'

'And my job is to protect him,' Maggie mumbled into the softness of Ethne's shoulder. 'I don't know what to do. I'd hoped coming home to the country would be the right move.'

'Kids find their own path, eventually. If they step off, you push back a little, guide them and nudge them away from sharp edges. But unless you're planning on clipping his feathers, Mama Bird, he's going to jump out of your nest one day and give his wings a serious workout.'

Maggie pulled away, smiled. 'You know more about kids than you think.'

Ethne snorted. 'I get to practice on those louts in the public bar. Believe me, love, you're a good mum.'

'Then why doesn't a mother see her child growing into a man?'

Holding Maggie at arms-length, her friend replied. 'Because they don't want them to grow into a man. You know the saying? A son's your son 'til he takes a wife; a daughter's your daughter for the rest of her life. You're wanting to hang on for as long as you can, Magpie. No different to any other mother. But it's you *I* worry about.'

'Why me?'

'The way you hide yourself away a little too much. You also have a life to live, love. You want to be enjoying it, not just looking after everyone else. Noah's getting to an age where you can start letting go a little. Look after yourself.'

'I'm not *not* living, Ethne.'

'I'm just saying, like them magpies you love, there comes a time when the juveniles are pushed aside to make way for the new ones.'

'Well, there are no new ones coming this magpie's way.' Unlike Tracy Ireland, Maggie silently reminded herself.

'I'm talking about making way for you,' Ethne said. 'In my experience, a neglected pot left on the stove to simmer will eventually boil dry. You don't want those juicy bits drying up too soon.'

'Your point?' Maggie's impatience showed as she fought back images of a luminous and still-juicy Tracy.

'You need to turn up the heat a little, stir things up, love. Put some excitement in your life.'

'I reckon I've had enough excitement to last me a lifetime.' Maggie sipped her wine and nudged the leftover crackers away. 'Not letting go of Noah isn't about me being alone either. As hard as I try to hang on, all the people I love slip away. I don't want my son leaving the minute he turns eighteen, and while I'm mad as hell at Fiona, she's not the evil witch I've manifested in my head; especially now I know Noah sees her as a friend and that's all.'

'I see,' Ethne chortled. 'And how did we draw such a conclusion?'

'I asked him. Straight out. He told me.'

'And you believe him?'

'Ethne, there's one thing about the Henkler boys. There's this thing they both do with their face when they're telling a porky. I can't explain it, but I'd know if he was lying. He's not interested in Fiona that way. She is not a problem.'

'Whatever you say, love.'

'That fiancé of hers—that Luke—worries me. He's so much older and Amber's father seems to be a never-ending source of conflict. At the funeral, Phillip gave the impression he wasn't at all happy about his influence on Fiona.'

Ethne leaned against the cool-room door, struggling to fold her arms across her ample breast. 'There's no better jury than the main bar on a Friday night, and as I recall, there were always plenty of opinions about that snake, Jack Bailey. None of 'em was good. If you ask me, he was a greedy, no good, son-of-a-bitch, and if he'd had his way, the Dandelion House estate would've been chopped up and sold off after old Gypsy passed away. Glad the old duck was smart enough to know it, and even smarter to leave the place to those girls.'

'But I can't imagine why a developer would want a chunk of land practically surrounded by water and virtually impossible to reach by car.'

'Not a developer,' Ethne said. 'Jack himself. I heard he'd had geology reports done years ago.'

'Looking for what? And if you tell me there's gold in *dem dere hills* you'd best prepare to race me.' Maggie laughed.

'Jack Bailey was always the type to want what he couldn't have, and he acquired things—people included—to stop anyone else from getting it. Old Barney told me Jack once cut in on a farmer from further west to sweep Cheryl off her feet and to impress Cheryl's well-to-do father. Making a buck and big-noting himself drove Jack Bailey. Owning something as unique as Dandelion House fit the bill. In my opinion, and I wasn't the only one to say so, his leaving town was the best thing to happen to Cheryl Bailey.'

Maggie was surprised. 'A marriage between Amber and the philanthropic Phillip Blair must have been like winning Lotto for the man you've described.'

'Like I said, love, Jack was all about winning any way he could.'

Maggie walked to the sink and tipped the last of her wine out, refilling the glass with water. 'Are you suggesting he's using Fiona?'

'I can only tell you Jack married to get ahead, used his own daughter to make himself look good, and he used Phillip to climb the Sydney social ladder.' Ethne went on. 'The autumn Amber stayed at Dandelion House was her wake-up call, especially when she discovered Jack had abused her mother. Luke looks to me like he has the makings of a young Jack, 'cept he's got his hands full with Fiona. Not as pliable as Cheryl was back then.'

'Oh?' Maggie queried. 'What makes you say that?'

'I happened to eavesdrop on Fiona and Luke on the Sunday. Heard her telling him to bugger off—engagement ring and all. Could be this thing with Noah has brought the girl to her senses and let her see what's important, like her mother did when she was here. Fiona's got to wake up sometime. Get rid of the boyfriend, get rid of the grandfather, and the girl might have a chance.'

Maggie sighed. 'And I kicked her out of the pub.'

'Oh no, you don't, Magpie,' Ethne chirruped. 'Feel sorry for the girl, sure, but she needs to fix her own problems. Now.' The barmaid picked up the plate and wine glass. 'How about you take yourself off somewhere? I'll look after things and do the breakfast shift tomorrow.'

'Thanks, Ethne, but I need to stay busy. I'll do brekkie.'

'Awright, love, but only because I know Luke has left town. Otherwise I'd worry about you dishing out a big manly serving of arsenic cereal.'

'And why not?' Maggie grinned—genuinely, for the first time in days. 'He served up a dose of God knows what chemicals to my son.'

'I know, love. Forgiveness—remember?'

30

C har-grilled salmon fillet and a warm honey mustard & corriander beetroot salad w/ minted cucumber.

'Yum,' Maggie said after reading the A-frame chalkboard on the veranda. 'But I think there's only one R in coriander, Ethne.'

The barmaid snorted. 'You think any of this lot will know or care if there's one, two or twenty? They see double most nights.'

'Good point! Here.' Maggie handed over the requested takeaway hot chocolate as the pair headed back to the bar. Apparently, nobody made hot chocolate better than Will. Or put six marshmallows on top.

'Sun's over the yardarm,' Barney said from his usual barstool. 'What's a bloke gotta do to get a beer?'

'Hold your horses, ya old bugger,' Ethne growled, turning back to Maggie. 'Things are definitely back to normal.'

'Except Fiona's still in town,' Maggie said, prising the plastic lid away from the paper cup. 'She and her grandmother were leaving the café as I arrived.'

'And I saw her in the beer garden yesterday while you were visiting your dad,' Ethne informed before licking the chocolate foam from the inside of the lid. 'And looking sheepish with the Drysdale boys and old Jim from out at Warnersvale. All seemed innocent enough.'

'Innocent?' Maggie harrumphed.

'Heard her asking Jim a few questions,' Ethne said, snatching a schooner glass in one hand and tilting it under the Tooheys Old tap. 'I'm thinking she's never heard about curiosity killing the cat.'

'What sort of questions was she asking?'

'Mostly about her mother and that muck-up day when young Willow died. Jim was around Amber's age. Here ya go, ya old bugger.' After slamming the schooner on the towelling bar runner in front of Barney, Ethne wiped beer from her hands. 'Should keep ya quiet for five minutes.'

Maggie couldn't recall the detail from twenty-odd years ago, and with Fiona occupying her thoughts she had no headspace to try.

'How can I stay mad at her when, until recently Fiona had never heard of Calingarry Crossing, much less suspect her mother grew up in the country. Makes me wonder how I'd feel if I found out the person I needed the most hadn't trusted me enough to be honest. I might have trouble forgiving them and I'm a grownup. Fiona's young and spoilt, but—'

'Don't forget arrogant,' Ethne added. 'And selfish, and shallow, and pompous ...' Ethne sipped her hot drink, the Mount Everest of milk froth building at the corners of her mouth and prompting Maggie to run a finger over her own lips in case.

'You have to feel sorry for her a bit,' she told Ethne. 'And I can't afford to alienate Fiona and risk alienating Noah.' For some reason, her son had connected with the girl.

'Most kids are smarter than we give 'em credit for,' Ethne said, unpacking the Keno cards and small red pencils from the box on the bar. 'And most secrets eventually come out.'

Maggie thought of the secrets she was protecting Noah from. Keeping his father's lifestyle from him went against everything she believed about trust and honesty.

'One thing I heard the girl ask old Jim was if her mother and that Dan chappy of yours—the persistent one you've been busy avoiding—were an item.'

'He is no chappy of mine,' Maggie insisted.

'Just saying, is all,' Ethne chirruped. 'Seems Fiona thinks he has some of those answers she's craving.'

'Honestly, Ethne, I'm not being mean when I say this, but if you'd listened to the gossip when we were at school ... Seriously, Amber Bailey got up to no good with so many boys. How much or how often she—you know—did it, I couldn't guess.'

'No doubt about it, love. The reputation we give ourselves while we're still kickin' will be the one we leave behind when we die.' Ethne polished glass after glass with perfunctory proficiency, then in an odd display of diplomacy lowered her voice and nodded towards the end of the bar. 'Like I was saying to old Barney before, does he want people to remember him as the bloke who never finished the boat in his backyard? Told him to pull his finger out, I did.'

Maggie chuckled, loving the way Ethne's eyes sparkled when she talked about Barnacle Bill. Why the barmaid had bestowed such a nickname on the man, Maggie didn't know. Possibly because of the boat, but more likely the name had something to do with the way he clung to the bar most nights. She called him a good barnacle—whatever that meant.

'From what I know, Ethne, if Amber and Dan ever did *it*, then he was one of goodness knows how many. So Fiona will need more than a chat with a few locals to find out who Amber got it on with on that night in particular, as opposed to any other—'

A sound coming from the adjacent dining room silenced both women. The pair turned around to find a bewildered, blinking Fiona staring back.

'Oh, gosh, Fiona.' Maggie's face grew hot. 'I'm sorry, I shouldn't have said that.'

The girl didn't respond straight away. She instead stood perfectly still, face scrunched, her brain possibly processing the words. She looked younger without a skerrick of makeup on her face, and shorter without a heel on her shoes. Wearing slippers in the middle of the day made her look child-like, small, sad, vulnerable. Then, as if injected with a dose of couldn't-care-less, she flapped a hand so violently she had to grab the doorframe to stop from falling.

'Don't apologise, marvellous Maggie.'

Slurred speech, wobbly boots and glassy eyes were not an unusual sight in a pub, except on a twenty-two-year-old girl and in the middle of the day.

'I guess everyone can't be wrong about my mother.' Fiona tripped towards the bar and when Maggie moved to help, Ethne tugged her back.

'Leave her be, Mother Magpie,' she whispered. 'A fall might do her some good.'

With a stern look and a whispered, 'Another patient is the last thing I need,' Maggie shifted to the front of the bar, ready to catch the girl should the need arise. 'Fiona, are you all right?'

'I'm just *grrrrreat*,' she announced. 'Although darling Amber will tell you I've never been quite good enough.' She raised a hand to flick her hair over one shoulder, missing her target entirely. 'I'm not even close to being like marvellous Amber—the *amaaazing* person that *eeeveryone* wanted to be around, like she was some kind of lucky charm. You know the sort: get a picture, be seen, rub shoulders and you too might be as *faaab-u-lous* as Amber Bailey-Blair.'

'Fiona,' Maggie said, dragging the bar stool under the girl's butt and making her sit. 'Don't judge your mother. We all did things when we were young. Kids make mistakes and bad choices, too.'

'Like one too many drinks,' Ethne mumbled, stifling a chuckle when Fiona's elbow slipped on the edge of the bar and her head jerked forward.

Maggie shot Ethne a warning look before addressing Fiona. 'Listen to me. It's what we do after those wrong choices, when we've grown up.'

'Here ya go, love.' Ethne slid a glass of water under Fiona's nose. 'Get that down ya gob and I'll give you another one.'

'Fiona, your mother had decisions made for her,' Maggie said. 'I understand it was similar for her mother—for Cheryl. They were easily controlled, but they both found the courage to stand up to your grandfather. You, too, can take control of your life.'

'Like you did, Maggie?' Fiona asked, brightening. 'I can't imagine anyone controlling you. Noah is *sooo* lucky to have you for a mum.'

Ethne slid the metal serviette dispenser along the bar and rolled her eyes. Maggie mouthed thank you and tugged out several paper napkins, shoving them in the hand not propping Fiona's bobbing head.

'Fiona, honey, I saw your mum for the first time in twenty years the night she arrived at Dandelion House and I can tell you, by the time she left Calingarry Crossing, she had wanted to make things right with you.'

'Well, she took her time about it.'

'Knowing where to start can be hard,' Maggie said.

'The truth would be a fairly universal starting point, wouldn't it?' Fiona asked, sounding sober all of a sudden.

Maggie didn't bother hiding the exasperation in her voice. 'Fiona, I'm not here to defend your parents' decision to keep the truth from you. This is a conversation for you and Phillip. Work on re-establishing a relationship with him. Once you have that, there won't be cause for secrets. You'll trust each other enough to sit down and talk about what matters.'

'Hmm, yeah, I understand. Like you and Noah, you mean?'

Maggie's nod was tentative. She stood and fetched a plastic bottle of Mount Franklin mineral water, loosened the screw-top lid and put it on the bar in front of Fiona. 'Take this, Fiona. I think it might be best if you sleep it off at Cheryl's.'

The girl looked up, her stare a challenge. 'So you and Noah talk about what matters? You don't keep secrets?'

Maggie considered her reply, keen to end whatever this was before it escalated. 'Noah and I do have a close and honest relationship.'

'So he can't possibly be keeping anything from you,' Fiona said, pointedly.

Something about the girl's tone was setting off warning bells in Maggie's head. What she'd thought was an apology was smelling like a set-up. If the girl's demeanour was because of booze, she was starting to sound like a vicious drunk.

'Enough, Fiona.' No way was Maggie prepared to make Noah a part of whatever this conversation was about. 'I'm suggesting you take this bottle and leave.'

'Hmm,' the girl said as if contemplating a request.

Maggie engaged her I'm-not-taking-any-crap-from-you voice. 'I don't know what you're getting at, Fiona. If this is to stir up trouble, or about Noah going to Sydney, he's already told me about your offer and I can assure you he's going nowhere with you, in that car or any other car. I am responsible for him until he's eighteen. I get to make the choice for him.'

'Not all his choices,' the girl mumbled loud enough for Maggie to hear. 'Noah is capable of making some pretty major life decisions without his mother's approval, which is why he wants to go to Sydney. Plus, he wants to talk to his dad. He misses him.'

Ethne's hand on Maggie's arm was firm, but it would take more than that soon. 'Noah doesn't need his father, Fiona,' she said, the sharpness in her voice surprising even Maggie. 'My son knows he can talk to me about anything.'

'Except about being gay.'

Maggie blinked to orientate the thought in her brain. 'What?'

'He *has* talked to you about that, right?'

Maggie backed away, not trusting herself. She'd never felt so close to lashing out. Then again, she'd never had her world bumped off its axis in this way, everything shifting out of kilter.

'Awright, girlie, that's it.' Ethne swung open the hinged counter, dropping it hard as she passed through to the public side of the bar. 'Time you left and sobered up.'

Fiona tried to shake the woman off. 'Let me go, you old bag. I'm not a baby.'

'If it looks like a brat, smells like a brat, and acts like a brat, in my experience it's generally a brat,' Ethne said, 'so get on out of here. Shoo!'

By now, most pub patrons had made themselves scarce, except for a couple of blokes playing pool and Barney and Louie firing up the jukebox. The Troy Cassar-Daley number tried, but there was no covering the hysterics at the bar.

'Noah's gay, Maggie,' Fiona shouted while attempting unsuccessfully to fend Ethne off. 'Let me go, you old witch. I'm trying to help Maggie. He's confused and too embarrassed to talk to her. He wants to tell his dad.'

'You might be wise to stop helping,' Ethne said, dodging Fiona's thrashing arms. 'And you, Maggie love, get yourself upstairs. I'll take care of things down here. Oi! You lot. Out!' she screamed. 'And you, Barnacle, can get over here and make yourself useful for once. Get this girl back to Cheryl Bailey's.'

Louie, whose nickname was The Fly because he worked for the council in waste management, stuck to his mate like a fly and sniggered. 'Now this I gotta see. The Barnacle rollin' someone else out the hotel door instead of the other way around.'

'Help him, you useless lump of dried cow dung. Get her to Cheryl's. She'll know what to do.'

Maggie wanted to get out. She would love nothing more than to escape the claustrophobic fug in the bar. Inside she screamed, *Get out! Get air!* But her body could barely muster the energy to move one foot in front of the other.

FIONA

The barmaid delivered a schooner of icy water and a warning. 'You've got a hide showing your face around here this morning, girlie. You'd best be on your way quick-smart.'

'Will she talk to me?'

'Maggie?' Ethne snorted. 'You're lucky she was raised to forgive. Anyone else would've knocked your block off for blurting out stuff that's none of your business. You're lucky I didn't. What did you think you were doing?'

'I didn't think.'

'No, because you were whacked out of your head. You need to start learning from all these mistakes.'

'I don't do drugs,' Fiona stated. 'Just pills. Luke left some behind. And I only took one. That's all there was, I swear.'

'Just pills!' Ethne's frenzied wiping of the bar kicked her wobbly arms into overdrive. 'Blokes who push pills on kids—on anyone—are parasites. That one of yours is worse. He's a bad barnacle if ever I saw one.'

Fiona whimpered as her frown sent a searing pain shooting across her forehead. 'A bad what?'

'There are good and bad barnacles,' Ethne explained. 'Bad ones are the worst kind of blasted parasite. The sneaky bastards attach themselves to anything they can, but always under the waterline to stay undetected—until the damage is done, that is. There they grow, getting stronger and feeding off their unsuspecting host. Those bad barnacles you've gotta scrape away good and quick before they suck you dry or drag you under.'

Fiona slid the glass towards Ethne for a refill, her other hand supporting her head that was growing heavier with every weird word sprouting from the barmaid's mouth. 'What *are* you on about?'

'Pesky, petty bastards like your Luke, pretending to be an oyster and thinking no one will notice he's actually a bad barnacle. You mark my words, girlie. The longer you allow blokes to stay attached, the harder they are to rid. And don't be fooled. No matter how much they might look like an oyster, a worthless barnacle can never produce a pearl, no matter how hard they try. Makes no sense keeping one around, does it?'

'How do you know I'm not a bad barnacle?' Fiona asked.

'Because I know my oysters from my barnacles,' the barmaid said matter-of-factly. 'Genuine oysters produce pearls. Their beauty is inside.' Ethne carved chunks of fresh lemon and with little regard for the splash factor on Fiona's shirt let the wedge plop into the glass. 'I believe there's a pearl in you, Fiona, but don't let yourself get caught up with the bad barnacles.'

'Why would you think that about me after yesterday?' she asked.

Ethne shook out a tea towel to wipe her sweaty brow before tucking a corner in the top of her apron. 'Because there's a certain irony in the creation of a pearl,' she said. 'A single grain, chosen from a sea of sand, grows and grows until it's irritated the bejesus out of the oyster and bingo! A pearl.'

Fiona fought through her hangover to understand. 'You're saying I have some growing to do, or that I'm annoying the whatever it was out of you?'

'The bejesus,' Ethne clarified. 'I'm not saying every regular barnacle is bad and every oyster forms pearls. Sometimes an irritation is just that— a blasted annoyance. Take old Barnacle Bill. They don't come more annoying, but he's a good barnacle. You, girlie, need to put all that rubbing everyone the wrong way to good use and let that pearl I know is inside you somewhere show.' The woman reached over the bar and poked a chubby index finger into Fiona's chest.

No one had ever lectured her like this, so Fiona didn't know if it was the berating or the kind words causing the steady trail of tears to flow over her cheeks. She knew only her anger and disappointment had pushed her to cross the line yesterday. Her intentions had been good; Noah needed help coming out to his mother because secrets tore families apart. Fiona had learned that the hard way. But the little dose of confidence she'd popped, the small pink one Luke had said would loosen her up, had loosened her lips too much.

'Do you think Noah will ever talk to me again?'

'You'll find out for yourself when he discovers what you've done.'

'I guess Maggie can't wait to tell him.'

Ethne smiled. 'You don't know our Maggie. She's upset, but I doubt she'll be broaching the subject with him. She's smart enough to know he has to *want* to tell her for himself. If I were you, I'd be thinking carefully about how you're going to get over breaking a confidence. If that's what you've done. In a way, I hope what you said isn't true.'

Fiona sat rigid. 'I'd hardly make it up. I figured if I was Noah, I would—'

'Bingo!' Ethne called with a cracking victory clap that startled Fiona. 'That's it right there, isn't it, girlie? You just said "If I was Noah ..." Well, I say, if you *were* Noah, you'd be happier because our boy has all those intangible things you crave. It's the stuff money can't buy that puts happiness in here.' Ethne placed a hand over Fiona's heart, patting twice. 'Lucky for you, Noah is like his mother. That doesn't mean they won't both be wary of you. You'll need to earn their trust, and I can tell you this ... Money and looks won't do you no good around here.'

'What will?' Fiona asked.

The old woman laughed. 'Dear God, girlie, are you seriously sitting there and telling me you don't know what you've got other than looks and money?' She huffed, she shook her head, she smiled. 'Look, I'm just the barmaid around this place. Go talk to your grandmother—or Phillip. Those intangibles you want are right in front of you. Open your eyes and shuck that heart of yours, Fiona-girl.'

32

MAGGIE

Today should have been another ordinary day for Maggie. The reunion was long over, the fair day decorations and street flags finally taken down, and plans were afoot for the end-of-year muck-up day pranks—a tradition and a rite of passage for those students finishing Year 12. For many in Maggie's day, the milestone meant an end to their formal education. Some would get a job locally or in one of the bigger regional towns; some might stay to work the family property. But today's farmers faced additional challenges with children leaving the land in search of a life without the hardship and heartache. And what parent didn't want that for the child they'd nurtured and watched grow for almost two decades? Instead, families are torn, with parents left behind to face the prospect of one day losing their land, their livelihood, and everything they'd planted and fed and watched grow.

What Maggie woke to today would be far from ordinary—her nurturing, her life, her dreams, her future uncertain. She must have managed some shuteye because she remembered crying herself to sleep several times, despite anger and despair coiling itself in her stomach. When her head refused to stop replaying Fiona's words, Maggie had tried counting sheep. When the sheep all looked like Fiona, she'd tried counting down through 'Ten Green Bottles'. When that had failed, she'd tried to count the number of ways she could inflict pain on that monster of a girl.

At some point, when panic, confusion and uncertainty fused with her anger, Maggie reminded herself this wasn't about Fiona. The girl deserved none of Maggie's energy—the little she had this morning. This was about Noah, and just thinking about having to face the day made her cry again. She dragged the pillow over her head to avoid the glimpse of morning sun and the relentless cry of the storm bird. The Channel-billed Cuckoo that lays its eggs in the nests of the Australian Magpie seemed to have taken up residence in one of the main street fig trees. All night its call had warned: rain is on its way, and protect your nests, Magpies.

Maggie wasn't cross with Noah for choosing to confide in Fiona, but it hurt. Then she pondered, had Noah told her himself, would she have known what to do or say? What if she'd reacted to his announcement with the same self-protective anger, rather than showing acceptance and support? She was a mother—torn and disappointed at the prospect of losing all she'd dreamed of for the son she'd nurtured and watched grow. That's the excuse Maggie was going with. The news had taken her by surprise. But why? How had she not realised? And how could she help her son when Maggie, herself, didn't fully understand? More importantly, how was she going to protect him in the future?

For one mad moment, Maggie thought about picking up the telephone and calling her husband. Being able to share the parenting load, with a subject as sensitive as this, might loosen the knot in her stomach. But she couldn't face Brian's neediness now. Not even the thought of the old mare waiting for her daily treat could hurry Maggie out of bed this morning. There was no time to feel sorry for the horse. Maggie was too busy feeling sorry for herself.

'DON'T SAY A WORD,' MAGGIE WARNED WHEN SHE WALKED INTO THE kitchen and saw the thin arch of one raised Ethne eyebrow. 'I know I look like crap, but I have to stay busy.'

'Awright, love, don't get worked up,' Ethne said. 'Cory's covering the bar so I can get these muffins done for dinner service. Have you talked to Noah yet?'

Maggie shook her head. 'I'm not sure how, or if any of this has truly sunk in.' Avoiding Ethne's glare—made up of two squinty eyes and pencilled eyebrows in pronounced arches that gave her a constantly questioning look—Maggie filled a glass with water from the tap before fishing out the Berocca tablet from the front pocket of her jeans. Almost immediately, the liquid turned orange, the effervescence slowly bubbling to the surface. Trying her best to act normal—whatever normal was now—Maggie raised the fizzing liquid to her mouth, the bubbles dancing on the tip of her nose. But she couldn't drink. She couldn't swallow. She couldn't think. Her brain was Berocca—one minute bubbling with determination, the next flat.

'Does needing time make me a bad mother?'

Ethne looked up from the muffin tins she was lining with a generous amount of butter. 'No, love, it makes you a wise one.'

Maggie scoffed. 'A wise woman would know what to do. I'm not even sure if I feel scared or sad or—'

'Love, listen, if there is any doing to be done, it's up to Noah.'

Maggie had lain awake asking herself why Fiona might make something like that up. The girl had to be lying. It wasn't possible that Maggie wouldn't know this about her son. She was Noah's mother. Had she not been so busy being a single parent, an only daughter, and a failed business owner, Noah would've told her himself. Wouldn't he?

Even before her son was born, Maggie had known the relationship she had wanted with her child would be very different to her father–daughter relationship with Joe. Though her mother had been a wise and caring woman, only after her death had Maggie understood the true role she'd played in all their lives. Without Mary, the Lindeman family had floundered. The loss had hit Joe hardest of all, and with Maggie the spitting image of her mother, he never stopped being sad. Then they lost Michael, and The Rev had nothing left in him, leaving Maggie to grieve in a greying world. That was until a father-son musical act returned to town one summer, bringing colour and noise with their banjos, ukuleles and guitars. By night the duo played on a small stage in the hotel's lounge. Nothing rowdy. Their repertoire was more sleepy country ballad style. But the daytime Brian was boisterous and waggish and his energy and enthusiasm addressed Maggie's longing for physical and emotional connection with another human being. That crazy, funny, carefree musician was the Brian she'd fallen in love with; the one before *iICON* came along.

These days, while Maggie struggled to influence her husband, her relationship and connection with her son remained as strong as ever. She was certain of it. Conversations between mother and son had never been awkward—never. In fact, as a youngster he'd been impossible to shut up. So many dinners had gone cold while they'd chattered about things he'd done at school, or what he and his dad had got up to on weekends while Maggie had worked.

Fifteen had been the beginning of the silent years. Should she have acknowledged those silences two years ago, rather than passing them off as growing pains? Maggie wondered. Had she missed an opportunity? Knowing what she does now, silence may have been Noah's way of asking her for help and she'd totally misread the cue.

'I'm terrified,' she admitted, watching Ethne drizzle batter into each muffin mould.

If Maggie didn't get her next move right she risked alienating her son or losing him to his father. *No!* She'd already lost too many years as a working mum. This was her time with Noah—their time, together. It would be so much easier if Noah had talked to her, but perhaps Ethne was right and it had to be at his pace and his way.

While Maggie's first instinct was to go to her son, wrap him tight in her over-protective wings and tell him he would never be alone, no relationship ever guaranteed constant companionship. Look at her marriage. And what about the homosexual couple who lived in the downstairs flat? One Christmas lunch, to appease unsuspecting family, the men had contrived relationships with women and invited 'regular couples', like Brian and Maggie, to support the lie. She and Brian had diligently played their part in the ruse, only to make fun of the pair over breakfast the next day. Had Noah heard them? Had he been in the room at the time?

Oh God! Maggie dragged an upturned crate out from under a bench and slumped onto the box. Then she buried her head in her hands, knowing her son's life, everything she'd wished for him (and for herself) —marriage, babies, the whole fairy tale—would never happen. Chink! Went another tiny piece of her heart.

'Oh Ethne, look at me. I'm crying. I cried all night. Why? He's not dead. He's just ... just ...'

'He's gay, love.'

'Shhh!' Maggie craned her neck to see around the corner of the kitchen door.

'There's no sidestepping the word. Be loud and be proud.'

'I'm not *sidestepping!*' She lied. Of course she was lying. She was avoiding the word because saying *it* aloud might make it real and ... 'It is real, isn't it?' She looked over just as Ethne was lobbing red-coloured berries at each mould of batter. 'My head's going in circles, Ethne. I feel so confused, so sad, and then so wrong for feeling so sad. I keep telling myself none of this is happening to me. It's poor Noah who's been coping on his own because he couldn't talk to me. Even if he had, though, I'm not sure I would've known the right thing to say.'

'Course you would, love.'

Maggie shook her head. Was there a handbook? Could she Google it? Isn't that how people got answers? Will a Google expert tell her to take the lead, or to wait for him to tell her? *If* he told her.

'Please, Ethne, please tell me what I'm supposed to do. I don't know.'

Ethne met her gaze with a tilt of the head. 'Maybe try not to over-think things, love. You're a natural carer. It'll come to you.'

Maggie's breath shook as she filled her lungs and slowly exhaled. 'You don't seem surprised.'

The barmaid-cum-cook turned from where she washed her hands in the sink. 'I've got my nothing-surprises-me eyebrows on today.' She winked with one eye, followed by the other so the painted arches danced up and down.

Maggie laughed. It was a sound she hadn't expected to hear from her mouth today. Or ever again. 'Have I said thank you lately, Ethne? I'd be lost without you.'

'You'll be right, love. So will Noah.' Ethne dried her hands, opened the oven door for the muffin trays and then focused on fitting a filter paper in the coffee machine.

'What if I leave the telling up to Noah and he doesn't? And why would he tell Fiona? She's not even family.'

Ethne stopped what she was doing to look at Maggie. 'She's a mate. You ever told something to someone when you were young, hoping they'd do the telling for you?'

Had she? Maggie wondered. The first thought was a berry-throwing Dan Ireland and their clandestine meetings after church. The rendezvous had been a Sunday ritual she'd looked forward to; something to get Maggie through punching out the same hymns her mother had played on the same church organ. One day, Maggie had told her brother Dan was cute. She remembered Michael had laughed and told her to rack off. Had she been hoping her brother would repeat her words to Dan to save her the embarrassment of a painful rejection?

'There was an occasion ...' Maggie confessed. 'Which means you could be right about Noah.'

Ethne smiled. 'Bottom line is, love, you and I can't imagine how hard it is for a boy to come to terms with such a thing, let alone tell his mother. Why not go with that explanation so you can stop beating your-self up?'

'But if he knows I know and I say nothing, how does that look?'

Ethne dusted coffee grounds from her hands on the tea towel, then patted the top of Maggie's hand where it rested on the counter. 'My advice is to let him see nothing's changed. Life is going on around him like always. Constancy and unconditional love are probably more reassuring than any words. Let him come to you.'

'And if he doesn't?' Maggie asked.

'It might take a while, love, and it might be in his own way when he does, but he'll let you know. Until then he's still Noah, still your boy. That's what matters.'

Maggie had to believe Ethne was right. She had nothing else, no alter-native solution, and no clue how to handle such a delicate situation. Besides, the advice made sense. He was still Noah, still her son, but still her heart ached.

'His life won't be easy,' Maggie said, sombrely. 'And I wanted so much more for him.'

'Such thoughts are natural, love, but try to see it this way. You've raised Noah to feel so secure and so self-confident that he's able to make a life-changing decision all on his own and feel comfortable enough to get on with life.'

'Hmm!' Disappointment seeped into Maggie's voice. 'Not so comfort-able and secure he can tell his mother, huh?'

'Drink this, my poor sleep-deprived publican.' Ethne slipped a coffee under Maggie's nose.

'Caffeine? You're giving me actual caffeine?'

'My herbal brews have their limits. Right now you're needing the big guns. Coffee, a muffin and a side order of distraction.'

'A side order of what?'

'Something to take your mind off your troubles, hopefully in a good way,' Ethne explained. 'This next bit of news will either make your day or not.'

Maggie braced. 'Tell me.'

'That Dan chappy called again. I told him you weren't here.'

'Oh,' Maggie responded.

'That's it? An "Oh" is all I get?' Ethne's piercing, pale-green eyes—almost spectral-like—homed in on Maggie. 'Come on, love, spill the beans.'

'It's nothing.'

'I see, so this Dan chappy is picking random names from the phonebook and calling to get his rocks off? I s'pose he just happens to have freakishly picked your name a couple of times. Either that or he loves the sound of my voice.'

'Dan and I sort of caught up at the reunion.'

'Sorta good, or sorta not good?' Ethne asked.

'Sorta married,' Maggie said. 'Dan Ireland married a friend from high school.'

Ethne's face looked like a goldfish at feeding time. 'Charlie's Dan? I remember you had quite the crush'

Maggie sighed. 'Michael's accident put an end to that, though, didn't it? Dad made sure it ended. I had no say in the matter.'

'There's always a choice,' Ethne said. 'A person just needs to be strong enough to make the one that's best for them.'

'Marrying Brian *was* the best one. We made Noah.'

'True,' Ethne said, 'but I'm speaking generally. I've got to know you pretty well since coming home. You need to start making choices that are best for you, love, not what everyone expects.'

'What are you getting at, Ethne?'

'You, Maggie, are the most obliging woman I know. Wouldn't hurt you to follow your son's lead. Be the person you want to be. Do want you want and bugger what everyone else thinks. Be selfish for a bit. When was the last time you did anything because you wanted to do it, *when* you wanted to do it?'

'Hmm, well, when you put it that way,' Maggie said, 'I was thinking of making myself scarce today. Maybe a long drive to think and some time with Dad. I need a good chat. Preferably one where no one chats me back.'

'Aw gee, love, sorry,' Ethne apologised. 'Not sure I can cover you today. Maybe next week?'

'Oh, sure, no problem,' Maggie flapped a just-forget-it hand in the air. 'I can wait.'

'Bingo!' Ethne whooped so loud Maggie's heart juddered in her chest, her hand clutching the front of her blouse. 'Wrong answer, love,' the woman announced. 'The correct answer is—repeat after me: "Ethne, I'm the boss and I'm taking some much-needed time out and leaving you in charge." Now your turn,' she challenged Maggie. 'Give the words a whirl.'

Maggie stopped her chuckling to clear her throat. 'Fine, okay …
Ethne, as I'm the boss and I'm—'

'Yeah, yeah, you got it,' Ethne quipped. 'Get going. Cory and I have
the place covered. Take your time and give the old bugger a hug from me.'

'Will do. And Ethne?' Maggie paused in the kitchen doorway.
'Thanks. I'm not sure what I'd do without you.'

'Me either, love. Scoot!'

33

'I'm late today, Roslyn. Sorry.'

'Late?' The nurse looked at her watch as Maggie neared. 'Slow down. Your dad won't notice the time.'

'Is having a bad day?'

'No, he's good today, Maggie,' Roslyn smiled. 'How are you doing?'

Had she let them, those four words said with a nurse's compassion could have been Maggie's undoing. The reason she'd been on the go for days was to avoid asking herself that very question.

She replied with forced bravado. 'I'm fine, Roslyn. Keen to see my favourite guy.'

JOE'S DOOR WAS OPEN, HER FATHER AWAKE AND PROPPED IN A BULKY recliner. 'Hi, Dad.'

'Magpie?'

Maggie smothered a small gasp behind her hand. He hadn't called her that in ages. She bent over and kissed his head the way she always did, the way her mother always did, and the way she kissed Noah, until her son started shying away from such affection. She'd hoped for—make that desperately needed—a good day for her dad, and here he was propped up in a chair with the rosy tinge staining beige cheeks reminiscent of old-fashioned baby portraits.

'Look what I brought today.' Maggie fished the camera from its protective carry bag, removed the lens cap and adjusted the aperture to suit the fluorescent brightness of the room. Ever since Fiona had gushed over Maggie's portfolio, the camera bag had been sitting in her room waiting for the right moment to get a good dusting-off. Today was that moment. 'I thought I'd start taking pictures again, Dad.'

'Why?'

'Why not?' she said, snapping her father's portrait in close-up, complete with creases and crêpy skin. 'I need a hobby.' *Because*, she might've added, *I don't have enough to do already and I need a distraction to stop me going mad.* 'The reunion inspired me to get my old photos out, Dad, which inspired me to get my old camera out, which—'

'Reunion?' he grunted.

'You remember, Dad. I told you about the school's centenary celebrations. About 200 people turned up. A few out-of-towners reneged at the last minute. The rain up north probably stopped them. I heard roads are still flooded, with detours in place. You should see the current in The Calingarry River.'

'*He* was there,' her father said, instant tears pooling in sunken eyes.

After all these years, Maggie knew who 'he' was. *He* was the one who'd featured in Joe's cries of, '*He* took our Michael away' all these years.

She slipped the camera back into the bag and squatted by her dad's chair. 'I didn't mean to upset you.'

'There,' was all he said, one long, gnarled finger pointing to the only cupboard in the room.

'What's there, Dad?' Maggie stood before walking over to slide the door open. 'What do you want out of here?'

'Box. Box.'

'What sort of box? Big box? Little box?' Maggie checked the cupboard floor and found only shoes, so she ran her hand along the top shelf, hitting something small and hard. With the tips of her fingers she worked the object closer, recognising the box Michael had made in woodwork class. He'd made two: one for himself and one for his father, each with their name etched onto the lid.

Maggie fought back the surge of emotion as she traced the letters M.I.C.H.A.E.L. The second box, carved with her father's name, was possibly at the pub, stored in an old tea chest containing her mother's mementos. Maggie would make a point of finding the box for Noah. At his age he'd appreciate the sentimentality of such keepsakes.

'Inside. Inside.' Joe waggled and poked a crooked finger.

After turning the tiny key and flipping the lid, she took inventory of the contents: the order-of-service card from Michael's funeral, a wad of sympathy cards, a small collection of photos tied with a white but yellowing ribbon.

'Bible. Bible.'

'Okay, Dad, okay. I'm getting there.' How many times had the church Bibles passed through Maggie's hands as she'd greeted the congregation each Sunday? But this Bible was different. This had belonged to her mother, Mary. 'What do you want with this, Dad?'

Without a word, Joe snatched the leather-bound book, arthritic hands thumbing the pages awkwardly until an envelope fell out.

'This.' He thrust the letter at Maggie, which she carefully unfolded.

The writing was messy, with frayed fold-lines obliterating sections, but the name and signature on the bottom was clear. She looked from her father to the letter again. 'Dan Ireland?'

What was it about this man? For twenty-odd years nothing, then— boom! The guy was everywhere: in her email inbox, in her overloaded mind, and in her trembling hands. Reaching out blindly for the visitor chair, she pulled it close and eased her body down, her eyes devouring the words.

Dear Sir,

I am not sure you will want to receive a letter from me now, or ever. I am sending this one in the hope you will one day be able to read it and know how sorry I am for the grief you have suffered. You blamed me for Michael's death and I accept I should have known better that night. Please know, while I can't bring your son back, I can and will never forget him. This letter is not about seeking forgiveness as I am yet to forgive myself. I do, however, need you to know what happened and I am finally free to share the truth.

It was my idea. It was my car. It was also my choice to drink so much that I handed my keys to Nate Parker. You'll remember Nate was always in strife with his dad. He wasn't supposed to associate with us at all, but he was there that night. So when Mike fell, I agreed to say I was driving. I was a juvenile—not yet eighteen. Nate was older and the grandson of a highly respected police officer. Understand, at that time we thought it was a stupid stunt gone wrong and Mike would get patched up and be home before we'd finished giving our version of events to the police. We didn't know about Michael's passing until after we'd set the lie in stone.

You might think I escaped punishment because I was young, but I'm punished every day of my life. I see the devastating impact of crashes on families and I understand there are no accidents, only a series of events that individually are not dangerous, but when combined—alcohol, inexperienced drivers, stupid dares, muddy paddocks—they allow the unthinkable to happen. In the end, it doesn't matter who did what that night, and changing our story afterwards wouldn't bring Michael back. You had lost your son and Maggie had lost her brother.

With Nate Parker gone—killed in a single-vehicle drink-driving crash not long after I joined the Police Force—I need you and Maggie to know it wasn't me behind the wheel the night Michaal died. Everyone's life changed that night. Mine included. I'm now a father with twins—a boy and a girl. I named the girl Emily. My boy, I named Michael. We go to church as a family every Sunday. (Please tell Maggie I actually go inside these days!) I regret never knowing what church and religion was when I was young, but you know what my father was like.

Believe me when I tell you, sir, that the grief I brought upon you and your family is with me always. I often wonder, as I'm sure you do, what might have been had that night played out differently, and while I wish I could turn back time I know we are dealt these challenges for a reason. I am certain one day that reason will become clear and, God willing, I will be wise enough and open enough to see it when it does.
Yours sincerely,
Dan Ireland

Maggie reread the last paragraph through a blur of tears, the flimsy notepaper trembling despite her firm grip. She turned away to reach for a tissue, not wanting her father to see her crying, but she need not have worried. The Rev had resumed the all too familiar slouch and drool position of slumber. Relieving him of the Bible, Maggie tugged the second envelope out from under his hand and read the addressee detail. Rather than the stilted, jerky script of an old man, the swirly penmanship was of a much younger scribe, a minister who once took pride in writing children's names on communion cards and hymn numbers on chalkboards. The addressee she also knew: Daniel Ireland.

'All okay in here?' asked Roslyn from the doorway, a compassionate and curious lilt to her voice.

Startled, Maggie stood and tucked both letters into the pocket of her shorts as if they were five-dollar notes she'd pinched from her father's wallet. 'He was here for a bit, Roslyn. Sleeping now. I'll head off. See you next time.'

Maggie bent to kiss Joe on the cheek, returned the box to the wardrobe, and took the Bible and the notes back home.

34

Concern etched two deep furrows in Ethne's large forehead, her pencilled eyebrows all but buried between them. 'What are you doing hiding out here, love?'

'Hiding!' Maggie had poured a beer and tucked herself away in a corner of the beer garden to make the most of the unexpected drop in temperature, thanks to increasing cloud cover.

Was nothing predictable? Not even the weather followed its usual pattern. After decades of drought, excess rain in the north was inundating inland New South Wales—a devastating blow for some farmers and a blessing for others. According to locals, the Calingarry River and its tributaries hadn't flowed so freely in years. Property owners with river access were even preparing to raise the pumps and machinery that sat high on dry banks most storm seasons.

'Let Noah know the cool room has a plate of snacks with his name on it.

'He rang to say he'd be late,' Maggie told Ethne. 'He rambled on about Cory and band practice but I worry he's avoiding me. What if I'm doing this all wrong by avoiding the topic?'

'He wants space and time,' Ethne said as she perched on a chair opposite Maggie.

'Well, too much thinking time is driving *me* crazy, and so is the damn storm bird with its incessant chanting. As if we don't know a storm's overdue!'

'Whatchya got there?' Ethne nodded at the table. 'Looks like your dad's old Bible.'

Maggie slipped the note out from underneath. Like a planchette on a Ouija board, she slid the single page over the table's surface. She recalled playing the Ouija board game after Mary Lindeman died. Tracy had sworn the spirit board could translate messages from heaven and Maggie had been craving connection any way she could. If she still believed in the power of the Ouija, Maggie would locate one and have a big chat with poor bloody Nate Parker.

Ethne's eyes narrowed at the letter. 'This has been around a while.'

'Yep.' Maggie shrugged and slipped the other note out from in between the Bible's pages. 'Here's Dad's reply.' She watched the frown on Ethne's face deepen.

'The Rev never posted this?'

In response, Maggie held up the addressed envelope with the pristine stamp. 'I've been sitting here for the last ten minutes trying to figure out what to do. Is it my place to send a letter like this after so long? And after what you said this morning, about Noah wanting someone else to do the telling, I had to wonder. Did Dad give me this letter to do his bidding?'

'I can't say, love, other than tell you we all want to right the wrongs before we meet our maker. You're worrying about dredging up bad memories for Dan, I suppose. You think he's put it behind him and moved on?'

'No. I know he hasn't—not entirely—even though we're talking about something that happened over twenty years ago.' Maggie had already noticed the significance of the letter's date. Dan had written on an anniversary of Michael's death. 'Dan works in crash investigation,' she told Ethne. 'That means every time he attends a crash and confronts a family with painful news he's punishing himself for his own misspent youth. Charlie Ireland should know that about Dan, and Dan should know Dad forgave him.'

'And you?'

Maggie shook her head. 'I never had a problem forgiving Dan. I never got mad, but I was sad for a while. What I can't believe is Dad's known all this time that Dan wasn't driving when Michael fell.'

'And Joe gave these letters to you today out of the blue and with no explanation?'

'Dad was having a good day,' Maggie explained. 'I mentioned the reunion and he brought up Dan. Other than that, I don't know why he thought about the letters today of all days.'

'And did your face light up when you mentioned Dan Ireland's name?' Ethne grinned.

'I beg your pardon?'

'I'm talking about the little pink blush that develops on your neck and face every time his name comes up.' Ethne slapped her hand with its chubby fingers and fat knuckles on top of Maggie's on the table, patting twice. 'Come on, where's that tough cookie I know and love?'

'Not feeling so tough,' she replied. 'What's that saying? It never rains, but it pours?'

'Ah, yes. When troubles come, they come together,' Ethne parroted.

'Until the reunion I've hardly thought about Dan Ireland.'

That wasn't entirely true. For the last two years she'd thought about him every time his father passed by the pub. Charlie Ireland's habit of checking in whenever heading off to throw a line in the river was still in force. Established by Joe when there'd been no mobile phones, Maggie maintained the precautionary ritual.

'What do I do with the letter, Ethne?'

'Love, don't you think you've got enough going on? That's been sitting undelivered for years. A little more thinking time won't hurt. Put it aside. It'll come to you.'

'You are a wise old bird, Ethne?' Maggie smiled.

'Oi, enough of the old!'

❧

IN HER ROOM, AFTER TUCKING THE BIBLE AND ITS TWO NOTES SAFELY IN her underwear drawer, Maggie fired up the old laptop to check emails. Deleting junk and ignoring another from Dan, Maggie double-clicked on Brian's and scanned her husband's latest scant and scatty communication. Today's message had all the markings of a down day—more down than usual from the lack of exclamation marks. Only a week ago Brain had raved in an email about the *iICON* producers bringing eliminated Season One acts back as surprise intruders in Season Three next year. They couldn't say more except the concept was under consideration, reminding all contestants that the same contract conditions applied and breaches of their confidentiality agreement would be costly.

This Brian email had few words: *They don't want me, Maggs.*

Maggie clicked the delete option, wishing she could erase some chapters of her life as easily. Then the cursor hovered over Dan's name. Best left unopened? Or might the words lift her spirits after Brian's depressing message; as long as the man wasn't apologising—again—or justifying his infidelity on the night of the reunion. Toying with the mouse, she clicked on the specials bulletins from the various food and beverage suppliers before manoeuvring the mouse back to Dan's name. *Delete unread or double-click?* She double-clicked and smiled at the message speckled with yellow emoticons.

Hi Maggie,
I'd prefer to talk, and I tried phoning but got mostly static by the name of Ethne! Since when do country pubs employ barmaids that double as bodyguards? I was deaf in one ear for a week after she hung up on me.

Anyway, if you would consider calling me, maybe we can talk. (Well, obviously not 'maybe we can talk'. If you called we'd actually be talking, wouldn't we? I mean, that's what people do when they call. They talk, right?) Bloody hell, I'm rambling. Sorry. I'm also sorry about not being honest and upfront. But like I said, I'm better in person, or at least over the phone.
I'm sending this email with my fingers crossed that you'll call me. It's okay if you don't, too. I'll understand.
Regards, Rambling Dan

Around midnight, unable to sleep or remember if she'd locked the hatch on the cellar, Maggie cursed her absent-mindedness and threw back the bedclothes. Stealing out of her room, she crept downstairs and over to the hotel. Checking was probably unnecessary—Calingarry Crossing was not the crime capital of New South Wales—but old habits die hard and sleep had been evading her, thanks to the storm bird and Noah's new night-time routine. He was staying out, missing dinner, and not coming home until Maggie was busy with closing time evictions. Saying nothing, her son would wave from the side door to the bar and motion he was tired.

Having confirmed the cellar hatch and all doors were secure, Maggie was returning to bed when she noticed a line of light from under Noah's door spilling across the floorboards. She hesitated, ashamed of herself and furious that Fiona had driven this invisible wedge of uneasiness between mother and son.

'Can I come in?' she said, inching the door open. 'What are you doing on the iPad at this hour? It's late.'

'I'm checking out all the cool apps. There's a Send-A-Card one. I'm downloading it so I can make Dad a birthday card. It's totally awesome.'

'Is there anything that gadget doesn't do?' Resenting an electronic device was ridiculous, but Maggie couldn't stop feeling jealous and wishing she was the person responsible for her son's grin, and not money-bags Fiona. Returning the gifted iPad with a thanks-but-no-thanks note crossed her mind, but that would only drive the wedge deeper.

Maggie was still paying off the computer equipment and the amplifier Brian had got 'a great deal on' four years ago. No way could she replace the 600-dollar iPad, nor afford the internet access, which Fiona's credit card was scheduled to pay monthly. In Fiona's world, one paid for their mistakes with a credit card. Maggie paid with her emotions.

'Check this out, Mum.'

Peering over the top, watching her son navigate the fancy touch screen like a pro, she said, 'What happened to hand-writing a birthday card and licking a stamp?'

'That's so dark ages, Mum. You should get one of these.'

'Really?' Maggie pictured her eyebrows disappearing under her fringe. 'And what will an iPad do for me?'

'For a start, it'll find you anything you want,' Noah said.

'Oh? Will it find me a cleaner for your room?' Maggie picked up a sleeveless hoodie from the floor. *Will it find me a life?* she asked herself. *Will it find the husband I used to know and who loved me more than anything in this world? Can an iPad find my sanity when I lose it—which could be any day?* 'I'll pass, thanks Noah.' Until an iPad could do those things, Maggie wasn't interested. 'Enough for tonight, bud,' she prompted while hanging the garment on the back of the door. 'I've read the brightness of the screen is bad for your eyes and can interrupt your sleep. Mum's not so dark ages, eh?'

He said nothing, his face eerily illuminated by the iPad's glow, eyes wide and innocent. Should Maggie take more interest in her son's online activities? Him doing anything foolish had never crossed her mind. Then again, she never thought Noah would take a pill from a stranger, ride on the boot of a car, or that he'd—

'Mum?' Noah said, letting the iPad fall back on the blanket.

'Sorry, bud, what?'

'Before you go, can I tell you something?' His eyes darted about the room before settling on the small rip in his top sheet. 'I've kinda been keeping it a secret.'

Maggie's stomach roiled. Was she ready? Did she want to hear it? She'd too easily satisfied herself that until the words came from her son's lips, Fiona's outburst was nothing more than hearsay from an unreliable source.

She took a deep breath, sat, and with a stranglehold on shaking knees said, 'Noah, buddy, you can tell me anything and never worry about what I might think or—'

'Chill, Mum. Geez! I'm not about to tell you I'm …' Maggie waited, chest pounding, heart bursting. 'I'm not like dropping out of school or anything.'

'Oh?'

'Nah, it's about Fiona,' he said, oblivious. 'She's kinda been working on a surprise for you.'

In lieu of an expletive, Maggie chose a lecture. '"Kinda" is not a word, Noah, it's two words—kind and of. And I've had enough surprises.'

'You'll love it, I promise, but I've gotta—I mean, I've got to—upload. Hang on a sec.'

Maggie was about to tell Noah not to bother when images appeared on the screen, one after the other. Images Maggie recognised. Images that looked amazing.

'They're my photographs!'

'I know. Cool, huh? You've got a website.'

'Why, Noah?' First shock, then scepticism infiltrated Maggie's thoughts. 'What do I do with one? And why would Fiona—?'

'Geez, Mum, what's with the interrogation? Fi wants to do something nice to make up. She reckons your pictures will sell. Something to do with photo stock and advertising. That's what she was doing all that time at Mrs Bailey's.'

Sell? Could Maggie make money out of her pictures online? Had she kept up with the technology explosion in early noughties, she might have a better idea, but she'd been busy earning money to pay the rent and fill the refrigerator.

'They do look good on the screen,' she admitted.

'That's because this iPad has over three million pixels. That's like four times the number of pixels in iPad 2 and a million more than an HDTV.'

'I see,' she said, only she didn't. Not at all. Old-fashioned cameras Maggie could understand. This iPad and her own website was too much to get her head around. What if no one bought her pictures? Had she not endured enough angst and heartache already? What if this website merely added to the growing list of disappointments in Maggie's life? 'I don't think so, buddy,' she said. 'Come on, sleep.'

Noah slammed the iPad on the bed. 'I knew I shouldn't have told you. I can't say anything without you getting angry.' Her son looked up with eyes like his father's; big, sorrowful puppy-like eyes that said they didn't understand why she was mad.

This was no way to gain her son's trust. *Chill, Maggie, chill!*

'Honestly, Noah, I'm not mad, or anything else.'

'Then why won't you let Fi do this? The site's not finished yet, but you get the idea. At least take a proper look.' Noah turned the iPad towards Maggie, flicking through the three tabs running across the top of the webpage:

MAGGIE'S PICTURES | MAGGIE'S STORY | MAGGIE'S CONTACTS

'When was Fiona going to tell me about this herself?'

'Soon,' he replied. 'When it's finished. She really wants to make up, Mum. You used to tell me forgiveness makes you a better person and that Pops should have been more forgiving when Uncle Michael died.'

Touché! she mused. 'So you do listen to me?'

'Mostly.' He grinned.

'Well, that's something, bud, and I'm glad you showed me. Maybe we can talk later—about a few things. Okay?' Noah's eyes again dropped to the hole in the bedsheet. 'No rush, buddy.' She bent over for a kiss and to tuck her son in tight. Old habits. 'Please don't stay up much longer. Love you.'

'Mum?' Noah said moments before the door closed. 'Love you too. G'night.'

BACK IN HER OWN ROOM, WHILE STILL IN A FORGIVING MOOD, MAGGIE considered phoning Brian. She was prepared to indulge his music obsession and the resultant self-pity only so long until his selfishness took her beyond forgiveness. Her next thought was of Dan Ireland. How had her marriage gone so wrong? Brian reinventing a life without Maggie in it, and her thinking every second thought about another man? And, just when life couldn't get any crazier, she discovered she has a website.

'I wonder,' she muttered, peeling back the bedsheet while the slideshow of images from Noah's iPad flicked through her head.

Brian needed reminding; Maggie had a dream to pursue, too. She also needed some idea of what she'd be doing in a week, a month, a year from now; not merely find herself a year older and no more inspired or, according to Ethne, with 'all her juices dried up'. People like her father wasted years waiting. Maggie wanted her days to be different, though not always exciting or ever-changing. She'd long ago got over the need for a life with colour and noise. Even planning to do nothing was a plan.

Maggie had unintentionally dialled Brian's mobile and was about to hang up when he answered. He sounded tired, maybe a little drunk. Probably both. Maggie talked anyway, telling Brian they couldn't afford the flat and to plan his move to Calingarry Crossing.

'Excellent, Maggs,' Brian said, his mockery unmistakable. 'I can see the banner: Welcome Home Brian-no-balls-Henkler—the bloke who chucked his career down the drain like his father. No bloody way, Maggie. I won't and you can't make me.'

'Don't!' The single word was a whack to the snout of his defiant puppy act. 'Grow up. You have responsibilities, Brian. Your son needs a male presence, someone he can talk to about …' Maggie pivoted, '… his music. He wants to do drama and music at university.'

'University?' Brian's voice softened. 'I didn't know.'

'You'd know if you bothered to return your son's calls.'

'I did,' he said, defensive again.

'When? One call out of how many messages, Brian? You raised him from a baby while I worked and—'

'Yeah, yeah,' Brian interjected. 'Here we go. Cue the violins for the *Oh Woe Is Maggie Having Given Up Her Career Concerto*—in fucking F Major.'

'It wasn't my career I missed,' Maggie said through gritted teeth. 'IT. WAS. MY. SON.' Silent rivers streamed over her cheeks. She was over trying and crying, hands muting each mournful sob, as usual, so Noah didn't hear.

'Maggie, Maggs, Magpie. Please, darlin', talk to me. I'm sorry. You know I love you. Please Maggie. Tell me what to do.'

'I-I can't,' she said. 'You decide what's more important, Brian.'

'But, Maggs, you might as well ask me to decide between living and dying.'

'Don't say things like that,' Maggie pushed the words out. 'Don't you dare talk to me about death and dying.'

'Why not? You're bloody killing me. You know that, right? Christ! You want me to beg? Okay, I'll beg. Please, Maggie, let me do this. One more try and I promise—'

'No Brian.' There was so much more she'd wanted to say, but nothing in his voice or words gave any cause for hope. She hung up, reefed the telephone plug from the wall for the first time in her life, then switched off her mobile so he couldn't call back.

This was not the life she'd agreed to when she'd said, 'honour and obey'. Brian was living the life he wanted, even if it was only in his head. Maggie needed to live hers.

35

Today was a fresh start and Maggie refused to let a restless and stormy night stop her from doing what she'd promised herself. The first hint of a sunrise tinged blue and lilac, and with a light cloud cover, would provide the perfect backdrop. All she needed was a quick snack, a pocketful of stale bread, her camera and a couple of hours. She left a note in the kitchen for Noah and Ethne, telling them she'd be back for the pub's opening.

Time to rediscover Calingarry Crossing, the Maggie Lindeman way. First stop: the old mare.

'G'DAY, GORGEOUS.' TO ENCOURAGE THE OLD GIRL TO THE FENCE, AND her nose to the bread scraps littering the ground, Maggie had crouched low and waited. 'Nothing wrong with a special treat now and then.'

Rising slowly, she raised her camera and snapped several pictures of the horse. When the mare wandered away, Maggie turned back along the same road and cut through the schoolyard to connect with the river walk. Although following the same path she and Dan had taken at the reunion, and wary of slithering things and spider webs strung between branches, the daylight allowed her to venture off-track and into the thicker scrub more comfortably.

'We artists must suffer for our art,' she told a resting butterfly while focusing the lens on perfectly patterned wings pressed flat to face the sun. 'And you must warm those magnificent wing muscles so you can fly, right?'

As if to answer, the butterfly spread its wings and lifted off, fluttering in front of Maggie's face—teasing her with its strength, its beauty and its freedom to fly away to someplace new. For a tiny second, Maggie wished she was a butterfly, too.

Every image she clicked reminded Maggie how different the world looked through a lens. With a camera, she could zero in on a tiny piece of her world while blurring the unimportant edges and capture that one moment when everything was just right—the perfect balance of content and composition. Landscapes were far more appealing than people. Except for baby Noah, human beings rarely caught her photographer's eye, even though Calingarry Crossing offered the odd, interesting character worthy of a creative study.

One such subject stood down river from Maggie. While suitably camouflaged by a tangle of blue morning glory vine and low-hanging tree limbs, she zoomed in on Charlie Ireland's hard and haggard face, confident he wouldn't notice her. Near-sightedness and a deaf ear were as much medical conditions as they were metaphors for the man's curt and ornery disposition most days. But if anyone was allowed to be cranky, old Charlie was—and not because he was Dan's dad. Like so many soldiers, Charlie returned home a changed man. When his wife ran off, followed shortly thereafter by his eldest son, Dan was left to withstand the worst of a man hollowed out by regret and anger. Bitterness and loneliness had devoured Charlie Ireland in the same way it had nibbled away at Joe.

Maggie thought about her dad's letter tucked away in her dresser drawer as she snapped a final photograph of Charlie. Standing on the river's edge, his fishing line carried by the fast-moving current, the man looked content as he waited for a fish to bite. Not Maggie. She didn't want to waste her life waiting or end up old with regrets. She'd take a leaf out of her son's book and decide who she was and what made her happy. This morning's photo shoot—metaphorically dusting off her dreams, while physically dusting off her camera—was a tangible beginning, while the emotional parts of her life were less straightforward. She supposed she could forgive Fiona, forget about Dan, humour her father, tolerate Brian, and be more present for Noah.

She could do all those, starting with Fiona.

❧

CHERYL BAILEY BRUSHED DIRT OFF GLOVED HANDS AND SHIELDED HER eyes to the intense early morning sun stretching along Konjulup Road.

'Hello, Maggie,' she said. 'What brings you out at this hour? I'm getting some gardening in before the heat. All this rain and now sunshine. Weeds are springing up as we speak.'

'The garden's looking lovely, Cheryl.'

'I'm planting a frangipani,' she said, some laughter leaving her eyes.

'Will frangipani grow out here?'

'Yes,' she said defiantly. 'They were Amber's favourite.'

'Of course.' Maggie remembered the coffin, laden with a massive frangipani wreath. 'Sorry to interrupt. I've come to see Fiona.'

'Yes, I thought as much,' Cheryl said. 'You'll find her inside, either on that telephone of hers or at my computer in the living room. A bit of a handful—like her mother,' Cheryl added, almost apologetically. 'But I admit to being quite spoilt having her here.'

'Spoilt?' Maggie sought to clarify.

'You're looking at a woman who's been defragged, had her RAM increased and her firewall upgraded. I feel sixteen again.' When the woman laughed, Maggie thought she looked younger.

Ordinarily, Maggie saw little of Cheryl Bailey; recovering alcoholics didn't frequent the local pub. But that hadn't stopped her learning about the woman's private life, including her marriage to Jack Bailey; not that the town knew how terrible things had been until recently. Other details about Cheryl had come from late-night whispers in the Manse when Maggie was young. The man with the loudest whisper had been the local GP. Doctor Wynter had been a frequent visitor, and whenever he arrived Joe Lindeman would close the kitchen door.

'I'm glad to hear that about Fiona, Cheryl,' Maggie said, smiling with her. 'It's her computer skills I want to see her about. I won't stay long.' Maggie wasn't planning a bigger scene than necessary.

'I hope Noah's doing okay,' Cheryl asked. 'I'm afraid Fiona takes after Amber when it comes to making the wrong choices. At least Luke's gone for good.'

'Yes, I heard she broke off the engagement.'

'A one-sided affair. A set-up is a more appropriate term,' Cheryl corrected. 'I'm afraid my ex, Jack—Fiona's grandfather—is still manipulating things to suit his needs.'

'Cheryl ...' Maggie hesitated. 'Did you know Fiona has been asking questions around town about her birth father?'

The woman squinted into the sun that was heating Maggie's back. 'Yes, Fiona has asked me if I knew anything.'

'What did you tell her? Do you mind me asking?'

Cheryl's shrug suggested indifference, not so the rueful, well-practised expression. 'What could I possibly tell her about those days? That I'm not proud about certain times in my life? That I failed miserably as a mother?' When Cheryl stiffened, raising a defiant chin, Maggie thought she was about to launch into an Alcoholics Anonymous affirmation. In a way, she was. 'I know I failed Amber when she was growing up. I was too drunk to know what was going on in her life. I'm trying to make up by being a good grandmother to Fiona.'

The woman wearing a brown cardigan over an apricot-coloured shirt and A-line skirt seemed to tire, shuffling to a shady garden bench and tucking her skirt into the back of her legs before lowering herself onto the edge. The cautious pose was all very June Dally-Watkins, albeit with dirt-crusted knees and a brown smudge on one cheek.

'That's the truth, Maggie dear. I have no idea who got Amber pregnant.' She smiled wryly. 'Of course, that's incorrect. Amber got Amber pregnant, but I don't know which boy it was. To be honest, I'm not sure Amber knew, but I'd never tell my granddaughter. Demeaning women and turning a child against their mother is what Jack does.'

'Amber tried putting things right with the family,' Maggie said.

'She did, didn't she?' Pride, then sadness washed over Cheryl's face, followed by a faraway look.

Maggie considered the woman before her. She was sweet but stiff, like a toffee shard. Brittle, Maggie decided. Three generations—Cheryl, Amber and Fiona—each damaged by the same man. She wondered if Jack Bailey was proud of himself.

Cheryl had not attended Amber's funeral. She'd told Sara before she and Maggie left for the drive to Sydney that aside from not being able to face Jack, she wasn't ready to say goodbye to Amber. She'd not long ago said hello to her daughter for the first time in twenty years. By not attending, Cheryl could go on believing Amber was still alive and grow frangipani trees in her memory. Strange logic, Maggie had initially thought. But wasn't she refusing to say goodbye to a marriage by holding tight to the memory of what her relationship with Brian used to be?

'I said, in you go, Maggie. You didn't come to see me.'

'Thanks,' Maggie said, as she headed up the steps to the porch.

THE OLD FLYSCREEN DOOR SQUEAKED AND SNAPPED SHUT BEHIND HER.

'Almost done, Gran, do you want to—?' Fiona had propelled the small office chair to one side and spun around, her heels digging into the rug to stop her mid-swing. 'It's you!'

'Your grandmother invited me in.'

A fresh, freckle-faced Fiona stared back. Even the lips, now pouting, were gloss-free and naturally rose-petal pink, while the wild curls were reined in at the nape of her neck. What a change from the overdressed and made-up mannequin that had whipped up a maelstrom of gossip after storming into town.

'Is there something I can do for you, Maggie?'

The words *Haven't you done enough?* almost made it to her lips. 'Noah showed me the website,' she said. 'The one with my pictures.'

'But he promised—' Fiona stopped short, her expression acknowledging the moral high ground was not hers to walk when it came to trust.

'I'm here to thank you, not berate you, Fiona. While I've no clue about websites, it was thoughtful and clever of you.'

A cautious smile twitched at the corners of Fiona's mouth. 'Not so clever. Pretty basic if you know what you're doing.'

'Which I do not.'

'Oh, I didn't mean … Maggie I-I wanted to do something nice. I stuffed up. I stuffed up real bad.' Fiona's nervousness played out by dancing the swivel chair from side to side, no trace of the pretentious penthouse princess. In fact, the girl looked at ease—even at home in the sun-filled room with its fresh flowers, framed needlecraft, and a wall of photos. So many pictures tempted Maggie to stickybeak.

'You'll be glad to know I've decided to go home to Sydney tomorrow.' Fiona's announcement snatched Maggie's attention back. 'I'm moving into Dad's—Phillip's—apartment, but I'd like to stay in touch with Noah. Only if that's okay with you,' Fiona was quick to add.

The magpie in her wanted to squawk and swoop and defend her baby until Maggie recalled how her father had forbidden her from having anything to do with 'that Dan Ireland'. Not that Fiona's attachment to Noah was, thank goodness, anything other than platonic. If only that was Maggie's quandary. Noah infatuated with a stuck-up, slightly older city girl was at least a situation she might know how to handle.

Maggie breathed deep, exhaling slowly, calmly. 'I will not say no, Fiona, mostly because I appreciate you asking. I also appreciate that between texting, email, Facebook and goodness knows what else, I have little hope of stopping Noah from communicating with whoever he wants, whenever he wants, but I will say this—'

'I know, Maggie, I know, believe me,' Fiona gushed. 'And I promise. I've learned my share of lessons. I'm even kinda glad I came to Calingarry Crossing.'

'*Kind of*, Fiona,' Maggie corrected. 'Kind of is two words.' And with that, Maggie turned on her heel. 'I have to get to work. Goodbye and good luck.'

M aggie stifled her yawn as she leaned down to kiss her Dad's
forehead. 'Mwah!'

Last night had been busy in the pub. She'd even dragged Noah off his
iPad to help Ethne during food service. Later, after locking up, Maggie
had crept past Noah's room and heard giggles and chatter. Something
called *Skype* was the new way to chat. Perhaps Maggie needed to learn
how if she was to nab time with her son. But today she needed to talk face
to face with her dad. Even though Joe was clueless to her yapping most
times, saying stuff aloud helped. Mostly Maggie liked the feel of her
father's hand in hers while she nattered, and the way his thumb softly
massaged her knuckles even though his eyes remained closed or fixed on
some distant point. Occasionally he'd surprise her with a laugh, often at
the most inappropriate times, like when she'd relived the horror hospital
trip with Noah. In the middle of her sad story Joe had ya-hoo'd, cackled
and barked out something unintelligible.

'I see you didn't save me any dessert,' Maggie called over the running
water in the tiny en suite. 'Oh well, I hardly need it, and you know what
they say? One minute on the lips, a lifetime on the hips.' She continued
her one-sided conversation while wringing the face washer.

Returning to her dad in the wheelchair where he sat hunched over a
tray table, Maggie cleaned the corners of his mouth, then dutifully dusted
the lumps of food from his cardigan and into her cupped hand. The larrikin

publican, the ratbag Reverend, the dutiful father, reduced to this. With so much focus on Joe's mental health in recent months, Maggie had missed his physical decline. His skin—loose and almost transparent—was oddly like that of a premature baby's, except a newborn's skin had colour. A baby's skin had life and hope and a future. Joe's mottled, greying, wilted flesh held no such qualities. He was fading away and Maggie, the protector, could do nothing.

'My Magpie.' Despite the words rolling out of Joe's mouth with the spitty-clickity sound of ill-fitting false teeth, Maggie smiled at the utterance and hoped today was a good day.

'Yes, Dad, it's me. How you doing?'

He shrugged his shoulders and his whole body—a mere fifty-seven kilograms according to his chart—shifted in the chair. He'd lost so much weight in the past few months. Doctors had tried to re-assure Maggie, reminding her there were aspects of a patient's health that medicine could not control, especially in lonely old people who were—'ready to go' was the phrase. But he's not lonely, she'd wanted to tell those doctors. *I'm here and I'm staying for as long as he needs me.*

'I thought we'd have a chat today, Dad. We can get some fresh air.' Maggie wrapped the bread crusts on his plate into his paper serviette. 'Would you like to feed the birds?' When his shrug suggested the glimmer of lucidity she enjoyed might be short-lived, Maggie didn't wait for the nurse's permission.

The breezeway between the independent and high-care wings of the nursing home was perfect on days like today. Orange jessamine topiary plants in pots scented the air with citrus, while the grevillea bushes dotted around the courtyard perimeter were favourites with bossy lorikeets and noisy honeyeaters, unperturbed by the proximity of humans, especially those bearing bread crusts.

'Dad ...?' Maggie sprinkled crumbs over the ground, enticing the birds closer to Joe. 'When I was telling you about the reunion, and about Noah's mishap ...' That's the term she was using now. '... you mentioned Dan Ireland.'

Though the change was too subtle for Maggie to know exactly what had shifted in her father's face, Joe had recognised the name. The reaction bemused Maggie. Was what happened to Michael so great it miraculously got through to that memory place in his brain most other life events failed to reach?

'Dan *was* at the reunion, Dad,' she told him. 'And we talked.' *Among other things!* 'And Dad, I realised how unhappy I am. How unhappy I was in the city. I'm loving Calingarry Crossing. Ethne is wonderful and I'm actually enjoying the pub. I have a purpose, you know? I'm even taking pictures again.' Maggie waited. Nothing. 'I'm sorry I didn't come home earlier. I wish you'd let me know how sick you were.' She was squatting beside his chair now, gently unfolding each finger to release the strangled bread crusts. 'Dad, I've been lying to everyone. Even you. Worse than that, I've been lying to myself. Brian and I ... We're over. I was hanging on for Noah's sake, or that's what I told myself. The truth is, I've been holding on for me. I was afraid to be alone. But, Dad, I've realised I'm already alone—and have been for a long time. Are you hearing me, Dad? You understand lonely, don't you?'

A tiny squeeze of his hand and Joe's eyes shifted to Maggie's face, staring as if filled with a thousand unsaid words. Then, using the word he'd invented when Maggie was young, he said, 'Smuddle?'

Maggie whimpered and wrapped both arms around her father's shoulders, her ear pressing on his chest, sensing each precious beat of a trying heart inside a tired body.

'Brian and I ... We're not like you and Mum,' Maggie said. 'What's the sense in being married and feeling alone?'

'With a child you're never alone.'

Maggie pulled back, stunned. Joe had spoken a complete sentence that made sense. So what if it sounded like the beginning of a sermon? Maggie didn't care.

'Noah is everything to me, Dad, but someone will come along for him and he'll move on with his life.'

'Brian's child,' Joe said.

'Yes.' She patted his hand for reassurance. 'Noah is his son, always. I would never—'

'Not Noah,' Joe said, frustration showing. 'Brian's child.'

Despite her efforts to hold in the frustration, Maggie sighed. 'Okay, Dad, time to head back inside. I'll bring *"Brian's child"* out tomorrow. I want to photograph you both together.'

'ETHNE?' MAGGIE HAD STOPPED IN ON HER WAY THROUGH TO THE residence to find the barmaid in a sweat. 'You look frazzled.'

'I've had to move those beer kegs this afternoon.'

'Noah usually helps you. Where is he?'

'Good question, love. Haven't seen him since Fiona lobbed. They sat in the beer garden for a while. A bit of a deep and meaningful in progress, if you were to ask me.'

'Fiona was here?' Suspicion stiffened Maggie's tone. 'Yesterday, at her grandmother's house, she said she'd be leaving for Sydney. I assumed early.'

'Sorry, love. I was too busy to keep tabs. Thought you were okay with the Princess. Besides, she's gone. Headed back to Sydney, as you say.'

'Oh?' Why did the news not comfort Maggie?

TWO HOURS LATER, WITH STILL NO SIGN OF NOAH, PANIC, MIXED WITH A mother's intuition, powered Maggie's dash into the residence. Dispensing with her customary knock and wait, she burst into Noah's room.

'No, no, no!'

What told a mother her baby had flown the nest when everything looked the same: the dirty laundry in the corner, the school locker smell of rotten socks and decaying fruit, the grating sound of silence without Noah's fuzzy music leaking from earphones. She hardly needed evidence of the missing backpack, beloved guitar case and treasured iPad to know the impossible had happened. Noah was gone.

After a frantic search of the Centenary Event planning file, Maggie located Fiona's mobile phone number scribbled on one of Jennifer's carefully typed meeting agendas. Shaking mad, she rushed to her bedroom, grabbed the landline's handset and punched out the number.

'Fiona!' The rage that had simmered all week boiled over. 'Turn around this minute and bring Noah back here.'

'Maggie? That you?'

'Yes,' she snapped, 'and I want Noah home.'

'He's not with me. He asked for a lift to Saddleton. I dropped him off on my way.'

'Saddleton? Why?' In the silence, Maggie pictured Fiona's casual shrug. 'Where in Saddleton did you drop him?'

'Outside the pool.'

'Did he have bags with him?'

'A backpack. And his guitar case. Said he was catching the bus to a mate's place in Springvale—somewhere like that.'

'A bus? There is no bus to Springvale.' Maggie visualised another annoying shrug and wanted to reach through the phone and throttle her. 'Fiona, if you're covering for him ...'

'Not a chance, Maggie. He was talking about seeing his dad but no way would I take him to Sydney,' she said. 'Can I do something?'

'You've done enough.' Maggie wanted to blame somebody, and Fiona seemed like the perfect person. 'I have to go. I have to find my son.' She disconnected the call and pressed Brian's quick-dial button while literally running with the handset from the residence and into the hotel. When the voicemail message played, Maggie cursed. If someone came at her with anything resembling a matchstick, she'd explode on the spot.

'You okay in there, love?' Ethne poked her head through the small servery window that separated the bar from the dining room.

'I would be if Saddleton had a bus route out to Springvale. Noah's taken the bus.' She paced over to the kitchen door.

'To Springvale?' Ethne's confusion deepened.

'To Sydney. Fiona claims she refused his request for a lift, instead dropping him at Saddleton swimming pool. There's a nightly bus to Sydney once a week that picks up from outside the council pool.'

'Well, lucky the boy's not silly.' Ethne guided Maggie back into the dining room and extricated the phone from her stranglehold before guiding her into a chair. 'And he's not a boy. Even though you don't see him as a grownup, he'll be eighteen soon.'

'Yes, and at eighteen I made the dumbest decisions. One of them was getting engaged.'

'He will obviously stay with his dad.'

'That's the worry.' Maggie slumped, head cradled in her hands, her elbows grinding into the tops of her knees until the surrounding skin pooled white. 'I thought I was doing a decent job.'

'You are, love. You can be a little over-protective, but nothing wrong with loving someone so much that you worry for them.'

'Or that you lie to them?' Maggie's body would no longer let her stay seated, the words *Liar, liar, pants on fire* pinging around her head. 'I should have told him the truth.'

'What's all this?' Ethne asked, her voice calm. 'What truth? Tell me.'

'I haven't been honest with Noah about his father.' Maggie spoke as if in complete control. She wasn't. 'I've let him, you and everyone else think the reason Brian can't be here with his family is because he's too busy with his flourishing music career.'

'He doesn't have a flourishing music career?'

'He doesn't have a music career, full stop. The last time we spoke he was high on something and I'm pretty sure it isn't life,' Maggie added. 'There is no special job, Ethne, nothing but the same old pub gigs where he's paid in meals and booze and God knows what else. At first I thought I wouldn't be away from Sydney for long. Brian promised he'd follow us out here, but ...' Maggie sat again and lowered her face into her hands. 'I've made such a terrible mistake, accepting every excuse. Brian cares about no one but himself and his ridiculous obsession with fame. I've stupidly let my son think his father is something he's not and now I have no idea what Noah will walk into at our apartment. Oh, what a mess.'

'You and Noah have a wonderful relationship. Why keep this from him?'

'Because, Ethne, I never, never, never want him to know the pain of being forgotten by the person who's supposed to love you. I naively hoped my husband would come around. And don't' tell me to calm down. There's no time. I need to go.' Maggie's eyes frantically searched the room as if looking for the packing list she'd never prepared to tell what she'd need for the trip she never dreamed she'd have to make. A trip to find her son. 'If I hurry I could be in Sydney by—' She glanced at her watch.

'Not on your life.' Ethne stood as if to make her point. 'The only person putting their foot down hard is me. You are not getting behind the wheel of Joe's jalopy in your state and driving in the dark. You got that car looked at by Mick at the garage yet?'

'I can't think about that, Ethne. I don't trust Brian to be sober, or even alone.' It was the first time she'd spoken those thoughts aloud. 'Last time I rang I heard a voice. He said it was the TV, but ... Argh, how stupid am I? I need to intercept Noah, or somehow get to Brian before him.'

'Have you tried calling Brian? You might be worrying for nothing.'

Maggie wouldn't admit the landline had been disconnected six months ago for non-payment of a bill. There was only Brian's mobile, which often went to voicemail. What sort of message would she leave? *Clean up your act and get whatever bimbo you have out of the flat because your son who admires you and wants to emulate you is on his way?*

'Ethne, if Brian's even home on a Saturday I'm afraid he'll be drunk or off his face. And if he's not home, what's Noah going to do then? Let himself in? That's if he remembered his key. Or else he'll sit in the stair-well until God knows what time.' Defeated, Maggie fell back against the wall, her fists clenched, their restrained thump, thump, thump on her thighs a slight release of her frustration.

'I have an idea.' Ethne reached out and took both Maggie's hands in hers, squeezing them tight. Then she gave Maggie that look—the kind a mother gives an irritable child. 'Didn't you tell me your chappy is a city copper?'

Maggie grimaced. 'Dan Ireland is not my *chappy* but, yes, he is a detective. And he's married, as am I, Ethne.'

'Then ring an old friend. He certainly seems to have no problem using the telephone.' Either Ethne's or Dan's name tricked Maggie's lips into a small smile. 'And while the man may not be your chappy, he is persistent.'

Maggie's shoulders slumped under the weight of her recollection. 'But I said something not so nice on the night of Noah's accident.' She didn't tell Ethne that Dan was the last person she would burden with her sorry state of affairs. 'What?' Maggie asked when Ethne shrugged and rolled her eyes. 'What's that look for?'

'Not sure about you,' Ethne quipped, 'but I find it helps to have someone share the burden. By calling, that's all you're doing.'

Sharing the load was exactly what Maggie had been craving, and while calling Dan sounded practical, she could hardly ask him to intervene without telling him the whole sorry story and exposing the lie that was her life. For some reason, the image of little Maggie Lindeman standing under a fig tree in the churchyard wagging a self-righteous finger at Dan after he'd stubbed his toe flashed before her. 'That'll teach you for throwing berries,' she'd chided.

Think, Maggie! There must be another option, but the quick tally of a short list—mostly friends and acquaintances linked to Brian and his music —yielded no alternative solution. The only other possibility was calling the local police near where they lived, but what would be the ramifications?

She sighed, resignedly. 'Maybe I *should* call Dan.' He was, after all, a friend and the only sensible choice—and she could trust him. 'I'll do it.'

She'd call Dan—for her son's sake. She'd do anything to protect Noah.

37

DAN

'It's Maggie, Dan. Maggie Henkler ... err ... Lindeman ... err ... Henkler. It's ... it's just me, Maggie. I'm sorry to call out of the blue. If now's not convenient—'

'Hey, slow down.' The edge in her speech told Dan this wasn't a social call, but he didn't let the fact take away from the momentary pleasure he'd taken in hearing her voice—tense or not. He'd given up the possibly of seeing Maggie again, and after emailing and leaving messages with the grumpy commandant at the hotel he'd about given up on hearing her voice. 'Tell me what's wrong?'

'Dan, I am so sorry. It's a long story—one I hardly have time to tell.'

'Then tell me what you need.' He heard a gasp on the other end of the phone. Not surprise or shock, more like catching that first breath after being underwater for too long.

'I need a favour. It's about Noah and ... and Brian.'

Had it been anyone but Maggie crying through a jumbled-up version of her relationship and marriage, Dan would feel compelled to ask more questions before agreeing to barrel into another bloke's apartment in a not-so-official capacity. The urgency in her voice, however, suggested this was no time for rules. Later, he would ask questions about her marriage—as a personal need to know rather than a professional one. At this point he didn't dare let himself think about the difference Maggie's admission of a failing marriage made to him. Did he have a chance?

The possibility was enough to squeeze his stomach tight. She'd barely been out of his thoughts in recent times, and with little more than reading to occupy his mind, this blasted long service leave was driving him crazy.

Grabbing the novel he hadn't got into, Dan walked to the bookcase and shelved the title, along with any cogitation about reconnecting and getting to know Maggie after all these years. The woman was asking for his help. She didn't need more complications. What did they even have in common, other than agreeing family came first? It was family loyalty that had kept the two of them apart as teenagers—that *and* Dan's self-destructive attitude—and his ongoing devotion to Tracy was why he'd held back on his feelings at the reunion. While keeping Tracy's promise might have been unfair on Maggie, no one could accuse Dan of being anything other than a good husband and father. Tracy had confirmed as much, regaling him with anecdotes about the many times he'd hugged away pain and those prickly prepubescent blues. He could also be a good friend and help an old one.

'What's the address, Maggie?'

Dan wrote what she told him. An area he knew well enough from his stint at The Cross. A wedge of the working class between the city centre and Sydney's trendy eastern suburbs: the good, the bad and the ugly. He could even picture the multi-storey, red-brick building from the seventies book-ended by similar units boasting why-even-bother balconies—too small for much of anything except a potted herb garden. And in relation to *that* neighbourhood Dan used the word 'herb' loosely.

'I'm worried for Noah,' Maggie was saying. 'Worried what he might find at the flat. I need to talk to him, to explain I wanted to preserve his and Brain's relationship.'

Dan wanted to reassure her, but she wasn't listening.

'I can't sit here trying to raise Brian on the phone. If I left for Sydney now—'

'Don't leave, Maggie!' he said—and not for the first time in his life. 'The drive may not be necessary. Let me drop by. If Noah is on the overnight bus, he won't hit Sydney for hours. I'll check the bus schedule to be sure, but from memory the Saddleton service has stops en route.'

'I-I'm not thinking straight, Dan. I'm not sure what the right thing is ...'

At the sound of her voice giving out, Dan wanted to leap through the phone and grab her. Maggie needed only a little propping up. She was strong. He'd discovered as much at the reunion. 'You know your husband and you know your son.'

'I know nothing, Dan, except that Noah has been at me for ages about his dad. When I saw Brian the day after Amber Bailey's funeral he was so different; nothing like the person we left behind two years ago.'

'Remember, Maggie, if Noah is coming to Sydney he's coming back to a city he knows. Leave it with me.'

'I sound like a crazy woman, don't I, Dan?'

'No, you sound like a mother.' He heard the sob she choked back; the sort he'd heard too many times; the sort a grieving parent holds in until the copper with the bad news leaves and the door closes. 'And you're protecting that all-important father–son relationship. I'm here for you, Maggie. Both of you.'

'Dan, I don't know what to say.'

'Say goodbye and say you'll stop worrying. I've got your number.'

❧

DAN SLEPT LITTLE, RISING EARLY FOR A RUN AND TO RECHECK THE BUS ETA. He needed time to call into Kings Cross station for a word with the Area Commander. Even an unofficial job called for prudence and observance of certain protocols. At the same time he'd look up Brian Henkler on the police database for any form, complaints, disturbance reports, known associates and outstanding warrants. He might get lucky and find a mugshot. Dan had no mental image of the bloke as he used to be back in Calingarry Crossing. What he remembered from the brief overlapping acquaintance when they'd been teenagers, both keen on the same girl, was a weird little guy whose intense passion for music had kept him on a natural high. Brian might have been soft around the edges, but he had talent, even if the smooth John Williamson-style singing voice seemed incongruent with his weedy stature and pock-marked complexion.

What had irked Dan on those few occasions he'd bumped into Brian— apart from him hanging off Maggie—had been an edginess that exaggerated the bloke's natural high. Henkler had always been like a helium balloon. One that goes up and up and up into the atmosphere, building pressure until—BAM!—it bursts and plummets. Unfortunately, that type of person took people down with them. This had bothered Dan more than anything. The louder and more hyper Brian became, the more Dan had wanted to scrunch up his face and stick his fingers in his ears to prepare for the inevitable pop. Despite what Dan had thought, the flashy bloke had obviously been more fascinating than the broody, rebellious Dan, whose idea of charming the girls—charming anyone—had been big-noting himself or making a scene. Dan had gone out of his way to be the bad boy in town, too stupid to understand that bad boys only ever ended up with bad girls—girls like Amber Bailey—rather than girls like Maggie Lindeman. How lucky he left town and scored that security job. Then Tracy came along and let him fall in love with her.

In *The Making of Dan Ireland*, which is what he called those early days of their relationship, Tracy had introduced a sceptical Dan to life's gentler side—pastimes like art and ballet. His first-ever live show was the Sydney Dance Company's interpretive performance of Romeo and Juliet. He knew little of the story beforehand, and by intermission was baffled until his wife explained the convoluted plot 'in Dan speak': 'This dude kills his girlfriend's brother, and even though an accident, the girl's parents forbid her to see the dude. Fantastic, isn't it?' Tracy had gushed.

STAR-CROSSED LOVERS, DESTINY AND TRAGEDY. THE MEMORY OF THAT ballet performance played on Dan's mind as he took a break from sorting through police records in a back room at Kings Cross local area command. With each find, Maggie's 'long story' needed less explanation. Brian Henkler—aka Reece Naylor—was a cliché crook and a time-waster for cops: a few DUIs, barred from every local hotel, and with several domestic noise complaints lodged against him. The rest Dan would find out in person.

38

D an pulled his car up short of a No Parking sign and slid a laminated police logo on the dash in case a local ranger had an itchy ticket trigger finger. Observing the red-brick block, Dan marvelled at the irony of Maggie having lived within a short drive of him for years. After a stint in Goulburn, where he attended the Police Academy, Dan and Tracy had favoured Sydney's north, buying a house in the leafier, family-friendly suburb of Lane Cove. When he'd moved out two months ago, he'd stayed close to be near his kids. It was a nice area. Maggie's apartment block, on the other hand, with Kings Cross her nearest train station, and the eclectic clash of haves and have-nots packed into surrounding streets, was a lot less salubrious but ultra-convenient for an ambitious musician.

After exiting and locking the car, Dan trod the skinny cement path that cut across a square of lawn littered with soggy junk-mail catalogues. From the foyer, he began the climb to apartment number eight on the second floor. When a long-haired, tattooed male teen—slight build, about 180 centimetres tall, Caucasian, with dark-brown eyes and a scar that split his right eyebrow in two—stopped dead on the stairway, the bloke eyed Dan as if emblazoned across his forehead were the letters C.O.P.

'You right, old man?' said the inked-up kid. Maybe he thought Dan was about to cark it mid-floors and bring the coppers.

'No longer in top nick,' he lied. 'You wait 'til you're my age.'

With a grunt, the tattooed teen continued his effortless descent, further rubbing his enviable youth and fitness in Dan's face.

On the second-floor landing, Dan stopped outside apartment-eight and heard the nasal twang of a country singer crooning a typical country song —the type that made you feel sad even when you're not. Dan's hard triple rap on the paint-chipped door worked like a remote control on the volume.

'Alright, lady!' a male voice called. 'You got superhuman fuckin' hearing or what? Go ahead. Call the fuckin' police, ya old bag.'

Dan knocked again, a friendlier rat-a-tat-tat.

'What the hell?!' The door flew open and a hollow, unnaturally tanned and unshaven face scanned Dan from top to toe and back again. 'Who the fuck are you?'

Dan was tempted to ask the same. After a glance to confirm the unit number, he engaged his well-practised policeman's poker face, eased his clenched jaw into a smile, and relaxed the fight-ready hands that had instinctively fisted by his side. He extended one. 'Brian, mate, you don't remember me?'

'Should I?' he asked, hesitating before limply shaking the proffered hand.

'You damn well better. Dan—Dan Ireland. How goes it?' He landed a heavy hand on Brian's right shoulder, almost pushing the inebriated bloke off balance when he barged into the unit. Stopping in the centre of the small, chaotic room, Dan silently inventoried the space, zeroing in on the coffee table stash by his left leg. 'Am I interrupting a party?' he asked, dangling a packet of six pills between his thumb and index finger.

Brian lunged for the bag, took possession, pocketed them. 'Where exactly do I know you from, mate?'

'You were in Calingarry Crossing, playing in a pub with your old man. About twenty years ago, I reckon.'

'Christ!' Brian smeared his oily fringe back over his head. 'Fucking hell, mate, you had me worried. Anyone ever said you look like a cop?' Brian chuckled. 'But I remember now. You had the hots for my Maggie.'

That unwavering smile of Dan's twitched. *My Maggie?* He wanted to thump sense into the undeserving dullard right there and then. This was exactly the scene Maggie had wanted to protect Noah from. Having seen the situation for himself, Dan checked his watch. *Plenty of time.* Not long now and he'd be talking to Maggie. Job done. Last night he'd ascertained a boy matching Noah's description had been collected from Saddleton bus terminal yesterday evening and confirmed his ETA in Sydney. Enough time to grab a strong coffee, intercept Noah at the terminal, and get him to call his mum.

'So ...' Brian said. 'You gunna just stand there? Do you want an autograph, or what?'

Dan was about to speak when a post-pubescent woman appeared wearing cut-off denim jeans that made Kylie Minogue's gold hot-pants look like pedal-pushers.

'Reece? Babe? Are you coming back to—? Well, hello there!' The beige halter top looked hand-knitted, although Dan doubted rosebud nipples poking through Grandma's knit-one, purl-one were part of the pattern. 'Are we having another party, babe?'

'This here's my old mate, Dan, from Calingarry Crossing.'

'Brian,' Dan said, his need for caffeine growing, 'we're not mates and I'm not staying to party. I've come here at Maggie's request.'

Nipple girl's gum chewing slowed; that, combined with her big brown eyes laden with mascara—and the nipples—made Dan think about a jersey cow.

'Who's Maggie, babe? And where's Calingarry Crossing?'

Brian ignored the woman, his shoulders squared firmly in Dan's direction. 'Oh, I get it. She's brought in the big guns. Well, if this is part of her get Brian by the balls and drag him back to Calingarry Crossing mission, you can tell her to forget it.'

'Reece? Who's Brian? I'm confused, babe.' Jersey cow's brain was battling, but she remained invisible to the two bulls locking horns.

'Listen, Brian.' Dan said, adopting his negotiator tone and stance—hands open, unthreatening. 'You've got a wife and a son in Calingarry who obviously ...' He was about to say love, but the word stuck in his throat. 'Who *care* about you. Family's important to Maggie. Call her, Brian.'

'Hey, mister, you got the wrong guy.' Nipple girl stuck both hands on her hips, pushed out her sizeable breasts and said, 'This man is Reece Naylor. The next big thing. Right, babe?'

'My name is Reece Naylor,' Brian repeated robotically. 'Soon to be the biggest name in country music, pal. Brian Henkler doesn't exist.'

'Not according to your wife.'

'What wife?' asked Nipple Girl.

Brian's uneasy pacing stopped so close to Dan he could taste every breath of stale booze the bloke snorted. Any minute Brian's foot would start pawing the ground. 'What's all this to you anyway, mate?' he said. 'You and my wife got something going on?'

Dan's fists clenched and unclenched by his side. 'Maggie is your wife, mate, and mother to your son.'

'Then what's it to ya?' Brian poked Dan's chest, urging him backwards and out of Nipple girl's earshot before lowering his voice. 'If you're here to push her bloody ultimatum, tell her there's no room in my life for family. She knows the importance of my music. Whatever her problem is, Maggie will have to handle it. I've waited too long, given up too much, and got too fuckin' close to my dream to pull the pin. According to my bio, I *am* Reece Naylor,' he announced. 'No way am I turning into my old man and throwing my career away to drop dead in a pub in a dusty country town. It does not suit me to have a wife or a son right now. You tell Maggie that from me.'

'Dad?'

Both men turned towards the front door. Dan swore under his breath, while Brian—after pushing Nipple Girl aside roughly—stumbled and lunged towards his son, arms flailing.

'No you don't, mate.' Dan redirected the stumble, shoving Brian back and onto a two-seater sofa as Noah took two terrified steps backwards, his expression morphing from confusion, to hurt, then anger.

'Geez, Noah, buddy, you surprised your old man. You're all grown up.'

'Screw you, Dad!' the boy shouted, side-stepping Dan and thwarting his attempt to stop him.

'Noah, wait up,' Dan called, closing the gap on the stairs and catching up on the outside path. 'I'm a policeman. Let's talk.'

Noah shrugged Dan's hand roughly from his shoulder and swung his backpack to the ground. 'I've done nothing wrong.'

'Listen, Noah, you probably don't remember me. I'm an old school friend of your mother's. My name's Dan Ireland. I was at the reunion.'

'Good on you.' Noah picked up his backpack, strode over to the kerb and drove his country boot into the parking ticket machine.

That's gotta hurt! Dan mused as he caught up. 'Listen, Noah, I'm sorry you had to see that just now. I was supposed to meet your bus.'

'I asked the driver to let me off. It was quicker. That against the law?'

Yes, Dan might have said. 'Your mum's worried.'

'Worried she didn't tell me my father's an arsehole?'

Another dent in the parking meter and the boy anguish grabbed Dan by the chest. After everything he'd seen on the job, a child's tears remained Dan's Achilles heel and this was Maggie's son. Dan wanted to reach out, to comfort and reassure. He resisted the urge. The boy was not Dan's to hug.

A Saab with a dented front fender nosed awkwardly into the No Parking spot in front of Dan's car. Recognising the vehicle first—who could miss the canary-yellow convertible and FIFI 001 plates—Dan recognised the young woman behind the wheel. Noah, too, he guessed, as the lad lowered his face to finger-combed his fringe; an attempt to cover red eyes, no doubt.

'Mum sent you, too, huh?' Noah mumbled.

'Are you kidding me?' Fiona shoved a pair of sunglasses on top of her head and exited the car. 'Your mother is freaking out. She just about accused me of kidnapping you. I tried calling her. No answer. Then, last night, I remembered we'd Googled your address on my phone one day. Figured it was worth a shot, if only to get back in your mum's good books.' Fiona turned to Dan, as though noticing his existence for the first time. 'I know you,' she said, almost accusingly. 'Is everything okay, Noah?' She reached out a hand, but the lad fended her off. 'You look like crap.'

He kept his head lowered and resumed his assault on the parking meter, his mark becoming more obvious with every boot to the thin metal sheeting. Dan knew he should stop him, but ... *What the hell!* Dan hated parking meters the same as the next guy.

'Quit with the kicking thing and look at me,' Fiona demanded.

'Shut up and leave me alone,' Noah retaliated. 'You're not my mother. You can't tell me what to do.'

'No, I'm not your mother, or your sister, or any relation, thank God. But I am a friend, and you, Noah, are a jerk if you don't let me help.'

'You wanna help, Fi? Start by not telling me what to do.'

'And you, Cowboy, can start by—'

'Okay, enough!' Dan interjected. 'You two sound no different to my fourteen-year-olds.'

Noah looked at Dan. 'Can we just get out of here, please?'

'Sure, mate, but I need one minute. You two stay put. An order, not a request. Got that, Fiona?' He glared at the girl and she responded with a look that said she wasn't a complete idiot.

Leaving the girl coaxing a reluctant Noah towards the Saab, Dan jogged into the block of flats, taking the stairs two at a time with ease, only to find Brian making a wonky descent, as anticipated.

'Back you go, mate.' Taking a firm grasp of Brian's left bicep, Dan turned him back up the stairs. The other hand grabbed Brian's belted pants with an upward twist—the proven technique an oldie but effective. The ball-crushing hold never failed to ensure cooperation.

'Get your hands off me. I gotta see my kid.'

'Not like this.' *And not ever, if I have any say.*

Dan pushed Brian across the second-floor landing and through the open door before shoving him onto the sofa for a second time. Within seconds, Nipple Girl was rushing to Brian's aid, a string of profanities vomiting from lips smeared with the remnants of fuchsia-pink lipstick.

'Who the fuck do you think you are?' she sprayed, flopping down next to Brian.

The police ID Dan flashed might as well have been a Taser. Initially shocked, as their gazes dropped to the coffee table with its inventory of smoking devices, booze and pill packets, the expressions switched to one Dan had seen many times—the struggle between fight and flight instincts.

'Relax,' he said, 'I'm not here to bust your arses. Not sure I can say the same for the guys at Kings Cross station. If you want to kill yourselves, I won't stop you. But Brian, you won't destroy your son, or Maggie.'

'Who's Maggie?' Nipple Girl whined.

'Maggie, Maggie, Maggie,' Brian jeered. 'She's got some nerve sending the cops around to force my hand. She might as well kill me.'

'Who's Maggie?' Nipple Girl's constant enquiry reminded Dan of a dripping tap, adding to his itch to flatten this stupid Brian bastard who Maggie had chosen over him.

No words would have prepared him for this sorry excuse for a man. Over the phone, she had alluded to Brian changing a lot in the last twenty-four months, but Dan was finding it hard to believe someone as smart as her would tolerate such base behaviour. Unless the man's downfall had been sudden, like a helium balloon—BAM!

'Wait!' Brian slammed a fist into the sofa. 'If this is about her wanting me out of the flat to save money, two can play at that game.'

Dan tensed, self-defence mode kicking in as Brian heaved himself off the sofa. Grabbing a shoebox from a low sideboard, he launched the contents at Dan. While the box fell short, Dan caught some contents mid-flight.

'She wants the place, it's all hers. Now, get the fuck out.'

As Dan walked away, still clutching the mess of envelopes to his chest, Nipple Girl's whining words, 'but Babe, who's Maggie?' echoed until he left the building and joined Noah on the footpath.

Dan was about to suggest they leave when Brian called from the tiny second-floor balcony. 'Oi, mate!' The man dangled a cardboard box over the railing. 'Tell her I've already started packing and I think this is hers.' He opened his hands and the carton fell, landing on the postage-stamp-sized front lawn and narrowly missing the small brick wall that housed the spewing letterbox slots. Then he disappeared.

Miraculously, the carton remained intact. Not so the contents—mostly ornaments, sports trophies and unknown objects in bubble wrap. As Fiona gathered the few items that had spilled over the lawn, Dan released the pile of paperwork over the top of the box ready to lift the lot.

'I'll do it,' Noah decreed, taking charge of the possessions as he looked back into the building.

With the lad's thoughts unknown, Dan made a point of slinging an arm across the boy's sagging shoulders to guide him towards the car. The move was both protective and precautionary should Noah ditch the box to dash up those stairs and beat the crap out of his old man. Lashing out is how a young Dan had dealt with his anger. But Noah wasn't him. Noah had grown up in a loving environment. He was solid with a sensible head on his shoulders. *When not under the influence of drugs!* Brian was the conundrum. Why Maggie would want anything to do with him was beyond Dan's understanding. He could only think she had good reason, and that reason was likely the scared and confused kid in front of him.

'I knew there was stuff happening,' Noah mumbled. 'I just wish Mum had told me the truth.'

'Right about now I reckon your mum's having that same thought,' Dan said. 'But sometimes keeping a secret is a choice we make because the time's not right to tell.' Dan thought he saw a spark of recognition in Noah's face, as if his words were getting through. 'Then stuff happens,' he added, 'and, well, before we realise it, the secret's turned into a lie. The longer you keep the secret, mate, the harder it is to tell the truth, especially if the truth will hurt someone you love. Get my drift?' When the kid nodded, Dan said, 'We'd best call Mum and get you back home. Let's go.'

Noah stood firm and shook his head. 'I asked Fi. She said I could stay with her dad and her. She's moving back in.'

Dan's head indicated his thought on the matter before Noah finished the sentence. 'I don't think your mother will go for that.'

'Won't know if we don't ask. I'll call Maggie,' Fiona offered, trying to fish her phone from skin-tight jeans. 'I'll put Noah on a bus back to Calingarry Crossing if she wants, or I'll drive him back myself in a couple of days. Her choice.'

'Maggie has a right to be annoyed, Fiona, and I can't blame her but if you want my advice …' Dan paused. This wasn't his call. These weren't his kids.

'Okay, yes, I made a stupid mistake and I'm a spoilt bitch,' Fiona snapped. 'Can we move on now? I've learned my lesson.'

'What say we hold off on any calls until we're sitting down? We can order food. You must be hungry, Noah,' Dan said. 'We'll get our bellies full and our heads clear and then you'll call your mum and ask about staying. What do you say?'

'I know the perfect place to eat,' Fiona replied first. 'My shout.'

'Noah?' Dan nudged the boy and grinned. 'I think we just got extra hungry.'

Dan watched from his own car as Noah climbed into Fiona's Saab and cast a final glance at his father's second-storey window.

MAGGIE

The dream woke Maggie; the one that had plagued her since putting Joe into care. Rather than frighten her, Maggie took comfort from the bright lights and glowing, ghost-like silhouettes and imagined Mary and Michael were looking over her. Not tonight, though. Tonight's dream had a sense of urgency, waking her at midnight.

Seconds later, the phone by her bed rang out. Maggie answered, and immediately Roslyn's tone told her all she needed to know. 'I'll be right there.'

Throwing on a track suit and running shoes, Maggie instinctively stopped by her son's room to check on him, but Noah wasn't in his bed. All three voices on the telephone earlier today had outnumbered Maggie three-to-one. Even Dan had vouched for Fiona, suggesting a day or two at the Blair apartment might be a distraction while Noah sorted out his head.

PANIC PUSHED MAGGIE'S FAST WALK ALONG THE LINOLEUM CORRIDOR into a jog as she neared the nursing station with its subdued night lighting. 'I got here as fast as I could, Roslyn. How is he?' Maggie didn't slow her gait, forcing the nurse to walk and talk.

'I'm afraid it was a bad turn, Maggie. Another stroke and some complications,' Roslyn said. 'Joe's resting comfortably but the doctor said I should call you, in case.'

In case of what? Maggie wanted to ask as she followed Roslyn into a room labelled: Special Care.

'Ring the buzzer if you need me,' the nurse said before leaving again.

Trying not to cry, Maggie swallowed back the sob that lodged in her throat at the sight of what was left of her father, what was left of the man —of his body suddenly withered by sickness and despair, yet still desperate to hold on a little longer. For what? Maggie wondered. For her? For Noah? Maggie wished her son was with her.

'My Maggie.' Even in the cruel silence of the stark ward, Joe's voice was barely audible. Maggie longed for the noise and hustle and bustle of a busy hospital room. Noise was good. Noise meant hope. Silence made the situation more profound, sadder.

'Hi Dad.' She smoothed the man's customary comb-over, patting the flimsy few remaining strands on the top of his head before leaning down to kiss his forehead, stopping long enough to breathe in the thousand memories. The man who'd taught her to smuddle still smelled like a big hug.

'So beautiful, so strong, so like my Mary,' he whispered while wiggling his fingers for Maggie to hold.

There was no truth in his words. Maggie wasn't strong. In marrying Brian she'd taken the easy path—the path of least resistance—and ended up lost and lonely. Only now was she taking control of her future—of those aspects she could control. Aware she could not stop her dad leaving, Maggie was here when it mattered the most, holding her father's hand and helping him to let go. How could he have deteriorated so quickly? Just the other day he was talking. Not the gibberish Maggie had become accustomed to, but actual conversation. It was almost miraculous, but the doctors had warned her ample times of the cruel progression of brain disease. Patients often came good just before the end, giving loved ones a final glimpse of the person they used to be.

The Rev's hands—twisted and tortured with arthritis—rested by his side, transparent tape crinkling thin skin. Without releasing her grip, Maggie dragged a chair over to the side of the bed and lowered herself gently. Then, pulling the seat closer still, she slipped her other hand over Joe's and recalled his hands as once powerful, protective, loving. She remembered him holding her as they danced around the living room, Maggie tippy-toeing while he waltzed in circles and Mary singing 'Moon

River'. She'd give anything to turn back the clock, to be six again, to still be dancing on her father's shoes. She applied the tiniest amount of pressure to his hand and, although her father's return grip was weak, it had the power to rip Maggie's heart from her chest.

'You're my strength,' he said as she bent down and rested her tear-streaked cheek where his hand rested.

'Get some sleep, Dad,' she said, glimpsing the big-faced wall clock ticking away in the hall outside. Three-thirty. Two more hours and the sun would signal a new day. 'One more, one more,' Maggie chanted the wish over and over. Anything to escape the clock's dire ticking.

'No more,' her father muttered. 'No more, Mary, I was wrong, so wrong and I'm tired of secrets. No more, no more.'

'Shhh, Dad, it's me, Maggie.' She sat up, staying close so she could whisper calming reassurances. 'And there are no secrets, Dad.'

'No strength to tell the truth,' he uttered. 'No strength to keep the lies. No more. It's time.'

Maggie's body stiffened, a mix of dread and confusion. Where was this coming from? 'The truth about what, Dad? The letters? Don't worry. I have them. Do you want me to give Dan his letter? Is that what you mean by "it's time"?'

'We have to go, Mary.'

The insistent sob that had been so determined to dislodge itself from deep inside Maggie's throat finally escaped. 'Go where, Dad? Where do you want to go?' She swiped the pad of her thumb over her father's cheeks one after the other. He was back making no sense.

The nurse appeared as if by magic, with only the sticky sound of soft, white shoes padding across the over-bleached floor. Maggie glanced at the nurse for a sign, any sign: a nod of reassurance, a glimmer of understanding, a hint of hope. Nothing.

'Mary?'

'It's Maggie, Dad. I'm here.' She tightened the hold on his hand as the nurse slipped away as silently as she'd appeared.

'A father's love never dies, but it's time.'

'I know, Daddy.' Maggie liked to think she could control everything, protect everyone, but she couldn't protect her father from this and his leaving broke her. 'A daughter's love never dies either, Daddy. I'll love you forever.'

'Maggie,' he mumbled, and she breathed a sigh at hearing her name, but not relief. 'Maggie ... Brian's daughter ...'

'No, Daddy, I'm Maggie—Brian's wife.' She stopped herself.

Why waste precious moments correcting the man? A fragmented conversation would not be her last memory. This room would not. But the clock's tick-tock was fading, the lights dimming, and nausea nudged its way into Maggie's throat. She gulped as the room whooshed around and around, then she lowered her head to the bed again to wait for the wave of sickness to pass.

A CHILL FEATHERED THE BACK OF HER NECK AS IMAGES FROM HER DREAM —the one with the silhouettes standing under a light—materialised. She heard her name just as the light banished the shapes. Gone.

'Daddy!' Maggie sat bolt upright in the chair, her eyes slamming wide open, her heart smashing against her ribs. There was another blast of cold air, as if a door had opened and sucked the warmth and life from the room, filling it instead with stillness and silence.

The *ba-boomp, ba-boomp* inside her chest slowly, slowly returned to normal and, just like in the dream, Maggie knew no fear, only peace. The Rev's hand was still on hers, still giving her courage as her father's final tear rolled down his face and disappeared into the feathery strands of grey sideburn. The struggle was over, finally.

'Say hello to Mum and Michael,' Maggie whispered, tears flowing free, her promise to not cry forgotten. *God, you have all three now.*

40

FIONA

With a wave of the remote, Fiona switched off the giant plasma TV. 'If you're just going to stare and be miserable I'm taking you back to Calingarry Crossing. Let's go, cowboy, move your backside.' She walked over to Noah sitting on the floor and dug the pointy toe of her black Prada pumps into his butt. 'Come on.'

'Quit it,' he said, making a swipe for her ankle.

'Or what?' she challenged. 'Get up. We've got the entire day.'

'To do what? Did you change your mind about getting me into a pub?' Noah asked.

'Do I look completely bonkers? As if I'd risk the wrath of Maggie one more time. Forget it. Besides, it's Sydney, it's summer, and I've got a brand new Megan Gale cossie to show off. Only cost 240 dollars.' Shifting the strap of her shocking pink mini dress, she struck a pose to reveal a matching bikini top.

Noah laughed. 'Are you still trying to impress me with your sexy gear?'

'Noah, I *never* tried to impress you. As if.' She tossed a beach towel at him before picking up her car keys and mobile phone from the glass dish on the table by the elevator. 'Coming or not? You can meet the gang. Molly's gagging to meet you.' Fiona activated the elevator and waited. 'Let's move it. I'll buy you a pair of togs at the surf shop on the way. You a boardies guy, or do you want budgie smugglers?'

'Board shorts, thanks.'

'Good. Not that I have anything against men with a cute arse. Better to leave some things to a woman's imagination, if you know what I mean. Although some blokes should never wear them, like Phillip.' She shuddered. 'A grown man wearing skin-tight swimmers is plain creepy. I told him he was too old and I bought him boardies.'

'Geez, Fi, do you ever stop talking?'

'I'll stop talking when you start walking. Move it, cowboy. I'm trying to make the most of your time before you go back home to the country. Besides clubbing, there must be things you want to do here in Sydney.'

'For sure,' Noah said as he jumped into the opening elevator ahead of Fiona. 'Like whipping your butt in the water.'

'Dream on, cowboy,' she laughed, pressing the carpark button repeatedly. 'No way am I getting these 240 dollars wet.'

PHILLIP LOOKED UP FROM THE STOVE, STEAM HAVING FOGGED HIS GLASSES to make him look less professional and slightly nerdy. 'How was the beach today, kids?'

'Bluebottles everywhere,' Fiona replied with her head in the refrigerator. 'Gross!'

'That's a shame. Do you two want a …' He looked at the Coke cans in Fiona's hands. 'Good-o. Dinner will be ready soon. Take the cutlery to the table on your way.'

'Your dad cooks?' Noah whispered as he followed her into the adjacent room and chose the carving chair at the head of the table.

'Yes, thank goodness! Most times Mum hardly ate, much less prepared meals.'

'You're sorta getting on with your dad now?' Noah asked.

Fiona shrugged, pulled out another chair and sat. 'I s'pose. Had our first deep and meaningful last night sitting right here. He told me stuff I already knew about my granddad, like he was a shit to Gran. I knew Jack Bailey was a control freak, but I figured he cared—about me. Mum suffered, too. Only he manipulated Amber while turning me against her. And you reckon you've got family problems.'

'Are you pissed at not finding your real father at the reunion?' Noah asked.

Fiona pouted. 'Part of me had hoped it would be as easy as landing in town and bumping into a lookalike in the main street. For sure I'd recognise his face, he'd recognise me and *voilà*! Happy families. Truth is,' Fiona added, her focus on the table runner edged with silky golden tassels. 'Luke convinced me I had a rich father out there.'

Noah snorted. 'The one you've got not rich enough?'

'I didn't care about the money part, but Luke would've enjoyed telling Phillip to piss off without jeopardising a potential inheritance. Got the surprise of his shallow freaking life after the reunion when I told him to bugger off,' Fiona giggled. 'Should've seen his face.'

'Because of me?' Noah asked.

'No, because Luke is a jerk and mean and totally under my grandfather's thumb. At least Calingarry Crossing let me see the loser he really is.'

'So you won't look for your real father again?'

Fiona stole a glance at Phillip in the kitchen. 'I might—one day. Dad said he was never happy about not telling me the truth. It was Mum. She was afraid people would look down on her, or she'd get turfed out of the golf club, or something. I dunno.' She looked at Noah looking at her, her next question rhetorical. 'Does a good person lie to those they love just to fit in?'

'Yes,' Noah answered without hesitating. 'That's after you've lied to yourself for years. You lie and lie and you keep who you are a secret so you don't disappoint the people who love you. At least that's what I did.'

'And I told your secret to Maggie.' Fiona spoke to the table runner. 'I'm sorry.'

'Yeah, well, at least I'm out,' Noah said. 'Saves *me* telling.'

'But Maggie's pretty cool. You're lucky. Why didn't you tell her?'

Noah fidgeted in the seat, his legs jigging up and down under the table. 'There was one night a while back. I heard her come upstairs after closing and I went to her room but she was on the phone talking to Dad—shouting more like it, only in a whisper—and telling him she was fed up, that she didn't like the person he was becoming, and insisting he change back or else.'

'Hmm,' Fiona hummed her understanding. 'And you assumed she wouldn't love you if you changed.'

'Maybe.' Noah shrugged. 'To be honest, Fi, I'm glad I'm out. You did me a favour.'

'But your mum *is* cool about you being gay, isn't she?'

'It's weird,' he said. 'I know she knows but … She hasn't said a word, like nothing's different.

'Nothing *is* different about you, Noah,' Fiona said, 'except your secret isn't a secret. In fact, everything's good.'

'Except my dad's a prick.'

'Hey, none of that language, thank you,' Phillip said on approaching the table, both hands laden with food bowls.

'Sorry, Mr Blair.'

'Call me Phillip. The name is trending around the house these days,' he said, sliding a smile Fiona's way. 'Hope you kids are hungry. No standing on ceremony.' He pushed the pasta dish towards Noah and a tossed rocket and parmesan salad—Fiona's favourite—to the centre of the table. 'Dig in. There's plenty.'

The trio helped themselves—Fiona mostly salad while Noah ate like he hadn't seen food for weeks. Partway through dinner, Fiona suggested a movie at the Double Bay cinema. They had a Doris Day/Rock Hudson film festival marathon showing all week—with movies playing on a loop.

AFTER DINNER, PHILLIP AND FIONA TRANSPORTED DISHES TO THE KITCHEN and Noah moved to the TV room where he'd left his guitar.

'What's that tune you were playing on the guitar earlier?' Phillip asked upon his return.

'Our collaboration,' Fiona answered. 'We'll play it for you. Okay, Noah?'

Noah shrugged, as usual, and after a few false starts the pair had played one soppy verse and a chorus before falling apart in fits of laughter.

'Bravo! Bravo!' Phillip applauded. 'While I cannot claim a scrap of musical knowledge, those harmonies sounded terrific.'

Fiona smiled, remembering Phillip's tone-deaf 'Twinkle Twinkle Little Star' from her childhood. Her mother's rendition hadn't been much better. While Phillip and Amber were patrons of the Sydney Symphony Orchestra, neither had a passion for music like Fiona did—the Dalewood School for Girls' Jesus Christ Superstar's Mary Magdalene two years running. Why had she never thought to question her parent's lack of musical prowess? And where did Fiona's come from?

'Hey,' Noah shoved her shoulder. 'Nice job, poodle girl.'

'You, too, cowboy.' Fiona shoved back, taking in the scratches and dodgy strings on the old guitar. Picturing the untouched instrument gathering dust in her old room up the hall, she announced, 'Hold your horses. I won't be a minute.'

Walking directly into her cluttered walk-in closet, Fiona located the guitar in its pristine case, leaning alongside two full removalist boxes. Who knew what was in the cartons? Nothing too important, she guessed. Lifting the lid on a plastic storage box, Fiona dumped the contents on the floor, cursing under her breath as she noticed the ridiculous, over-the-top outfit she'd worn to her mother's funeral was amongst the pile. What an idiot. What a total brat, she'd been that day. She might've blamed grief for her bad behaviour at the funeral, only Fiona had been too busy being mad to be sad. With bitterness and her brattish behaviour almost ruining the relationship with Phillip, she worried Noah's resentment towards either parent would see him follow the same sorry path as her. Kicking his butt into gear was partly why Fiona had asked Noah to stay with her and Phillip. Luckily, Dan had agreed and dealt with 'the Maggie issue'.

Poor Maggie, Fiona thought, fancy being married to a dropkick like Brian.

Taking the emptied plastic box in one hand and the guitar case in the other, Fiona stopped by the mangled carton of Maggie's belongings sitting in the entry hall. 'Better in the apartment than in the boot of her Saab,' she'd told Noah. Not even a security system and steel mesh gates kept crooks out of the basement parking area. Sitting cross-legged on the cool terrazzo hall tiles, Fiona transferred objects from the broken box into the sturdier plastic crate. Amongst the damaged knick-knacks where two Best and Fairest awards engraved with Noah's name, a stuffed bear, and a scented candle. Also, a framed black-and-white photo—the family of four, including a young boy and girl, huddled together on the steps of a small church. The glass and wood frame had survived the fall. Had the family?

Fiona absentmindedly flattened each window envelope, refolding the loose bills, statements, and financial marketing letters Dan had indiscriminately crammed inside the box until one envelope stood out from the bunch. While the mottled parchment, too flimsy for a printer, pricked Fiona's memory, the flamboyant handwriting with a squiggly knotty curly flourish on the capital B set her heart racing inside her chest.

The note began: *Dear Brian*. And by the time Fiona had read: *Best wishes, Amber Bailey-Blair*—with all the frilly letter B's—her body, all the way to her ears, pulsated so hard she didn't hear Noah at first.

'What are you staring at?' She fumbled with each fold of the hand-written letter before jamming the envelope into the back pocket of her jeans as she stood.

'Thought we were going to the movies.'

'SHAME YOU'RE HEADING OUT,' PHILLIP SAID AS FIONA HURRIED INTO THE kitchen and into the shoes she'd left in the middle of the floor. 'I'm enjoying the company.'

Fiona braced a hand on the countertop, hopping from one foot to the other as she positioned the heel straps. Keen to get out and to the cinema so she could sit in the dark without conversation and think about the letter, Fiona instead stood, frozen in a fug of melancholy. The man she'd always called Dad—until recently—had slipped a lonely mug under the espresso machine, pressed the one-cup button, and was tapping a finger on the bench while he waited.

Outside the kitchen window, Sydney's neon skyline flickered, The Harbour Bridge and Luna Park's smiling face dazzling. Fiona, along with twelve of her best friends, had celebrated her sixteenth at the iconic amusement park. It had cost Phillip a bomb. How spoilt she'd been all her life. She caught sight of Noah in the next room fiddling with the TV remote. He'd never been to Luna Park, Dreamworld, Sea World, or Disneyland—nothing. Instead, the seventeen-year-old got excited by a big-screen TV. *But what a jerk of a father!* The cross barmaid in Calingarry Crossing had told Fiona off one day. She'd called her a barnacle and suggested Noah had everything she wanted. But the old bag had been wrong. Noah didn't have a father who loved him. Fiona did.

'Fiona?' Phillip was standing opposite her at the breakfast bar offering her a tissue for the tears she didn't know until then she was crying. 'What's wrong, honey?'

'Nothing.' She sniffed, grabbing the tissue to blow her nose. But there was.

Phillip wasn't her biological father, and yet he adored her. He'd given her everything, looked after her, protected her and loved her like a father loves his daughter. Fiona only had to love him back, and she did. The man need not be alone tonight, or ever again. No matter what had happened in the past, or where she ended up in the future, he had her. Fiona was Phillip's daughter—always.

'You know what?' she said, kicking off both shoes. 'We don't need the flicks, and Noah won't care. He's totally in love with your TV. If that's okay ... *Dad*.'

Phillip smiled, nodded.

'Besides, it's been ages since I beat you at Chess.'

🖎

BY 10 PM, WITH PHILLIP AND NOAH BOTH CRASHED OUT IN THEIR ROOMS, Fiona tried counting sheep. Then she'd counted the neon lights of Sydney's skyline. Knowing he was out there on the edge of the city, Fiona got out of bed, dressed in jeans, a T-shirt, and a hoodie, and crept out of the apartment.

The drive was not long, but it might as well have been to the other side of the world.

🖎

ONLY ONE THING—FIONA'S HEART—BEAT HARDER THAN HER FIST pounding the front door of the flat.

The door opened with a flurry, a putrid whoosh of stale booze and smoke assailing her. The man in blue-striped pyjama pants stared bleary-eyed, his hair standing at odd angles from his skull. 'Who the hell are you?'

'You know who I am,' Fiona said, steeling herself against the urge to slap his chest and his face. 'Take a good look because this is the last time you'll see me.'

Bug-eyed, his mouth dropped open. 'You're her! You're—?'

'No one—not to you,' she interjected. 'I came over to tell you I don't care what my mother wrote in the letter you threw away. You can't possibly be him.'

'Threw away?' Brian seemed to snap awake. She had his attention.

'I knew there had to be a reason I didn't want to look for you,' she told him. 'I now understand. You're an arsehole, Brian—or Reece, or whatever the hell you're calling yourself. I have a father who is more real that you'll ever be. He loves me. Noah is also better off without you. We all are. So go to hell.'

❧

SHE'D GIVEN BRIAN NO TIME TO RESPOND. IN WHAT HAD FELT LIKE ONLY seconds, she'd hit hard and hit fast—a storm without warning and unconcerned for the damage she might cause. As Fiona slammed her car door closed, he would still be reeling.

'Good!' she screamed from inside the closed convertible. 'Good freakin' riddance, jerk-off!' Locking the doors, Fiona rested her forehead on the steering wheel and cried. She cried for herself and for Phillip. She cried for Noah, too, who would go home later today with the box of broken bits. As for the letter … Fiona could only cry more for her mother's broken life.

41

MAGGIE

The sun was climbing into a pomegranate-pink sky when Maggie
walked out of the nursing home and stepped carefully around car
park puddles—evidence of a reasonable overnight rain event. When an
ambulance pulled in, lights flashing, Maggie turned away, emotionally ill-
equipped to witness any more grief or pain until a noise sounded. One
Paramedic was extracting a woman on a gurney, while the driver escorted
a man wearing red pyjamas shorts and a loose shaving coat. He was
carrying a squawking bundle of white, which he delivered to the patient's
outstretched arms. Milling around the entrance, Emergency staff in their
scrubs laughed and applauded as the paramedics bowed and a couple
bearing a bouquet wrapped in blue paper raced from their car. Another
cheer erupted. Another baby born. A boy.

Maggie dropped her head into cupped hands without shedding a tear.
She had none left. Instead, a rumble started in her chest and ground its
way out in a low, mournful moan. Maggie had never felt so alone; nor had
she ever felt such a need to hold her son.

❧

THE TOWN OF CALINGARRY CROSSING WAS YET TO WAKE FULLY, THE MAIN
street's motley pattern of morning sunshine and shadow courtesy of fig
trees in full bloom. To one side, the hotel stood silent—too silent for

Maggie's liking. After parking the car, she crept upstairs, even though there was no one to wake. Noah wasn't in his room. Sitting on his bed, oblivious to odours which would ordinarily have her searching the floor, Maggie remembered her phone was still switched off. As soon as the device powered on, the message tone sounded, delivering an update from Dan via voicemail. *At last!* He'd accompanied Noah to Fiona's home, met Phillip Blair, and enjoyed fancy wine and a fancy view. 'Nice guy,' he'd said, before telling her to do the impossible: 'Don't worry, Maggie.'

Tempted to return the call, wanting his comforting voice in her sad solitude—maybe bringing a smile to her lips like his message had done—Maggie flopped back on her son's unmade bed and hit the replay function on the phone. Hearing Dan's message multiple times was better than the sound of silence where there should have been noise.

MAGGIE'S EYES FLUTTERED OPEN. HAD SHE SLEPT? NOT FOR LONG according to the bedside clock, and not long enough to face another day—a day that had no familiarity to it until certain sounds grew louder. The hotel was waking.

From her son's room, Maggie listened to the sounds that shaped her Calingarry Crossing existence: the hum of delivery trucks; Ethne's shrill response when a driver told her the latest joke; the clinking of empties from the night before, because chucking cans and bottles in the recycle *after* closing was too noisy. She heard the constant squeaks and clunks that came with living in a century-old building with rattling windows and hard-to-open doors—or those that closed too easily and too loudly. These were things she could live with. What bothered Maggie was walls as thin as paper, especially during those whispered arguments at night with Brian.

Maggie was so lost and lonely without Noah she'd welcome an argument with her husband. Anything to distract her and stop her worrying about breaking the news about Joe to her son, but only once he's safely home. For the next twenty-four hours, Maggie would sleep, and when the pub reopened after the day of mourning that Joe Lindeman would have pooh-poohed, the bar will fill and Maggie can pretend her dad is not gone forever and her boy will be closer to home.

UNSURPRISINGLY, SLEEP ELUDED HER, WITH EVERY 'YOU-HOO!' OUTSIDE the residence ignored. The entire town—or so it seemed—took turns to leave cards, flowers and gifts in the courtyard. Someone brought her wine. Maggie smiled at the thought. Who knew the right thing to say or do at a time like this? Except Sara. Sweet, sweet, Sara had lost so many loved ones, she could find a glass-half-full way through any situation. If not for the café owner inviting herself to dinner that night, Maggie might have stayed in bed, covered her head with a pillow and ignored everyone. But Sara had sealed the dinner deal with one of Will's favourite sayings: 'No one ever got strong by staying in bed.'

Joe had thought Maggie was strong. And she would try, if only to get through the official funeral, day after tomorrow. Making the loss more painful was learning her father had wanted no fanfare, no church service, and no sad farewell. With Ethne's help, he'd instructed the home's administrator to arrange a brief ceremony and immediate burial alongside his Mary in the old Calingarry Crossing cemetery. Maggie need to do nothing except be strong while she broke the news to her son.

With a groan shutting out another shouted sympathy message, she forced herself up, straightened her frame, sucked some brightness into her voice and echoed her father's sentiments. 'You are strong, Maggie. You are.'

4 2

Maggie looked up from the last of the drenched pews she was drying to see Charles Ireland riding towards the pub, a fishing rod strapped to the old bicycle and a tackle box and yellow rain jacket stuffed in a wire basket on the handlebars.

'Never rains but it pours, eh?' he said, dismounting like a septuagenarian might. Maggie held her breath each time he stumbled.

'You can say that again.' How many times had she looked into the man's face seeing nothing but an old man? Today she saw a smidge of life. He had Dan's eyes, only without the hope.

'How's tricks?' he said in his gravelly voice, the roll-your-own glued by spit to his bottom lip bobbing up and down as he spoke.

'Better with Noah back from Sydney. How about you?'

'Trying to get a spot of fishing in before tonight's storm.'

'Storm?' Ordinarily, Maggie would see the nightly weather report on the television in the main bar. Last night, around news time, she'd been on her second bottle of wine and rolling drunk. Not that she remembered the rolling bit; the pounding in her head this morning told her as much. Sara had dropped around again for dinner and while ordinarily two bottles of wine might not have been such a problem for two people, her drinking partner was pregnant and therefore, technically, not a drinking partner.

'They're tracking a big one coming our way from the north,' Charlie was saying. 'The rivers are already flowing. With the right spot you could be eating fish for a month.'

'And which spot is that?'

'Ha! You sound like your father, Maggie. Always keen for me to tell.' He hesitated before saying, 'Joe was an outstanding human being. Folks around town thought the world of him, obviously.' Charlie's gaze shifted beyond Maggie to the remaining floral tributes adjacent the pub's main doors. 'I'll be lucky if someone cares enough to nail my box shut to keep the grubs out.'

'Hey, Charlie?' As Maggie stepped off the veranda, she shielded her eyes with a hand. 'If you do catch one of those big bastard fish, drop by on your way home and I'll dig out the what-a-whopper pan of Joe's. I'll cook.'

He looked at her, frown lines scribbling their way across his forehead. She thought he was about to ask her why—why after all this time was she interested in getting to know the crusty old guy who'd managed to chase off everyone in his life? The answer might have had a little to do with missing her father—and those Dan eyes staring at her.

'That's kind of you, Maggie-girl, although I doubt there's a pan big enough.' The faintest tinge of pink brightened the man's dull, grey complexion. 'Then again, if there's a beer on offer you'd best hang onto this to make room in my basket for the catch.' He fished the yellow rain-coat out of the wire basket. 'Rain's not due until tonight. I'll be well back by dinner.'

'If you're certain, Charlie. I'll hang it inside where the brollies go.' Maggie took charge of the musty-smelling plastic. 'Well, I'd better get back to work.' She was returning to the veranda when Charlie's gravelly voice reached her.

'That son of mine was an idiot,' he called. 'Always a bit of a no-hoper. You did well riddin' yourself of him.'

Maggie turned around, prepared to tell him he was wrong. Instead she said, 'See you, Charlie. Be careful out there.'

&.

SARA AND WILL BRAVED THE LATE AFTERNOON CLOUDBURST TO ENJOY their regular Sunday after-work treat—a beer and a meal cooked by someone else, while the monster-in-law took the grandkiddies. Maggie would never say it aloud, but she suspected Ethne enjoyed impressing Will with her weekend specials, and the pair was always a welcome gust of good spirits.

'What culinary creation have we got on the board tonight? Ooh, nice!' Will winked at Maggie from the main door but projected his voice enough to reach Ethne on the other side of the small servery window behind the bar. Making a miniature rain shower when he collapsed the umbrella, Will left it with a half-dozen others in the old milk tin that had sat in the same spot inside the door for a century. 'Couple of the usual, thanks barmaid.'

Maggie chuckled as the pair settled at the bar. 'I'd back off on the barmaid thing, unless you want to wear your beer.'

'Hardly going to matter given the drenching we just got,' Will remarked. 'Where did this lot come from?'

'At least Noah's home and not travelling in this weather,' Sarah said. 'Glad he's back safe, eh?'

'Delivered, as promised, by a subdued Fiona,' Maggie replied, topping up Sara's mineral water with ice.

'Subdued? Are we talking about the same woman?' Will asked, taking the beer Maggie handed him.

Maggie nodded, grinned. 'Yep!'

Fiona did seem very different. If someone asked Maggie to rate on a scale of one-to-ten how changed she seemed since arriving back in town, Maggie would suggest an eight, if not a nine, simply for the way Fiona had stuck by Noah at the cemetery where the small gathering had farewelled Joe.

Did funerals bring people together, perhaps? Sharing the grief of losing Amber and spending time together in Sydney had deepened Maggie's friendship with Sara. Her pregnancy news had further cemented their bond and for the first time in a long time Maggie felt connected enough to open up and be herself with a friend. But too much wine over dinner with Sara had relaxed Maggie too much. Not until the cold, hard light of a hangover had she realised, she'd over-shared about her marriage, about Brian's ridiculous fame obsession and, worst of all, about her son's sexuality. *Brilliant, Maggie!* One minute she was berating Fiona for betraying a confidence and the next she's doing the same with Sara.

'Maggie, honey?' Sara said. 'I was asking how Noah's doing.'

Maggie apologised, only to have the words drowned out by another rumble of thunder and Jackpot's barking. 'He's quiet, sad, confused and keeping to himself. Ethne's looking after the pub tomorrow so he and I can take a drive and a bushwalk through Cedar Cutters Gorge. We'll find a spot to talk. I can't be tiptoeing around my son.'

'Smart move,' Will chipped in. 'Jasper and I are planning a boys-only fishing adventure next week. Nothing teaches kids about patience better than dropping a line and waiting.'

Maggie gasped and twisted around to check the time on the clock behind the bar. 'Bloody daylight saving! I'm worse than a dairy cow adapting to the time change.'

Will slurped noisily through his beer froth, earning a swift jab in the ribs from his wife. 'We keeping you from something, Maggie?' he asked.

'No, but you mentioned fishing and Charlie Ireland came by earlier, going on about a new fishing spot.' Had he said where? Maggie racked her brain to think. She'd been so caught up analysing the features in his face and comparing them to Dan's she'd only half listened.

'I'm not seeing the problem, Maggie.' Will stared at her over the rim of his beer glass.

'Charlie usually checks in his way back home,' she explained. 'He said he would today and he hasn't, as far as I know, and that's his raincoat hanging on the hook.'

'Ethne might've seen him,' Sara suggested.

'Someone mention my name?' Ethne joined Maggie behind the bar.

'Have you seen Charlie Ireland, Ethne?'

'Not today,' the woman said. 'It's late though.'

'I know.' Maggie took the pen Ethne wore behind her ear, picked up an empty glass and tapped the pen repeatedly on the side. Once the room fell silent she sung out. 'Anyone seen Charlie Ireland? He went fishing.'

As the ripple of murmurs and unanimous grunts rose in volume, Louie called back from the pool table. 'You saying he was s'posed to check back in and didn't? You sure, Maggie, darlin'?'

'Yes. He was bringing me a fish in exchange for a beer.'

Someone guffawed. 'Not like old Chuck to miss out on a free beer.'

'One of you needs to go out to his place, just to be sure,' Maggie said.

'No worries, darlin', I'll go,' Louie replied in his usual laid-back drawl. But as he left his half-finished beer, Maggie knew. Behind the calm exterior was genuine concern for a mate, because it was very unlike Louie The Fly to leave a beer unfinished.

'Where did he say this great spot was?' Cricket asked.

'I don't think he did. What should we do?'

'You keep the beer cold, Maggie. I'll call the new copper at the station. What's his name again? Callum?'

Maggie smiled. Callum had been part of the community for over twelve months, yet he was still 'the new bloke'.

After a general mumbling of consensus and nodding, there was an effort to resume normality in the bar while they waited on news from Louie.

'Relax,' Sara said, taking her friend's hand and rubbing it between her own. 'Why so worked up over crusty old Charlie Ireland? Louie will call any minute to say he's found the guy washing down his fresh fish with a home brew.' Sara squeezed her friend's hand tighter, guiding her along the bar to the service gap at the end. 'Come over and sit with me.'

Slumping in a seat, Maggie gestured hopelessly. 'Oh Sara, I'm so over being a pathetic mess. This isn't who I am. I'm just so easily overwhelmed.'

'Sweetie, look what you've been through: Amber's funeral, the reunion, Noah's accident, Brian, your dad, the pub not selling ...'

'... Losing Dan's father!' Maggie added as Will joined them at the table.

'Steady on,' he said. 'If Charlie Ireland is lost, he's got *himself* lost. You are not to blame. And as I recall, Maggie, plenty of kids were always telling him to get lost. He never did. Too damn stubborn.'

The telephone managed what Maggie rarely could—a still bar. Letting Ethne take the call, she sat pin-straight and watched from the table, but the barmaid had the best poker face, even as she hung up and placed the portable handset on the bar counter.

'Louie says "No sign at the Ireland property".'

Callum appeared in the doorway to the main bar, his full-length Driza-Bone beaded with water, his face glistening from rivulets of rain dripping from his hair.

'Geez, Callum looks like a walkin' water feature,' someone muttered.

'If you're afraid of water, I suggest you stay put,' the policeman fired back. 'She's bucketing down.'

Callum was used to the shenanigans of 'pub dwellers', as he called them whenever Maggie needed help getting a patron out at closing. He always tried being one of the blokes, while very aware of his position, his young age, and his lack of the required 'local' status. Tonight, however, Callum wore his serious face.

'Tonight's weather will get worse before it gets better and it's looking like Charlie Ireland might've run into a spot of trouble somewhere along the Calingarry.'

'We need to set up and search the riverbank—both sides,' a voice said, followed by a flurry of activity and hat grabbing. No one was joking anymore.

Callum held up two hands, palms out. 'Agreed, but all the water coming down from the hills won't make our job easy. Any tick of the clock she'll be pitch out there, so delaying is not an option. Those of you with property boundaries on the river, you need to go home and check. The rest of you, we need a controlled search while we're waiting for the Saddleton SES crew. For now, pair up and stay on designated tracks.' Callum instructed. 'No going off-road and beware of a wash-away reported near Coolabah Gully Road. There's likely to be more, so keep your partner close.'

'But mate—' someone said.

'No buts,' Callum insisted. 'We do it by my rules until I hand over to the SES. We're rescuing one person only tonight.'

Everyone in the main bar moved in unison, except for Maggie who did the only thing she could. She dialled Dan's mobile number and prayed she would find the right words.

FIONA

Glad to find the main bar almost empty, Fiona walked over to Maggie sitting at a table with Sara and Will. 'Do you have a minute, Maggie? I need to show you something.'

'Not a good time, Fiona,' Maggie said, eyeing the plastic crate in her hands. 'Whatever it is will have to wait.'

'It's already been too long,' she retorted. 'And I wouldn't ask if it wasn't important to us both. We'll talk in the dining room.' She was not taking no for an answer.

After placing the plastic container on the corner staff table, she waited for Maggie to stop by the kitchen on her way and speak to the barmaid.

'I'll be in the dining room, Ethne. Come get me the minute you hear.'

Fiona observed the woman's approach. Maggie seemed as on edge as Fiona was feeling despite having practised the impending speech on her grandmother a dozen times. Cheryl had offered to accompany Fiona to the pub for support, or have Maggie come to the house, but Fiona needed to do this herself.

'What can't wait?' Maggie asked, sounding unusually impatient. 'What have you got there?'

'This is the stuff … The box … The one your husband … You know?' Fiona flicked the clips on either side of the crate, lifted the opaque plastic lid, and watched as Maggie unpack pieces of smashed china from a bubble-wrapped parcel.

'Oh!' the woman whimpered. 'My mum's tea set. I was saving it to give to Noah's fiancée when … Well, anyway … Not all is lost. Whoever *he* turns out to be, will just have to be sweet enough without sugar. I'm sure he will be.' Placing the broken sugar bowl to one side, Maggie delved deeper, arching her brows while inspecting the cup, saucer and matching milk jug that had miraculously survived.

Just as Fiona was deciding Maggie might need time alone to go through the contents of the box, the woman pushed the crate to one side distractedly. 'Thank you for delivering this to me, Fiona, and thank you for being such a friend to Noah these last couple of days. I appreciate your care. Adults can learn a lot about forgiveness from their children. I'll take a look at all this another time.'

'There's one thing, Maggie.' Fiona dug into the box to retrieve the pile of correspondence. Weak-kneed, she dropped into an adjacent seat and slid the pretty, parchment envelop over the table. Her gaze stayed on the letter as she confessed. 'I've read it. Sorry. I recognised the notepaper first. Then I saw the handwriting and suddenly I … I didn't mean to read your letter. Well, not *your* letter exactly either. Please, just read it and you'll see what I mean.' But the woman seemed super distracted, her attention drawn to a noise in the main bar. As she made to stand, Fiona reached over and slapped her hand on Maggie's. 'No, this letter can't wait.'

The woman blinked for a million seconds before sitting slowly and unfolding the note even slower. Fiona did the same with the scanned copy and read with Maggie in silence:

Dear Brian,

I suspect this letter comes as a surprise and you will be more surprised by the news. I won't go into detail about my recent stay in Calingarry Crossing. I assume Maggie mentioned she and I caught up.

Going home to the country changed me. I hadn't realised how important family was until I had the chance to reconnect with that part of my life. What stands out the most about Calingarry Crossing today is small towns do have big hearts, and country people are generous, forgiving and genuine. Honesty and openness are an important part of who I am now and who I want to be as I reconnect with my daughter. Our daughter, Brian.

I've made woeful choices. The worst was lying about the night I fell preg-

nant and agreeing we tell no one it was yours. I was immature enough to think a reputation was more important than the truth. But you and I know the truth, as does Phillip. You were my first time, but you had dreams and ambition. You wanted nothing to do with me or the baby and I understood then, as I understand now. That's why this letter is not about blame. That night, I was drunk and went looking for trouble. I found you.

What we wanted back then is not as important as what we should want for our daughter's future. I sincerely hope you have enjoyed success with your music and you can connect with Fiona in some way. She needs to know her real father. At least she needs to have the choice of knowing you. I also hope you understand and agree telling her is overdue. Your willingness to be a part of her life will make such a difference—to me and to Fiona. Please contact me as a matter of urgency to discuss.

'Maggie? Maggie, are you okay?'

The parchment paper floated to the floor, wafting from side to side in slow motion, like a single leaf falling from a branch. Maggie looked ready to fall, too.

4 4

MAGGIE

O nce she'd done staring at Amber's words for what seemed like an eternity, Maggie looked up and across the table at Fiona. There were tears of genuine sorrow and disbelief in the girl's eyes, but Maggie would not be joining her misery fest. Not here. Not now.

Toying with the letter she asked, 'How does the news make you feel?'

Fiona's reply shrug also described Maggie's feelings: numb, shocked, but not hurt. Why not? Shouldn't Maggie feel betrayed, angry, sad? Shouldn't she question the validity, the letter's origin, the timing? The date underneath Amber's flowery signature was three months ago. Brian had known about the letter and Amber's wishes when sitting with Maggie in the Newtown café after the funeral, yet he'd said nothing to her. Worse still, her husband had been aware of Fiona's existence before marrying Maggie, when he'd vowed to 'forsake all others'.

Relief ... another word to describe Maggie's response to the news. *How strange!* How odd that she would be so unruffled, unless Brian's letter was that calm before the storm people referred to. Cyclone Fiona *had* just blown the lid off a lifetime of secrets and the reunion had brought home more than memories for Maggie. One of those memories—Dan Ireland—was on en route to Calingarry Crossing. Maggie couldn't focus on her own feelings until he arrived she knew Charlie was safe. Yes, she felt bad for Fiona, but she was guilt ridden about Charlie and felt partially responsible. As much as Fiona might need mothering, Maggie had only so much to give right now.

'Maggie?' Fiona was staring. 'Maggie, are you feeling okay? Your face ... It's gone all weird.'

Weird? she mused. Funny how, out of all the ways to describe an expression, Fiona used the same word as Noah. Then the words *half-sister* hit Maggie.

'Fiona, who else knows about this letter?'

'Only you and Cheryl—and the arsehole.' Fiona looked sheepish. 'Sorry, Maggie.'

'You confronted Brian with this? When?'

'The other night, before I left Sydney, I went over to your flat. It was late. When he opened the door and I saw the kind of man he was and how he'd upset Noah, I lost it.'

'I'm sorry you saw him like that, Fiona. To have known him as a passionate young musician with ambition was ... Well, he was fun to be around. We had dreams and ...' Maggie stopped herself. There was so much that needed saying. A rushed conversation wasn't right for anyone. 'Fiona, can we agree to keep this between us until we're thinking clearly? I'd like the opportunity to tell Noah. We can do it together, okay?' Maggie said, fingers crossed.

Fiona nodded. 'Yes, we need to protect Noah.'

The slightest grin curled Maggie's lips. 'We all need time and clear heads.'

Fiona looked up as Maggie prepared to leave. 'Can I tell my dad? Oh, and ...' The words stopped Maggie mid-stride. 'Can I can ask him to come out to Calingarry Crossing?'

'Great idea,' Maggie said, feeling impatience creeping into her rushed replies. 'Fiona, I really must—'

'Oi, Maggie!' Will called from the door. 'Ethne needs you to man the bar. Our favourite Jaffa Ball is suited up and heading out.'

'Sure,' she replied. 'I'm coming, Will.'

DAN

On any ordinary day in Sydney, Dan Ireland would wake to the screech of an alarm and throw on his jogging gear to thrash any sleeping cells awake with a fast jog around the leafy Lane Cove neighbourhood. After that, life would grind to a halt as he inched his way along the motorway—for which he paid dearly in tolls.

Now in his car with the lights of oncoming vehicles whipping by in the dark—one dazzling burst of retina-destroying light after another—Dan cursed his father. Then he cursed the rain. Even the stupid weatherman with the irksome banter and sickly smile who'd forecasted blue skies had earned a profanity or two from Dan's lips while he drove through a night alternating between downpour and drizzle. Finally, Dan cursed himself for being a bad son. Northern New South Wales was in for a hammering and his old man was lost in the middle of it and all Dan could think about was seeing Maggie.

Yesterday's early evening telephone call had caught Dan by surprise. Already tired from a broken sleep, he'd spent the morning shouting from the sidelines at Mike's soccer finals and Emily's basketball gala. In the afternoon, after a thrashing by his old partner on the squash court, Dan had stopped by the supermarket to find the biggest, meatiest T-Bone and a pre-made salad. Cooking up a hearty protein hit might ease both his boredom and the jadedness he'd been experiencing since returning from the reunion. Not until later in the evening, about to indulge in a Scotch and some mind-numbing television, had Dan thought to check his unusually quiet mobile to discover a flat battery. Immediately after plugging in the charge cord, his kitchen had echoed to the chorus of notification tones—multiple messages, all from one person. Maggie Lindeman had sounded scared.

He'd called without delay, and before hanging up, said, 'My old man's been fishing the same river for decades.'

It was the truth. Charlie knew the place better than anyone. He *would* turn up and Dan *might* get a grunt of recognition out of the old man for his trouble. The all-drinking, all-smoking Charlie Ireland was famous around town for saying, 'It hasn't killed me yet.' But Dan's job had taught him that everyday practices could easily turn fatal. Complacency and familiarity were significant factors in motor vehicle crashes, with drivers coming to grief most often when close to home. People are quick to presume driving in a city, with its glut of vehicles, congestion and tangle of roadways, is more hazardous. In reality, the city network—even a lousy one—was more predictable than a rural road at night with wild animals, straying stock, soft shoulders and wash-aways, to name a few.

For that reason, Dan needed to focus if he was to make it to Calingarry Crossing in one piece and give his father a hard time. After which, he'd take the opportunity while in town to have that long-awaited chat with Charlie. Numerous times in the past he had sought Tracy's advice on how he might reconnect with a father whose estrangement was the result of the very land he'd loved. 'Whatever strategy, hon,' she'd said, 'it will need to be acceptable to a father who's never known how to be one.' Dan had been at a loss until Charlie fell off his quad bike in the field one day. Pinned there until the next morning when a neighbour dropped by to borrow the slasher, Dan had found his reconnect strategy.

'S'pose it makes sense,' Charles had grunted over the phone he'd received in the mail. Dan had bought, charged and set up quick-call numbers for emergencies, packaging the mobile with a brief note. 'But I'll be paying you back,' Charlie had told Dan, the man's pride clear even though the phone reception wasn't. That had been three years ago.

And just where is the mobile phone now, eh Dad?

Picturing the device flat as a tack, sitting in a cupboard or in Charlie's car rather than in his pocket for emergencies worsened Dan's headache that was already the wrecking ball kind that perforated eye sockets and distorted vision. The *Welcome to Calingarry Crossing* sign sure was a sight for his sore eyes.

❦

THE MANY TIMES DAN HAD IMAGINED SEEING MAGGIE AGAIN, NEVER HE pictured the scene that greeted him as he entered the pub's main bar: a room full of mostly unshaven, bleary-eyed blokes who smelled like wet dog. The elders eyeing the newcomer were likely the same locals who'd once branded Dan a no-good lout. Dan's gut tensed until spotting Maggie.

'Thank goodness, Dan!'

Even with tension in her smile and in the fine lines around puffy, bloodshot eyes, Maggie was his instant cure-all. She hurriedly delivered a steaming mug of something to a woman in orange overalls before continuing towards Dan. 'You're here. I worried about you driving in these conditions.'

'I've done worse. Thanks for worrying, though.' Dan would've preferred meeting somewhere without the eyes of the town. He also would've liked a hug hello. As beautiful as her smile was, he deemed it a poor substitute in the circumstances. 'I gather there's no news?' Maggie could only shake her head.

Diverting Dan's attention from Maggie was the orange overall woman with a voice that belied her tiny stature.

'Okay, folks, rally around! I'm Kylie Swift. We are your fresh crew, in from Saddleton and keen to start a first-light search. We hoped we weren't needed, but ... We'll do our best. Can we get these overhead lights on?' Unrolling a large map on the pool table she anchored the corners with a mix of two-way radios, her coffee mug and a crew member's hand. Mid-thirties, short and stout, she wore glasses perched on the tip of a ski-lift nose still dotted with a twelve-year-old's freckles that were as clear as anything when she bent down under the fluorescent lighting. Dan took a step back, pleased that a woman was in charge. His experience of female detectives was all good, especially when a case demanded attention to detail. Kylie clearly had the respect of her unit, and good commanders got results. That was all the reassurance Dan needed. They would find Charlie. Exposure would not be a problem for the old bugger. How many times throughout winter had Dan's mother pleaded for a fire, only to be told, 'Being cold never killed anyone.'

You remember that, Dad! You hear me!

'Hey, yeah you!' Kylie eyeballed Dan. 'Step closer and focus. We're searching by grid this morning.' The commander handed out a smaller, simplified version of the same map she'd unfurled. 'Take a printout and take a partner. If your map has a red cross in the corner, see Callum. He has two-ways powered-up. You'll call in every half hour with coordinates and an update. Clear? The rest of you, staying closer to town, will use your phones.'

As Dan watched the fresh surge of orange overalls and peak caps clash with the drenched and bedraggled locals returning, he heard a voice behind him.

'Where do you want us?'

'What the ...' Dan muttered. Fiona looked like a giant orange Gumby in over-sized SES overalls pinched in at the waist with a plaited leather belt. An orange cap concealed her curls and large hoop earrings dangled below, reminding Dan of Emily's Hula Hoops.

Commander Kylie appeared as gob smacked as Dan. 'Us?' The woman looked from Fiona to Noah and back to Fiona. 'Adults or trained personnel only, I'm afraid, but do me a favour and stay close, will you, lass,' she said to Fiona. 'If our communications drop out those earrings of yours might help re-establish radio reception.'

Noah's snort landed him an elbow to the ribs and Fiona was about to huff away when Dan stepped forward, hand extended. 'Detective Dan Ireland. The man missing is my father.'

'You should've said so.' Kylie's handshake was as curt as her response.

'Yeah, well, I'll take responsibility for these two. I was about to head out to my dad's house. It's fine,' Dan said when Kylie looked close to objecting. 'Another check of the property can't hurt. I do know all the nooks and crannies.'

'Fair enough,' said Kylie. 'Assuming you can keep in touch by phone out there?'

'Why do you think I'm taking Hula Hoop girl with me?' He winked. 'Let's go, you two.'

'Hang on, Dan!' Maggie rushed over to the door of the pub and yelled over the sound of heavy rain on the metal awning. 'Fiona, you can't do this.'

The girl's expression suggested she was unaccustomed to hearing the words 'Fiona' and 'can't' in the same sentence. 'But I want to help, Maggie. I'll be fine.'

With an arm braced on the doorframe, Maggie leaned down and yanked her Blunnies off, one boot at a time. 'You might be fine but those little canvas espadrilles will last two minutes in mud. These should fit. And for goodness' sake, stick together.'

≥∞

AFTER CHECKING THE OLD HOUSE, THE TRIO OF DAN, NOAH AND FIONA criss-crossed yards and paddocks and shone torches into the old sow sheds and various tumbledown structures housing dilapidated machinery parts. Having spent his youth staying clear of his father's strap, Dan knew how many places there were to hide. Fiona kept up, her grit surprising Dan until she walked through a spider web. Such a hullaballoo he had never heard as she thrashed about, screaming at Noah, 'Get it off me! Get it off me!'

All three were quiet on the return drive, except when Noah did an impersonation of Fiona's spider dance.

≥∞

BACK AT THE HOTEL, THE TRIO PEELED OFF WHATEVER WET THINGS THEY could before entering. Without stopping, Fiona disappeared up the stairs to the accommodation while Noah took one of two towels Maggie offered and impersonated Fiona and her web dance for his mother's amusement. Dan was happy to see the resultant smile on Maggie's face.

'Very funny, Noah. Hit the shower. Go!' Holding out a second towel, she waited until Dan had hooked his borrowed Driza-Bone on the wall-mounted hat rack inside the front entrance. 'Any sign of him?' Her smile was gone, replaced by a rush of tears.

'Try not to worry, Maggie. I'm not.' Dan hoped he sounded convincing. 'Tough old bastards like him don't go down too easy.'

'Charlie is not a tough old bastard.' Maggie shoved the towel into Dan's chest before turning on her heels and calling over her shoulder. 'You don't know him and you should—before it's too late.'

'Hold on!' Dan hurried after her, rubbing the towel through his hair and along the back of his neck before letting it drape over both shoulders. 'Sorry for being an insensitive clod.' When Maggie wiped a tear from her cheek, he reached out and wrapped both arms around her shoulders, hugging her close until her forehead was against his chest, his own face buried in the sweet-smelling tangle of Maggie's hair. When she didn't pull away in a hurry, as he'd expected, Dan knew he should. 'Look at me,' he

279

said, hands firm on her shoulders as he took a step back. He was not letting go of her completely. 'I'm sorry about The Rev.'

'I'm not crying over my dad, Dan. I feel responsible for not realising Charlie might be in trouble until it was almost dark.'

'You're shaking. Come and sit.' Dan led her to a chair before perching on one opposite, dragging it close until their knees knitted together. 'Blaming yourself does no good,' he told her. 'Besides, Charles Ireland is not your responsibility. None of these characters are. You told me your father spent the last part of his life in the pub administering his special spiritual guidance. You are not obliged to carry on the tradition.'

'But, Dan—'

When he hushed her with a finger to her lips, worried eyes stared back, confused and blinking in perfect synchronicity with Dan's heartbeat. He was sitting so near to her; close enough to reach out and tuck the one stubborn tress of hair behind her ear; close enough to hold her hands as he confessed to thinking about her every second since the reunion. When they did eventually find the old bugger—and they would—Dan must remember to say thank you for dragging him out to Calingarry Crossing in the middle of the night.

'Maggie, you're no more your dad than I'm Charlie. But you do protect people. You always have done, and I admire you for your compassion.' Dan saw questioning in her eyes. He smiled. 'Don't look so surprised. I remember every detail and you haven't changed. You're still protecting people. You've protected your son all his life. You're still protecting Brian—God knows why. And while you're doing all that, Maggie, who's protecting you?'

'You know nothing about my family, Dan.'

He cursed under his breath. Maligning her family was stupidity on steroids. He'd dared get too close to the nest. 'All I'm saying, Maggie, is since the reunion I've been going crazy thinking about you.'

Maggie pulled away, her torso stiffening, protective armour in place. 'What are you on about? I don't fit into your life, Dan.'

'You could,' he said. 'I want my life to change and I want you to be a part of it.'

'That's ridiculous.'

'No, Maggie. Ridiculous is me—a grown man whose existence is so desperately mundane I was preparing to watch a Tom Cruise movie on TV. Thank goodness I checked my phone. Your message saved me. Let me protect you.'

Maggie didn't laugh with him. She didn't smile, grunt—nothing. She simply sat, staring and blinking with big, beautiful, mind-blowing brown eyes.

'So, let me get this straight, Dan,' she said. 'Telling me you want me, even though you know I'm married, is your way of protecting me? Seriously?' Maggie rose so fast the chair fell backwards, crashing to the floor. 'I don't think so. And you don't need *me* to bring about change, Dan Ireland. Babies tend to do that all by themselves. You have Tracy to think about.'

'Hey, slow down.' Dan's palms waved in truce. 'I love Tracy—as the mother of my children—but our marriage is over. What she does with her life is not my business. I need to find my own happiness.' Maggie wanted to speak, her jaw dropping, but Dan had more to say. 'And while I know you're married I don't think you should be. Not to Brian. Not anymore.'

Maggie gasped. 'My marriage is not your business.'

'Actually,' Dan said, 'you made it my business when you asked me to intervene.'

'And now I'm asking you to butt out.' The only thing more intense than Maggie's stare was the silence between them, making the moment more awkward, her glare more piercing. 'Focus on your own growing family, Dan, and your father who's missing, in case you've forgotten that's why you've come.' She rose, resisting the tug to her hands, and a single tear rolled over her cheek as she looked down at him.

He cursed under his breath, physically exhausted and emotionally drained. Yes, he'd timed his confession poorly, but an empty pub was rare. Any minute the SES crew would be walking in with his missing father. Maggie needed to hear what he had to say—the lot—and he'd sit right there until he was done.

'Please, Maggie, I don't want my past, and that includes my family who I love very much, to define me. Can't a guy want more from life and move on?'

'What is it with you men?' Maggie exploded. 'You decide on a whim it's okay to dump the parts holding you back, but as long as you say you still love them everything is hunky-dory. Have I got that right?'

'Maggie, Maggie, slow down.'

'Don't Maggie, Maggie me, Dan. What are you doing?' Her body seemed to concertina back into the chair. 'I've loved seeing you again, but this is terrible, Dan. Terrible.'

The craziness of the situation warranted laughter. If she hadn't looked so serious, Dan might have given her a thump on the knee and told her to buck up, like he did with Emily. He didn't do either.

'What are you talking about?' he asked. 'What's so terrible that you have to say it twice?'

Maggie merely shook her head. This was definitely not the reaction he'd hoped for.

'So, you loved seeing me and you felt something between us on the night of the reunion. I'm not mistaken, am I, Maggie? Let's talk about that.'

If morality had a face, Maggie's was it as she implored with him. 'Please, Dan, now is hardly the time. You should be more concerned about your father. Whatever you think of him, he's a human being with feelings and he's alone out there, cold and wet and probably scared.'

Dan sighed. Nothing spoiled the moment like being castigated by the woman you're falling in love with.

'My father, yes.' His voice took on the same ticked-off tone. 'That would be the man who turned his back on me when I needed him but, for some crazy bloody reason, I am concerned for him, which is why I've driven through the night to walk into a pub where the same old locals are eyeing me as if I'm still trouble. Until a few minutes ago, talking to you had been a helpful distraction. So no, Maggie, I am not a heartless bastard. I do care.'

'I know you care, Dan. I didn't mean … I'm just … I'm thinking about the baby.'

'Baby?' His voice bumped up an octave.

'Dan, calm down and listen.' Maggie used her mothering tone, the kind he guessed she'd used to sooth an unsettled baby Noah. To his surprise, the dulcet timbre worked—until her next question tightened his gut. 'Don't you care about Tracy having a baby?'

'Do I care?' he retorted. 'I especially care about Tracy having a baby —*at her age!* I'd care even more if the baby was mine.'

Maggie's head jerked as if someone had pulled her ponytail. 'It's not yours?'

'No, Maggie.' Dan was sounding exasperated, but this conversation was wearing him down fast. 'I told you, Tracy and I separated.'

'Sort of.'

'I beg your pardon?'

'You said you were "sort of" separated and that you were staying together until the kids—'

His laugh refused to stay put. 'I meant we were in no hurry to do the official divorce thing. Trace and I haven't been together for a while, and not in a baby-making manner for a bloody lot longer.'

'Not. Your. Baby,' Maggie repeated as though the words and the concept didn't quite compute. She looked even more beautiful when thinking.

Dan's shook his head. 'I knew Trace was seeing a guy. My wife—soon to be ex-wife—keeps a secret like a dirty beer glass keeps a head. You and I both know it doesn't, Maggie,' he added. 'While our arrangement might sound strange, it's totally mutual and Trace couldn't be happier. Yes, we made a conscious decision to keep the status quo for the kids—for a while. We figured starting high school was a big enough adjustment. We pushed on with the official divorce once she told me about the new bloke.'

'New bloke?' Maggie blinked.

'That's when I moved out,' Dan explained. 'Guess I should be flattered. Apparently he's like me "only better".' He shrugged his shoulders and laughed, pleased to see Maggie's lips waver into some semblance of a smile. 'By not telling you all this outright I've stuffed up badly. I wasn't deliberately keeping a secret from you at the reunion, or since. I'd made a promise to Trace and my situation didn't seem to work into our conversation at the start. I had no idea how distracted I'd be seeing you again, Maggie, or how tongue-tied.' He shrugged again. 'I didn't want to destroy the moment we had going. Then you up and left early, so I went after you. I intended telling you while we walked, but …'

'Sara found us,' Maggie muttered.

'Yes, and when Tracy said the two of you enjoyed a big deep and meaningful the morning after the reunion, and she told you about the baby … By the way,' Dan added. 'I only found out about it a few hours before you. I assumed she'd told you about the father as you chatted. The guy's name is Roger, and he's a real doofus. Mike's word, not mine. I also assumed she'd told you about us. Well, not about us as in *us* as there is no *us* which is what I should have said when … Damn, listen to me, Maggie. Can I possibly make a bigger mess? If only we—'

'Dan, stop,' she said. 'There is no we. I *am* still married, remember?'

'Cripes it's wet out there!' Callum, followed by a small army of orange, burst into the pub and Maggie's previously empty, early morning confessional became a busy bar again.

'Conversation over, Dan,' Maggie whispered, as she gathered dry towels in the arms Dan desperately wanted to be in.

'Great news, mate.' Callum slapped Dan's back. 'Your dad's at home and you can thank Ethne. I'll let her fill you in on the details.' The constable winked and delivered a second round of congratulatory back pats. 'We left old Chuck refusing to be fussed over and demanding we leave. Louie's staying the night, despite Charlie's protests that he was—and I'm quoting here: "No poof, so I won't have no bloke in my bedroom and no bloke watchin' me sleep".'

'Yep, I'd say that's getting close to normal, wouldn't you, Maggie?' Dan had chuckled at the inappropriate Charlie-ism. Maggie had not. She wasn't smiling at all and her face had a look Dan didn't have a label for. He only knew he was desperate to patch things up and the sooner the pub cleared, the better.

'Well done, constable.' He shook Callum's hand. 'You guys have earned your sleep—what's left of the night. My thanks to everyone,' he shouted over the rabble of relieved voices, scanning the drenched army busily drying their hair and faces with Maggie's towels. 'I guess the next round is on me. Shame it's not drinking time.'

'You kiddin', mate?' Came a voice from somewhere. 'It's always drinkin' time.'

Maggie, back in her comfort zone behind the bar, tapped the pen to a glass. 'Right, you lot, coffee's hot in the dining room. Those of you preferring a beer, sit down and I'll fill some jugs.'

Like good working dogs, the majority sat on command while Maggie mouthed a quick head count, took four chilled beer jugs from the fridge and began filling them two at a time. Some crew members opted for coffee in the dining room and a few headed for home. Dan helped ferry full jugs and clean glasses, declining a beer for himself but lingering at the tables long enough to be sociable and show his genuine appreciation. Soon enough, once relief and exhaustion washed over him, he would excuse himself.

MAGGIE

S itting on the edge of her bed, unable to nap despite her tiredness, Maggie recalled Dan patting a lot of backs before he'd left the pub last night. Saving a final hug for her, he'd whispered in her ear, 'Forgive me'.

Now couldn't shake the words. *Forgiveness for what?* Dan had asked for Joe's forgiveness and the carefully worded letter with its ecclesiastical declaration of forgiveness of sins had implied absolution and fulfilled the church minister's obligation. Sadly, the father in him could not. Joe's battle to forgive, which had started with Mary's death, had altered so many lives. But Maggie would not perpetuate past failings. If she could forgive Fiona for hurting and betraying her son, forgive Noah for breaking her heart when he ran off, and forgive Brian for being—well, Brian—then she could forgive Dan Ireland for doing no more than making her feel sixteen again and wanted.

A contrite Fiona had delivered Noah home, but the girl was different— as was Noah. Maggie had expected to greet an angry, hurt boy. Instead, he was a son worried for his mother. And he'd grown, as evidenced the night mother and son had passed each other outside the bathroom. Showered, his hair wet and dripping, he'd hugged Maggie with powerful arms and the soft scent of soap, whispering, 'Hey, Mum, got time for a smuddle?'

Noah was home, different, grown, but still her boy. For that she'd forgive Fiona.

Yesterday's quiet post-search day had been hard on Maggie. She'd had no choice but to open the pub, as usual, but with little to no sleep overnight, the day had dragged. She'd expected—hoped—to see Dan, but he remained a no-show, putting Maggie on edge and forcing her to replay their conversation over and over. Fiona was nursing sore muscles and, according to Noah, Mrs Bailey was treating her granddaughter as if she was the sole survivor of a Mount Everest expedition; not someone who'd opened and closed a dozen farm gates, slipping several times in the mud, and destroying a spider's hard work and dinner prospects. By hanging out with Fiona while she convalesced, Noah had milked some grandmotherly love for himself. Mrs Bailey apparently baked the best scones—*ev-ar!*

While last night she'd slept like the dead, Maggie was now wide awake, the golden glow of sunrise a welcome change from two days of cloudy skies and rain. With the day shaping up to be a stinker, and with a good dash of humidity thrown into the mix, she threw on a pair of track shorts and a sports top and tiptoed downstairs. Stopping in the kitchen, she filled a bag with carrots and apple quarters. *Time for a little girl talk!* And a brisk walk back before the heat of the day kicked in.

RED-FACED AND PANTING, MAGGIE DARTED IN THE PUB'S BACK DOOR AND into the kitchen for some ice to add to her water bottle. Aware of her of her post-run appearance—sweaty skin, hair clamped into a chaotic mess on top of her head, her breathing laboured—her breath became shorter still when Dan's gaze grazed her body. What was the man doing standing in her kitchen looking and smelling squeaky clean and laughing with the staff? Ethne was supposed to be having a day off after her heroic efforts during the search and here she was sharing, by the smell of it, one of her special brews.

'What's so funny?' she asked, struggling to ignore Dan. His stare was the practised type that pinned a person to the spot until he was ready to let them go. He had something to say, but Maggie was not prepared or willing to hear him out. Not this morning, not in the pub's kitchen, and not looking the worse for wear. She instead focused on Ethne and her version of the search story making the rounds. Spreading as far as Saddleton Provedores, their delivery driver had lobbed not long ago and, in typical Chinese whispers style, regaled Ethne with the updated account of the rescue. Everyone was talking about Calingarry Crossing's feisty barmaid with the big knockers who'd saved old Charlie Ireland by improvising with her 'flotation devices'.

'Old Barnacle seemed particularly impressed with my ingenuity,' Ethne sniggered.

The gaiety in the kitchen subsided quickly; Maggie's low-key laughter the most likely cause. She was acting like the sour, sober party-pooper who sucked the fun from the room, but she wasn't in the mood.

'Hilarious,' she offered in place of a smile. 'I hope Charlie sees the funny side.'

'I'm going to sit down with Dad today,' Dan said. 'But I was hoping before I do you and I might—'

'No, I can't.' Maggie was already on the move and calling over her shoulder. 'I have rooms to service and a bar business to run.'

LATER THAT DAY, THE POCKET-SIZED AND BLISSFULLY PREGNANT SARA rushed into the pub, desperate for a bag of ice. Maggie would have liked her to stop awhile so she could chat, but planning a birthday for little Jasmine, while dealing with the woman Sara referred to as the fun-sucking monster-in-law, meant her hands were full enough with her family.

After the lunch sitting, Maggie was back in the main bar, listening at another local's version of Charlie Ireland's rescue—with full action replay —when Dan walked up and perched on a stool as far away as possible from Louie the Fly and his workmates.

'Maggie.' He nodded straight-faced.

'Dan.' Maggie responded with the same polite nod and deadpan lilt as she walked to the end of the counter. 'About this morning ...' She fussed with the bar runner, smoothing the frayed edge of a freshly laid towel. 'This morning I was ... Well, hopefully a free beer and my telling of the latest Ethne story will make up for being in a rush earlier.'

'Sure.' Dan replied. 'I believe a beer and an ear would be the tradition of this bar "business" you have "to run".'

'Hmm,' she grimaced. 'I did say something like that, didn't I?'

Dan's lips broke into a smile. 'How many versions of the rescue are we up to?'

'You know small towns!' she said. 'Nothing like them when it comes to storytelling. But the best version by far is ...' Maggie recalled the most amusing anecdote of the day, her narration fading as she noticed him staring dully into the empty glass his two index fingers nudged from side to side. 'Not funny enough for you?' she asked him.

'The bit about small towns frustrates the hell out of me. When I think about the irony ... Some of those locals so quick to come to a bloke's aid and laugh at his jokes are the first to condemn him when he screws up.'

'You didn't screw up, Dan,' Maggie stated. 'And people were wrong to judge you. Especially Charlie.' But Maggie knew country people could come across as laid-back, open and friendly, when often they were the opposite, while old-timers like Charlie Ireland could be quite insular and wary, especially of newcomers. She'd seen it a thousand times. 'People protect each other around here, Dan. You know what it's like.'

Dan toyed with the empty glass. 'Even your father blamed me for Michael's death. And don't worry, I've paid for that night. If it wasn't punishment enough to be rejected by the entire town, I've let my job punish me all these years.'

'I know, Dan, but it was an accident. A stupid, sad, tragic accident.'

Dan huffed. 'No such bloody thing, Maggie. It's called a *Crash* Investigation Unit for a reason. Crashes happen not by accident, but by our own foolish decisions. We make a wrong choice or a mistake, or we accelerate through a red light or talk on the phone. We speed to make up time, or we fail to get enough sleep. And when the facts are examined, it's always that initial choice made.'

'I'm not sure I follow,' Maggie said.

'By getting in the car with the wrong attitude,' Dan explained. 'Or we drive after drinking, we drive tired, we drive angry, we drive fast when we don't plan enough time to make our destination. We make mistakes, feel invincible, and speed like bloody morons. Not content to screw up our own lives with our choices, we screw up somebody else's.' He slammed the glass on the wooden counter so hard it should have shattered. 'Crash Investigation 101, Maggie. There are no accidents.'

She wrung a cloth and was lifting his glass to soak up the circle of beer underneath, when Dan's hand wrapped around hers. 'Speaking of decisions. Adding alcohol to sleep deprivation is one a bad one. I'd best stop —both the drinking and the lecture.'

Was it also a mistake to let his hand linger on hers? Maggie wondered.

'I didn't hear a lecture, Dan. I heard passion—and I understand. You have a love–hate relationship with your work.'

'I have a love–hate relationship with my life,' he muttered. 'Experts espouse the only way to stop kids killing themselves on our roads is to put an old head onto young shoulders. I'm proof aren't I? If I'd known back then what I know now I would never have let Michael climb onto the back of my ute.'

'Michael made his decision, Dan. You weren't to blame.'

Maggie thought about the letters she'd found in her father's old Bible. But was this the right time? Dan was trying to connect with Charlie. Might sharing the letter make Dan question how Joe Lindeman could forgive him for his misdemeanours, but not his own father? The contents might interfere and muddy the waters and Maggie, more than anyone, appreciated how debilitating complications could be.

'Thank you for your honesty,' Dan was saying. 'Knowing you don't harbour any resentment means the world.'

He returned her smile, and the pair stood facing each other like starstruck teenagers until Louie's exaggerated throat-clearing and goofy grin ignited a warm tingle on Maggie chest and neck.

After pouring two beers—faster than she should've—delivering them with froth oozing over the sides of the glasses, she returned to Dan.

'I have an idea.' With her eyes fixed on her fingers fighting to loosen tight apron ties knotted low on her belly, she explained. 'Ethne's out back. No way will she take a day off until she's milked every drop of attention and glory. I say we take advantage of that and try a river walk in the daylight. This time with no interruptions. We can't talk here'

Within a heartbeat, Dan was standing. 'Let's do it.'

'I'll tell Ethne and change. Here.' She took a leather Akubra from the hat hook on the wall behind the bar. 'You'll need a hat in this heat. Back in five.'

In her room, she threw on shorts and a top before tucking her hair under a Bundy Rum baseball hat and racing downstairs to double-check with Ethne.

'I'm as good as I was five minutes ago when you asked, love. Your chappy said he'd be waiting in the park. Off you go.'

Maggie's eagerness was reminiscent of those earlier summers when she'd dashed home, dropped her school bag, wriggled into her cossie on the run, and skipped all the way to the swimming hole. But one look at a dorky Dan wearing the-one-size-too-small Akubra and Maggie's heart skipped.

'Good grief! And you call yourself a country boy? Take this,' she chuckled, swapping her cap for the ill-fitting Akubra. 'Shall we?'

Their walk started out pensive, with the track's narrowness taking Maggie back to the reunion. Too much champagne had let her forget she was married, and she'd fallen into the trap of fantasising over the brush of Dan's shoulders and grazing of their hands. Amazing the difference daylight made.

'Dan,' she started, tentatively, 'I like remembering how things were with you and Michael. And Nate, of course. You three sure made a commotion, and I loved noise, but I only knew half the stuff you got up to back then.'

'And the stuff we didn't, we still got the blame for,' Dan added. 'Like poor Will when Amber's father went after any bloke who'd ever looked at his daughter. People have to blame something or someone when the person they love is hurt.'

'Like I blame Brian's obsessive pursuit of fame on those *iICON* people when in truth,' Maggie said. 'I should be angry with him. I was so shocked when I saw him in Sydney after Amber's funeral. He's happy to change for *iICON* and yet, when I ask one small thing of him he can't …' Maggie tempered her voice, her pace slowing. Bringing Brian into the discussion was more cringeworthy than commenting on the weather.

Before she could switch to a different, more positive topic, Dan said, 'You still love him.'

Though not a question, Maggie responded. 'He's the father of my son.' Then she let the silence hang between them.

'Speaking of fathers and sons,' Dad announced cheerily. 'The prospect of meeting Emily and Mike has tipped Charlie into agreeing on a trip to Sydney.'

'Wow!' Maggie was genuinely delighted. 'That's great news. Good on you for persisting.'

'Truth is, Maggie, it was you talking about losing The Rev, and something you said about leaving things too late that got me thinking. I told Charlie he and I had a second chance. The grandkids sweetened the deal, but I believe the night spent clinging for dear life to a submerged tree branch was the kicker. While I was with him at the hospital, he had a coughing episode and his heart spasmed. Doc said it wasn't a worry but suggested X-rays and easy access to a major hospital until the chest congestion cleared. So I said, "What about Sydney?" and he agreed.'

'You'll be going soon then,' she said, not bothering to hide her disappointment.

Dan scoffed. 'Nah! The old man doesn't do much in a hurry and everything he does do he repeats—at least once. A couple of days, I reckon.'

'Well then,' she said, wondering if her straight spine and perky response was as noticeable to Dan as they were to her. 'We'd best make the most of the time. Is there a place in particular you feel like revisiting?'

'As a matter of fact there is,' he said, taking her hand and hastily leading her away.

She might be decades older and not exactly skipping along the track but there was no denying the buzz and the giggle she forced back down. Maggie was that young girl again, carefree, full of wonder, and crushing on Dan Ireland.

🦋

THE SWIMMING HOLE WAS LESS CROWDED THAN MAGGIE HAD EXPECTED, evidence of the deluge still apparent in the high water line lapping over the sandy strip locals called Calingarry Beach. In her youth, the scorching summer days brought people in droves to wade, or swim, or dive from the makeshift pontoon moored in the deepest section. There'd been few luxuries when Maggie was young. Nowadays, simple outdoor pleasures like tree swings and swimming holes were forgotten in favour of air-con, spa tubs and gaming consoles. A small group of teenagers had swum the fifty metres out to the pontoon, the four males taking turns to dive bomb and splash the two squealing sun bakers in bikinis.

'Do you remember being their age?' Maggie asked.

Dan laughed. 'Geez, you make us sound ancient, but yeah. I remember a lot.'

She slipped her hand from his grip and removed her shoes, stepping into the current until water swilled around her calves. 'It's cool,' she said over her shoulder, glad Dan was doing the same. 'Feels good though.' She bent down, cupped her hands and splashed her face and the back of her neck.

'Let me help,' Dan said. At the same time he launched three quick sprays in Maggie's direction.

When he sprayed her three more times, she squealed like the sixteen-year-olds now watching silently from the pontoon. 'Right, mister, this is war.'

Maggie retaliated, wildly kicking water with little accuracy. Spray after blinding spray she kicked until her belly-laughing, combined with the inability to breathe, made the smallest kick impossible.

Clothes drenched, hair bedraggled, and a hand raised in surrender, Maggie caught sight of the six pontoon dwellers gawking at the old fogies. 'I guess we'll be the talk of the town now.'

Dan waded back to shore with her hat and plonked it on her head. 'Do you care?'

'I have to. They go to Noah's school. Look at me.' The cheesecloth top, now glued to her skin, showed off her favourite aubergine-coloured bra.

Dan grinned mischievously. 'Let's get out of here.'

'If you expect me to go strolling back into town looking like this—'

'You're right. We should dry off, and I have the perfect place. This way.'

Waiting until they were out of sight to take Maggie by the hand, Dan led her off the well-formed pathway and onto a snaking, overgrown track, prompting her to ask, 'Where are you taking me?'

'If my memory serves me correct, over there, beyond those bushes is a special bridge.'

Maggie giggled, child-like. 'Bridge? There is no bridge near here, Dan. Where are we going?'

'Trust me,' he said as the path came to an end at a thicket of tall gums and tangled undergrowth that skirted the river's edge. There was no going through the scrub and no way around it.

'You intending to walk on water?' Maggie wisecracked.

'Nope,' he replied, pointing. 'That's our bridge across the water there.'

A massive tree trunk lay where it had toppled, likely the victim of a flood many years ago. Despite established root systems, sandy footings were often not enough to support the abundant crown of foliage. A fall usually meant death for a tree, but this one had leaves—still green with new shoots.

'How is it still alive?' she asked.

'Amazing, eh?' Dan squeezed Maggie's hand. 'I remember the year she came down. It was the same year Mum left. I'd come here every day, expecting to see it slowly dying and wanting to curl up and die with it,' he said. 'Instead, what might've been lost lived by adapting to the changed conditions. You'll see what I mean when we get to the other side. Come on, Baby.' He leapt onto the trunk and with a Patrick Swayze finger curl motioned for her to follow.

'I am not your Baby,' she said, watching him demonstrate his balancing prowess. 'I'll fall.'

'No, I won't let you, Maggie.'

'Didn't I mention my aversion to balance beams at the reunion?'

Dan laughed. 'I'll protect you. Come on, adventure girl! Take my hand and put one foot on the biggest branch, there.'

Crossing her mind as she dug deep for the courage were all the times Brian had accused her of not being adventurous enough, and all the name calling he'd delighted in: uptight, scaredy cat and wimp. Steeling herself, she gripped Dan's hand and launched herself onto the log where they both teetered precariously, until steadying each other, hands on shoulders. As Maggie's heartbeat calmed, she found her balance and her voice.

'Okay, so far so good. What now, adventure boy?'

'When I turn around, put your hands on my waist.' He pirouetted, wobbled, and cursed under his breath. 'Whoa! That was close. Okay, follow me, right foot first. Slow and steady.'

They were doing it, crossing over water, the trunk a bridge to a point of riverbank beyond the dense clump of she-oaks, and onto a secluded quarter-moon patch of pristine sand.

'I did it!' Maggie cheered, even though her legs trembled so violently they were close to folding underneath her.

'I never doubted you,' Dan said, settling back against the exposed portion of twisted roots towering well above his head. 'Your balance beam prowess would impress Mrs Whoseywhats from school.'

'Hmm,' Maggie hummed, giving in to Dan's tug on her hand and dropping onto the sand beside him. With fingers still entwined, their hands rested on Maggie's thigh. 'I'm not so sure my PE teacher considered this scenario when telling me balancing skills would come in handy one day, but thanks for sharing your secret spot. Why didn't I know this was here?'

'Nobody knew,' Dan said.

'How could you be sure?'

'Because I'd leave signs behind each time: a scribbled pattern in the sand, a cairn made of river pebbles, a structure made from branches. They were always undisturbed. This was my special place and there was only one person I've ever wanted to bring with me,' Dan said. 'Only took me a few decades.'

'What did you do when you came here on your own, apart from your designs?'

His focus fell to their fingers, where the pad of his thumb fondled the freckled skin on the back of Maggie's hand. 'I came to think, to wish, to dream. Then,' he added, his voice brightening. 'I grew up and stopped wishing in favour of smoking pot.'

Maggie feigned shock.

'If you think that's bad, I have another confession,' he said, 'Pot helped me fantasise, and this scenario—you and me—featured. It featured a *lot*.' Together they chuckled and leaned into each other, ridiculously content, until Dan fell serious. He let go of her hand and moved to face her. 'Did you … *Do* you ever think about us together?'

Reaching for her hand still on her thigh, the tip of his finger traced the peaks and troughs of her knuckles.

'Dan … I'm sorry, I …'

'No, I'm the one who should be apologising. I'm being selfish. I've dragged you here and now I'm making this all about me and my feelings. If you tell me you want to go, I'll take you back to the pub. No pressure. Do you want to go?'

Knowing the answer, a fusion of fear and excitement fired through Maggie; the kind that trembled a body from the inside out; the kind you know is wrong but you want it—need it—anyway. In her youth, Maggie *had* been adventurous, and sitting here with Dan she yearned to be that brave, young girl again. To be thirteen again with a matchstick in her hand, sneaking out in the dark to light her first-ever firecracker—the

Catherine wheel her father had fixed on the old outhouse door. She'd known playing with fire was wrong and that her father would be mad as hell, but such things were every kid's rite of passage come Cracker Night. Driven by the need to take a risk, do something crazy, break out of her own protective cocoon and spread her wings, she hadn't thought twice about risks back then, and danger didn't deter her now.

Maggie sat up and repositioned her body so she was knelling before Dan. Then, reaching out, she began tracing the scar that began by his ear and zig-zagged to the cleft in his chin. 'You asked if I ever thought about us. Thinking and doing require different paths, and we're no longer kids, Dan, we're grownups.'

Rather than disappointment, his mouth curled into a slow, seductive grin and he redirect her fingers to his lips, kissing them.

'You're right, Maggie, we are all grown up.'

A hot *whoosh* in her tummy was like that spinning firecracker in the backyard—the one that had hurled sparks into the night sky and threatened to tell the universe, not just her dad, how close she'd come to getting burned. Three decades on, Maggie was that crazy girl and someone was handing her one more matchstick.

'I've wished and dreamed and waited a long time to kiss you, Maggie Lindeman.'

As their mouths locked with enough force to break teeth, Maggie ripped the shirt from his body like a wild woman. After she'd de-shirted Dan, Maggie thrust her arms high into the air, her desire to feel skin on skin and rediscover the warmth of intimacy dominating any rational thought. He obeyed her silent command, peeling the still-damp top up and over her head before flinging it to the sand. As Dan's hands feasted on her breasts, his fingers eager to sneak inside her bra, her lips devoured eyes, earlobes, mouth and neck. He tasted salty and sweet all at once, the synthesis of bare skin and sweat a heady concoction. Warmth rippled through Maggie, the kind she'd long ago forgotten when she and ...

'Brian!' She gasped, her eyes catching a bemused Dan's as she pushed off his chest. 'Oh no, I ... That wasn't what I ... Oh, Dan!' She sat back on her knees and lowered her shaking head into her hands. 'What am I doing?'

'Maggie, Maggie, please, I'll do anything—or nothing. If I have to apologise, I will. If you want to just sit, we can. I want to spend time with you. I want to know you. I want to know what I've missed, but not if it's hurting you. I'd never deliberately make you sad, Maggie. Never.'

Concern carved Dan's words, shaping them into something soft and beautiful, something she wanted to take away, like a tiny memento, and keep somewhere safe so when she was down or desperate for its warm hug, she could take it from her secret hiding place and put it under her pillow at night to remember today.

Mortified about blurting Brian's name and feeling self-conscious in her semi-naked state, Maggie didn't look at Dan. Instead, she grabbed the top he'd earlier tossed and hugged the sandy cheesecloth to her chest. 'I'm not sad, Dan. I'm trying to be strong.'

'You are strong.' Dan sounded like an echo of her father's last words. 'What should we do? What do you want?'

Maggie lifted her shoulders and let them fall. She was tired of deciding, tired of being the responsible person, and tired of trying to hold the fort, fill the breach, take over the reins, carry on, manage. Maggie's life was like an inside out umbrella in a rainstorm; she was only just holding on and yet still drowning. Knowing what she wanted was one thing. Being able to have it, Maggie told herself, was another thing altogether.

She shrugged again, but with a long exaggerated sigh as her shoulders dropped. 'Lately, Dan, my son has been telling me to chill, as in be cool, you know?'

'I understand the lingo, Maggie,' Dan said, that same mischievous Clooney grin making a comeback. 'I have two fourteen-year-olds.'

'Yes, well, I'm thinking my seventeen-year-old son is more grownup and more in control of his life than I am at this point. That changes right here, right now. Get up, Dan.' Maggie stood, hand extended and tightening around his as she helped him up and the pair made for the waterline. 'Noah's right about staying cool, don't you think so, Dan?' she asked, leading his through the water towards the start of the tree bridge.

'Sure,' Dan agreed. 'Staying cool makes sense to me.'

'Glad to hear you say so.' And with that, Maggie yanked on Dan's arm so hard she unbalanced them both so they stumbled forward and fell.

Dan broke the water's surface gasping and threatening revenge, and like teenagers they splashed and squealed, touched and teased, and chased each other deeper and deeper to wrestle. When their feet could no longer touch the bottom and they were both too aroused to laugh, they sank, their limbs in a tangle beneath the water, before the pair spluttered back to the surface, breathless and laughing again.

'This isn't as easy as it looks in the movies,' Dan said. 'I'm in a spot of bother. My jeans are lead.'

'Then let's get to the bank,' Maggie laughed, 'before we drown each other.'

Side by side on the sand, shirtless and panting—Dan on his stomach, one arm draped possessively across Maggie's purple bra—she squinted into a gloriously blue sky, unable to wipe the smile from her lips. And there they fell asleep under Dan's tree that refused to give up.

MAGGIE

E thne's face resembled Luna Park's entrance when she bailed up
Maggie sneaking through to the private residence.

'Well, well, someone's looking happy.'

A nonchalant flick of Maggie's hair resulted in a leaf fluttering down
the front of her crushed and sand-covered shirt. She'd spent the walk back
from the river trying to finger-comb foliage and grit from the tangle and
regretting she'd insisted Dan hang back on the track for five minutes. The
suggestion had only wiped the sheepish smile from his face and made
what happened between them seem sordid.

Adding a new level of awkwardness was Ethne's eyebrow arch and a
general mien that was both mother and best friend, both chastising and
cheering as if saying: 'What have you been up to, young lady?' and
insisting Maggie 'Spill it, girlfriend. Every juicy detail.'

'Have a nice time, did we, love?'

'Err, I don't know what you're talking about, Ethne. Noah in? I was
on my way to his room.' She declined to admit her need to see Noah
was a much-needed reality check after the interlude with Dan. Her son
would remind her she was a seventeen-year-old's mother, still someone's wife, and this—whatever she was doing with Dan Ireland—was
not real. Neither are candlelit dinners, and yet she'd agreed to dinner
before she and Dan had parted laughing, any guilt complex left behind
on the riverbank. She thought she'd left it behind until seeing Ethne's

cat-swallows-canary look, and something else Maggie couldn't work out.

'I believe Noah might be in his room, love, but …' the woman paused. 'I'd suggest before seeing your boy you might want to take a look at yourself in the mirror.'

Maggie baulked. Was there a lecture coming about infidelity and responsible parenting? 'Exactly what do you mean "Take a look at myself in the mirror", Ethne?'

The barmaid laughed. 'Relax, love, relax, I'm not talking figuratively. No business of mine what you do on your time off. But about bloody time,' she added from the side of her mouth. 'What I mean is *physically* take a look in the mirror. Unless inside-out is a fashion statement I've missed this season, you'll be wantin' to fix that top of yours before seeing your son.'

A FEW MINUTES LATER, MAGGIE STOOD IN THE BEDROOM AND GROANED AT her just-had-wild-sex-outdoors reflection. *If only!* How they'd stopped when they did—how Dan had stopped—she didn't know. *Poor man!* Giggling at the memory, she grinned to herself while stripping off and jumping in the shower. Then, checking all clothing items were the right way around, Maggie walked down the hall to her son's room. She went to knock before entering, as was her habit lately, but stopped short at hearing Noah speaking on the phone—or Skyping, or whatever it was called. Maggie could wait. She'd come back for her dose of reality another time.

DAN ARRIVED IN THE MAIN BAR AT 7 PM, AS ARRANGED. THEY'D previously agreed Maggie should wait up the street, away from prying patrons, but she'd rung him and changed their meeting point to the pub, telling Dan what she'd once told Brian. 'Best to be upfront from the start. There's no gossip in something that's out in the open.' Should she bump into one person she knew in Saddleton, the news about Dan would be all over town before they ordered an entrée.

Choosing a back corner table at the Fortune Cookie, they ordered a banquet for two, ignoring the fortune cookies. While they found plenty to talk about—Noah, Fiona, Charlie, Dan's twins—the conversation soon turned to their 'romp'. Dan's word, not hers.

'Can we talk about today?' he asked. 'Are you okay?'

'Of course!' I'm not sixteen, she wanted to add. *I may have come across as a pathetic, desperate born-again virgin, but ...* 'And you, Dan?'

His grin was answer enough. 'Seriously, Maggie, I don't want to pretend today didn't happen. We've talked about everyone except us and—'

'Dan, there is no 'us'. Today happened, yes, and it was fun after a stressful few weeks. Plus, the start of storm season has been extra hot and humidity makes people crazy.'

'You're blaming the weather for what happened by the river?'

Maggie poked at her plate with the chopsticks, recalling how she'd wanted to poke her eye out with one of Fiona's to escape another Centenary committee meeting. Sitting here with Dan's eyes burning into the top of her head had Maggie contemplating the same. She didn't want to ruin their night by deconstructing what had or hadn't happened. The reality was, Dan would be gone day after tomorrow.

'Look Dan, about—'

'Uh-oh.'

Maggie flinched at both his flippancy and the smirk on his face. 'What's with the uh-oh?'

'I might not have dated a lot since Trace and I split up,' he said, 'but I know the start of a this-was-all-a-mistake line when I hear one.'

Maggie pushed her plate away before reaching for her wine. But as the rim of her glass hovered at her lips she returned the glass untouched to the table. She needed a clear head.

'Dan, things did get out of hand, don't you think? I mean ... Today was nice but ...' She swallowed, her mouth dry. 'Look, seeing you has been amazing, Dan. I'm so grateful for the reunion.' She leaned close to whisper, even though the Chinese family at the enormous banquet table were being noisy enough to mask the discussion. 'To be honest, I felt like Cinderella at the ball, only slightly older and a lot more complicated.' The joke fell flat.

Without a single twitch of those lips, much less a smile, Dan's eyes narrowed. 'What's complicated about it? Is this where you say, "I'm married"?' Dan sat back in his seat and folded his arms. 'I don't see complicated, Maggie. You either love Brian, or you don't. You're happily married, or you're not.'

My life is more complex, she wanted to say until The Rev's favourite marriage service line came to mind. 'Marriage isn't about losing your dreams,' he'd say. 'It's about having someone to share your dreams with.' And yet here was Maggie, his daughter, struggling to find that connection. Maybe she hadn't lost her dreams so much as herself when she'd married Brian, and perhaps her husband hadn't so much rejected or abandoned her, he'd forgotten her. It was about as obvious as an inside-out top, only it had taken someone like Ethne to point that out to her. Now Dan, looking wounded and confused, was questioning Maggie, pointing out something just as obvious about her marriage. She and Noah were second to Brian's dreams. Not only was she living a life she didn't remember agreeing to, when marrying Brian she hadn't said 'I do'. Inadvertently she'd said, 'I don't'—I don't live for myself; I don't enjoy what I want; I don't even know what I want any more. Dan Ireland turning her life inside-out was not as easy to fix as a top too hastily thrown on after a romp in the river. She had more important considerations, like her son. Maybe she needed to take that good look in the mirror, figuratively speaking.

'Well, Maggie?' The unexpected harshness in Dan's voice snapped her attention back. 'Are you married or not? This isn't complicated. I spend half my time investigating why someone seventeen, eighteen, twenty, ends up dead on a dry, straight, level stretch of expertly engineered highway, or on a breathtakingly beautiful country road in broad daylight. The other half I spend watching parents fall apart, believing they've somehow failed their children. Some wail about having wasted years loving their kids, investing in them, and teaching them right from wrong, only to lose them. That's what I call complicated, Maggie.'

'Years spent loving someone isn't ever a waste, Dan.'

'Except when they don't love you back, Maggie.'

'Brian loves me.' The assertion sounded as childish as plucking petals off a daisy—he loves me, he loves me not. 'He does love me, but he's vulnerable and he's confused.'

Dan recoiled from the invisible slap, his eyes flaring. 'Vulnerable and confused? Seriously, Maggie? That's what you call his behaviour? Is that how your son described the father he walked in on at the apartment?'

'Noah was up front, Dan. He told me he'd found his father drunk and stoned, just as I was afraid he would. My son's angry but he'll come around in time. We raised him to forgive, and Brian is his father.'

Dan opened his mouth to speak, closing it again as he huffed and shook his head. 'You need to talk to Noah. He's like you, Maggie. He's protective. He's protecting you.'

'From what?'

'Talk to him, Maggie,' Dan replied. 'Make him sit down and tell you how he feels about Brian after that day.'

A nervous cackle erupted from Maggie's mouth. 'I'm not sure what you think you know, Dan, but I can tell you what you don't know. You're still to learn there is no making a seventeen-year-old sit down and do anything. Boys Noah's age are making their own choices—big, important, life-changing decisions that I can't help him with, even though I'm his mother.'

'Maggie, you're a good mother. One look at your son tells me so.'

'Wrong again, Dan. I can't take the credit. I worked all day. But Brian … Brian was an amazing dad. That's why he doesn't deserve to lose his family because he's made a few wrong choices. We all make those.'

Dan opened his mouth as if to speak, before snapping it shut without a word and pinning his bottom lip with his teeth.

'I thought, if I could get Brian out here and away from all those city influences we could start over and Noah would have his father.' Or maybe it is too late for us, Maggie was about to add when Dan cut her off, his voice, eyes and shoulders heavy with defeat.

'You're right, Maggie. I don't know Brian, but I know you, and I see the man Noah's growing into. He's Maggie Lindeman's son; he protects the people he loves. Saying anything that might hurt you, even if it is the truth, would not be easy for him.'

'I know the truth without Noah telling me, Dan. I'm not an idiot or naïve. I know Brian drinks—and worse. Nothing would surprise me and the man is far from perfect, *but*—'

'You don't understand, Maggie.'

She bristled and growled an expletive under her breath before glaring in Dan's direction. 'Tell me, Dan, are they the first words they teach a man? "You don't understand!" Brian says the same all the time and to be honest, I—'

'You're comparing me to Brian?'

'Argh!' Maggie slapped her serviette on the table. 'Why are we here having this conversation? Why do you know so much about my marriage and since when is it your business, Dan Ireland?'

'Since you asked me to help you with your drop-kick of a husband.'

'And that was my first mistake. Don't even ask what my second one was.'

Maggie hardly recognised her own voice. It wasn't the familiar fed-up exasperation she heard when arguing with Brian. Despair and heartache had brought a bitterness to words she'd fired indiscriminately, like a gunman inflicts maximum hurt. And she'd succeeded. Dan looked wounded. Though Maggie had heard the description a dozen times, never had she seen someone actually turn ashen, and so quickly.

Apologise, Maggie, she told herself. Only to realise remorse doesn't *unfire* a gun or turn a bullet back. The smart thing to do was leave, so she stood, calm but determined.

'Maggie, please.'

'No, Dan, dinner was a mistake. Everything is a mistake. If it's okay with you, I'd like to go home. I want to see my son and I want to say goodnight. This is over.'

'Come on, Maggie, not like this. It's not as if I live down the street or a few suburbs away. When I go back to Sydney—'

'The fairy tale ends.' She finished the sentence for him. 'I don't need to tell you my priority is protecting the people in my life. If, as you're suggesting, things are worse for Brian than I know, he will need support and understanding. Dad, in his publican days, used to say, "People who rely on drink aren't bad people. They're sad and drinking to escape. If we care about them, we stick around, support them, and guide them back so they don't get lost".'

'Support, yes,' Dan agreed, 'but it doesn't have to be from you, Maggie.'

'I can't stop caring about Brian because of the choices he's made, any more than I would stop caring because of Noah's choices. My son will need me too.'

'And what will you need?' Dan asked.

Maggie didn't answer.

DAN

'G'day, Ethne.' Dan's quick nod acknowledged the barmaid before he dared look at Maggie behind the cash register. 'Good morning!'

'Hello,' she returned with the same forced formality.

'Well, if it isn't my favourite Detective,' Ethne chirruped, the old bird looking wise to a problem. 'What'll it be? The sun's not quite over the yardarm but you look like you could do with a strong shot or two.'

Thank goodness Ethne was in barmaid mode because Dan was in no mood for a battle with the bodyguard version. This morning's mission—to spit out what had kept him tossing and turning since dinner two nights ago —required more time than Charlie had granted him.

'Look, Maggie, I wanted to see you yesterday but preparing the old man for this trip took more work and time than expected, so I'll come straight out and say this, okay?'

Maggie's expression was the picture of panic, her eyes darting around the near-empty bar before resting on Ethne, her mute message prodding the barmaid into action.

'Well, I'm out of here,' she announced. 'I'll be in the kitchen hunting for some eye-gouging chopsticks.'

Dan had no idea what Ethne was talking about, but the turn of phrase made Maggie smile. A positive sign, considering the circumstances.

'Maggie, this won't take long. It can't take long. I dropped Dad up the street. He insisted on getting a haircut before we leave. No trustworthy barbers in Sydney!' He smiled, but Maggie didn't move, except to close the till drawer and put a glass of water on the bar for him. 'You read my mind,' he said, revealing a small bunch of wildflowers from behind his back. She stared at the flowers he dropped haphazardly in the makeshift vase, then up at Dan questioningly. 'At the reunion you mentioned I owed you a corsage. I hope these might help me apologise for dinner the other night, and I hope you didn't mean to finish us like that.'

Maggie sighed. 'Dan, I know you hate me using the word complicated and believe me, I hate that it makes me sound pathetic ...'

'You are far from pathetic, Maggie.'

'Overwhelmed may be a better choice of word. I'm overwhelmed, Dan.'

He nodded. 'You've had a lot going on. I get that. I was having a coffee at Will's yesterday and Sara—' Maggie's panic-stricken face forced Dan to slow down, but it wasn't easy to do with his heart beating wilding in his chest. 'Relax, Sara didn't tell me anything except ... Now what were her exact words? Oh, yeah, I believe she said words to the effect of "Don't be a dickhead, Dan. Get your"—I think she may have slipped in a flattering adjective or two—"arse over there and tell Maggie you'll give her the time she needs." At least I think that was the gist of her advice.'

While there was no smile, eyes like Maggie's didn't lie; his joke had done its job and tweaked her pressure valve. Itching to reach across and take her hand in his, the public bar was Maggie's domain, and Dan respected her desire to keep her social life separate from her publican life.

'In fact, Maggie, so very persuasive and expressive was Sara's advice, I slept on it; although restful is not exactly the word to describe the hours from 9 pm to 6 am. Still, here I am with minutes to spare, telling you to take all the time you need. And before you say anything, know this, Maggie ...

'I haven't stopped thinking about you since dinner, since the reunion, and since we were kids when I threw fig berries to get your attention. But I'll keep to the current facts.' *The current facts?* He sounded like an investigator with a case to solve. 'I didn't want to come back to this town; Tracy asked me to accompany her and I never could say no. I've loved her as a wife and as the mother of my children, and Trace has loved me back. She's put up with me for so long. She asked for my support at the reunion and I wanted to do that one small favour if it made her happy. Naturally, I'd wondered if you'd be in attendance.'

'G'day, Maggie love,' Barney said as he and Cricket sidled over to the bar.

'Oh, ah, hi, fellas,' Maggie said without barely a glance in their direction. 'The usual?'

'Picked it in one, girlie.'

Dan must have groaned aloud because when he looked up, Barney and Cricket were staring intently, like a couple of expectant working dogs.

'Listen, guys,' he said. 'Do a bloke a favour, will you?'

'Name it,' Cricket said with gusto while Barney slurped the head from his beer. 'Does it involve catching criminals?'

'Actually, it involves taking your beers and buggering off.'

'Dan!' Maggie hushed, sliding Cricket's drink across the counter.

Ignoring her censorious stare he said, 'Five minutes, fellas. You know what it's like to be this close to telling a woman you're falling in love with her, don't ya?'

Barney stood and slapped Dan on the back. 'Onya, mate. You want any advice from these old heartthrobs, we'll be in the beer garden.' While the pair trundled out of the main bar chuckling, Maggie lifted the servery and stepped out from behind the bar.

'Dan—' she began.

'Let me finish, Maggie, please. Then I promise to apologise and leave you in peace.' He settled on a bar stool and positioned one for Maggie, who also sat, but in a tentative fight-or-flight fashion. 'On one hand,' Dan started. 'I dreaded returning to Calingarry Crossing, but coming back has enlivened me and I'm not sure 'enlivened' was a word I'd ever used before now. My kids are my happy button, but you've made me come alive, Maggie. I feel positive for the first time in years. I'm picking wildflowers and having a deep and meaningful with Barney and Cricket about falling in love.' He silently revelled in having made her smile again. 'Look, I won't push. God knows you've had enough to deal with of late. But I don't want to be one of those guys who lets life pass him by—the one who could have been more, had more, loved more if only he hadn't been such a monumental dickhead.'

Another smile. This was good.

'My bad decisions go way back, Maggie, and I'm not talking about Michael. If I'd trusted my heart early, I would've thrown fewer fig berries and made a move. I wasn't sure what a kid like me had to offer a girl like you. I'm still not sure but, Maggie, I had to tell you how I feel before I leave on a nine-hour road trip with a man I haven't had a relationship with in, err, well ever. Could be a whole new take on Thelma and Louise. Guess I should stay away from cliffs and canyons.'

'*You* know Thelma and Louise, Dan?' Maggie chuckled. 'Which one are you?'

A bigger smile. Now you're really getting somewhere, Dan, mate.

'Actually,' he said, smiling smugly, 'I always fancied myself as the Brad Pitt character.'

'Wasn't he a crook on the run?'

Dan was on a roll. *Laughter and words!* One touch from Maggie's hand would make the full trifecta.

'I believe the guy was out on parole, but if you'll bear with me, Maggie, and know I don't want to leave today. I want to stay and talk, but my kids need to meet their grandfather before he changes his mind about going. I know I said some things at dinner the other night and—'

'You were right,' Maggie interjected. 'Noah was protecting me. We talked about his father. I asked him to be honest.'

'Oh, Maggie, I'd give anything not to have been right.'

'I know. At least there are no more secrets. But I owe Noah all my time and understanding at this point. Brian and I have talked, and he's in a dark place that requires more than I can give him. While you were right, too, about Brian needing time to see for himself, I can support him and make sure he gets the help he needs. Don't look at me like that, Dan. Brian and I might not have a marriage, but we have a history and a son.' She seemed to know he was about to speak again and raised a silencing hand. 'I've seen how losing someone you love destroys a person. Cheryl Bailey had her daughter taken away, Fiona lost her mother, your mother destroyed your father when she walked away, and Dad was never the same after losing Mum.'

'Maggie Lindeman, you haven't changed,' Dan said, feeling a mix of relief and hope. 'You cope and you care and you accept people, even boorish berry-throwing numbskulls. I will go today and give you time, Maggie, but you have to do something for me.'

'What, she asked.

'Tell your bodyguard to take it easy when I call.' He grinned. 'And I will call, and email, and text, and—'

'Okay, okay, I get it,' she said, laughing.

Dan looked at his watch and saw the time ticking away. 'I'm not sure how long I'll keep the old bugger in the city. We haven't even left town and he's asking me when I'm bringing him home. I'll want to see you, Maggie.'

Another nod and a smile. 'We should catch up, Dan. We have so much to talk about. We might even ...'

'What?' Dan asked. 'Why did you stop speaking?'

Maggie rested her index finger on her chin and tapped twice. 'I, um, I'm not sure I've ever used the word 'we' so many times while describing my life. I like saying 'we', Dan, and yes there is plenty I want to say when time's on our side. Go do what you have to do with your dad. When you get back, we will have all the time in the world to talk.'

5 0

When Maggie found Noah in the dining room eating a sandwich, he offered her half, as usual and she declined, as usual. The mother-son ritual was the boost she needed to believe their lives would return to a kind of constancy, even if punctuated with panic over exams and up-coming assessment tasks for Noah.

'School exams are important, bud, but grades are not a measure of how successful you can and will be,' she'd told him after yesterday's mathematics meltdown.

'But I want you to be proud,' he'd replied.

'Never doubt that, Noah. You need to be proud of yourself and make sure the choices you make are the ones that make you the happiest. I know music is your passion and I understand the importance of creative accomplishments.' She also understood what it felt like to take second place to a passion, but she didn't share that with her son. 'What worries me, bud, is you're doing music for the wrong reason—to be famous. You can do all the wrong things and become famous,' Maggie said over the top of her phone ringing. She plucked the device from her pocket and thumbed the screen. Seeing a message from Brian, the phone went back into her pocket. Maggie had Noah in an actual conversation—an important one requiring assurances and understanding. She refused to let Brian butt in, like always, and take Noah's attention away. 'Where were we?' Maggie asked.

'That was Dad,' Noah stated, her son's perceptiveness never failing to surprise Maggie. 'I don't get why you didn't tell me about him.'

She sighed. 'I thought I was protecting you. He couldn't be a good husband, father and famous all at once. Something had to give, and his choice put me and him on different paths.'

'Didn't you try to change his mind?'

'Please trust me, Noah. I did enough. There comes a time when you have to step away and let people make their own decisions. I know *you* understand that, bud, and if you need to talk to me ...'

When Noah's gaze held firm, Maggie held her breath. But, no, her son averted his eyes—opportunity lost.

'Noah, I'm not walking away from Dad, but I won't put my dreams on hold any longer. Knowing where I stand will allow me to support Dad better. He'll need that. And you need to focus on your schoolwork.'

After contemplating his sandwich filling for an inordinate amount of time, Noah said, 'I'm angry.'

So am I, Maggie wanted to say, nodding instead. 'If it helps, bud, try to think of your father as addicted to fame. The other stuff is the result of that addiction.'

Noah's eyes zeroed in on Maggie's. 'You're doing it again, Mum.'

'Doing what?'

'Protecting him,' Noah replied. 'I accused you once of not caring about Dad.'

'I was protecting you at the time, Noah.'

'I know, Mum, and I love you.' Noah cocked his head to one side.

'What's that look for?'

'I was about to tell you to chill, but you kind of are chilled.'

'Chilled?' Maggie felt a flush creeping up her neck and over her cheeks. 'Let's keep to the matter at hand, Noah. About your dad and fame,' she said. 'Do what you love, but without it ruling your life. Always keep part of yourself for those you love. Whoever they end up being, Noah.'

'Mum?'

'Yes, Noah?'

'I won't end up like him.'

Maggie exhaled through a smile. 'I know, buddy, and do you want to know how I'm sure?' It was time. Maggie was done skirting around the edges of the subject, testing the water by dipping the occasional toe. 'I know you're not like your father, Noah, because you know who you are.

More importantly, you're brave enough to be that person—to be you and not care what others think. You've chosen a life and a path that will, I fear, have many challenges, but I'll help you and love you and support you, always. You've taught me something, bud.' She stopped short of confessing she'd chosen the easy path when she'd been his age and missed out on the fairy tale with the happy ending. 'You'll never, never have to be sorry or apologise to anyone for being you. Okay?'

'Mum?' Noah said, in such a way Maggie braced herself. She watched his hand slowly reach over to rest on her cheek. She pressed her face against the warm palm, closed her eyes and …

'Ouch!' Noah tugged her ear. 'Stop that!'

'Am I *ear-i-tating* you, Mum?'

'Hey, you little bugger!' Maggie launched herself off her seat and chased her son around the furniture like they'd done when he was young. 'Come back here, piker!' she yelled as Noah ran across the dining room and out to the residence.

'Homework first,' he called back. 'Then dogs!'

Flopping into the seat, Maggie laughed and laughed until tears started rolling down her face. She and Noah would be fine. Talking will not only get easier, it will help Maggie through each phase towards acceptance. She'd recovered from the shock, fought denial, wrangled with guilt, and was tired of being angry. The bargaining phase might hang around, which was silly. She believed in her boy; she trusted him to know himself. Maggie would always be scared for Noah and disappointed for herself. She would miss out on a wedding and grandchildren, but they were her dreams, not her son's. He had his own path to travel and Maggie simply had to be there for him in case he crashed.

'I'm here, Mrs Henkler,' Cory announced while struggling, as usual, to tie the bar apron at the small of his back. 'Ethne asked me to do a shift this afternoon.'

'Oh, okay, thanks. And Cory, you can call me Maggie.'

'No worries. Will do, Mrs Henkler.'

Maggie smiled as her mobile rang out. 'I'll leave you with it then,' she said, glancing at the caller ID.

Her smile faded as she took the call. Brian had been worse than ever since Noah's Sydney trip, phoning her several times a day, often leaving a voice message or a text. Most were soppy apologies for something he'd said or hadn't said, done or hadn't done.

'Maggie, Maggs, Magpie, hear me out,' he said as she hurried through the dining room, passed the kitchen, and towards the residence. 'I don't want to be that guy—the one who could have been something if only he'd stuck with it long enough. You don't understand, Maggs. You never have.'

'Stop, Brian, I'm tired of you telling me I don't understand, because I do,' she said. 'And I feel so sorry for you and all those like you hanging on to that tiny thread of hope in the hands of strangers. Noah and I won't try anymore. No—' She cut Brian off. 'Me hanging on to the dream of being a family is as pointless as you holding out for those blood-sucking producers. One of us has to let go, Brian. One of us has to give in and it will not be me this time. We were so good once and I miss us. I miss being a family, but that's my dream, not yours. If you'd agreed to live in Calingarry Crossing, we might have had a chance. You didn't choose me, Brian, and I'm okay with that now. Honestly, I am. I'll talk to you again when you're sober.'

LATER, IN BED, HAVING FINALLY TURNED HER MIND OFF AND READY TO sleep for what seemed like the first time in goodness knows how long, Maggie remembered the text message that had come through over dinner. Fumbling in the dark for the telephone, she looked at her husband's latest —*Sorry I wasn't good enough* message—before returning the phone to her bedside table.

For the first time in ages Maggie didn't lie awake mulling over something Brian had said or hadn't said. She thought instead about Dan and Charlie, wishing she'd been a fly on the wall during their nine-hour Thelma and Louise trip. They'd left town later than planned, with Dan pulling up outside the pub briefly after having collected his dad. After tooting the horn, those in the bar and the beer garden had joined Maggie on the veranda to wave old Charlie off, knowing a drawn-out goodbye would mean driving into the night. As it was, once they made the Pacific Highway south of Newcastle, Dan would encounter the exodus of city weekend warriors, their cars creating an endless ribbon of blinding and mind-numbing headlights all heading north. Never ideal driving conditions; worse still at the end of a long trip when so close to home. Maggie was glad he'd stopped by though, especially seeing Dan's expression when she'd shouted a final, 'Don't forget to stay away from those cliffs and canyons, Thelma!' She smiled again, picturing his exaggerated panic as the pair drove away from the pub.

❧

THE DOOR KNOCK CAME JUST AFTER 2 AM, THE SOUND CATAPULTING Maggie out of bed. As she padded barefoot across the creaking floorboards in full flight, hurriedly dragging on her dressing gown, a sleepy Noah stepped into the hallway, his hand smearing his fringe back over his head.

'Go back to bed,' she called while racing towards the breezeway, her dressing gown billowing. Another knock as she approached stopped Maggie short.

'Callum?' What could it be? Surely there was no room for any more tragedy in Maggie's life. This had to be somebody else's grief and Callum needed assistance. Helping is what Joe had done, long after he'd given up the church. Maggie would do the same.

Flinging the door wide, she asked, 'How can I help, Callum?'

Concern deepened the lines on the young policeman's forehead. 'There's been a crash, Maggie. I wanted to come over personally to tell you.'

Afraid to release the supportive grip on the door handle, as if she no longer trusted her legs to keep her upright, Maggie's first thought was to close the door again.

'No, no,' she said with a shake of her head.

'I'm sorry to have such bad news, Maggie, but I must inform you of a single-vehicle crash that took place ...'

White noise and blackness filled her head. She couldn't think. What was she supposed to do? Invite the policeman in and offer tea or a comfortable chair so he could watch as she fell to pieces? She was already on a precipice. A nudge was all she'd need.

'And Charlie?' she asked, the name almost lost in another sob. 'This can't be right. I don't understand ...'

'Take a breath, Maggie.' Callum edged forward; both his hands extended in readiness should Maggie pass out. 'We found Charlie. He's fine. You need to sit down.'

'He is? You're certain?'

'Of course, Maggie.'

Irritation straightened her spine. Callum's words and his tone sounded so condescending. Or had Maggie skipped shock, denial and guilt to move straight to anger?

'Just bloody say it, Callum. If Dan's dead and Charlie is in a hospital—?'

'No, no, Maggie, this isn't about Dan or Charlie.'

Maggie's eyes blinked so hard she felt lightheaded. 'Then who? I'm confused.'

Callum's Adam's apple sliding up and down twice was all Maggie could focus on. 'I'm instructed to inform you ... single-vehicle ... male ... Brian Henkler.'

Maggie's mind scrambled to recall the last conversation with Brian, but all she recalled was her anger and the message he'd sent straight after: *Sorry I wasn't good enough.*

'Maggie?' Callum's voice penetrated the fog. 'Can I do anything?'

'Were fine,' she heard Noah say. 'I can look after Mum.'

51

DAN

Dan was ill-prepared for a three-hour traffic jam in heatwave conditions on the Pacific Highway and with his old man fiddling non stop with the air-conditioning, despite Dan thrice explaining electronic climate control. He should be grateful their southbound snarl was at least moving and they weren't part of the stalled north-bound lanes. The convoy of emergency vehicles—police, fire rescue, ambulance, all with lights and sirens—suggested a fatality. He could phone in and get the lowdown, deciding instead to fill in time tomorrow while Charlie was at the X-ray place.

'AREN'T YOU ON LEAVE, IRELAND?' SAID SERGEANT FRANK DOWNEY, who'd been investigating road crashes since before horse-drawn trams— so the joke went. 'Getting under the missus's feet, are you?'

'Under my old man's skin,' Dan replied. 'Dad and I were stuck on the Pacific Highway late yesterday.'

'There were a few messes out that way,' Frank said. 'Including a tricky single-vehicle recovery job further west on Nine Mile Mountain Road.' The old copper flung a wad of paper at Dan. 'Lucky this one didn't take anyone out with him. If you wanna top yourself, don't put others at risk.'

'Vehicular suicide?' Dan shook his head. He knew it happened. Isn't that what the town had thought when he'd crashed into the barbed-wire fence? 'Wouldn't be my choice,' he told Frank. 'No certainty a crash will kill you.'

'Bastard covered his bets,' Downey snapped. 'Booze and more. Tox report pending.'

When Dan's eyes stopped on the deceased's name—Brian Steven Henkler—his first thought was to get in his car and start driving, to be there for Maggie, and to be the one to deliver the news and comfort her, but Dan knew the protocol. As the local bloke would've already done the dreaded door knock, Dan had to wait to contact the victim's grieving wife.

DAN DIDN'T HAVE TO CALL MAGGIE. A WEEK LATER, MAGGIE CALLED him, her voice on the other end of the phone sounding distant, small, brittle.

'I didn't know who else to ring, Dan.'

'It's all right, Maggie. I didn't know *when* to ring. You can call me anytime. How are you?'

'I need to know if it's true; if Brian purposely drove off that road.'

Dan's automatic response was to pull on the well-practised persona. Professionalism was a coping mechanism, especially when family, desperate to know if their loved one had suffered, begged him for detail. Mostly they wanted to know if the person had said anything before they died.

Detach, Dan, don't make it personal, he told himself. But this was Maggie asking, and that made it very, very personal.

'Do you have reasons to believe otherwise, Maggie?'

'Maybe I shouldn't ask, Dan. It's just … I have to know and Callum either won't or can't say if Brian's accident … Was it an accident, Dan? And don't give me one of those "there is no such thing as an accident" lectures. Don't make me say the word aloud, Dan.'

'Do you have a reason to suspect he might have done something like that on purpose?' Having studied the crash scene analysis and reconstruction over one long sitting, questions remained unanswered, with the cause of death up to the coroner. 'I'm asking off the record, Maggie. Talk to me.'

'What was he doing on Nine Mile Mountain?' she asked. 'We chatted the night before and he messaged me, but if he was coming here because I said something … If I put him behind the wheel then …'

Dan wanted to fling his receiver at the wall, or climb through it somehow so he could be with her. 'No lecture, Maggie, I promise. But know this. You weren't a contributing factor. You didn't make Brian pump himself full of booze. Brian made a choice to drink and take drugs.'

'But if I forced him to—'

'Don't, Maggie! We'll never really know.'

'But I didn't mean it, Dan.'

'Didn't mean what? Say it,' he urged, knowing the Band-Aid had to come off. 'You'll feel better. Trust me.'

'I didn't say it to make him come to Calingarry Crossing. I would never have abandoned him.'

'Say what, exactly, Maggie?'

'Even though I knew his answer, I said, "me or music". I selfishly left him to choose so Noah wouldn't blame me. I've told myself I didn't lose my husband in that crash, that I'd lost him years ago, but not knowing what happened for sure … And if Noah ever thought—'

'Maggie, stop. You're not to blame—not for the crash or your marriage. Noah's smart enough to know better,' Dan said. 'And until we complete the investigation, there are no certainties. I'll see what I can find out; only if you promise not to blame yourself, no matter what the coroner finds.'

She didn't promise. She simply said, 'Thank you, Dan,' in a way that added a double hitch to the knot in Dan's stomach.

5 2

When Dan had cut short his leave to return to work, the boss didn't say no. From his city desk he would keep tabs on the Henkler case. Plus, the festive season meant busier workloads for the crash team. Dan's early call of vehicular suicide had changed after a witness reported seeing an unmarked B-double in the Nine Mile Mountain area. Though not a truck route, second-vehicle involvement had to be eliminated first.

On the home front, Dan took the kids at night—when the job allowed. Tracy was having a tough time with the pregnancy and Emily and Mike were keen to escape 'kooky Roger with the goo-goo baby noises'. Once the kids were in bed, Dan and Maggie would talk, their conversations slowly shifting from sad things like Brian and who was to blame, to Ethne and Barnacle Bill's amusing bar room barnies. Sara's monster-in-law jokes and Noah's squabbles with his pain-in-the-butt half-sister were also something to laugh over.

One night Maggie had surprised Dan, telling him carefully about her son's sexuality. That chat had lasted for three hours and she'd cried one minute, laughing the next. She told Dan about Phillip's offer—at Fiona's suggestion—to have Noah board with them should Sydney University accept him. Noah had decided a Bachelor of Music degree would let him teach music as a fallback. Sensing Maggie's reluctance, particularly regarding Fiona's influence, Dan had offered her his thoughts and observations of a very changed young woman who he saw from time to time in that impossible-to-miss canary-yellow Saab convertible. Dan had also dined at the Blair's and while chatting to Phillip he'd learned Maggie's easy forgiveness had helped the girl heal.

Tonight when Dan dialled Maggie's number, she answered before the second ring. He was glad. He had something important to talk about. The letter in his hand, written years before, by The Rev. Joe Lindeman. Forgiveness. Finally.

53

MAGGIE

Joe's faithful station wagon, packed with boxes, had completed its last return trip to Sydney. They were close to Calingarry Crossing when the car's front tyres dug into the soft shoulder at Wilson's Corner, the sudden sideways skid snapping Maggie from her stupor.

'You okay, Mum?' Noah asked. 'I can drive again, if you want.'

'I know you can drive, but I have the licence.'

'For now,' he said pointedly, the grin warming Maggie's heart.

'I'll be fine, Noah. I am keen to get home though.'

For the first time in a long time, the word home didn't sound strange. Calingarry Crossing *was* home again. Her only home. She'd closed the door on the flat for the last time, sold her furniture, and walked away with remarkably few remnants of married life.

Brian's Sydney funeral had been a sad, small occasion for a man who had talked big and wanted a big life. Long-haired, leather-clad heavy metal types mingled with country belt-buckled blokes, all perfunctorily paying their respects to a fellow musician. Maggie didn't know most of the people, or what they might have been to her husband. She'd felt like a stranger. Thank goodness for Fiona; not words Maggie had ever envisioned thinking. Despite her own grief and confusion, she'd stood by Noah and deflected curious mourners away.

Noah had not only been quiet since his father's funeral, for most of the drive his focus had stayed on the guitar case filled with a lifetime of musical memorabilia. Covered with scores of ancient stickers providing a virtual tour of small-town New South Wales, Victoria and Queensland, the battered case had belonged to Brain's father. Although to Maggie, it had been an under-bed obstacle to vacuum around. The contents—surprising her and delighting Noah—appeared to be a kind of time capsule of an almost-famous father's life and filled with another almost-famous musician's exploits—Noah's grandfather. From her cursory glance at the flat, the keepsakes included pages of yellowing sheet music, autographed record covers and photographs from Mr Henkler's early career as a support act to big-name performers. 'Always the bridesmaid, never the bride' she'd heard the man repeatedly tell his son.

Of course! Why was Maggie only thinking of that now? Early in their marriage, Mr Henkler would drop names and retell the same story about sacrificing his career for family, which was how he'd ended up on the country pub circuit. Unable to forgive his dad for 'throwing his career away', the Henkler duo broke up, leaving Brian to dream of being something else, something more, something better.

'Mum?' Noah was saying. 'Do funerals get any easier when you've had to say goodbye so many times?'

'No, buddy, they don't. But you do learn to deal with them differently.' Possibly the hardest lesson for Noah—harder still on Maggie—was accepting they'd never really know what had led Brian to that road, on that perfectly beautiful day, and into a ravine. Not even the experts agreed. 'How are you feeling about stuff, buddy?'

'I guess I sorta know how Fiona must have felt when her mum died,' Noah replied. 'But after Dad dying … I mean, he was her dad too, right?'

'Yes, bud, we're all going to need time to adjust. Fiona more than anyone.'

'She's still got Phillip,' he mumbled, his face turned so Maggie couldn't see if the thinness of her son's voice was from his tears or tiredness.

'And we've got each other,' Maggie said with a pat to his knee. 'I'm glad Fiona's wised up and is at least giving Phillip a chance. What changed her mind?'

Noah faced Maggie, his nose and eyes crimson. 'You did, I reckon. She says you're an all-right mum. The accident and that Luke crap taught her a lesson.'

'At your expense, bud.' Maggie bit back the tiny speck of anger that would probably never go away. Noah had turned out fine, no lasting physical injuries, and Maggie knew anger or blame did little more than destroy lives. There'd been enough lives ruined.

'I reckon Fi would do anything to take all that back,' Noah said.

Maggie had to concede, while Ethne's prediction on that first day of storm season had been spot on, they could be grateful Fiona turned out to be a Category One storm only.

'Fiona will always be welcome in our lives,' she told Noah. 'I can hardly lecture her about Phillip and espouse the virtues of giving people a second chance and not do the same.' Maggie reached across and ruffled Noah's hair, lamenting those times she'd been able to slip her fingers through her son's fringe before he started gluing it in place with styling putty. 'I think you'll be good for her.'

'Quit it, Mum.' Noah jerked his head away, smoothed the hair back over his eyes and returned his attention to the rusted metal clip on the guitar case he'd been fingering. Maggie had asked him to close the case several times, concerned about losing her concentration with each, 'Check this out, Mum!'.

'I have an idea, buddy.' Flicking her indicator on, she veered off the road. The car handled much better after the much-needed wheel alignment and service—and all for next to nothing. For reasons beyond her under-standing, Cory had worked on the car without charge—with Noah's help. Maggie flung open her driver's door. 'You can drive the last leg.'

'Serious?' said a bug-eyed Noah as Maggie walked to the passenger side.

He'd already driven on a good dual-carriage section of highway and, although supervising a learner driver was hardly a break for Maggie, it would mean relegating the guitar case to the back of Joe's old station wagon to rattle around with the residue of life with Brian.

'Yep, drive us home, buddy.'

5 4

W ith storm season over for the year, and March temperatures at night making sleep easier, Maggie woke refreshed and ready to seize a day filled with promise. Yawning, she let the sound grow into a squeal at the end while she stretched and wriggled the painted toenails peeping out beyond the bedsheet.

'You awake, Mum?' The door to her room creaked open and Noah's face appeared.

'Come in, bud.' She sat up to wedge a pillow behind her shoulders and fuss with her skew-whiff singlet top to cover her belly.

After Noah swaggered across to the bed and flopped next to her, angling his head to share the same pillow, Maggie detected the day-old downy shadow on his chin and top lip. What a metamorphosis! From fragile, premmie baby boy to the courageous and capable young man beside her.

'Thanks, Mum,' he said.

'What for, buddy?'

'Everything. Trusting me. Saying yes to Europe after school. I'm not sure who was more excited. Fi or me?'

Phillip had rung, preparing Maggie for the ambush and to explain the Amber Bailey-Blair Trust would fund Noah's gap year in London, where Fiona and Noah would base themselves with Phillip's good friend who lived not too far from the famous Abbey Road recording studio.

'Every musician's Mecca,' Noah had announced.

'Only if I can tattoo my conditions on your arm,' Maggie had said.

He'd smiled. 'Yeah, yeah, I know. Homework, dogs, bar job, Facebook —and in that order.'

The pair were side by side listening to the early morning sounds of Maggie's hometown when Noah curled into a foetal position to face her. 'Mum?'

Maggie did the same. 'Yes, bud.'

'I want to feel good about Dad, not angry. I miss him and I feel sad, but is it okay to feel happy? I mean, because of him I have a pain-in-the-butt sister.'

'Of course, Noah. Happy is good.'

A loud bang catapulted Maggie off the bed and to the window over-looking the side street. Fiona stood by her canary-yellow Saab with the roof up, the cabin crammed with balloons.

'Yes, you have big muscles, Cory!' the girl yelled. 'Be gentle.'

Even from where Maggie stood on the veranda, the body language and flirtations were obvious. 'Cory and Fiona?' she asked Noah, incredulous.

'Since the cocktail party,' he replied. 'You didn't notice him hanging around like a bad fart, doing all those extra shifts recently and working on Pop's car?' Noah laughed. 'Worst case of Fiona fever *ev-ar*, and why he insisted on helping today, even though I said balloons and him were not a good combo if he's wanting to impress Fi.'

'But ... I thought Cory was *your* friend,' Maggie said before she could stop herself.

'Nah! Not my type, but a good mate,' replied Noah with a candour that belied her early fears that awkwardness might distance mother and son moving forward. 'Good drummer, too,' he added with a wink.

'And why so many balloons?'

'Ethne's Priscilla moment,' Noah said. 'Fi's idea.'

Maggie eyed her son. 'Her Priscilla moment?'

'You'll see,' he winked, headed for the door. 'Better go do my bit.'

A purple balloon escaped and Maggie followed its path into a perfectly beautiful autumn sky. Last night's red sunset had promised a sailor's delight by morning, and the folklore looked like proving true. Storm season was finally over and so too was the wettest summer on record, with unprecedented flooding in south-east Queensland affecting towns in the southern state.

'A bloody miracle' was how locals explained Calingarry Crossing escaping the inundation that had struck so many river towns. Major down-pours in catchments across north-western New South Wales had taken Charlie by surprise. Only by being a strong and stubborn old bugger had Charlie held on for help to arrive. While Calingarry's loss, both stock and crop, had been minor, devastating losses elsewhere had made the new year a reflective one, and what better way to celebrate a new beginning than with a big announcement. A March wedding in town was the perfect pick-me-up: something old, something new, something borrowed, something blue. *And something wonderful.* After three funerals in six months, Maggie needed some wonderful back in her life.

Another crash witness had come forward. A tourist remembered seeing a car driving erratically and speeding on the treacherous hairpin bends on Nine Mile Mountain. The actual crash site—a sweeping bend close to where the road plateaued, where a break in the guardrail allowed tourists to stop and observe the breathtaking vista across the ranges—had not a single skid mark. The investigation eventually ruled out second vehicle involvement, mechanical problems and environmental causes, and the coroner concluded the low quantity of ecstasy and alcohol in Brian's system were unlikely to have been contributing factors. With the text message Brian had sent to Maggie deemed inconsequential and with no suicide note, the inquest recorded an open finding, meaning they'd never really know what happened on that mountain.

But Brian did leave a note. Just like Joe had replied and never posted a letter to Dan, Brian had replied and kept Amber's un-posted letter and some lyrics in a folder. Also containing old press clippings—mostly social page pictures featuring Amber and Phillip Blair with baby Fiona—was a dossier on the daughter he'd longed to know. The day Noah sat at the Pianola and played the song, Maggie had cried: for herself, for Brian, and for Fiona, whose mother was thrust into a new life; one a poor pub musi-cian could never compete with. Still, Brian kept that torch for Amber burning throughout his marriage to Maggie. Not that she would condemn him for clinging to memories. Hadn't she secretly held a torch for Dan Ireland since school?

What Brian's letter to Amber had made clear was the reason he'd not made a fuss over Fiona. He'd alluded to the same in his last text to Maggie. *Sorry I wasn't good enough.* Given the chance, Maggie would've told Brian he had been a good father. He just wasn't a good husband. That said, his passing taught her a lesson: no sense yearning all your life for something when with a little courage it could be yours.

'No more wishing, no more fantasising,' Maggie muttered, glancing at her watch. 'Time to make a fairy tale come true.'

After laying out her clothes and kicking off her pink scuffs, Maggie slipped into new shoes. The satin sandals might not be Cinderella glass, but at least the wedge heel made them slightly more practical for a country wedding than stilettos. She inspected herself in the mirror. How long had it been since she'd owned an outfit so fancy and so feminine with its frilly, flowing layers in hues of emerald green and turquoise? Outside the fitting room in Saddleton, Noah had made a comment about peacocks, while Fiona hadn't looked twice at the out-of-this-world price tag before handing over her credit card to the surprised boutique owner. Even Ethne received a string of pearls for the wedding, along with a handwritten note that had made her guffaw.

While everyone had changed this past season, Fiona's growth had perhaps been the greatest, as was the evolution of her expressions the day Maggie and Phillip had presented Brian's keepsakes and the song he'd written for Amber. First joy lit Fiona's eyes, then confusion, and finally anguish over another person lost before she'd had the chance to know them.

Startled by a wolf whistle from behind her, Maggie whipped around to see Dan leaning a shoulder against the doorframe of her bedroom, feet crossed at the ankles, one hand shoved in the side pocket of navy trousers, and he wore a pale blue, partially unbuttoned shirt, the sleeves rolled up to his elbows to expose tanned farmer's arms.

'I don't believe you should be here, Mr Ireland.'

'I came to make sure you're ready for that walk down the aisle, and here you are looking like the Lindeman girl I once knew.'

'And you, Dan Ireland, look like a gorgeous version of a boy I once knew.' As hunky as he was right then, when he'd walked into the pub a week ago in dusty Wrangler jeans and RM Williams boots, she'd seen her mad crush from twenty years ago. 'What have you done with Charlie?'

'He's downstairs grumbling about wearing a flower in his buttonhole. Says he looks like—' Dan stopped short, a silent apology in his eyes taking the place of unsaid words.

'A poof?' Maggie finished, trying to smile but failing. 'Yes, I can hear him now.'

Would thoughtless turns of phrase ever not hurt a mother's heart and remind her of the times she'd laughed along whenever Charlie told one of his poofter jokes in the bar. Unkind comments made Maggie want to cry.

But she was learning to adopt a poker face and do what her son would have to do for the rest of his life: tolerate bigots and fools who didn't mean any harm and didn't know any better.

'Hey, buck up, this is a happy day.' Dan pushed off the doorframe and sidled up to Maggie, inspecting the two of them side by side in the mirror. 'We look good together.'

'I always thought so,' she said. 'The truth is, I thought our names—Lindeman and Ireland—were a good omen. I even wrote a letter to Lindeman Island Resort asking if we could honeymoon for free—once we married.'

Dan turned her to face him, his hands big and comforting on her shoulders. 'I'm learning to love that laugh of yours.'

'And yet for a while I wasn't sure I'd ever laugh again.' Maggie sighed.

'Last storm season proved one thing,' Dan said. 'Let things simmer for long enough and they're bound to boil over, especially when you bring new people into a small town and turn up the heat.'

'There's no keeping a lid on some secrets,' Maggie said, 'but we're all the better for the truth.'

Dan nodded. 'We are, and I'm glad things look like working out for Phillip, too. And glad Fiona was smart enough to see what's good for her. Phillip Blair must be the nicest bloke on the planet.'

'Besides you.' Maggie winked and grabbed hold of Dan's arm for support, lifting one foot at a time to adjust the new slingbacks over her heels. 'I guess everyone's waiting to go to the church?'

'Yes, and I managed a glimpse of Fiona and Noah's handiwork before they hustled me away. The 'Just Married' job is the best I've seen. Reckon they've got enough balloons?'

Maggie chuckled. 'Fiona, the event manager, has been whipping Noah and his mate into line, and she has more surprises to come, apparently.'

'Noah sure has taken to having a half-sister like a horse to hay,' Dan said. 'Speaking of horses, old Charlie can't figure out why you'd pay Clive Peters anything for that old nag, but she's settled nicely into our stables and Charlie's enjoying the company and the responsibility. Dare I ask about Fiona's other surprise?'

'She and Noah have written a song together for the wedding today? Plus, they have plans to bring the pub into the twenty-first century.' Maggie saw the surprise on Dan's face. 'Yes, I accepted Fiona's offer—with conditions.'

'The offer to invest a portion of her inheritance into the pub, you mean?'

'Yes and no,' Maggie said. 'I don't want her money, but she's keen to lease the bistro. Apparently the all-new, soon-to-be-refurbished and renamed Edge Restaurant will be blogging, tweeting and Facebooking. Business plan and all,' Maggie added with a grin. 'She's qualified and quite the expert!'

'Some turnaround,' Dan commented.

'Phillip helped by sharing a secret from Amber's stay at Dandelion House. I don't know what it is about that place that changes people for the better, and I'm not expecting Fiona to put down roots, but she's committed to revitalising the bistro and she has Ethne's approval. Plus, she'll be here to help until Noah finishes school. Works for me,' Maggie said, picking up the camera from the dresser. 'I have lots more photo ideas to pursue in my new spare time. First things first, though.' Maggie breathed deep and flattened a palm against her belly. 'You should get to the church first.'

'On my way,' Dan said. 'Just had to check on you.'

'Thanks, I'm fine, Dan. Happier still at seeing Ethne so over the moon.'

'And I'm happy to be on the right side of her,' he joked.

'Until you're late to the church, so go!' Maggie shooed. 'I need to settle this queasy feeling in my stomach. It's been a while since I walked down an aisle.'

'I'll be right there, at the front of the church, Maggie. Focus on me.'

'And if I trip in these snazzy shoes? I've never given a bride away.' Slinging the strap of her camera over one shoulder she added, 'And I'm not looking forward to Ethne being away sailing the high seas.'

'I heard Barney found a buyer for his boat. Good on him.'

'Yes, they're taking it to Coffs Harbour on the back of a giant semi which is how Ethne's Priscilla idea came about. She planned on riding on top of the boat—wedding dress and all—until Noah advised against not wearing a seatbelt.'

Dan laughed and took the wrapped wedding gift Maggie handed him. 'Your gift to the bride and groom, I assume?'

'Yes, when Ethne told me they were leaving after the service I had to rethink the reception gift idea. So, I emailed a photograph through to The Camera House and they posted the print back as a giant canvas.'

'The photo is one of yours?

'Yep, and guess what else?' Maggie teased. 'I've been keeping this news a secret but …'

Dan made a play for her, grabbing Maggie by the waist. 'Do I need to tickle it out of you?'

'It's about the pictures Fiona put on the website,' she said, slapping his hand away. 'A book publisher emailed me about using the picture of our fig tree at the churchyard as cover art for a new novel. My first sale!'

'That's great news, Maggie! As is my secret.'

Maggie stepped back. 'What? Tell me.'

'Soon. After the service, when the newlyweds are on their way, wait at the church for me. Gotta go,' Dan said over the blast of a horn and hurried out of her room.

§.

MAGGIE WIPED TEARS OF JOY FROM HER EYES AND WAVED GOODBYE TO the back end of Barney's semi-trailer with its 'Just Married' sign trailing a million purple balloons, and with Ethne's wibbly-wobbly arms waving frantically out the passenger window.

'I thought the next wedding might be yours,' said Sara, pressing a tissue into Maggie's palm, encouraging her fingers to curl around the scrunched-up white ball.

Maggie sighed and dabbed her cheeks. 'The thing about fairy tales, Sara, is not everyone gets the happy ever after. Dan's reality involves his kids and there's not much call for crash investigators in the country. At least with old Charlie swearing he'll be carted out of his house feet first, Dan will visit more often. I'm seriously okay with a happy-for-now ending and it is happy: Dan gets his dad back, you get a new baby soon, Ethne gets her prince, and I get to be a wicked step-mother to Fiona.'

Sara's laugh turned the heads of the last wedding guests leaving the church. 'Fiona's lucky to have you, Maggie.'

'Come on you two,' Will urged from the doorway. 'Time to get to the pub and break in the new bar-*man*. Maggie, love, what were you thinking hiring a bloke?'

Sara thumped Will on the shoulder. 'Nothing wrong with a bit of eye-candy for the girls. Well done, I say, Maggie.'

'His name's Aiden and it's temporary,' she explained. 'He's keen and happy with long shifts to make his travel time from Coolabah Tree Gully worthwhile.'

'That *is* keen.'

'His uncle owns the pub there, so he knows his way around one. He's also a qualified chef. I mean *really* qualified, and from a fancy Sydney restaurant that got the big tick from Fiona. The timing couldn't be better.'

'What are we waiting for?' Will asked.

'You and Sara head off,' Maggie suggested. 'I'm waiting for Dan. He's supposed to be here.' She escorted Will down the ramp and glanced around the church grounds, even craning her neck to peer around the corner of the church to the old outhouse. No trace.

'Okay, gorgeous wife,' Will said. 'You push. I'm preserving the strength in my arms for drinking games. Plus, you need pram practice. Come on, Little Mama. *Mush! Mush!*'

Maggie looked at her watch, then checked inside the empty church one last time. Still no Dan, just memories of Sundays from her childhood. The old organ was gone, replaced with a tinny-sounding amplifier and pre-recorded music, which was why today Maggie had accompanied Ethne down the aisle to Noah's composition. The same melancholy turned Maggie towards the fig tree and to wondering what the next few years might hold for her.

Where was Dan? Had she misunderstood his request to hang back?

'Ouch!' She flattened a palm on her head and rubbed. 'Ouch!' Another single plop on her skull preceded a scattering of berries on the ground around her feet.

There was one very big fig bird in that tree and Maggie had guessed it answered to Dan Ireland.

She slammed her hands on both hips. 'You don't think that hurts just as much all these years later?'

'Just getting your attention.'

'Well, you have it. Now what?'

'Come closer,' he said from his tree perch.

Stumbling on the uneven ground, she lifted one foot after the other and with the flick of a finger the slingbacks were off and dangling from her hand. She moved under the tree, careful to avoid tripping on buttress roots clawing their way over new ground. When she was close enough to see his laugh lines—white in his newly bronzed face—she was reminded of how much Dan had laughed since coming back to Calingarry Crossing.

'What is this tree obsession, Dan? Are you part monkey? Come down before you hurt yourself?'

'I want to tell you something.'

'Like what? You're a fig bird?'

'I'm resigning.'

She felt a rush of happiness to her heart. 'From the police service? But why?'

'Because I'm staying in town.'

She held back the tiny gasp and the accompanying smile with four fingers pressed against her mouth.

'No cross-examination, Madam Prosecutor?'

'What about your life in Sydney?'

'My kids are looking forward to coming out in the holidays, especially after I told them there was internet. I've also bought an X-Box. In the meantime, I plan to make amends with the old man, who'll need help—not that he's admitting it. The property could do with some TLC and I wouldn't mind being a country boy again, especially now I have a horse and a hat.'

'Well, wow, that's great … about your dad. I'm so pleased things are working out for you both.'

'Don't go popping the cork on the champers just yet.' Dan jumped to the ground, grunting as he almost tripped over a tree root before regrouping with a laugh. 'I have one more thing to figure out with a woman who has never been far from my thoughts.'

'Dan,' Maggie said in a cautionary voice as his two strong hands grasped her shoulders. 'Be warned. My heart won't weather more disappointment.'

'I'm not aiming to disappoint, Maggie. I'm aiming to hang around and help while Ethne's away. I know you're capable, but you shouldn't have to do it all on your own. Let me share the load. I can be quite useful, not to mention resourceful.' He winked.

'Resourceful, Dan Ireland?'

'Yes, Maggie Lindeman. I've finally figured out a place I can take you for dinner. Once Ethne's back, we'll go there.'

'Where?' she asked.

'A lovely little place you might've heard about, set in a resort: intimate dinners for two, breakfast in bed every morning, sunset walks on the beach. It's a little spot in the Whitsundays. I hear Lindeman Island is particularly wonderful in winter. What do you think?'

Tightly she cuddled him and tighter he hugged her back. 'I think I'm ready for a wonderful winter.'

Maggie Lindeman's past, present and her future had converged and was standing right in front of her—not a storm cloud in sight.

Amber Leaves

A father's love is kind of special,
Nothing else can take its place.
With no chance to show the love I have,
My heart's a cold and empty space.

The child I never got to know,
No chance to play my part.
I know you would have loved me if you knew,
If I hadn't kept us apart.

~

Amber leaves, broken hearts,
And a winter frost sets in.
It's a long, cold, lonely life for me,
If I never hold you in my arms again.
Amber leaves, broken hearts,
And a winter frost sets in.
It's a long, cold lonely life for me,
If I never see my baby girl again.

~

And I can't stop thinkin' 'bout the choice I made,
How I never gave myself a chance.
I know in my heart, if I don't see you again,
My life's a long, cold, lonely dance.
The baby I never got to hold,
No chance to play a part.
I'd been a fool to think our lives would cross,
Once Amber left and broke my heart.

~REPEAT CHORUS~

HOUSE FOR ALL SEASONS (2013's #5 top-selling debut novel)

Four women, four lives unravelled. The truth will bind them forever.

Bequeathed a century-old house, four estranged friends return to their hometown of Calingarry Crossing after 20 years to stay a season each at the century-old Dandelion House where they each discover something about themselves and a secret that ties all four to each other and to the house - forever.

HOUSE OF WISHES

In 1974, two teenage girls—strangers—make a pact to keep a secret.

Forty years later, Beth is fulfilling her mother's last wish by heading to an obscure country town to scatter the ashes. On the outskirts of Calingarry Crossing, when Beth comes across a place called Dandelion House Retreat, she hopes it's a place to stay so she can begin to heal.

Instead, when a local cattleman, Tom, relays tales of the cursed, century-old river house and its reclusive owner, Gypsy, Beth begins to question her mother's wishes.

When meeting Beth leads Tom to uncover his own family's disturbing connection to the old house, he must decide if the truth will help a grieving daughter, or will it hurt even more.

Should Dandelion House keep its last, long-held secret?